Buffy the Vampire Slayer™

SEASON EIGHT VOLUME 8

LAST GLEAMING

Script JOSS WHEDON AND SCOTT ALLIE

Pencils GEORGES JEANTY

Inks ANDY OWENS

Colors MICHELLE MADSEN

Letters RICHARD STARKINGS & COMICRAFT'S JIMMY BETANCOURT

Cover Artist JO CHEN

Commitment through Distance, Virtue through Sin
Script JANE ESPENSON
Pencils KARL MOLINE

Cover Artist JO CHEN

Executive Producer JOSS WHEDON

Dark Horse Books®

President & Publisher MIKE RICHARDSON

Editor SCOTT ALLIE

Associate Editor SIERRA HAHN

Assistant Editor FREDDYE LINS

Collection Designer AIMEE DANIELSON-GERMANY

This story takes place after the end of the
television series *Buffy the Vampire Slayer*,
created by Joss Whedon.

Special thanks to Debbie Olshan at Twentieth Century Fox, Jane Espenson,
Nicki Maron, and Daniel Kaminsky.

EXECUTIVE VICE PRESIDENT Neil Hankerson · CHIEF FINANCIAL OFFICER Tom Weddle · VICE PRESIDENT OF PUBLISHING
Randy Stradley · VICE PRESIDENT OF BUSINESS DEVELOPMENT Michael Martens · VICE PRESIDENT OF BUSINESS
AFFAIRS Anita Nelson · VICE PRESIDENT OF MARKETING Micha Hershman · VICE PRESIDENT OF PRODUCT DEVELOPMENT
David Scroggy · VICE PRESIDENT OF INFORMATION TECHNOLOGY Dale LaFountain · DIRECTOR OF PURCHASING Darlene
Vogel · GENERAL COUNSEL Ken Lizzi · EDITORIAL DIRECTOR Davey Estrada · SENIOR MANAGING EDITOR Scott Allie ·
SENIOR BOOKS EDITOR Chris Warner · EXECUTIVE EDITOR Diana Schutz · DIRECTOR OF DESIGN AND PRODUCTION
Cary Grazzini · ART DIRECTOR Lia Ribacchi · DIRECTOR OF SCHEDULING Cara Niece

This volume reprints the comic-book series *Buffy the Vampire Slayer* Season Eight #36–#40, and *Buffy
the Vampire Slayer: Riley* from Dark Horse Comics.

Published by
Dark Horse Books
A division of
Dark Horse Comics, Inc.
10956 SE Main Street
Milwaukie, OR 97222

DarkHorse.com

To find a comics shop in your area,
call the Comic Shop Locator Service toll-free at (888) 266-4226.

First edition: June 2011
ISBN 978-1-59582-610-7

1 3 5 7 9 10 8 6 4 2
Printed at Interglobe Printing, Inc., Beauceville, QC, Canada

Buffy the Vampire Slayer™

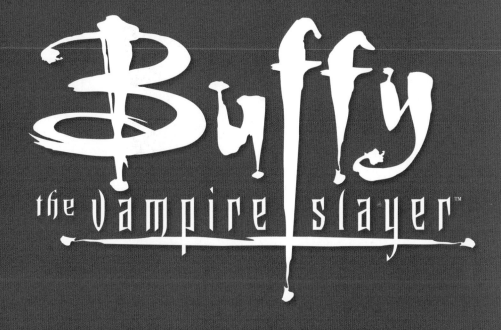

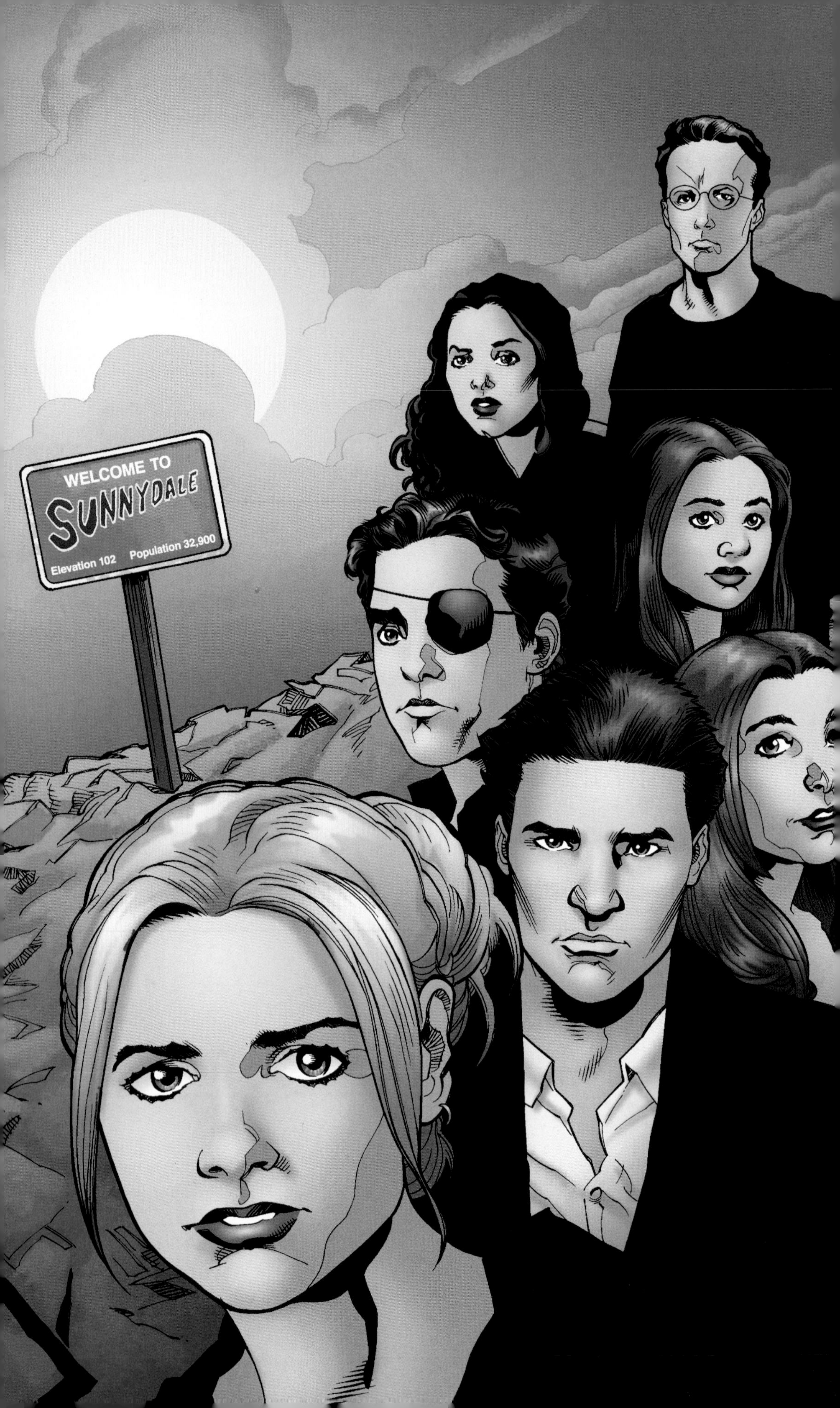
WELCOME TO
SUNNYDALE
Elevation 102 Population 32,900

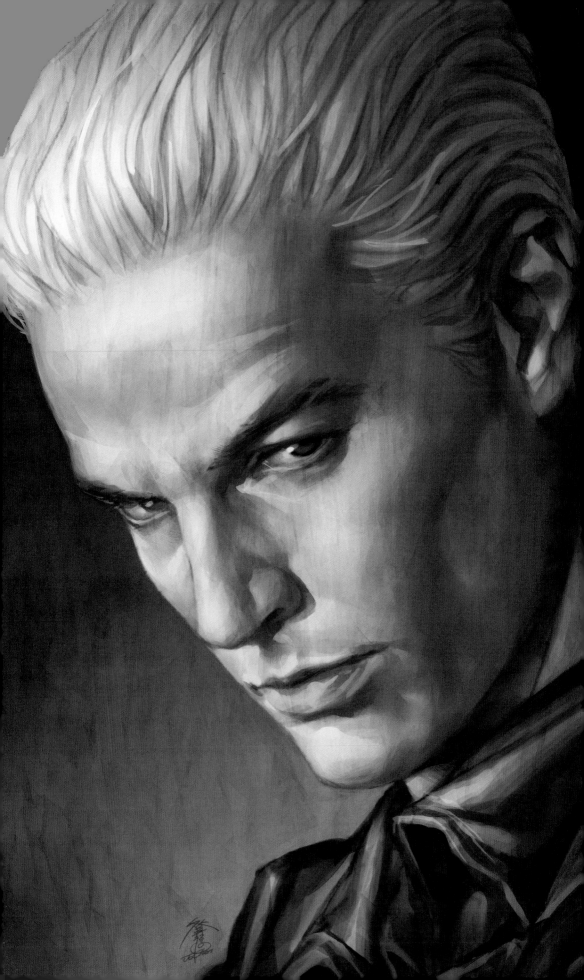

LAST GLEAMING

PART ONE

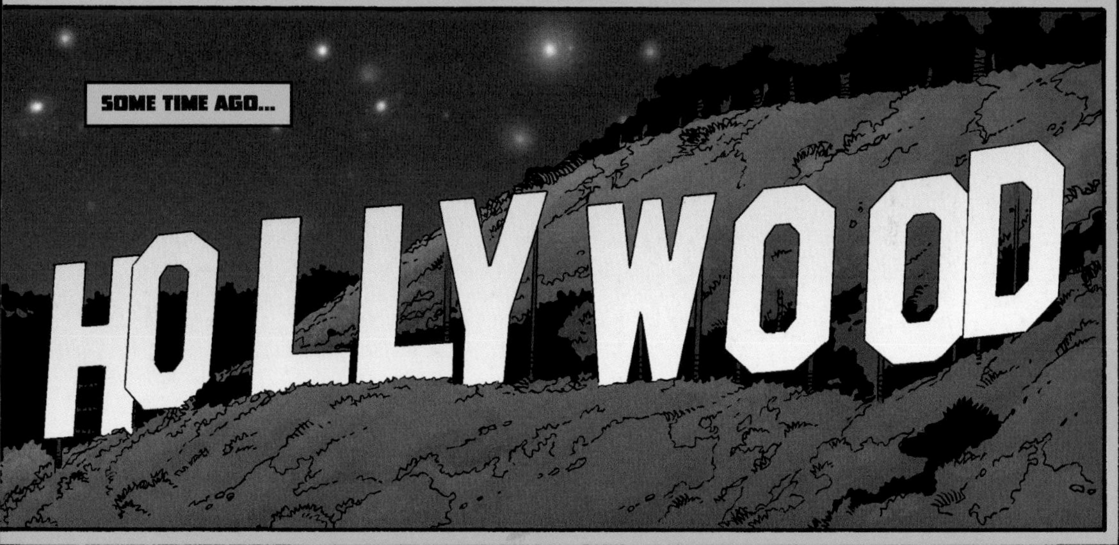
SOME TIME AGO...
HOLLYWOOD

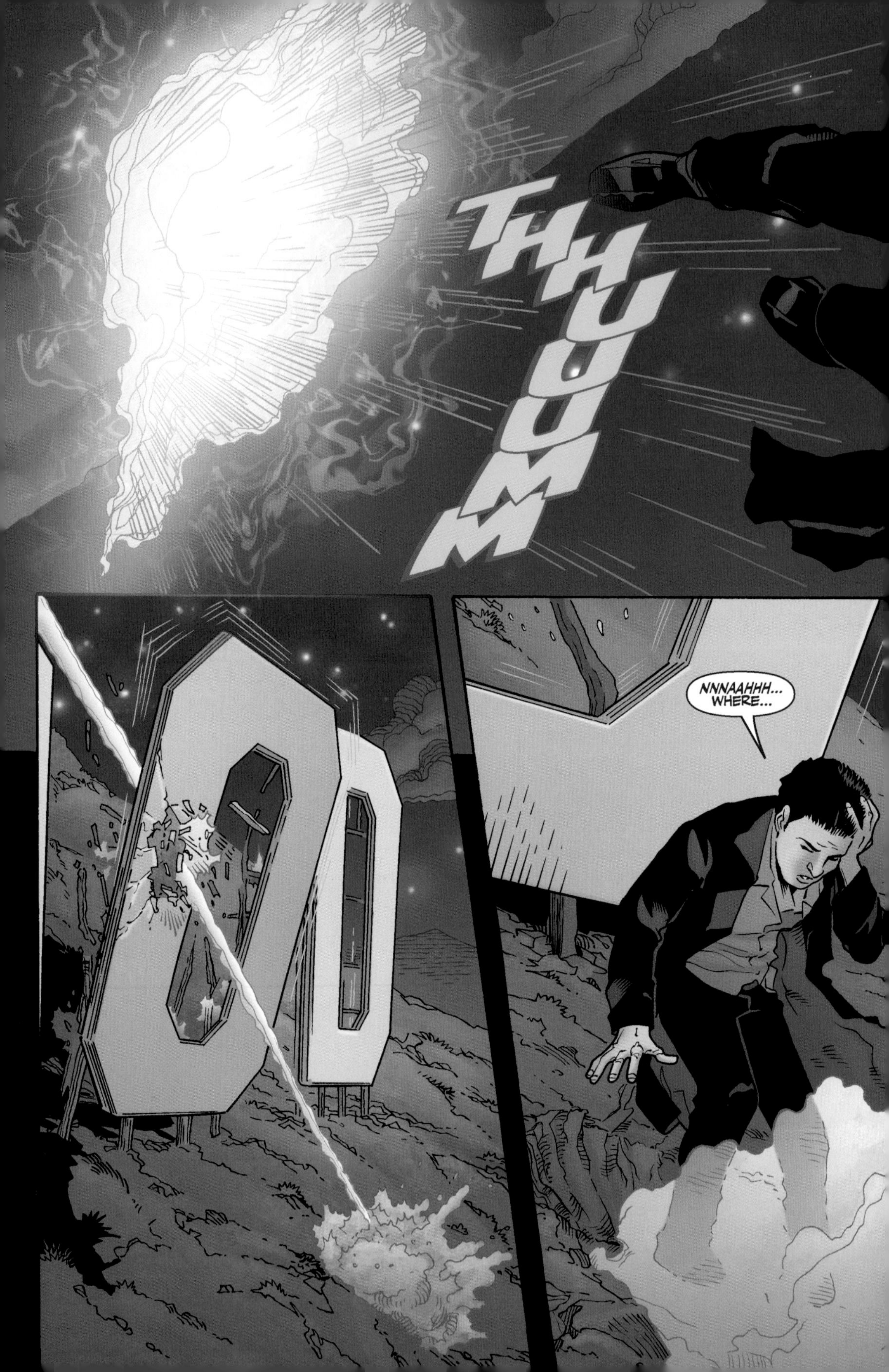
THHUUMM
NNNAAHHH... WHERE...

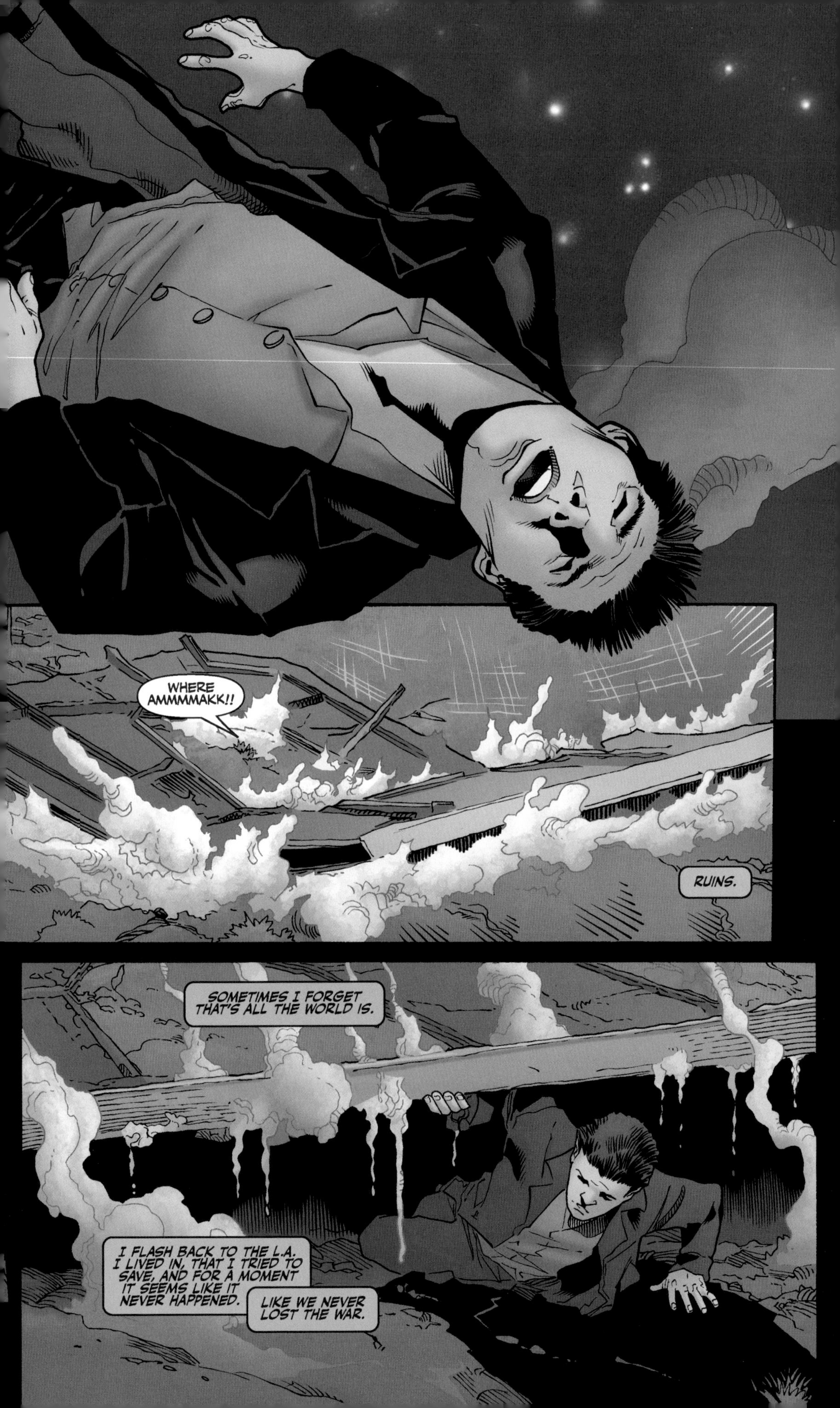
WHERE AMMMMAKK!!
RUINS.
SOMETIMES I FORGET THAT'S ALL THE WORLD IS.
I FLASH BACK TO THE L.A. I LIVED IN, THAT I TRIED TO SAVE, AND FOR A MOMENT IT SEEMS LIKE IT NEVER HAPPENED.
LIKE WE NEVER LOST THE WAR.

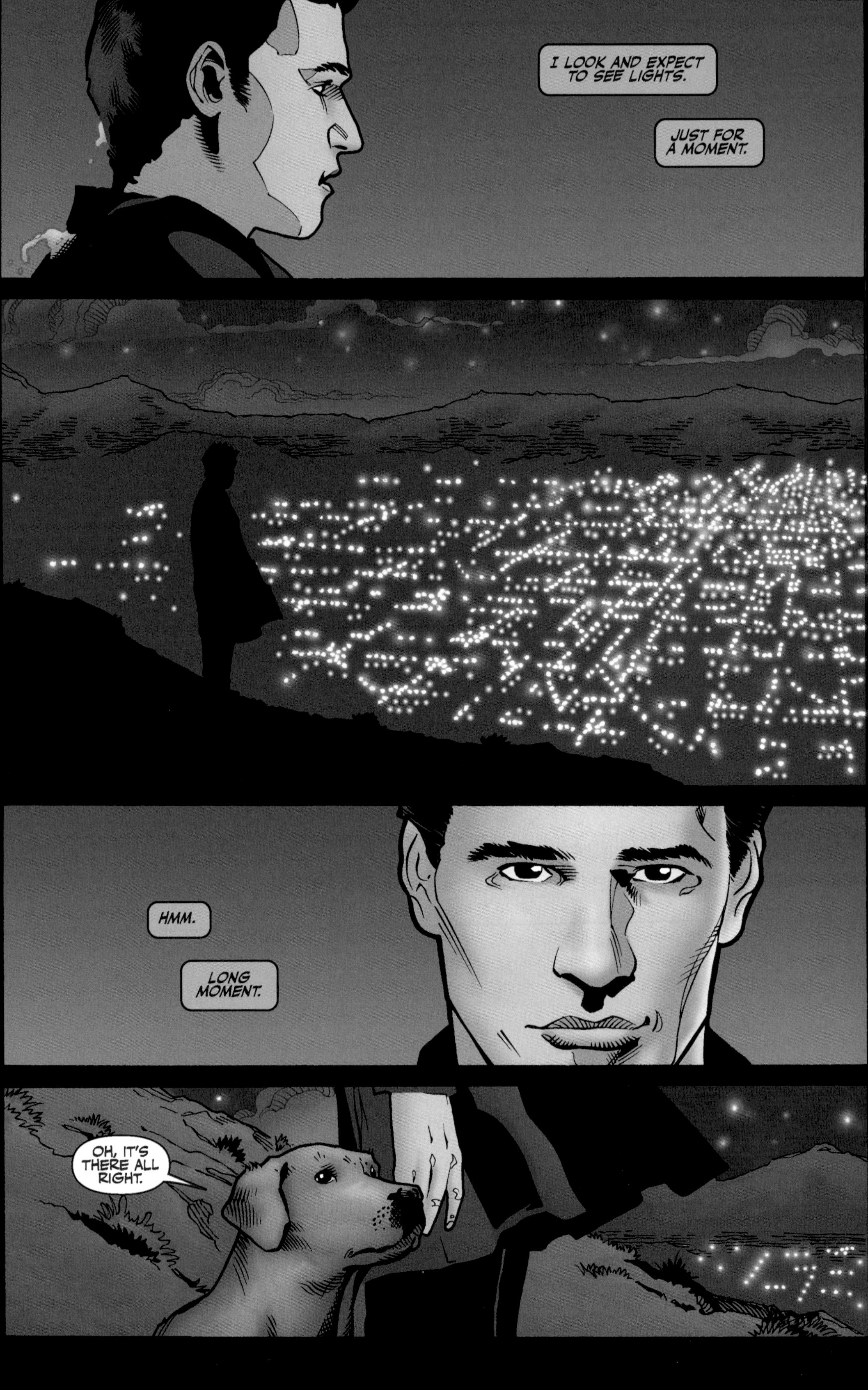
I LOOK AND EXPECT TO SEE LIGHTS.
JUST FOR A MOMENT.
HMM.
LONG MOMENT.
OH, IT'S THERE ALL RIGHT.

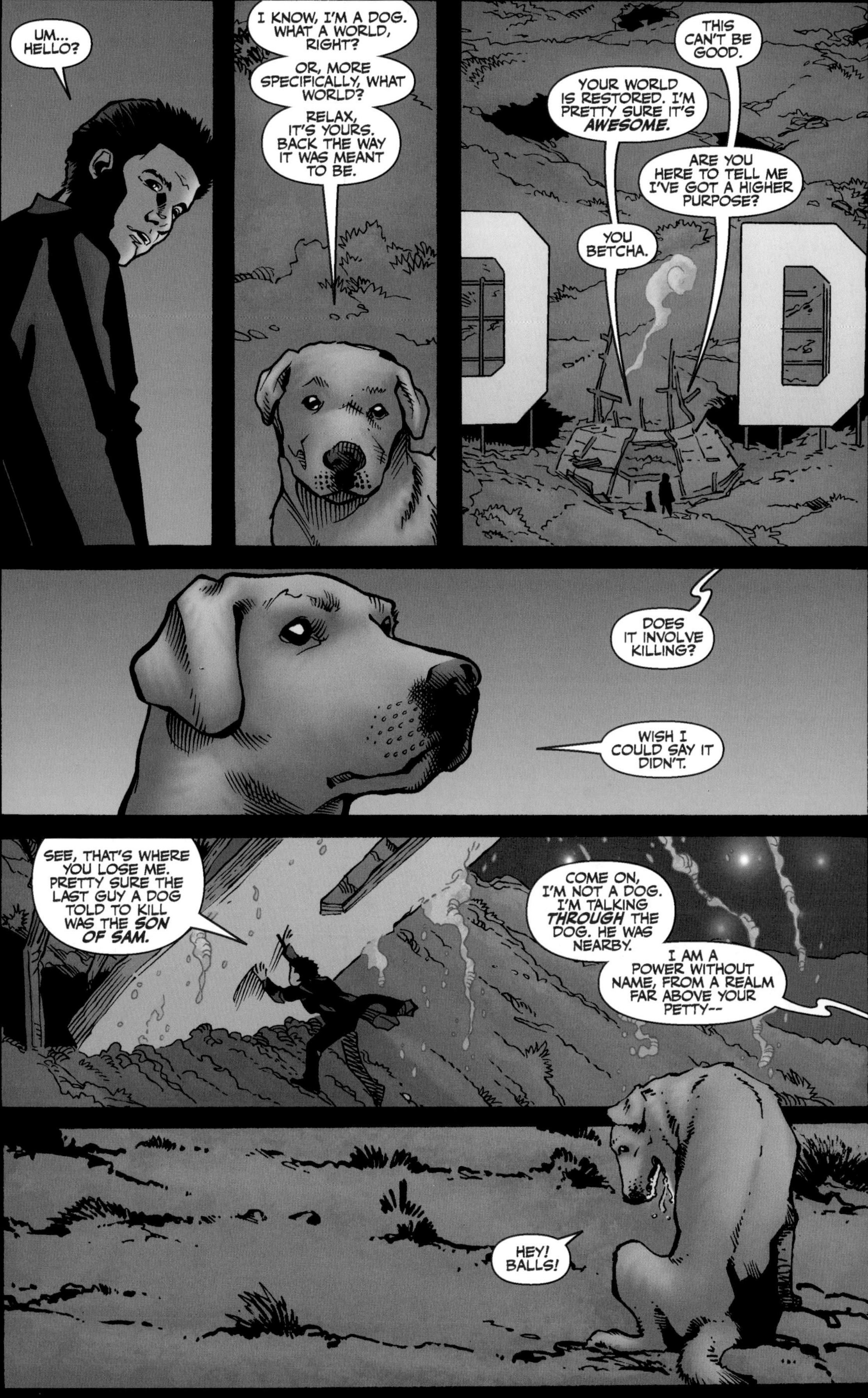
UM... HELLO?
I KNOW, I'M A DOG. WHAT A WORLD, RIGHT?
OR, MORE SPECIFICALLY, WHAT WORLD?
RELAX, IT'S YOURS. BACK THE WAY IT WAS MEANT TO BE.
THIS CAN'T BE GOOD.
YOUR WORLD IS RESTORED. I'M PRETTY SURE IT'S *AWESOME.*
ARE YOU HERE TO TELL ME I'VE GOT A HIGHER PURPOSE?
YOU BETCHA.
DOES IT INVOLVE KILLING?
WISH I COULD SAY IT DIDN'T.
SEE, THAT'S WHERE YOU LOSE ME. PRETTY SURE THE LAST GUY A DOG TOLD TO KILL WAS THE *SON OF SAM.*
COME ON, I'M NOT A DOG. I'M TALKING *THROUGH* THE DOG. HE WAS NEARBY.
I AM A POWER WITHOUT NAME, FROM A REALM FAR ABOVE YOUR PETTY--
HEY! BALLS!

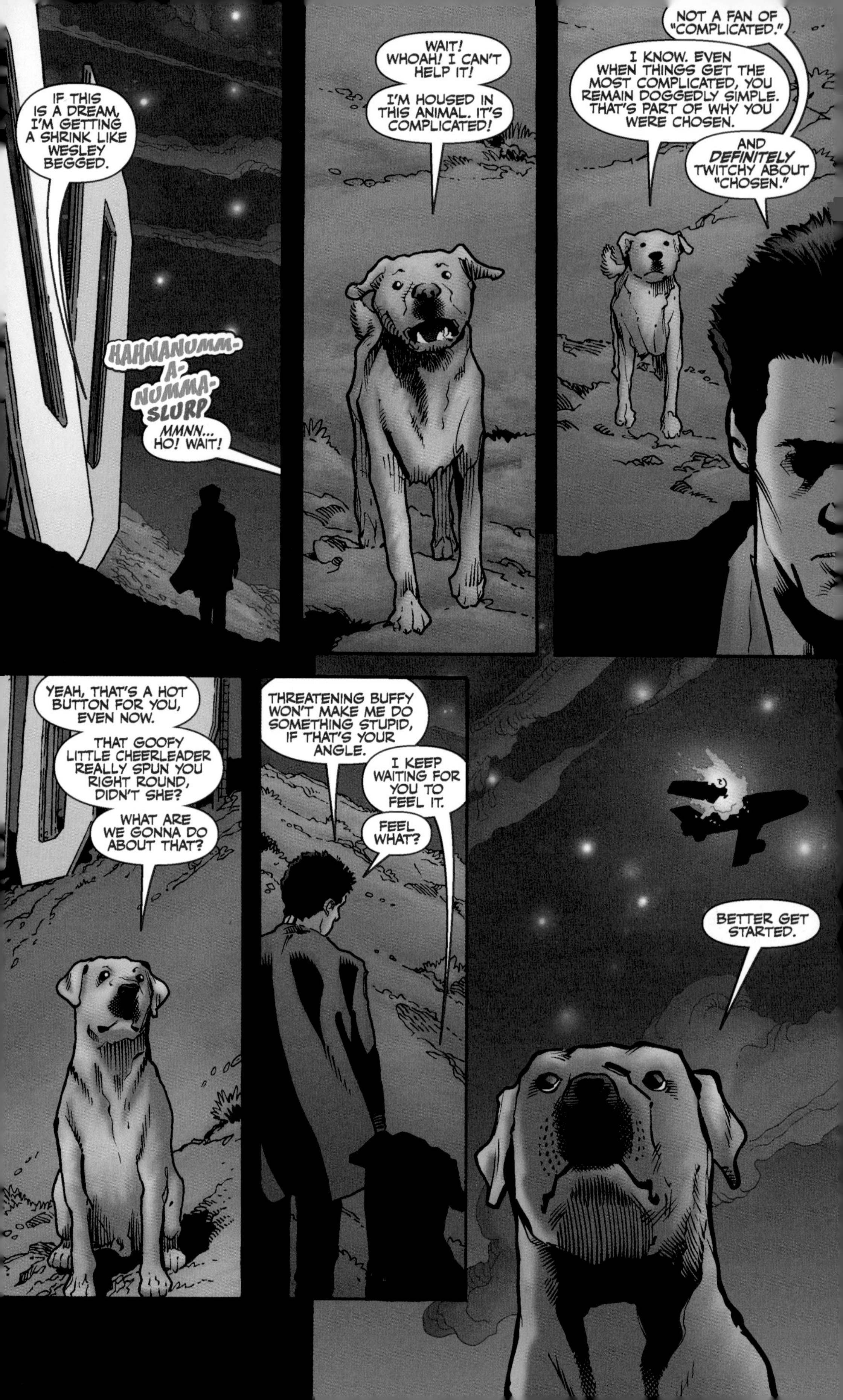

IF THIS IS A DREAM, I'M GETTING A SHRINK LIKE WESLEY BEGGED.
HAHNANUMM-A-NUMMA-SLURP
MMNN... HO! WAIT!
WAIT! WHOAH! I CAN'T HELP IT!
I'M HOUSED IN THIS ANIMAL. IT'S COMPLICATED!
NOT A FAN OF "COMPLICATED."
I KNOW. EVEN WHEN THINGS GET THE MOST COMPLICATED, YOU REMAIN DOGGEDLY SIMPLE. THAT'S PART OF WHY YOU WERE CHOSEN.
AND *DEFINITELY* TWITCHY ABOUT "CHOSEN."
YEAH, THAT'S A HOT BUTTON FOR YOU, EVEN NOW.
THAT GOOFY LITTLE CHEERLEADER REALLY SPUN YOU RIGHT ROUND, DIDN'T SHE?
WHAT ARE WE GONNA DO ABOUT THAT?
THREATENING BUFFY WON'T MAKE ME DO SOMETHING STUPID, IF THAT'S YOUR ANGLE.
I KEEP WAITING FOR YOU TO FEEL IT.
FEEL WHAT?
BETTER GET STARTED.

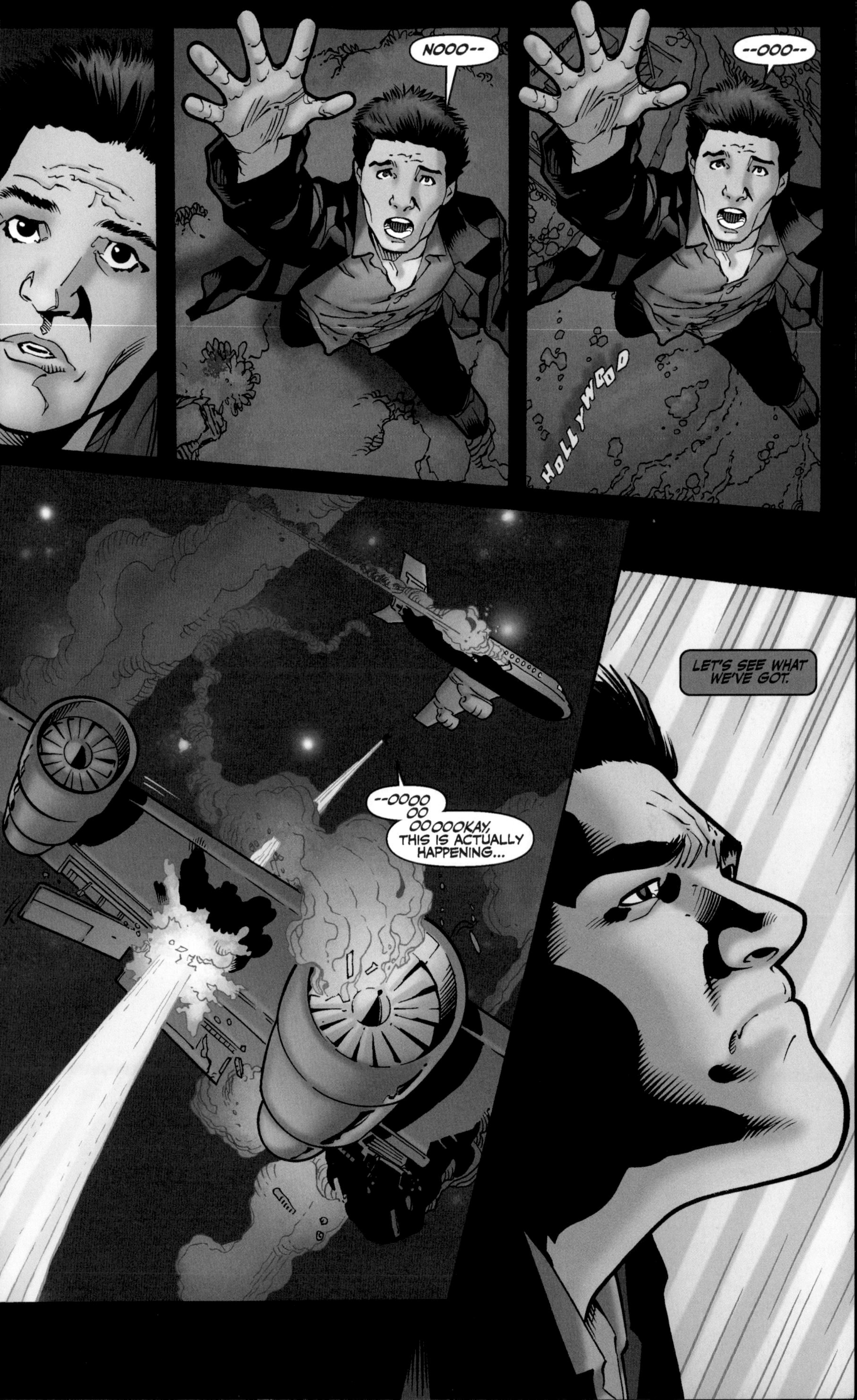
NOOO--
--OOO--
HOLLYWOOD
--OOOO OO OOOOOKAY, THIS IS ACTUALLY HAPPENING...
LET'S SEE WHAT WE'VE GOT.

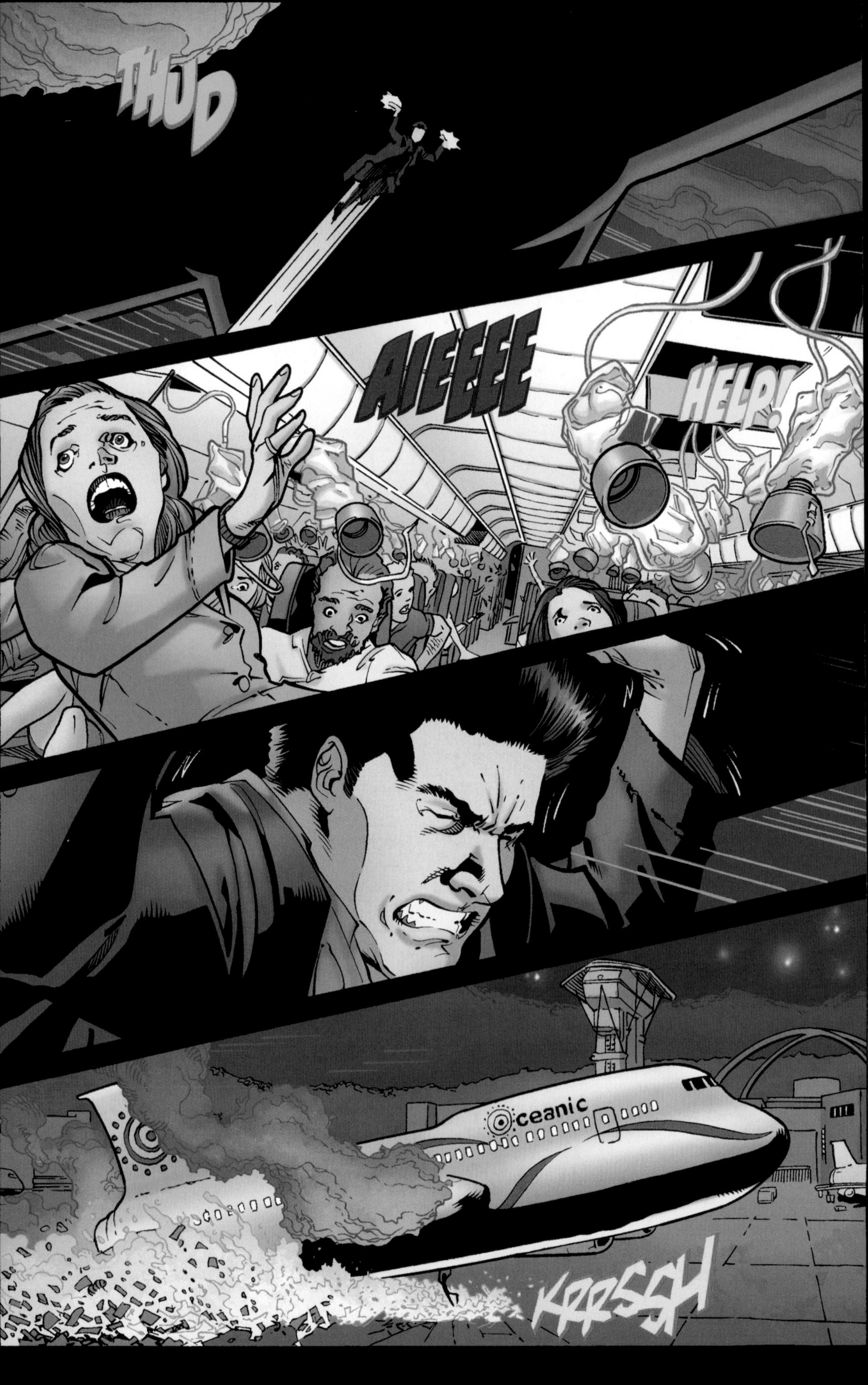
THUD
AIEEEE
HELP!
oceanic
KRRSSH

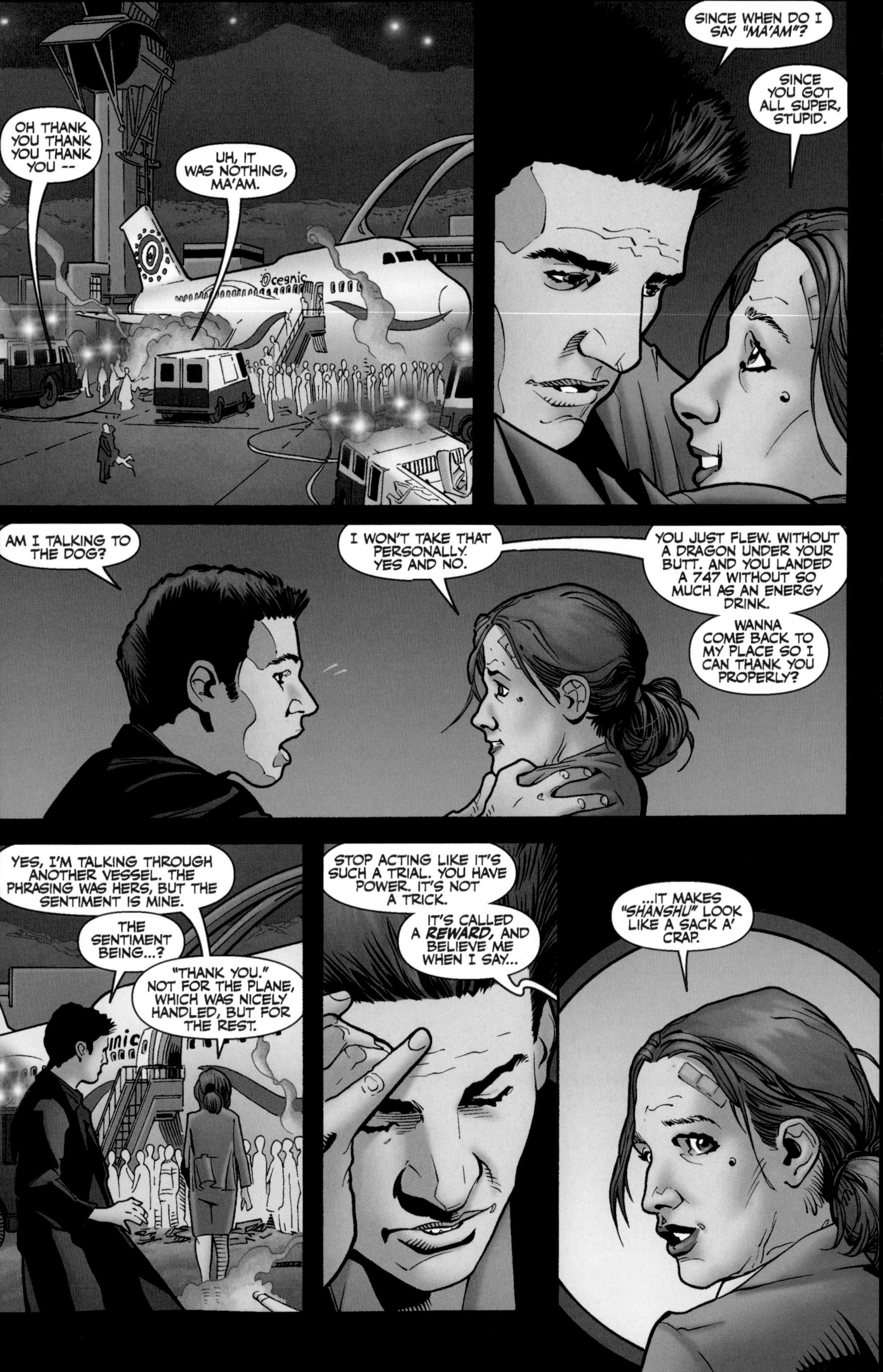
OH THANK YOU THANK YOU THANK YOU --
UH, IT WAS NOTHING, MA'AM.
Oceanic
SINCE WHEN DO I SAY "MA'AM"?
SINCE YOU GOT ALL SUPER, STUPID.
AM I TALKING TO THE DOG?
I WON'T TAKE THAT PERSONALLY. YES AND NO.
YOU JUST FLEW. WITHOUT A DRAGON UNDER YOUR BUTT. AND YOU LANDED A 747 WITHOUT SO MUCH AS AN ENERGY DRINK.
WANNA COME BACK TO MY PLACE SO I CAN THANK YOU PROPERLY?
YES, I'M TALKING THROUGH ANOTHER VESSEL. THE PHRASING WAS HERS, BUT THE SENTIMENT IS MINE.
THE SENTIMENT BEING...?
"THANK YOU." NOT FOR THE PLANE, WHICH WAS NICELY HANDLED, BUT FOR THE REST.
STOP ACTING LIKE IT'S SUCH A TRIAL. YOU HAVE POWER. IT'S NOT A TRICK.
IT'S CALLED A ***REWARD,*** AND BELIEVE ME WHEN I SAY...
...IT MAKES "*SHANSHU*" LOOK LIKE A SACK A' CRAP.

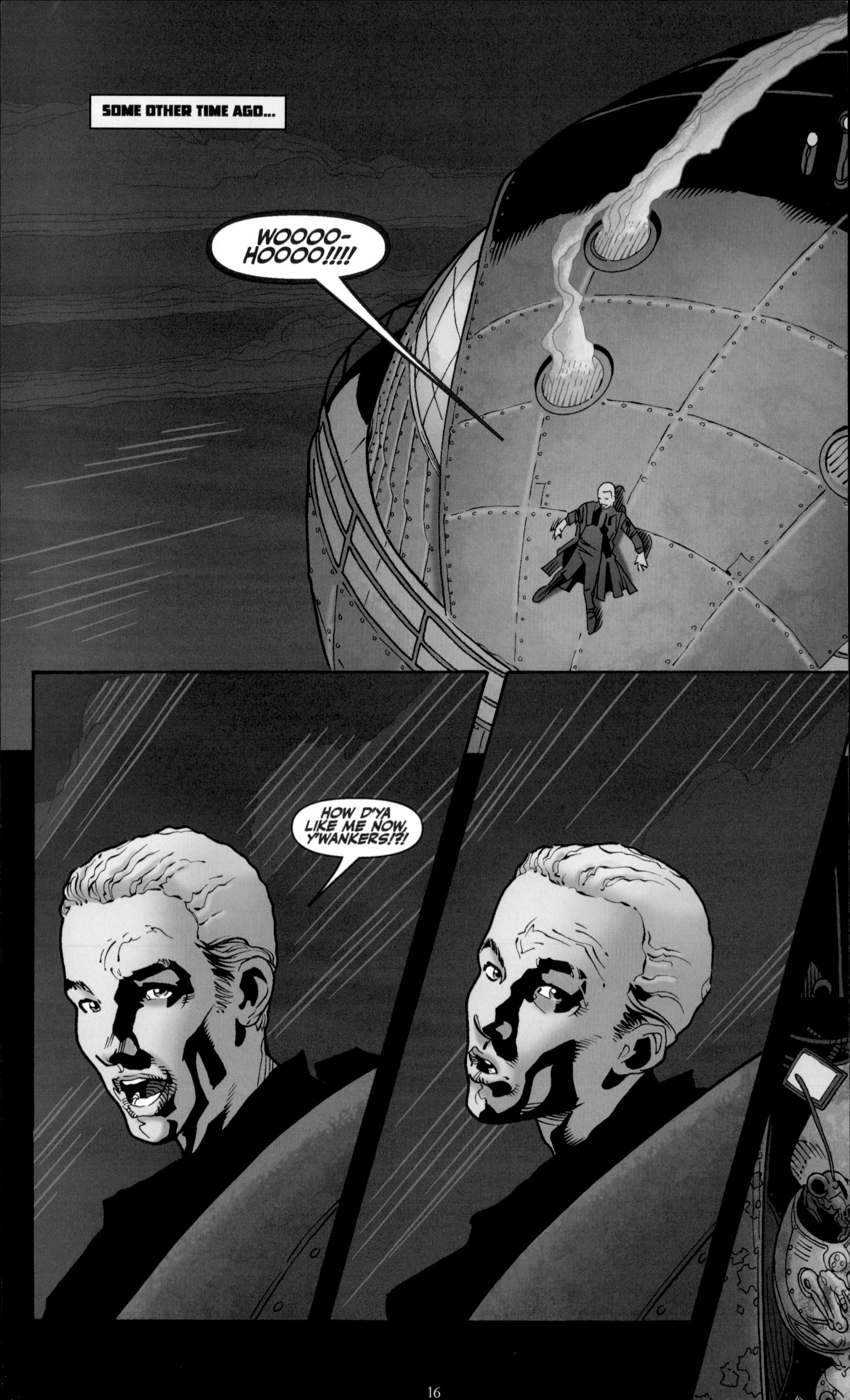
SOME OTHER TIME AGO...
WOOOO-HOOOO!!!!
HOW D'YA LIKE ME NOW, Y'WANKERS!?!

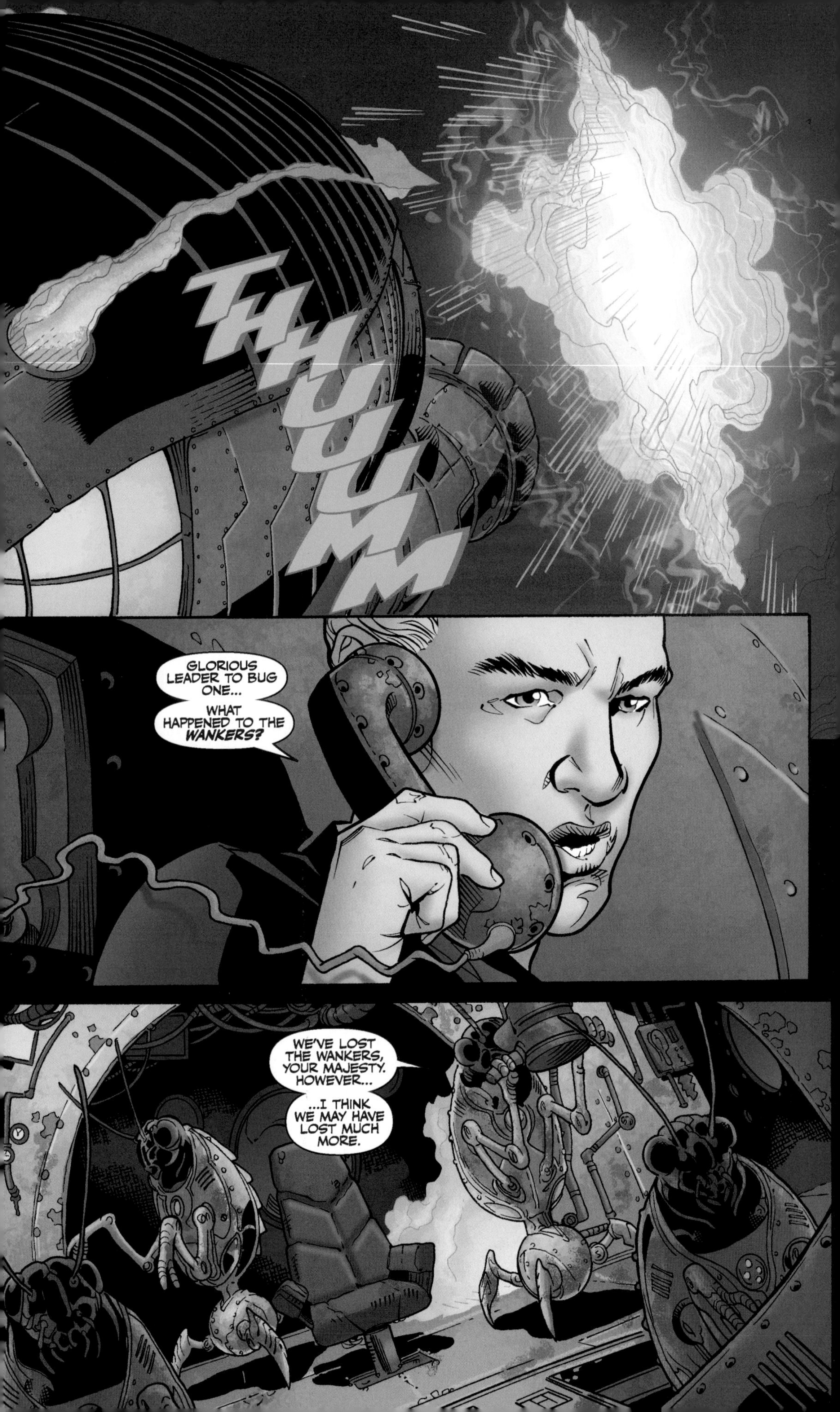
THHUUMM
GLORIOUS LEADER TO BUG ONE...
WHAT HAPPENED TO THE *WANKERS?*
WE'VE LOST THE WANKERS, YOUR MAJESTY. HOWEVER...
...I THINK WE MAY HAVE LOST MUCH MORE.

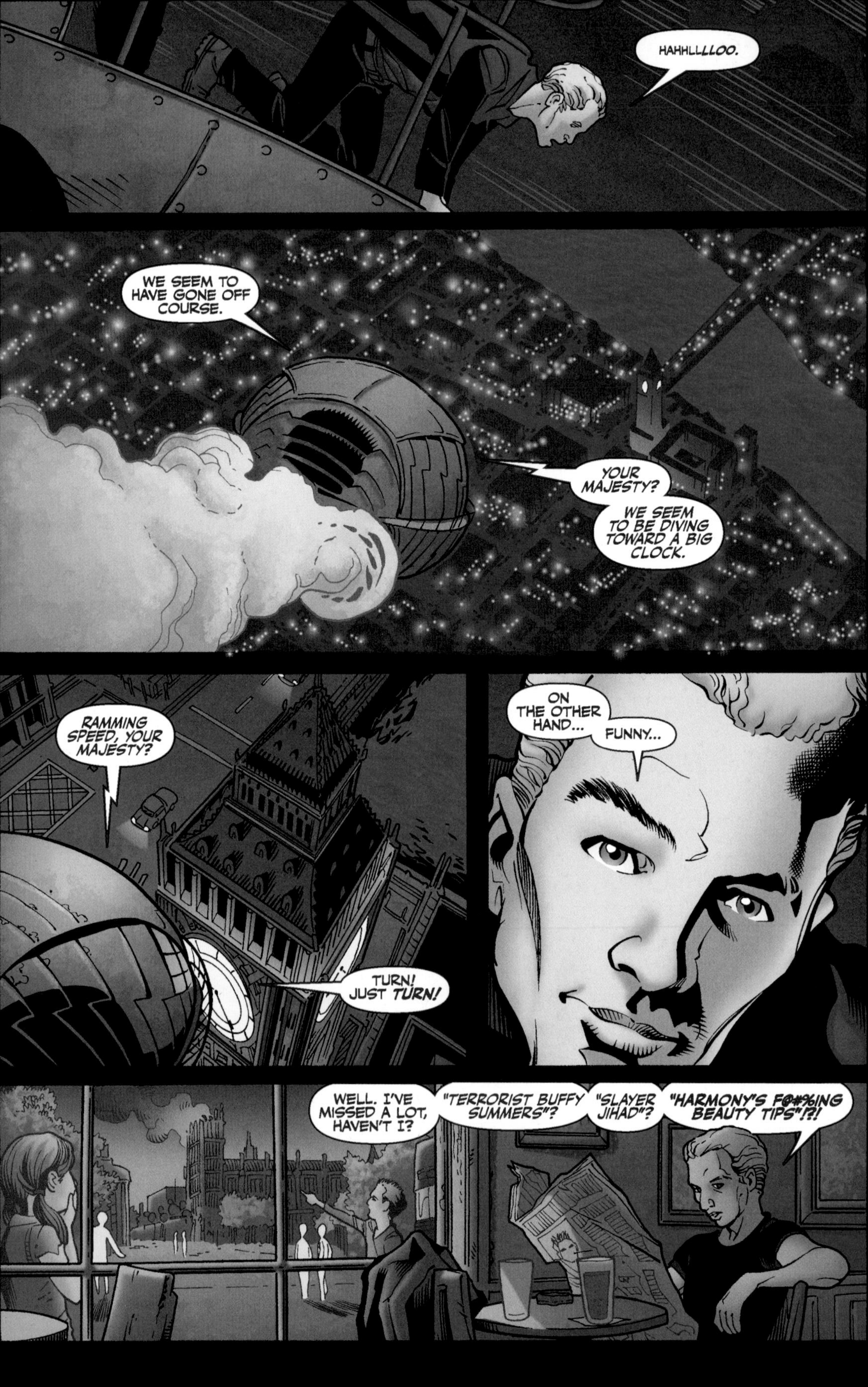
HAHHLLLLOO.
WE SEEM TO HAVE GONE OFF COURSE.
YOUR MAJESTY?
WE SEEM TO BE DIVING TOWARD A BIG CLOCK.
RAMMING SPEED, YOUR MAJESTY?
TURN! JUST TURN!
ON THE OTHER HAND...
FUNNY...
WELL. I'VE MISSED A LOT, HAVEN'T I?
"TERRORIST BUFFY SUMMERS"?
"SLAYER JIHAD"?
"HARMONY'S F@#%ING BEAUTY TIPS"!?!

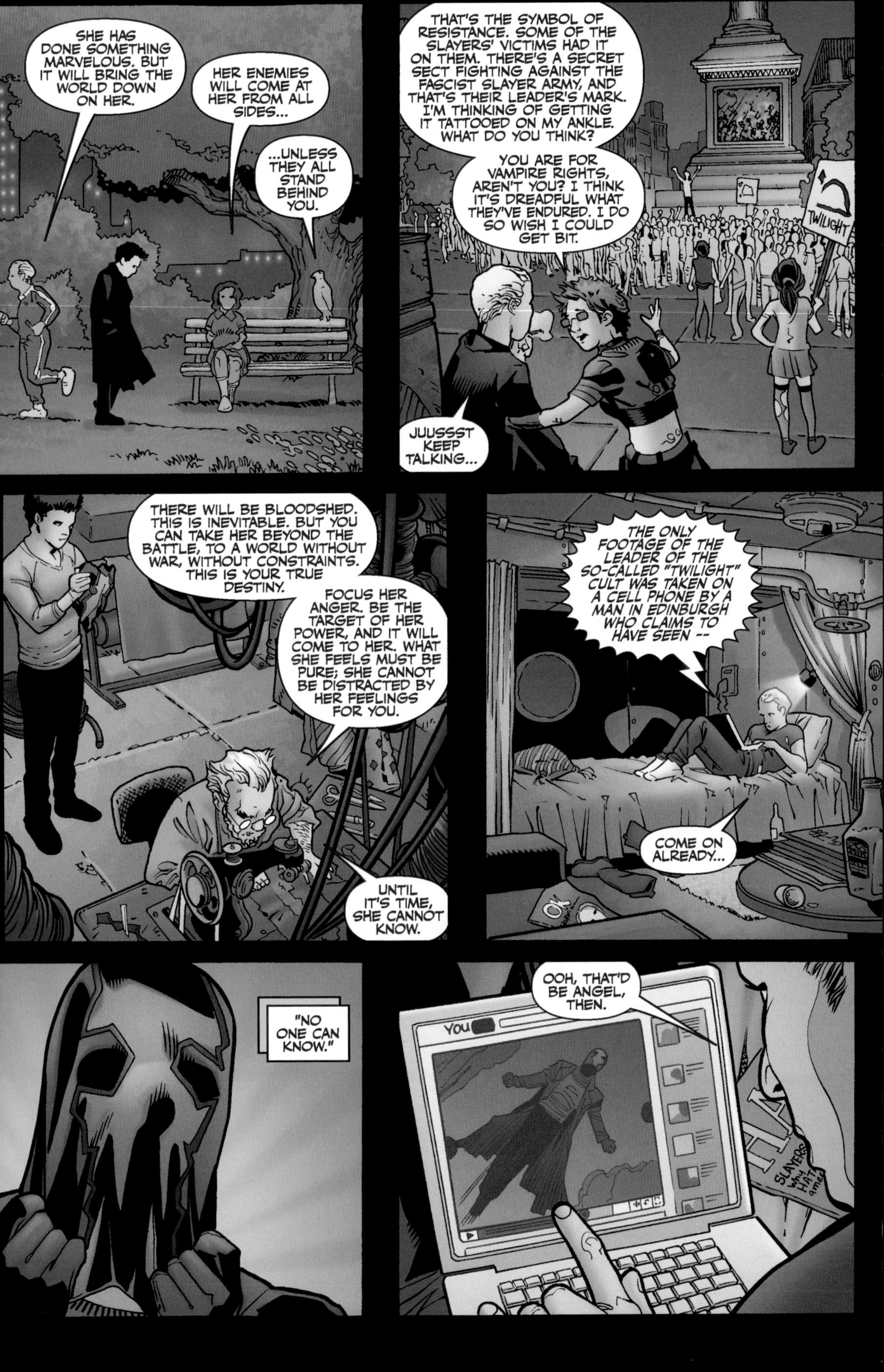

SHE HAS DONE SOMETHING MARVELOUS. BUT IT WILL BRING THE WORLD DOWN ON HER.
HER ENEMIES WILL COME AT HER FROM ALL SIDES...
...UNLESS THEY ALL STAND BEHIND YOU.
THAT'S THE SYMBOL OF RESISTANCE. SOME OF THE SLAYERS' VICTIMS HAD IT ON THEM. THERE'S A SECRET SECT FIGHTING AGAINST THE FASCIST SLAYER ARMY, AND THAT'S THEIR LEADER'S MARK. I'M THINKING OF GETTING IT TATTOOED ON MY ANKLE. WHAT DO YOU THINK?
YOU ARE FOR VAMPIRE RIGHTS, AREN'T YOU? I THINK IT'S DREADFUL WHAT THEY'VE ENDURED. I DO SO WISH I COULD GET BIT.
TWILIGHT
JUUSSST KEEP TALKING...
THERE WILL BE BLOODSHED. THIS IS INEVITABLE. BUT YOU CAN TAKE HER BEYOND THE BATTLE, TO A WORLD WITHOUT WAR, WITHOUT CONSTRAINTS. THIS IS YOUR TRUE DESTINY.
FOCUS HER ANGER. BE THE TARGET OF HER POWER, AND IT WILL COME TO HER. WHAT SHE FEELS MUST BE PURE; SHE CANNOT BE DISTRACTED BY HER FEELINGS FOR YOU.
UNTIL IT'S TIME, SHE CANNOT KNOW.
THE ONLY FOOTAGE OF THE LEADER OF THE SO-CALLED "TWILIGHT" CULT WAS TAKEN ON A CELL PHONE BY A MAN IN EDINBURGH WHO CLAIMS TO HAVE SEEN --
COME ON ALREADY...
"NO ONE CAN KNOW."
OOH, THAT'D BE ANGEL, THEN.
YOU
SLAYERS

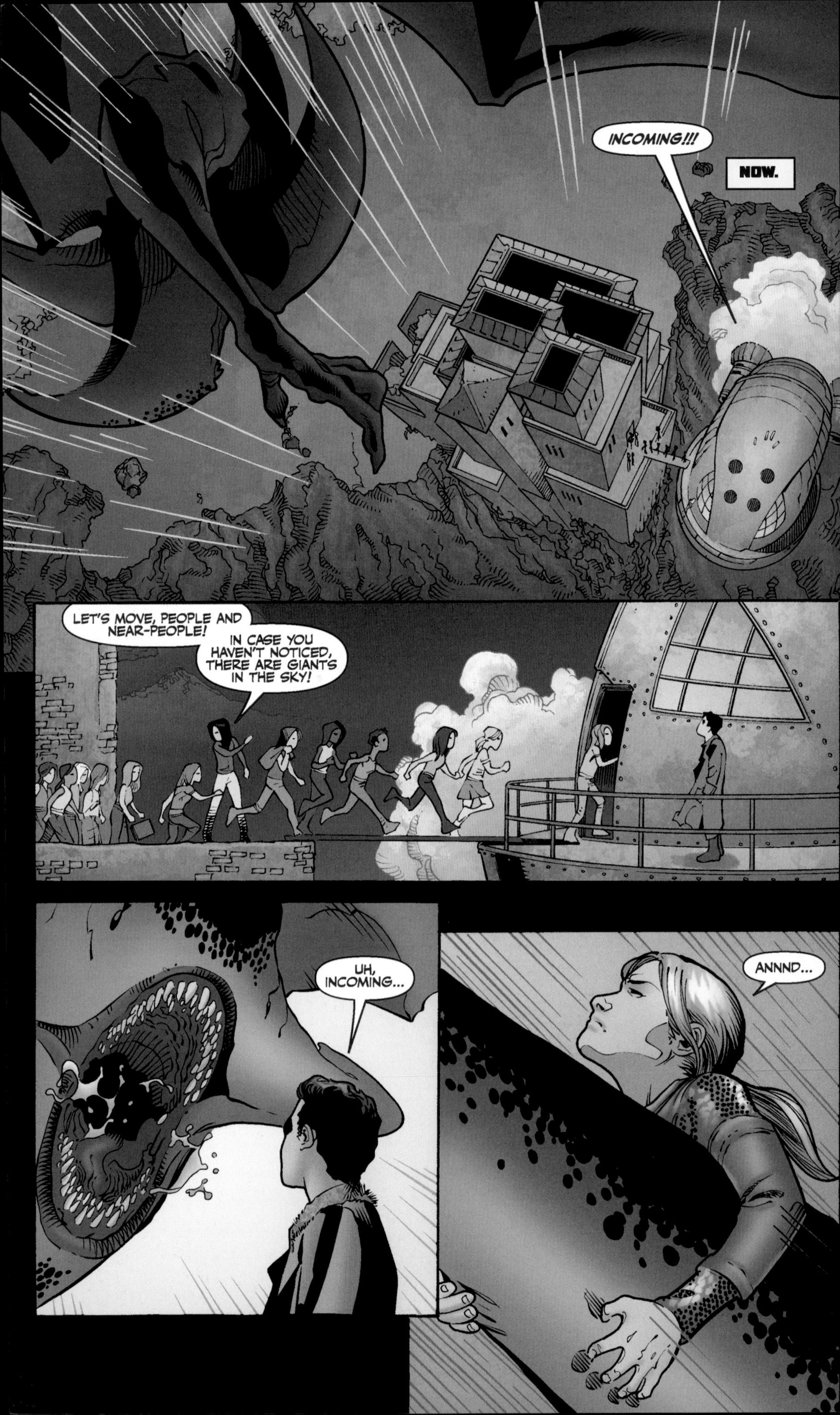
INCOMING!!!
NOW.
LET'S MOVE, PEOPLE AND NEAR-PEOPLE!
IN CASE YOU HAVEN'T NOTICED, THERE ARE GIANTS IN THE SKY!
UH, INCOMING...
ANNND...

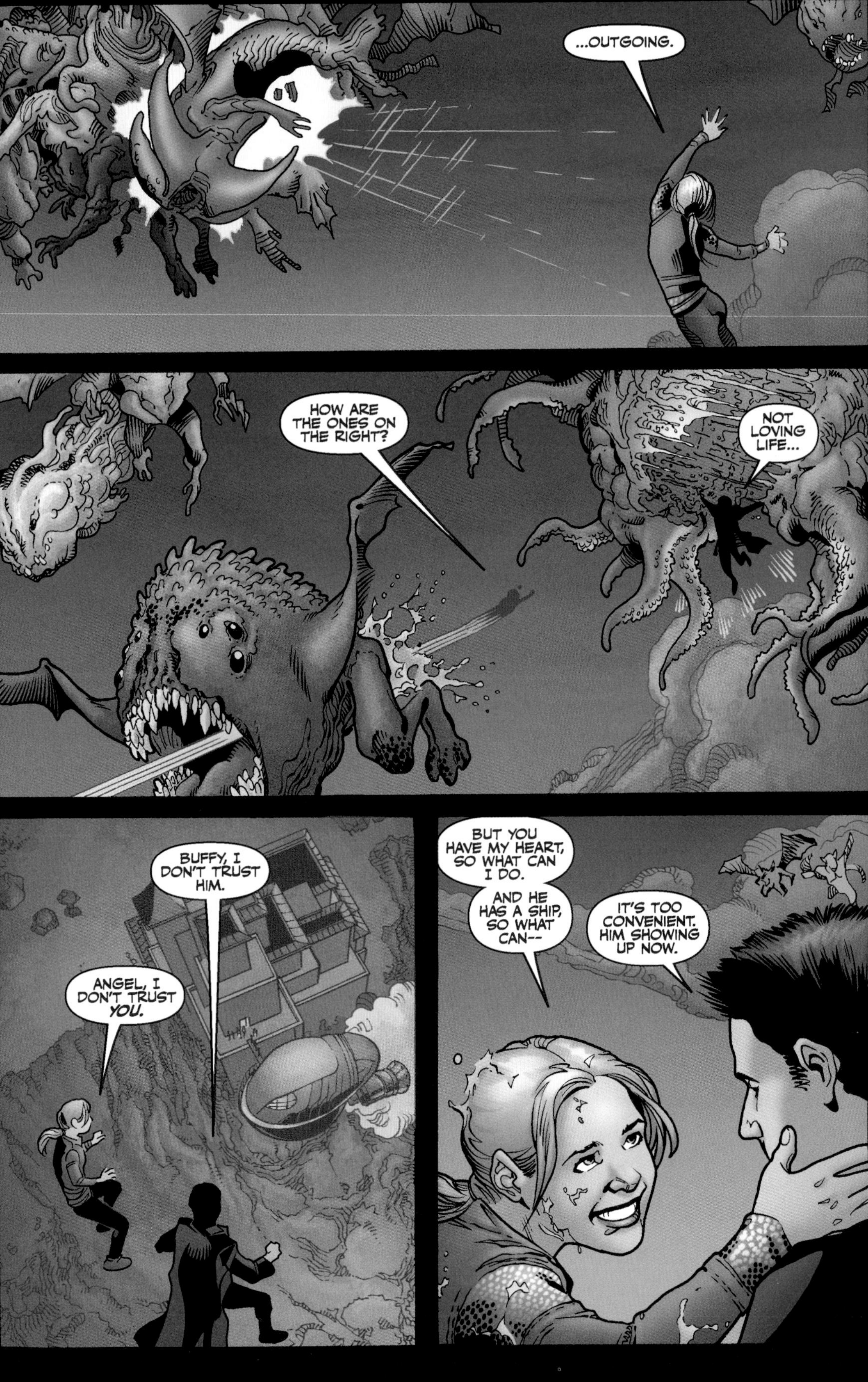
...OUTGOING.
HOW ARE THE ONES ON THE RIGHT?
NOT LOVING LIFE...
BUFFY, I DON'T TRUST HIM.
ANGEL, I DON'T TRUST *YOU.*
IT'S TOO CONVENIENT. HIM SHOWING UP NOW.
BUT YOU HAVE MY HEART, SO WHAT CAN I DO.
AND HE HAS A SHIP, SO WHAT CAN--

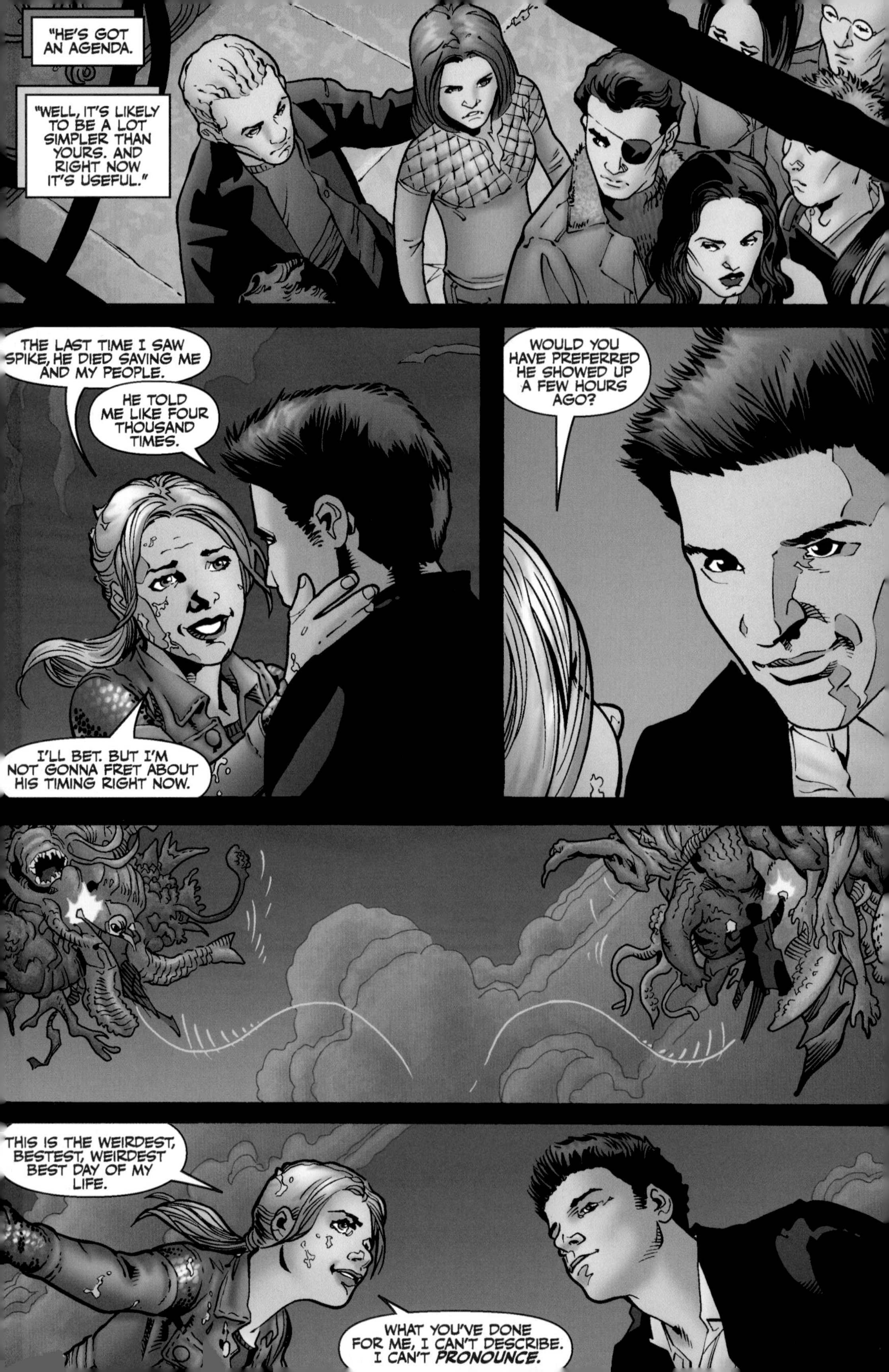
"HE'S GOT AN AGENDA.
"WELL, IT'S LIKELY TO BE A LOT SIMPLER THAN YOURS. AND RIGHT NOW IT'S USEFUL."
THE LAST TIME I SAW SPIKE, HE DIED SAVING ME AND MY PEOPLE.
HE TOLD ME LIKE FOUR THOUSAND TIMES.
I'LL BET. BUT I'M NOT GONNA FRET ABOUT HIS TIMING RIGHT NOW.
WOULD YOU HAVE PREFERRED HE SHOWED UP A FEW HOURS AGO?
THIS IS THE WEIRDEST, BESTEST, WEIRDEST BEST DAY OF MY LIFE.
WHAT YOU'VE DONE FOR ME, I *CAN'T* DESCRIBE. I CAN'T ***PRONOUNCE.***

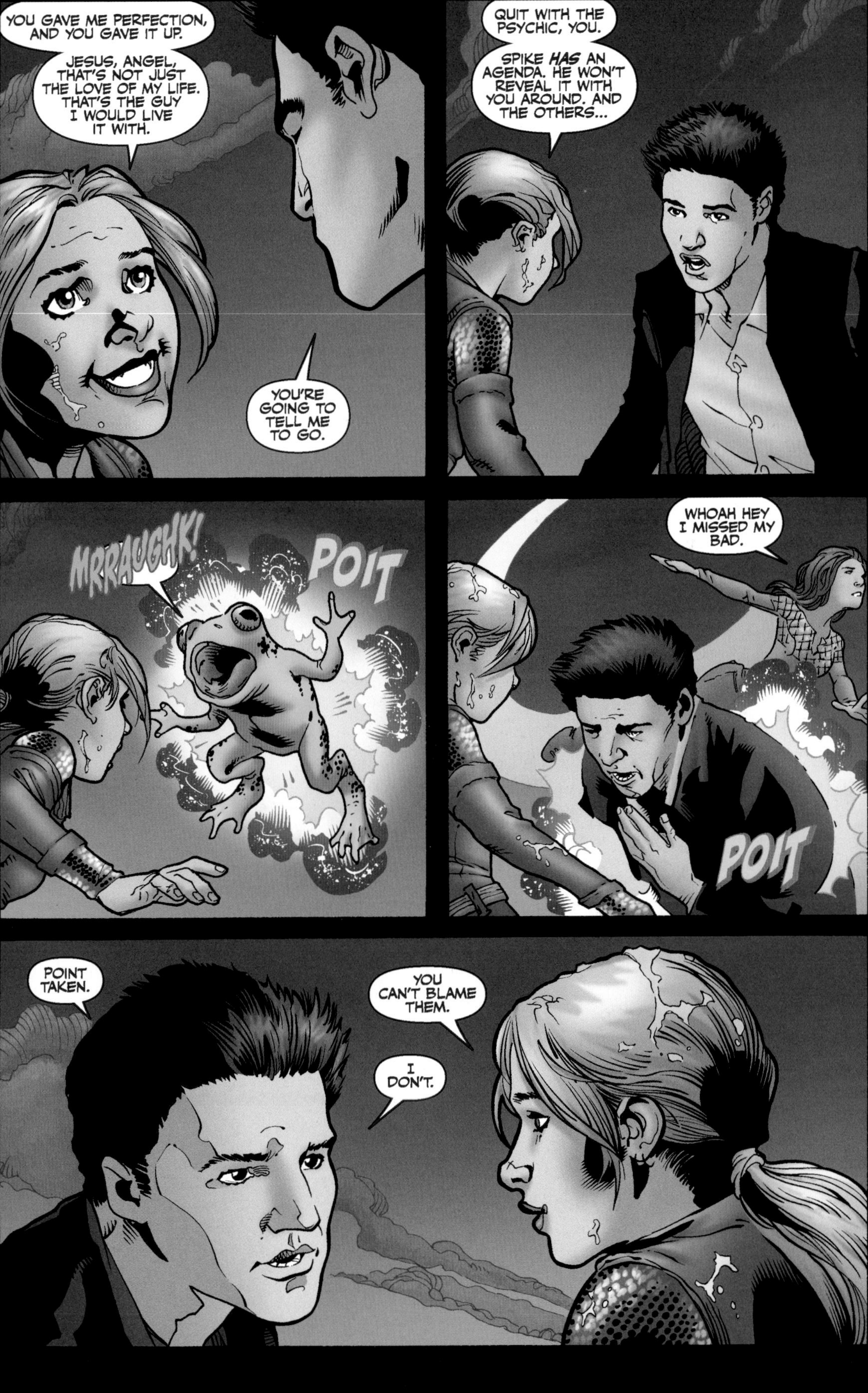
YOU GAVE ME PERFECTION, AND YOU GAVE IT UP.
JESUS, ANGEL, THAT'S NOT JUST THE LOVE OF MY LIFE. THAT'S THE GUY I WOULD LIVE IT WITH.
YOU'RE GOING TO TELL ME TO GO.
QUIT WITH THE PSYCHIC, YOU.
SPIKE HAS AN AGENDA. HE WON'T REVEAL IT WITH YOU AROUND. AND THE OTHERS...
MRRAUGHK!
POIT
WHOAH HEY I MISSED MY BAD.
POIT
POINT TAKEN.
YOU CAN'T BLAME THEM.
I DON'T.

WHAT WE DID... IT RELEASED THESE DEMONS. ALL OVER.

THEY'RE GONNA TARGET SLAYERS.

ARE YOU SURE--

WELL, EVERYONE *ELSE* HAS. YOU CAN MAKE UP FOR A LOT OF DAMAGE, ANGEL. I NEED YOU TO.

I THINK YOU NEED IT TOO.

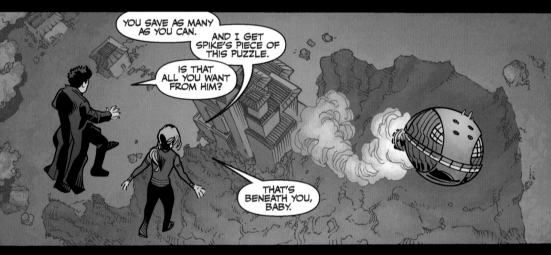

YOU SAVE AS MANY AS YOU CAN.

AND I GET SPIKE'S PIECE OF THIS PUZZLE.

IS THAT ALL YOU WANT FROM HIM?

THAT'S BENEATH YOU, BABY.

I GOT MORE POWERFUL, NOT REMOTELY MATURE.

I'LL FIND YOU SOON.

YOU BETTER.

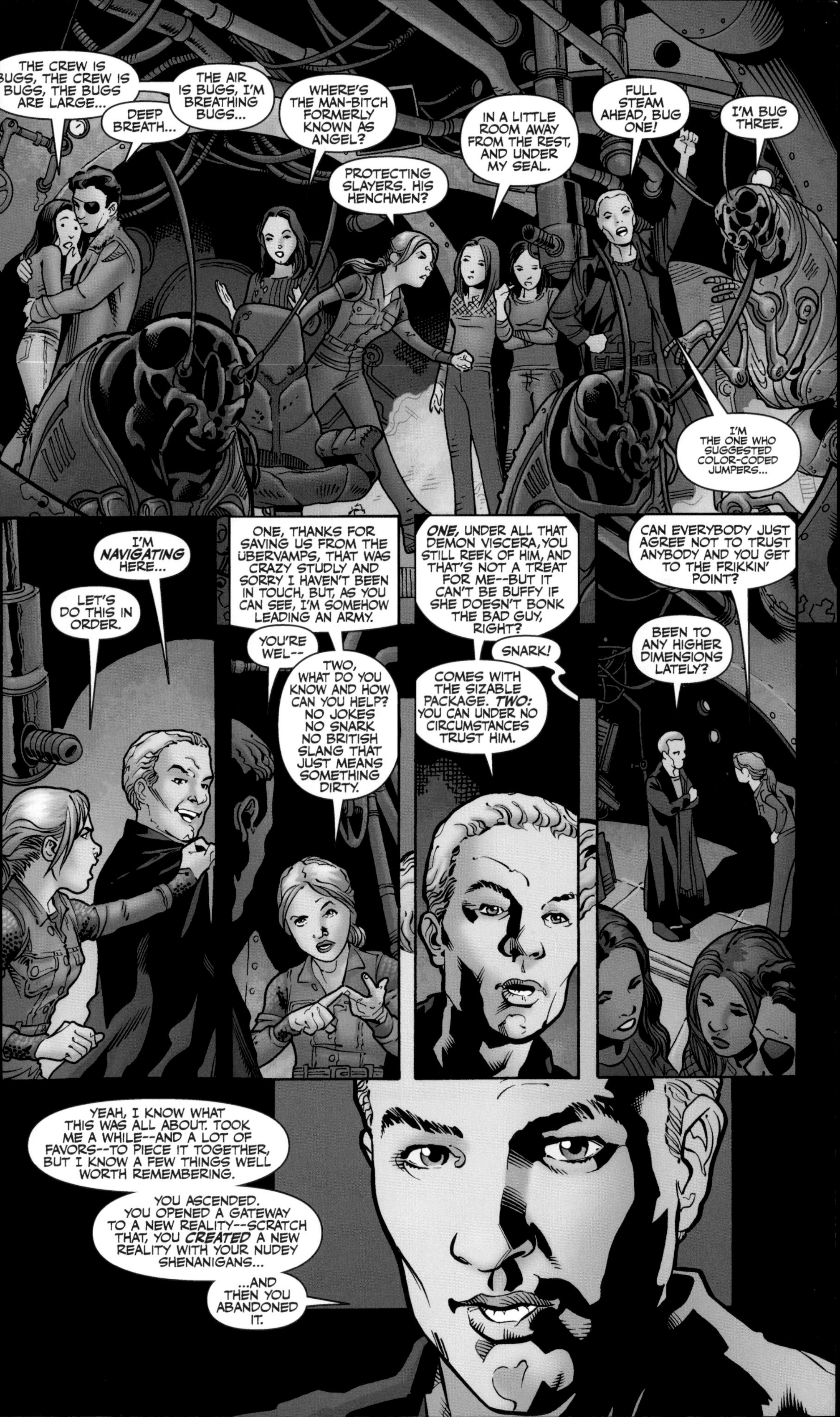

THE CREW IS BUGS, THE CREW IS BUGS, THE BUGS ARE LARGE...
DEEP BREATH...
THE AIR IS BUGS, I'M BREATHING BUGS...
WHERE'S THE MAN-BITCH FORMERLY KNOWN AS ANGEL?
PROTECTING SLAYERS. HIS HENCHMEN?
IN A LITTLE ROOM AWAY FROM THE REST, AND UNDER MY SEAL.
FULL STEAM AHEAD, BUG ONE!
I'M BUG THREE.
I'M THE ONE WHO SUGGESTED COLOR-CODED JUMPERS...
I'M NAVIGATING HERE...
LET'S DO THIS IN ORDER.
ONE, THANKS FOR SAVING US FROM THE ÜBERVAMPS, THAT WAS CRAZY STUDLY AND SORRY I HAVEN'T BEEN IN TOUCH, BUT, AS YOU CAN SEE, I'M SOMEHOW LEADING AN ARMY.
YOU'RE WEL--
TWO, WHAT DO YOU KNOW AND HOW CAN YOU HELP? NO JOKES NO SNARK NO BRITISH SLANG THAT JUST MEANS SOMETHING DIRTY.
ONE, UNDER ALL THAT DEMON VISCERA, YOU STILL REEK OF HIM, AND THAT'S NOT A TREAT FOR ME--BUT IT CAN'T BE BUFFY IF SHE DOESN'T BONK THE BAD GUY, RIGHT?
SNARK!
COMES WITH THE SIZABLE PACKAGE. TWO: YOU CAN UNDER NO CIRCUMSTANCES TRUST HIM.
CAN EVERYBODY JUST AGREE NOT TO TRUST ANYBODY AND YOU GET TO THE FRIKKIN' POINT?
BEEN TO ANY HIGHER DIMENSIONS LATELY?
YEAH, I KNOW WHAT THIS WAS ALL ABOUT. TOOK ME A WHILE--AND A LOT OF FAVORS--TO PIECE IT TOGETHER, BUT I KNOW A FEW THINGS WELL WORTH REMEMBERING.
YOU ASCENDED. YOU OPENED A GATEWAY TO A NEW REALITY--SCRATCH THAT, YOU CREATED A NEW REALITY WITH YOUR NUDEY SHENANIGANS...
...AND THEN YOU ABANDONED IT.

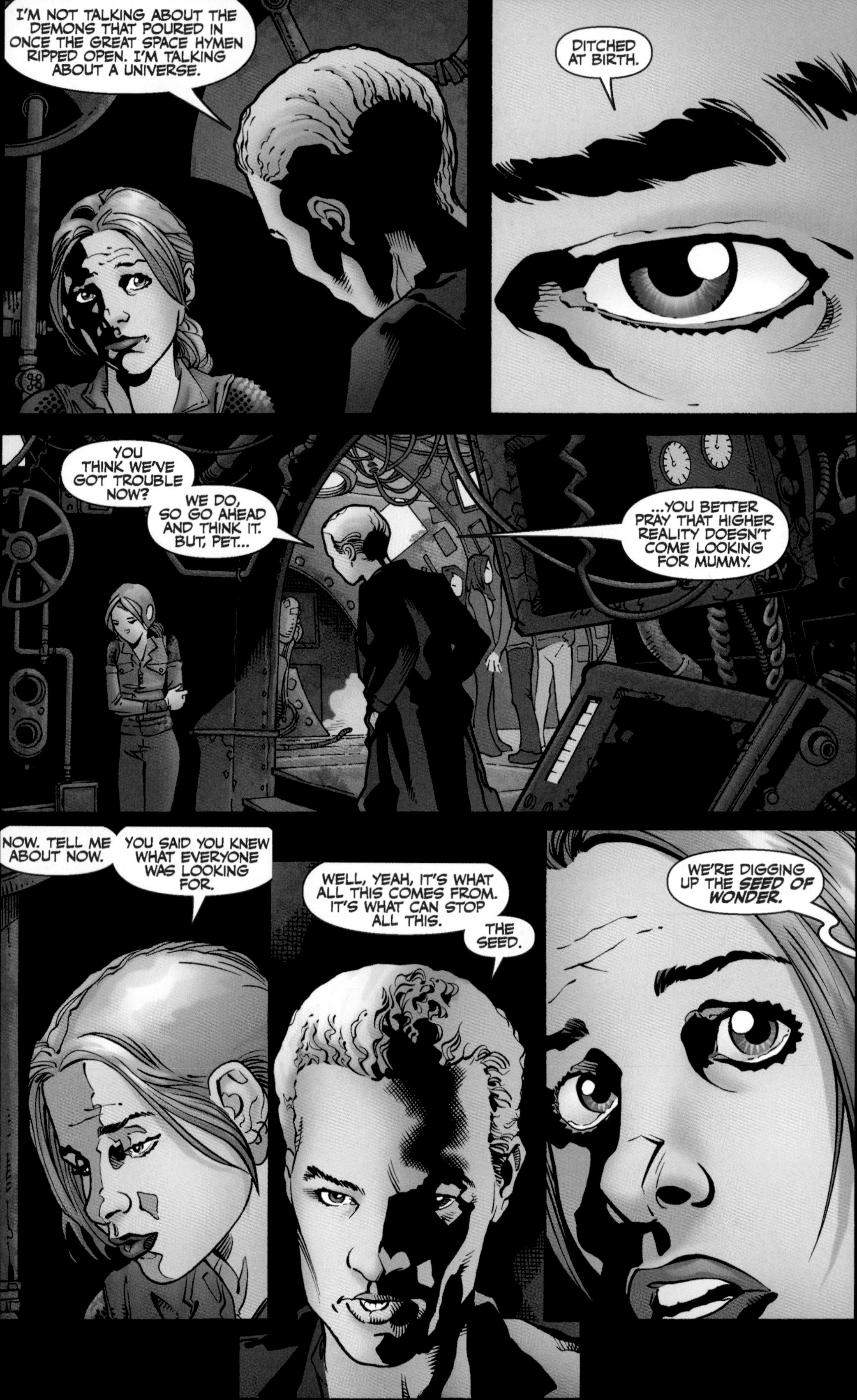

I'M NOT TALKING ABOUT THE DEMONS THAT POURED IN ONCE THE GREAT SPACE HYMEN RIPPED OPEN. I'M TALKING ABOUT A UNIVERSE.
DITCHED AT BIRTH.
YOU THINK WE'VE GOT TROUBLE NOW?
WE DO, SO GO AHEAD AND THINK IT. BUT, PET...
...YOU BETTER PRAY THAT HIGHER REALITY DOESN'T COME LOOKING FOR MUMMY.
NOW. TELL ME ABOUT NOW.
YOU SAID YOU KNEW WHAT EVERYONE WAS LOOKING FOR.
WELL, YEAH, IT'S WHAT ALL THIS COMES FROM. IT'S WHAT CAN STOP ALL THIS.
THE SEED.
WE'RE DIGGING UP THE *SEED OF WONDER.*

THIS IS YOUR CAPTAIN SPEAKING.

WE ARE CURRENTLY ON COURSE TO THE HEART OF ALL MAGIC ON EARTH, AND SORRY, TREE FANS: IT'S NOT STONEHENGE.

THERE WAS, ONE TIME, A HOUSE OF WORSHIP... SWALLOWED UP BY THE EARTH.

OVER WHICH THEY BUILT A CITY...

...ALSO SWALLOWED BY THE EARTH.

WE'RE HEADED FOR THE HEART, MY FRIENDS...

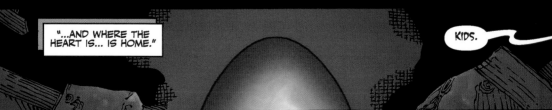

"...AND WHERE THE HEART IS... IS HOME."

KIDS.

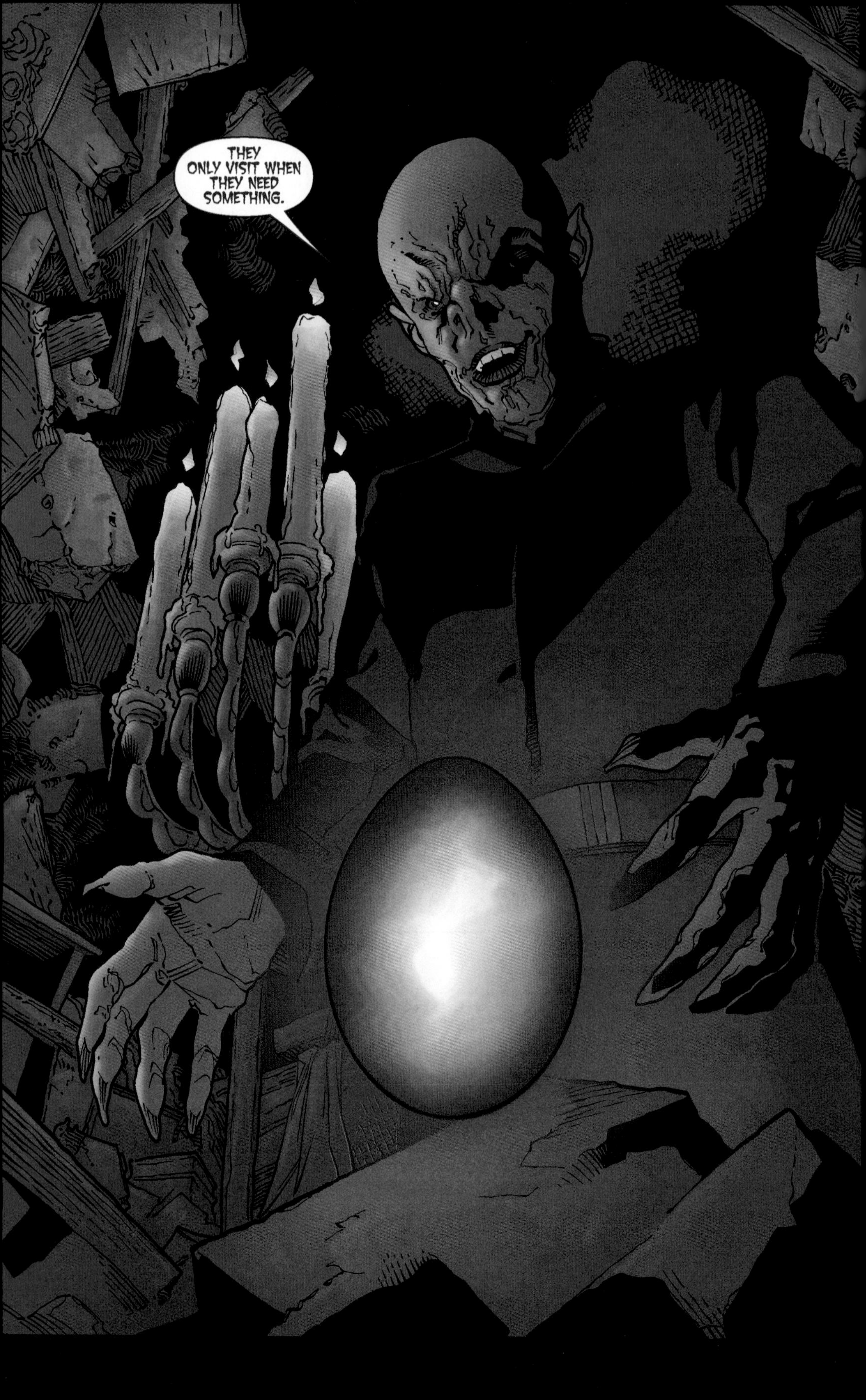
THEY ONLY VISIT WHEN THEY NEED SOMETHING.

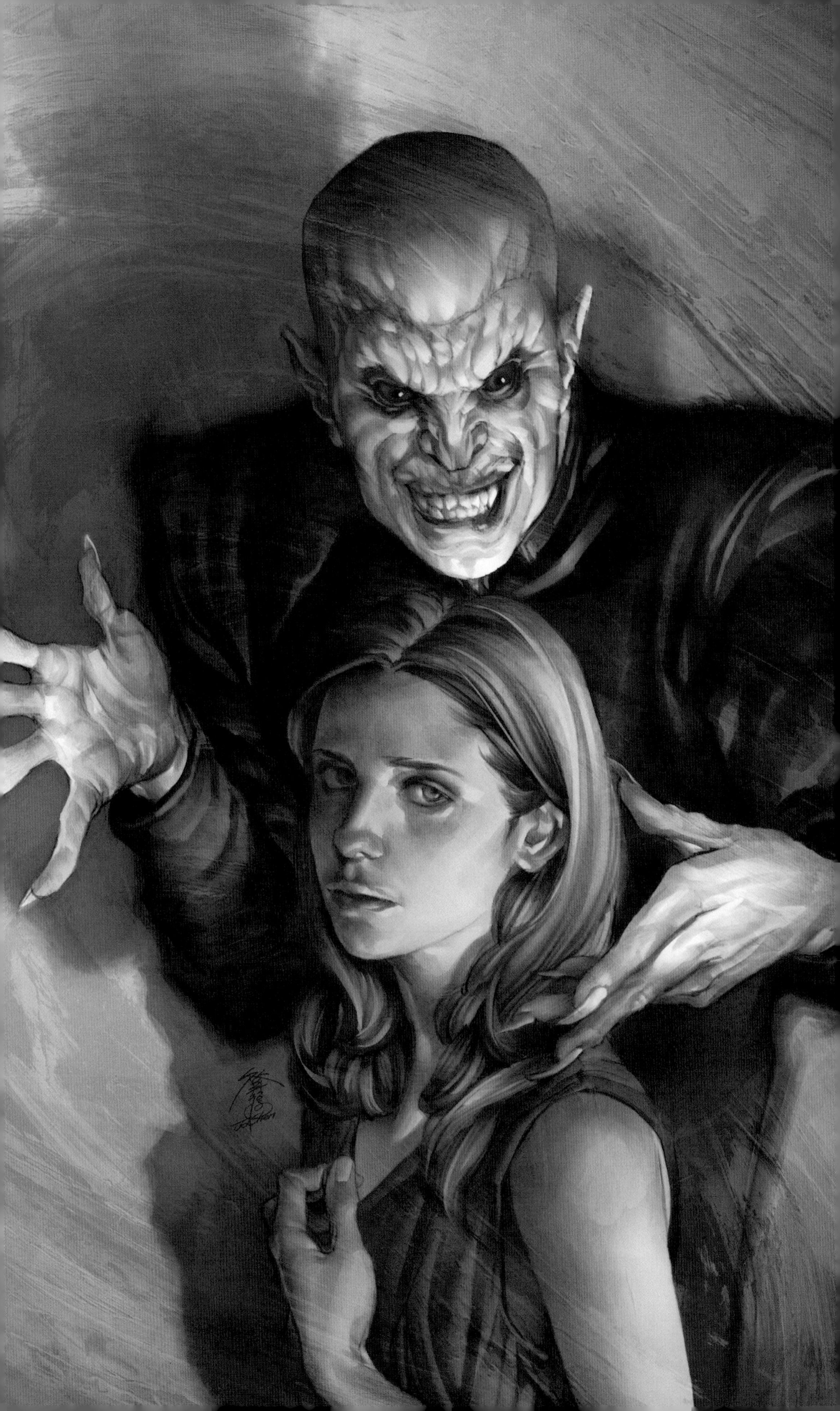

LAST GLEAMING
PART TWO

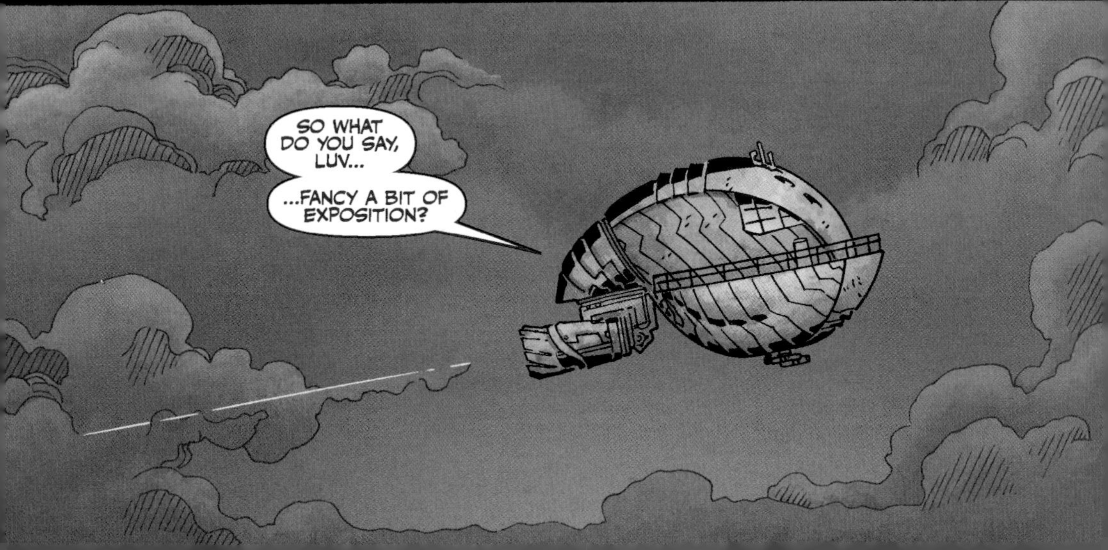
SO WHAT DO YOU SAY, LUV...
...FANCY A BIT OF EXPOSITION?

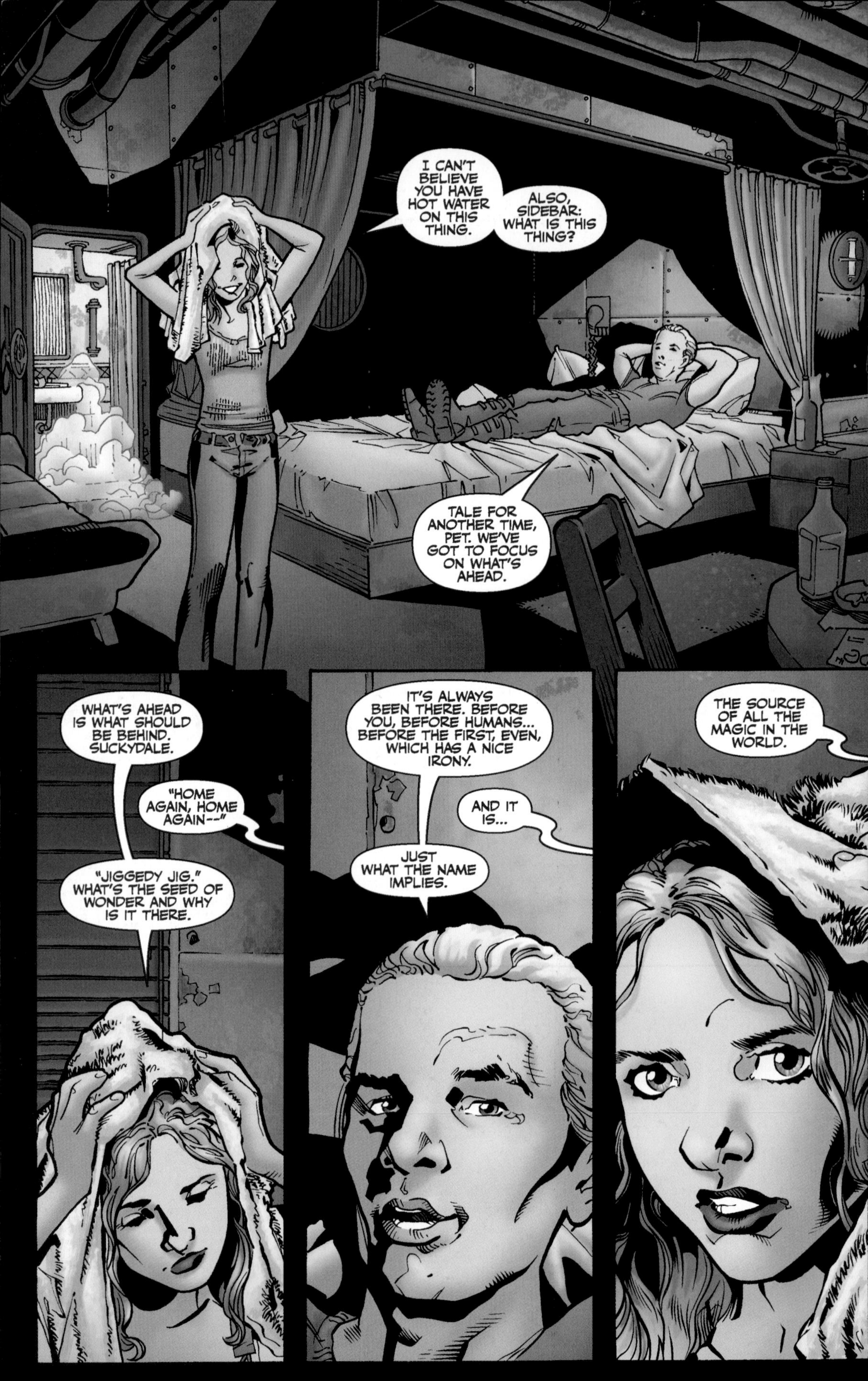
I CAN'T BELIEVE YOU HAVE HOT WATER ON THIS THING.
ALSO, SIDEBAR: WHAT IS THIS THING?
TALE FOR ANOTHER TIME, PET. WE'VE GOT TO FOCUS ON WHAT'S AHEAD.
WHAT'S AHEAD IS WHAT SHOULD BE BEHIND. SUCKYDALE.
"HOME AGAIN, HOME AGAIN--"
"JIGGEDY JIG." WHAT'S THE SEED OF WONDER AND WHY IS IT THERE.
IT'S ALWAYS BEEN THERE. BEFORE YOU, BEFORE HUMANS... BEFORE THE FIRST, EVEN, WHICH HAS A NICE IRONY.
AND IT IS...
JUST WHAT THE NAME IMPLIES.
THE SOURCE OF ALL THE MAGIC IN THE WORLD.

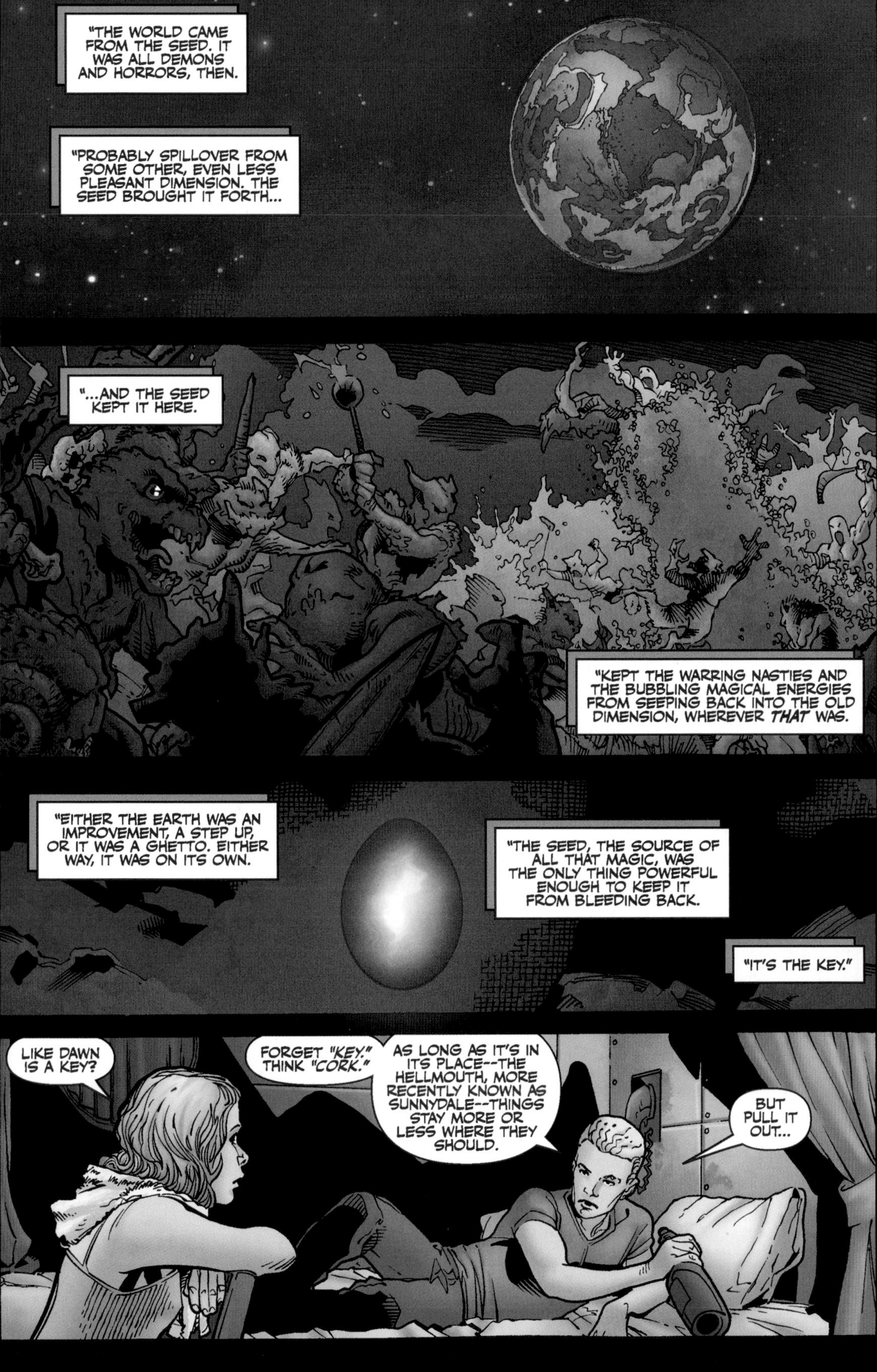
"THE WORLD CAME FROM THE SEED. IT WAS ALL DEMONS AND HORRORS, THEN.
"PROBABLY SPILLOVER FROM SOME OTHER, EVEN LESS PLEASANT DIMENSION. THE SEED BROUGHT IT FORTH...
"...AND THE SEED KEPT IT HERE.
"KEPT THE WARRING NASTIES AND THE BUBBLING MAGICAL ENERGIES FROM SEEPING BACK INTO THE OLD DIMENSION, WHEREVER *THAT* WAS.
"EITHER THE EARTH WAS AN IMPROVEMENT, A STEP UP, OR IT WAS A GHETTO. EITHER WAY, IT WAS ON ITS OWN.
"THE SEED, THE SOURCE OF ALL THAT MAGIC, WAS THE ONLY THING POWERFUL ENOUGH TO KEEP IT FROM BLEEDING BACK.
"IT'S THE KEY."
LIKE DAWN IS A KEY?
FORGET *"KEY."* THINK *"CORK."*
AS LONG AS IT'S IN ITS PLACE--THE HELLMOUTH, MORE RECENTLY KNOWN AS SUNNYDALE--THINGS STAY MORE OR LESS WHERE THEY SHOULD.
BUT PULL IT OUT...

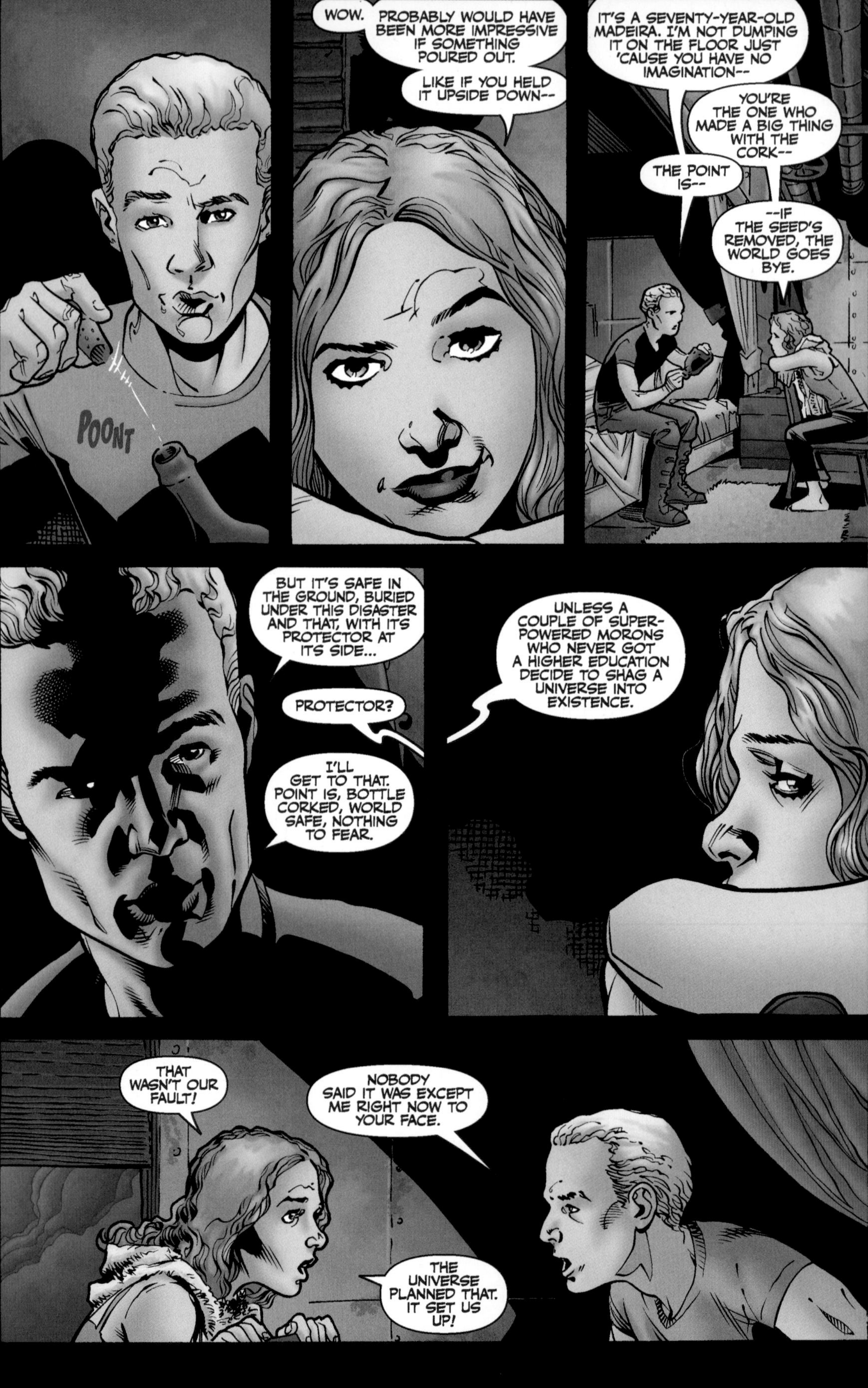
POONT
WOW.
PROBABLY WOULD HAVE BEEN MORE IMPRESSIVE IF SOMETHING POURED OUT.
LIKE IF YOU HELD IT UPSIDE DOWN--
IT'S A SEVENTY-YEAR-OLD MADEIRA. I'M NOT DUMPING IT ON THE FLOOR JUST 'CAUSE YOU HAVE NO IMAGINATION--
YOU'RE THE ONE WHO MADE A BIG THING WITH THE CORK--
THE POINT IS--
--IF THE SEED'S REMOVED, THE WORLD GOES BYE.
BUT IT'S SAFE IN THE GROUND, BURIED UNDER THIS DISASTER AND THAT, WITH ITS PROTECTOR AT ITS SIDE...
PROTECTOR?
I'LL GET TO THAT. POINT IS, BOTTLE CORKED, WORLD SAFE, NOTHING TO FEAR.
UNLESS A COUPLE OF SUPER-POWERED MORONS WHO NEVER GOT A HIGHER EDUCATION DECIDE TO SHAG A UNIVERSE INTO EXISTENCE.
THAT WASN'T OUR FAULT!
NOBODY SAID IT WAS EXCEPT ME RIGHT NOW TO YOUR FACE.
THE UNIVERSE PLANNED THAT. IT SET US UP!

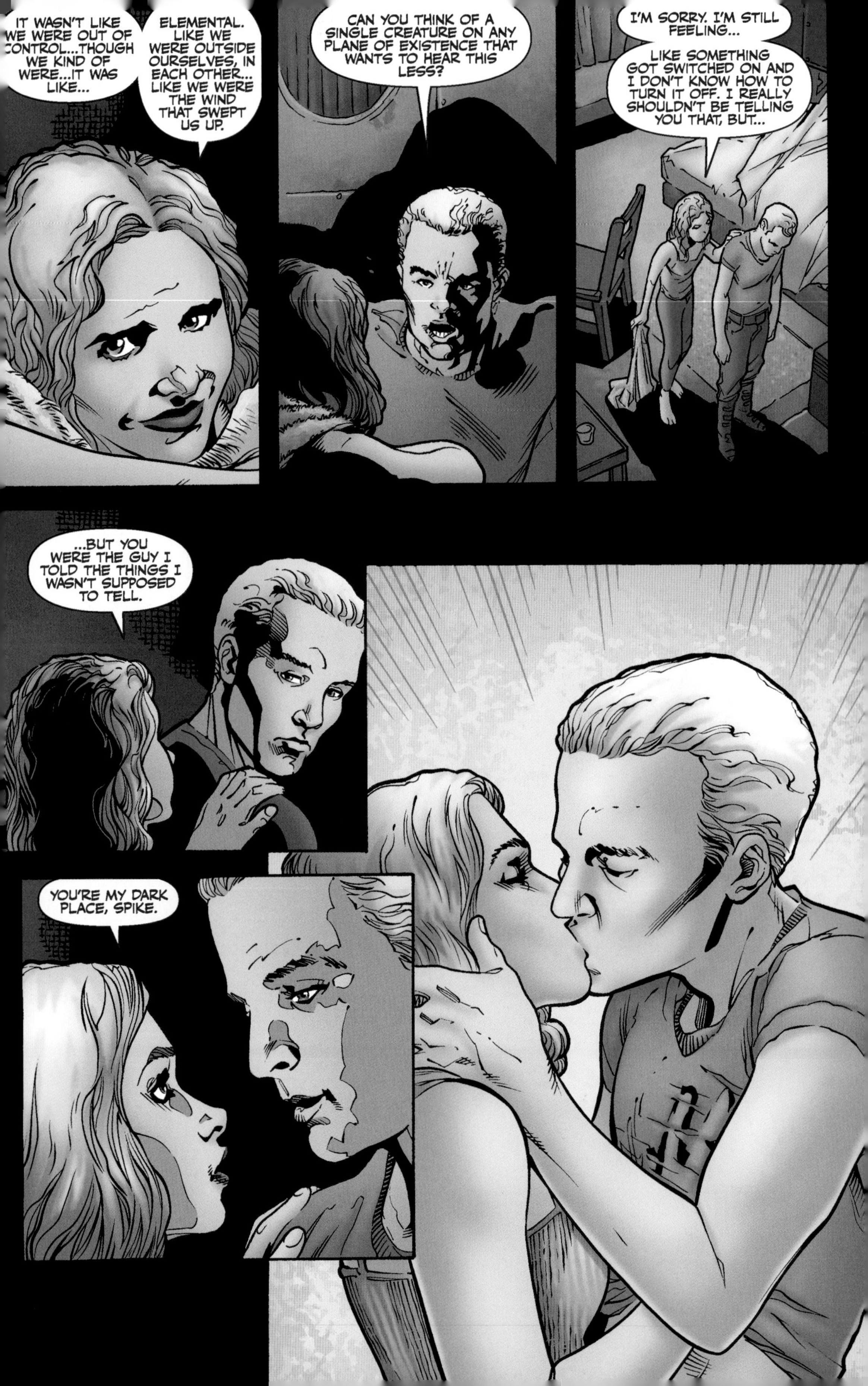
IT WASN'T LIKE WE WERE OUT OF CONTROL...THOUGH WE KIND OF WERE...IT WAS LIKE...
ELEMENTAL. LIKE WE WERE OUTSIDE OURSELVES, IN EACH OTHER... LIKE WE WERE THE WIND THAT SWEPT US UP.
CAN YOU THINK OF A SINGLE CREATURE ON ANY PLANE OF EXISTENCE THAT WANTS TO HEAR THIS LESS?
I'M SORRY. I'M STILL FEELING...
LIKE SOMETHING GOT SWITCHED ON AND I DON'T KNOW HOW TO TURN IT OFF. I REALLY SHOULDN'T BE TELLING YOU THAT, BUT...
...BUT YOU WERE THE GUY I TOLD THE THINGS I WASN'T SUPPOSED TO TELL.
YOU'RE MY DARK PLACE, SPIKE.

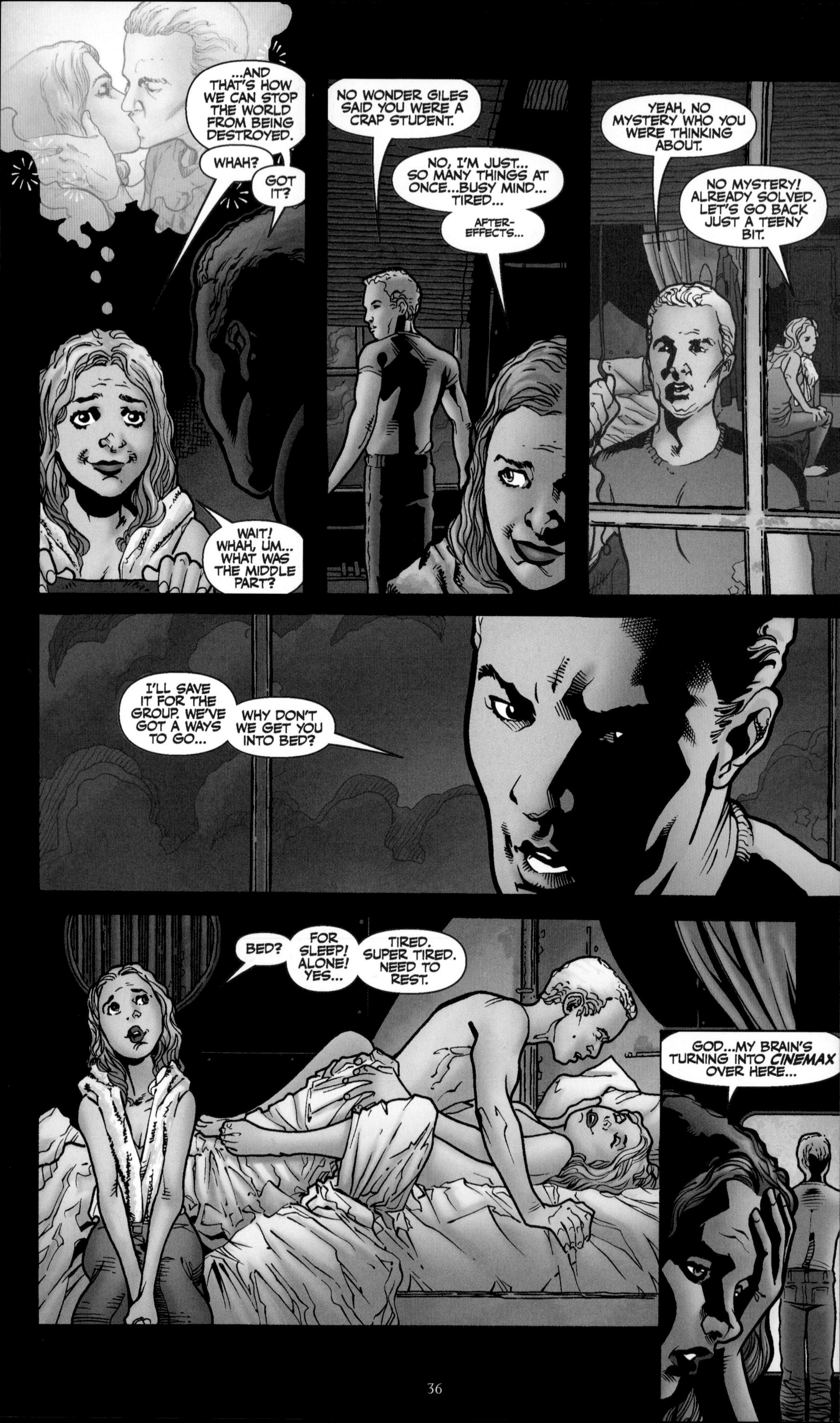
...AND THAT'S HOW WE CAN STOP THE WORLD FROM BEING DESTROYED.
WHAH?
GOT IT?
WAIT! WHAH, UM... WHAT WAS THE MIDDLE PART?
NO WONDER GILES SAID YOU WERE A CRAP STUDENT.
NO, I'M JUST... SO MANY THINGS AT ONCE...BUSY MIND... TIRED...
AFTER-EFFECTS...
YEAH, NO MYSTERY WHO YOU WERE THINKING ABOUT.
NO MYSTERY! ALREADY SOLVED. LET'S GO BACK JUST A TEENY BIT.
I'LL SAVE IT FOR THE GROUP. WE'VE GOT A WAYS TO GO...
WHY DON'T WE GET YOU INTO BED?
BED?
FOR SLEEP! ALONE! YES...
TIRED. SUPER TIRED. NEED TO REST.
GOD...MY BRAIN'S TURNING INTO *CINEMAX* OVER HERE...

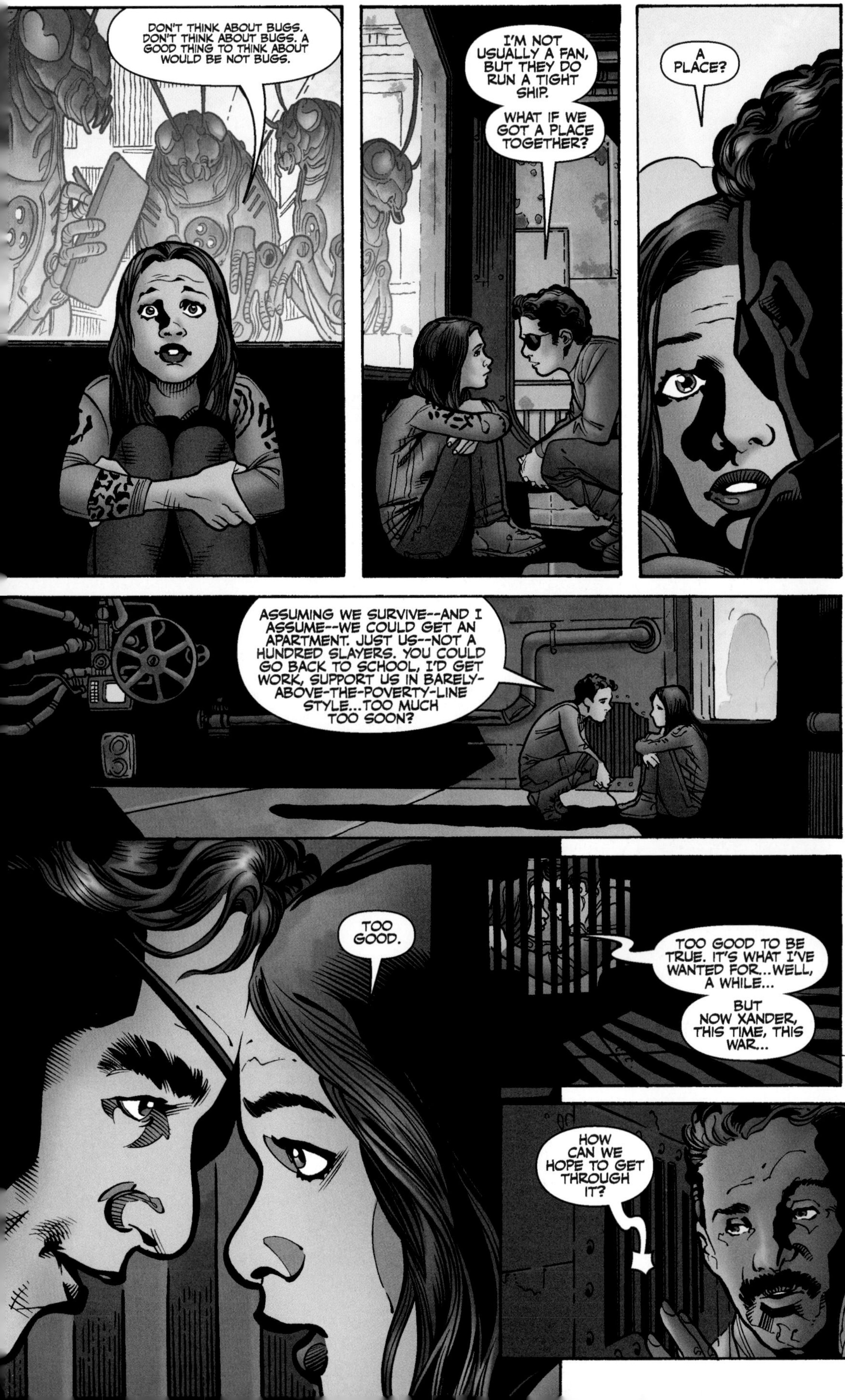
DON'T THINK ABOUT BUGS. DON'T THINK ABOUT BUGS. A GOOD THING TO THINK ABOUT WOULD BE NOT BUGS.
I'M NOT USUALLY A FAN, BUT THEY DO RUN A TIGHT SHIP.
WHAT IF WE GOT A PLACE TOGETHER?
A PLACE?
ASSUMING WE SURVIVE--AND I ASSUME--WE COULD GET AN APARTMENT. JUST US--NOT A HUNDRED SLAYERS. YOU COULD GO BACK TO SCHOOL, I'D GET WORK, SUPPORT US IN BARELY-ABOVE-THE-POVERTY-LINE STYLE...TOO MUCH TOO SOON?
TOO GOOD.
TOO GOOD TO BE TRUE. IT'S WHAT I'VE WANTED FOR...WELL, A WHILE...
BUT NOW XANDER, THIS TIME, THIS WAR...
HOW CAN WE HOPE TO GET THROUGH IT?

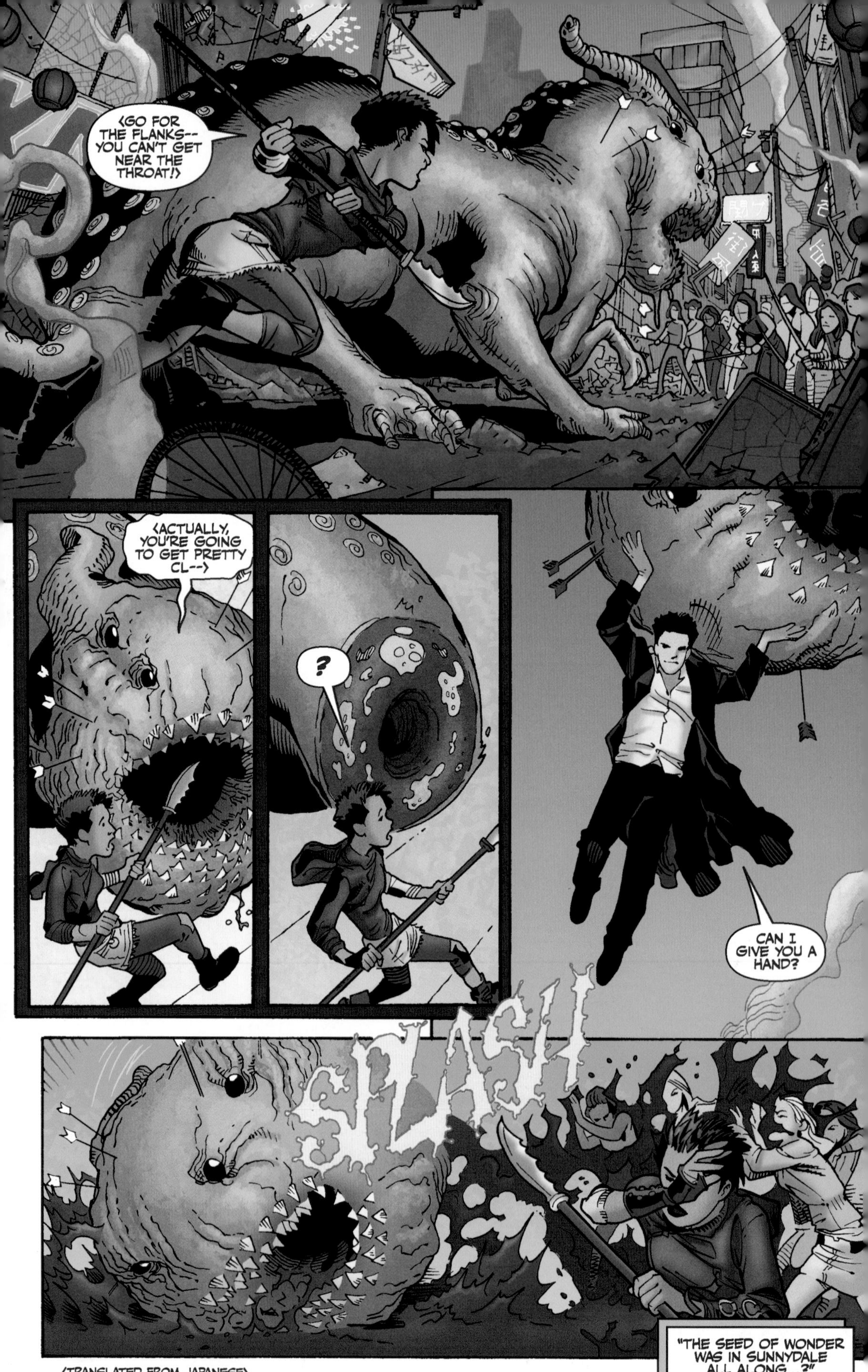
‹GO FOR THE FLANKS-- YOU CAN'T GET NEAR THE THROAT!›
‹ACTUALLY, YOU'RE GOING TO GET PRETTY CL--›
?
CAN I GIVE YOU A HAND?
SPLASH
"THE SEED OF WONDER WAS IN SUNNYDALE ALL ALONG...?"

‹TRANSLATED FROM JAPANESE›

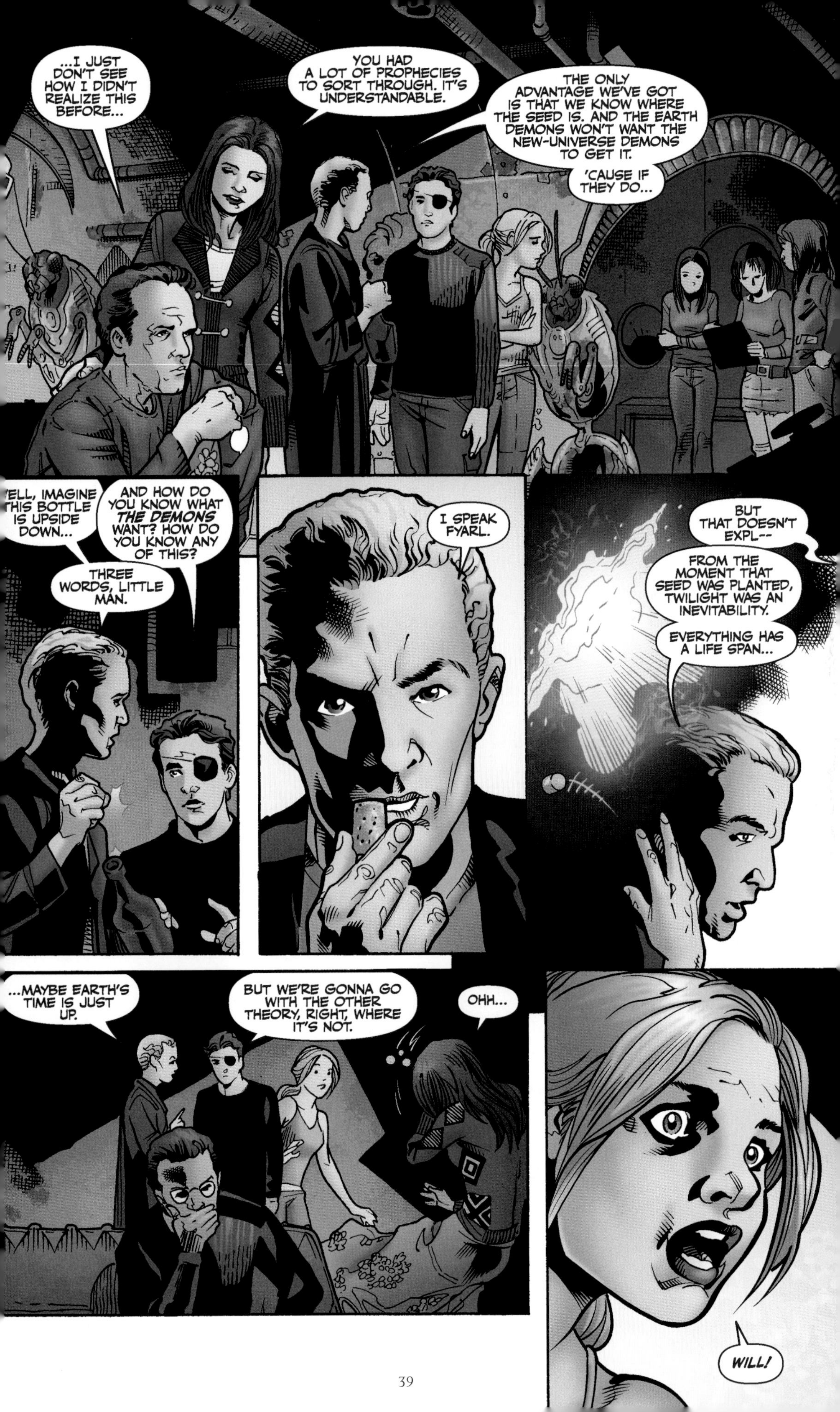
...I JUST DON'T SEE HOW I DIDN'T REALIZE THIS BEFORE...
YOU HAD A LOT OF PROPHECIES TO SORT THROUGH. IT'S UNDERSTANDABLE.
THE ONLY ADVANTAGE WE'VE GOT IS THAT WE KNOW WHERE THE SEED IS. AND THE EARTH DEMONS WON'T WANT THE NEW-UNIVERSE DEMONS TO GET IT.
'CAUSE IF THEY DO...
WELL, IMAGINE THIS BOTTLE IS UPSIDE DOWN...
AND HOW DO YOU KNOW WHAT *THE DEMONS* WANT? HOW DO YOU KNOW ANY OF THIS?
THREE WORDS, LITTLE MAN.
I SPEAK FYARL.
BUT THAT DOESN'T EXPL--
FROM THE MOMENT THAT SEED WAS PLANTED, TWILIGHT WAS AN INEVITABILITY.
EVERYTHING HAS A LIFE SPAN...
...MAYBE EARTH'S TIME IS JUST UP.
BUT WE'RE GONNA GO WITH THE OTHER THEORY, RIGHT, WHERE IT'S NOT.
OHH...
WILL!

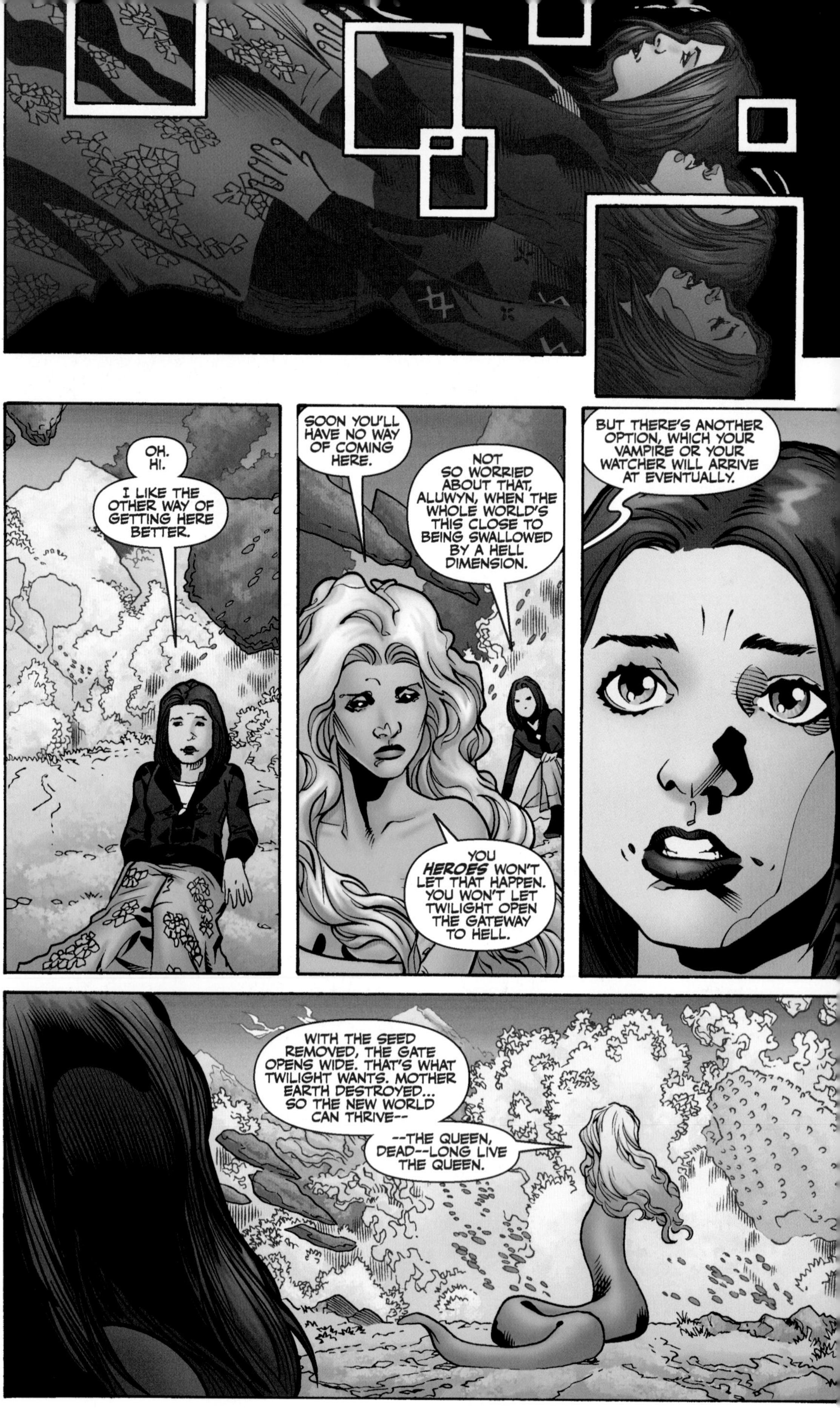
OH.
HI.
I LIKE THE OTHER WAY OF GETTING HERE BETTER.
SOON YOU'LL HAVE NO WAY OF COMING HERE.
NOT SO WORRIED ABOUT THAT, ALUWYN, WHEN THE WHOLE WORLD'S THIS CLOSE TO BEING SWALLOWED BY A HELL DIMENSION.
YOU *HEROES* WON'T LET THAT HAPPEN. YOU WON'T LET TWILIGHT OPEN THE GATEWAY TO HELL.
BUT THERE'S ANOTHER OPTION, WHICH YOUR VAMPIRE OR YOUR WATCHER WILL ARRIVE AT EVENTUALLY.
WITH THE SEED REMOVED, THE GATE OPENS WIDE. THAT'S WHAT TWILIGHT WANTS. MOTHER EARTH DESTROYED... SO THE NEW WORLD CAN THRIVE--
--THE QUEEN, DEAD--LONG LIVE THE QUEEN.

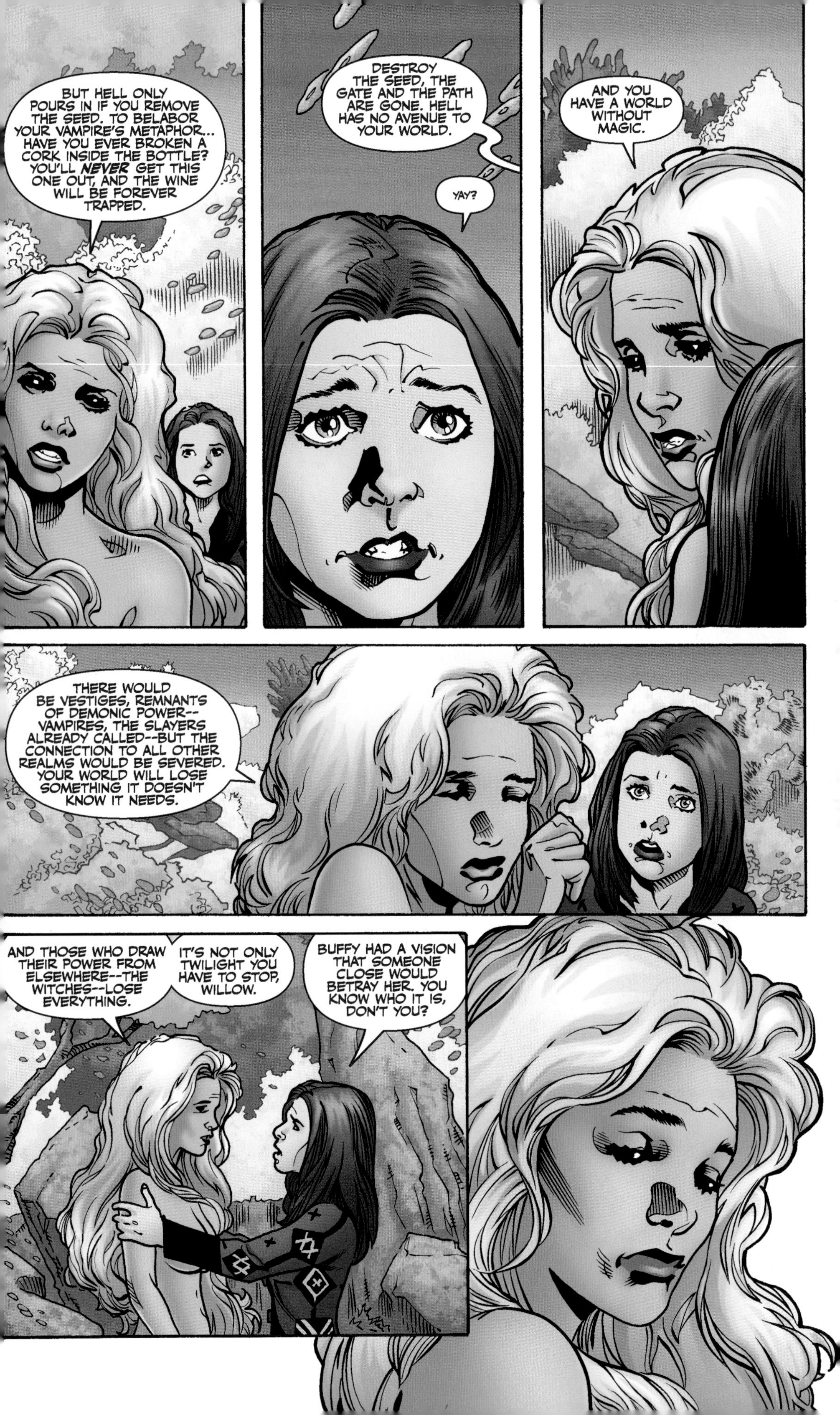
BUT HELL ONLY POURS IN IF YOU REMOVE THE SEED. TO BELABOR YOUR VAMPIRE'S METAPHOR... HAVE YOU EVER BROKEN A CORK INSIDE THE BOTTLE? YOU'LL NEVER GET THIS ONE OUT, AND THE WINE WILL BE FOREVER TRAPPED.
DESTROY THE SEED, THE GATE AND THE PATH ARE GONE. HELL HAS NO AVENUE TO YOUR WORLD.
YAY?
AND YOU HAVE A WORLD WITHOUT MAGIC.
THERE WOULD BE VESTIGES, REMNANTS OF DEMONIC POWER--VAMPIRES, THE SLAYERS ALREADY CALLED--BUT THE CONNECTION TO ALL OTHER REALMS WOULD BE SEVERED. YOUR WORLD WILL LOSE SOMETHING IT DOESN'T KNOW IT NEEDS.
AND THOSE WHO DRAW THEIR POWER FROM ELSEWHERE--THE WITCHES--LOSE EVERYTHING.
IT'S NOT ONLY TWILIGHT YOU HAVE TO STOP, WILLOW.
BUFFY HAD A VISION THAT SOMEONE CLOSE WOULD BETRAY HER. YOU KNOW WHO IT IS, DON'T YOU?

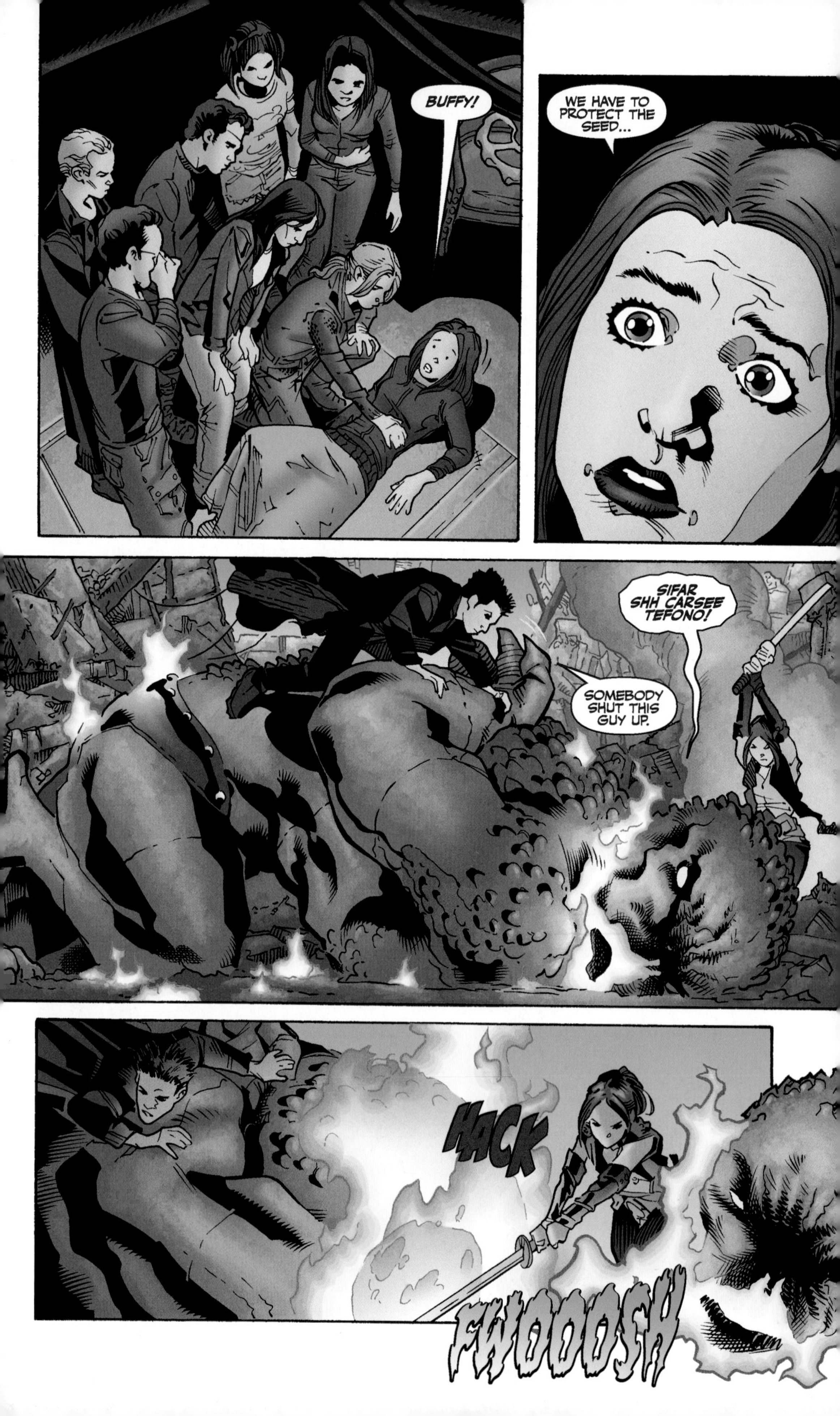
BUFFY!
WE HAVE TO PROTECT THE SEED...
SIFAR SHH CARSEE TEFONO!
SOMEBODY SHUT THIS GUY UP.
HACK
FWOOOSH

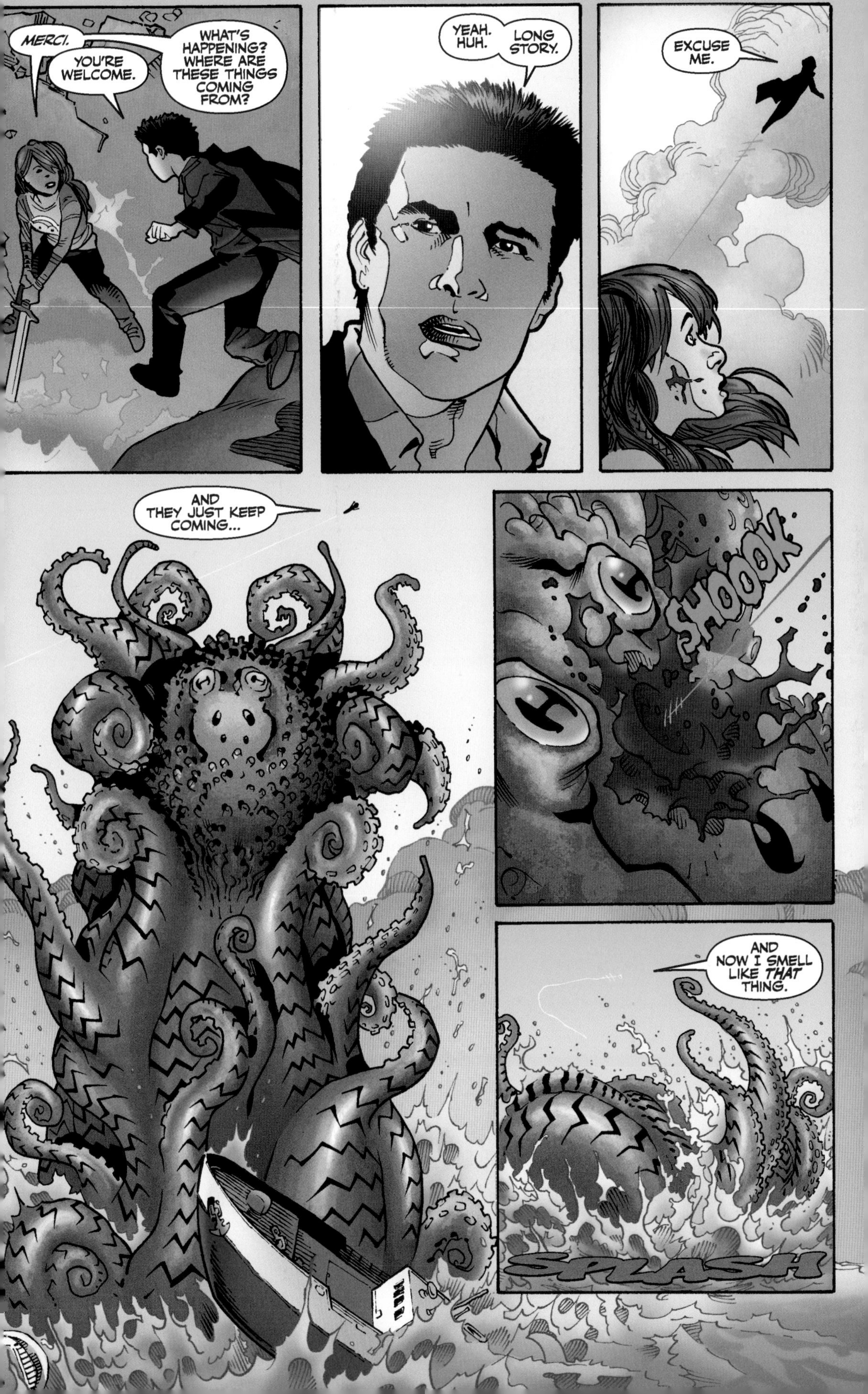
MERCI.
YOU'RE WELCOME.
WHAT'S HAPPENING? WHERE ARE THESE THINGS COMING FROM?
YEAH. HUH.
LONG STORY.
EXCUSE ME.
AND THEY JUST KEEP COMING...
SHOOOK
AND NOW I SMELL LIKE *THAT* THING.
SPLASH

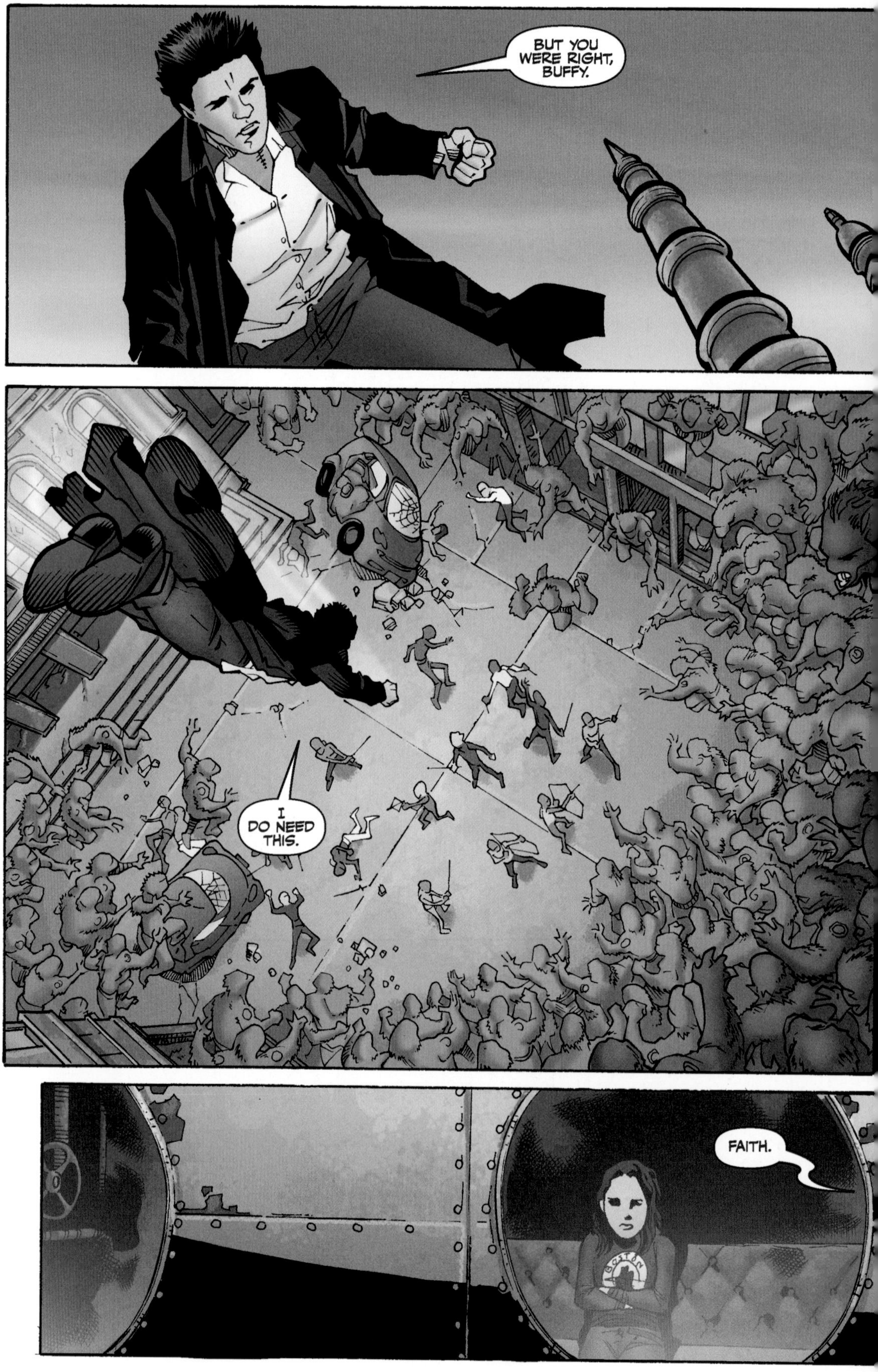
BUT YOU WERE RIGHT, BUFFY.
I DO NEED THIS.
FAITH.

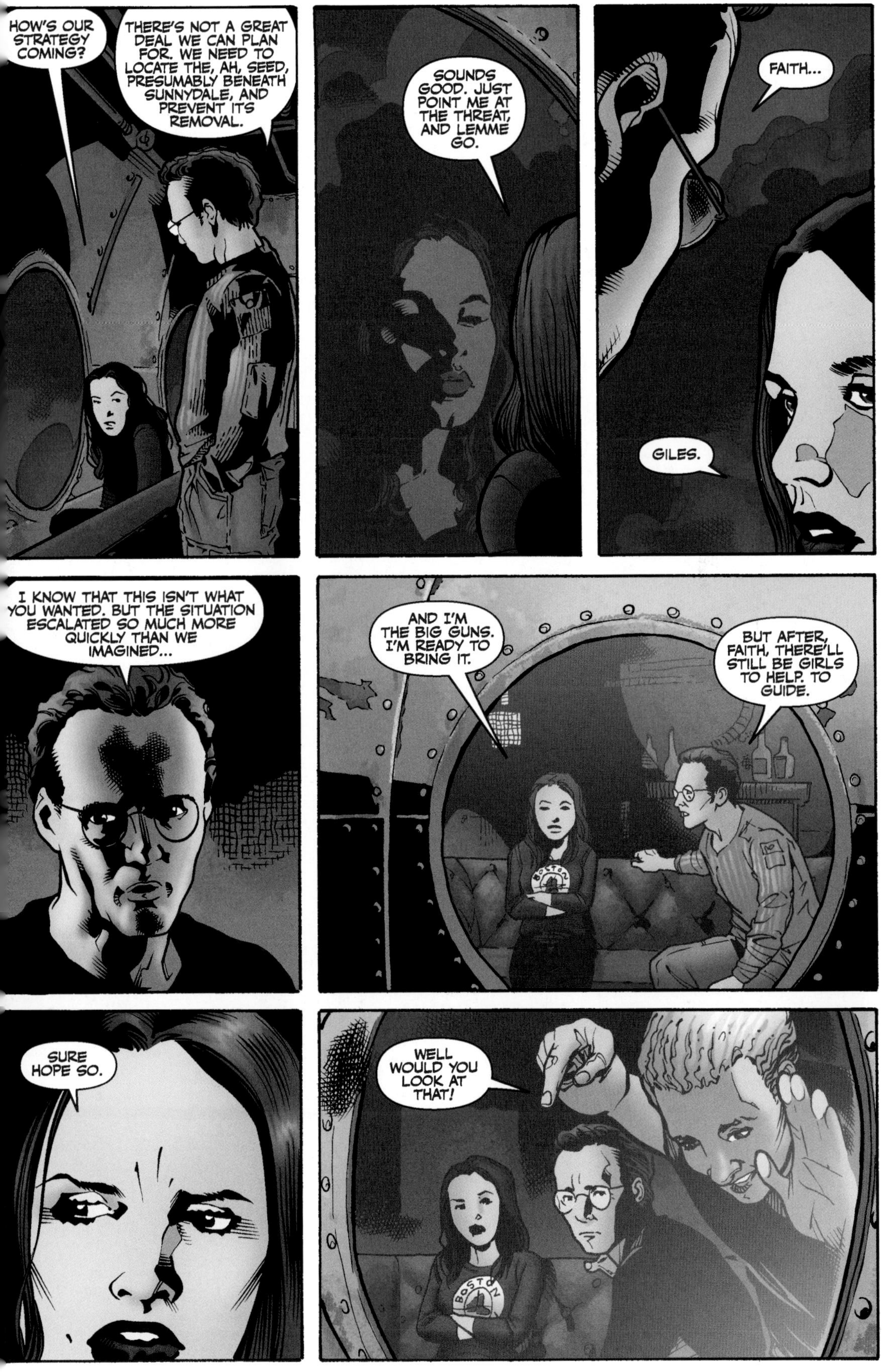
HOW'S OUR STRATEGY COMING?
THERE'S NOT A GREAT DEAL WE CAN PLAN FOR. WE NEED TO LOCATE THE, AH, SEED, PRESUMABLY BENEATH SUNNYDALE, AND PREVENT ITS REMOVAL.
SOUNDS GOOD. JUST POINT ME AT THE THREAT, AND LEMME GO.
FAITH...
GILES.
I KNOW THAT THIS ISN'T WHAT YOU WANTED. BUT THE SITUATION ESCALATED SO MUCH MORE QUICKLY THAN WE IMAGINED...
AND I'M THE BIG GUNS. I'M READY TO BRING IT.
BUT AFTER, FAITH, THERE'LL STILL BE GIRLS TO HELP. TO GUIDE.
SURE HOPE SO.
WELL WOULD YOU LOOK AT THAT!

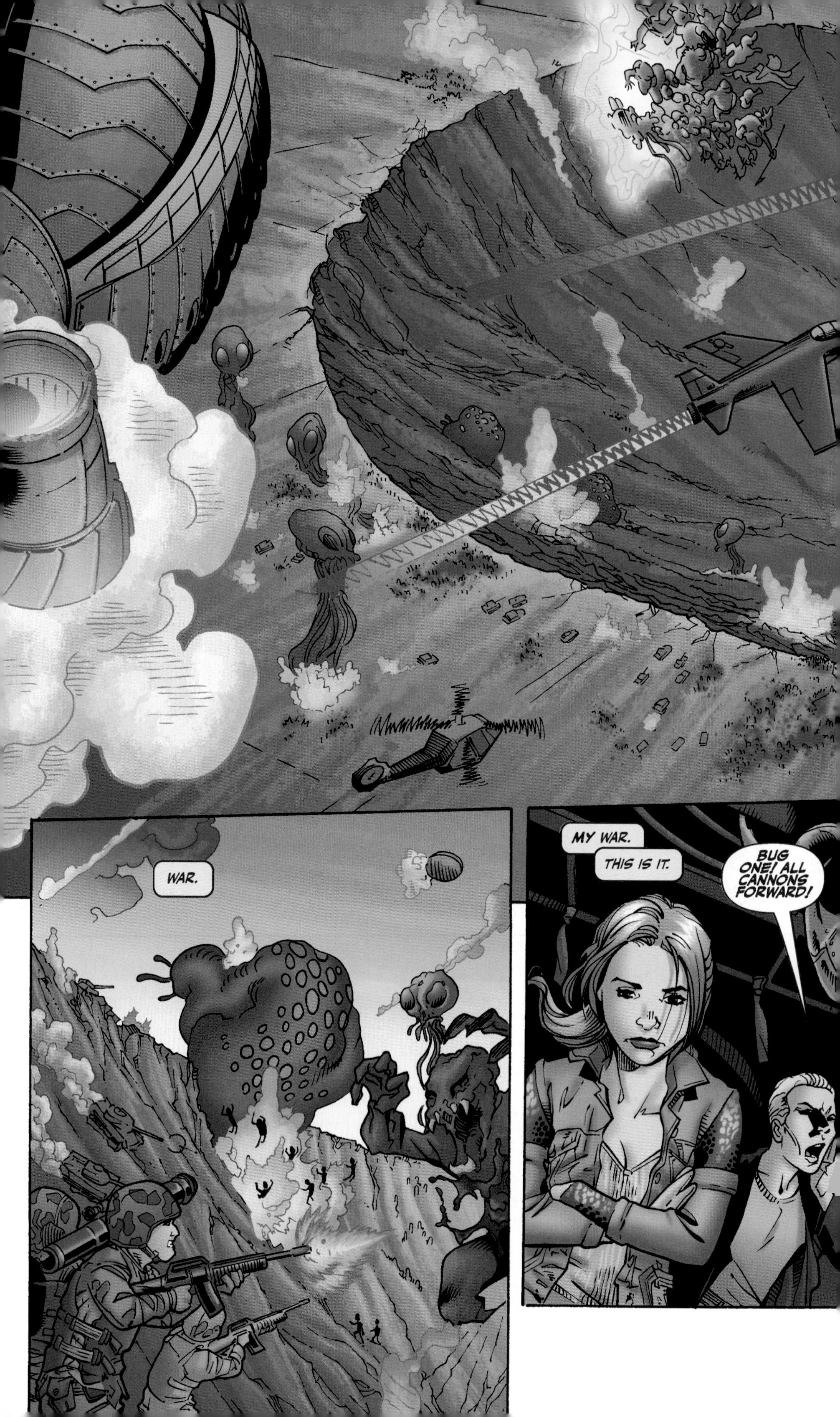
WAR.
MY WAR.
THIS IS IT.
BUG ONE! ALL CANNONS FORWARD!

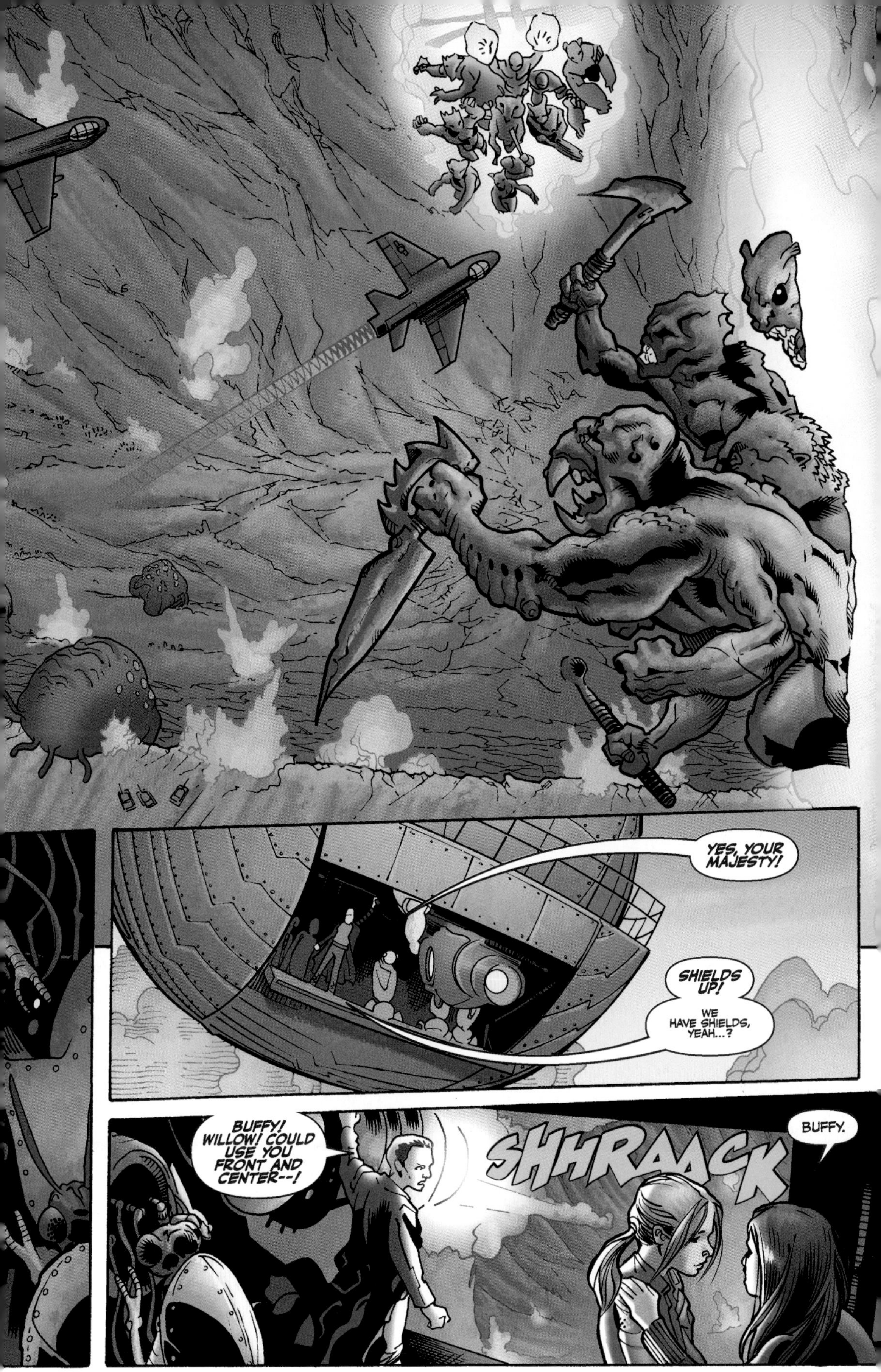
YES, YOUR MAJESTY!
SHIELDS UP!
WE HAVE SHIELDS, YEAH...?
BUFFY! WILLOW! COULD USE YOU FRONT AND CENTER--!
SHHRAACK
BUFFY.

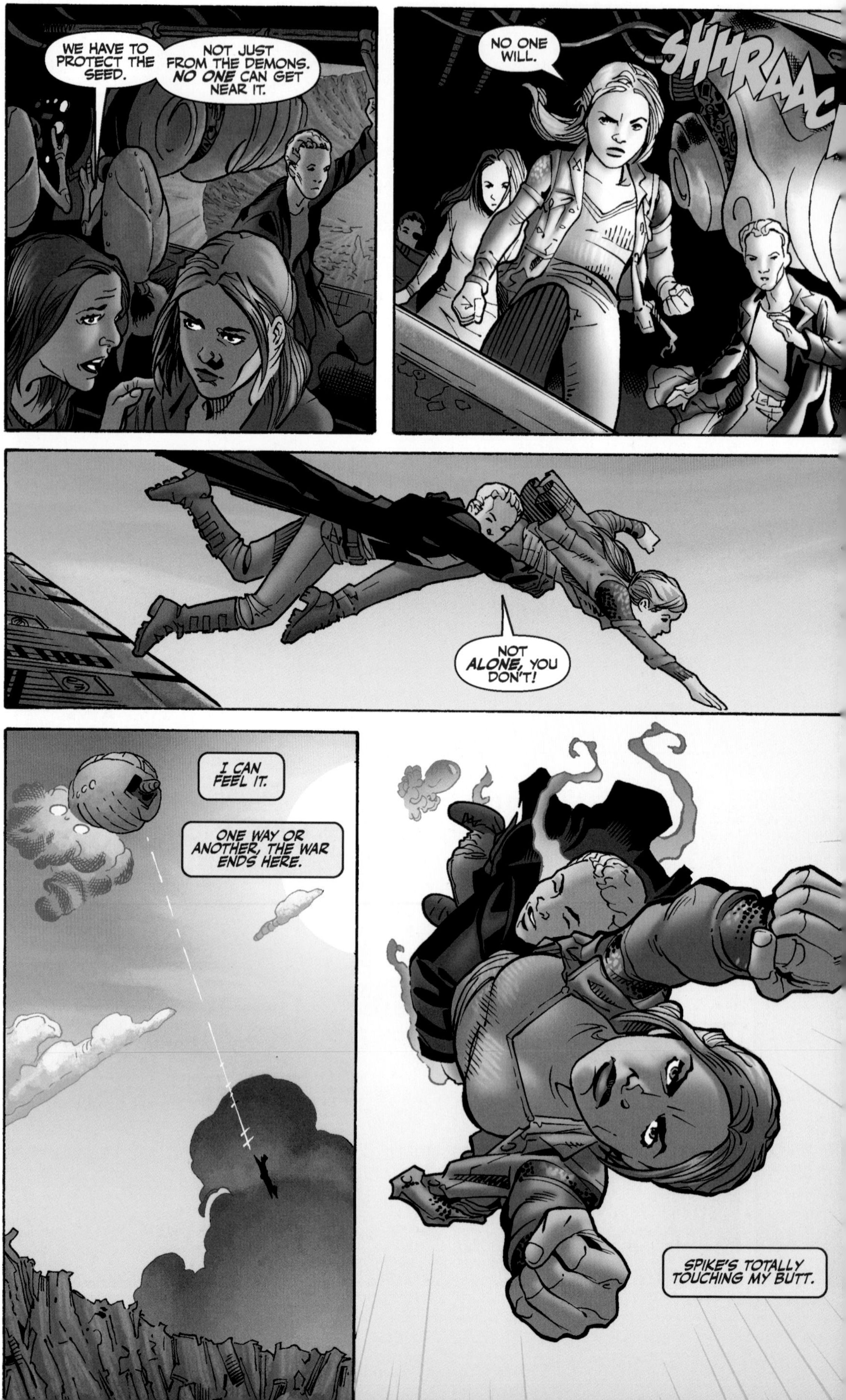
WE HAVE TO PROTECT THE SEED.
NOT JUST FROM THE DEMONS. NO ONE CAN GET NEAR IT.
NO ONE WILL.
SHHRAAC
NOT ALONE, YOU DON'T!
I CAN FEEL IT.
ONE WAY OR ANOTHER, THE WAR ENDS HERE.
SPIKE'S TOTALLY TOUCHING MY BUTT.

WILL, WAIT!

SHHRAACK

IT'S SUNNYDALE.

YOU CAN'T LEAVE ME OUT OF THIS.

TAKE US HOME.

WHOA WHOA WHOA!

DID *I* DO ALL OF THIS?

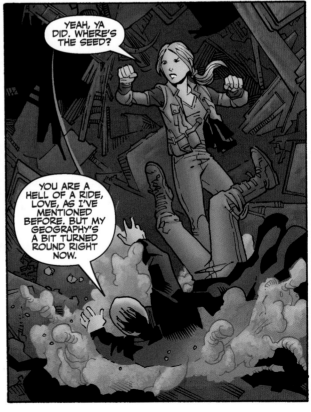

YEAH, YA DID. WHERE'S THE SEED?

YOU ARE A HELL OF A RIDE, LOVE, AS I'VE MENTIONED BEFORE. BUT MY GEOGRAPHY'S A BIT TURNED ROUND RIGHT NOW.

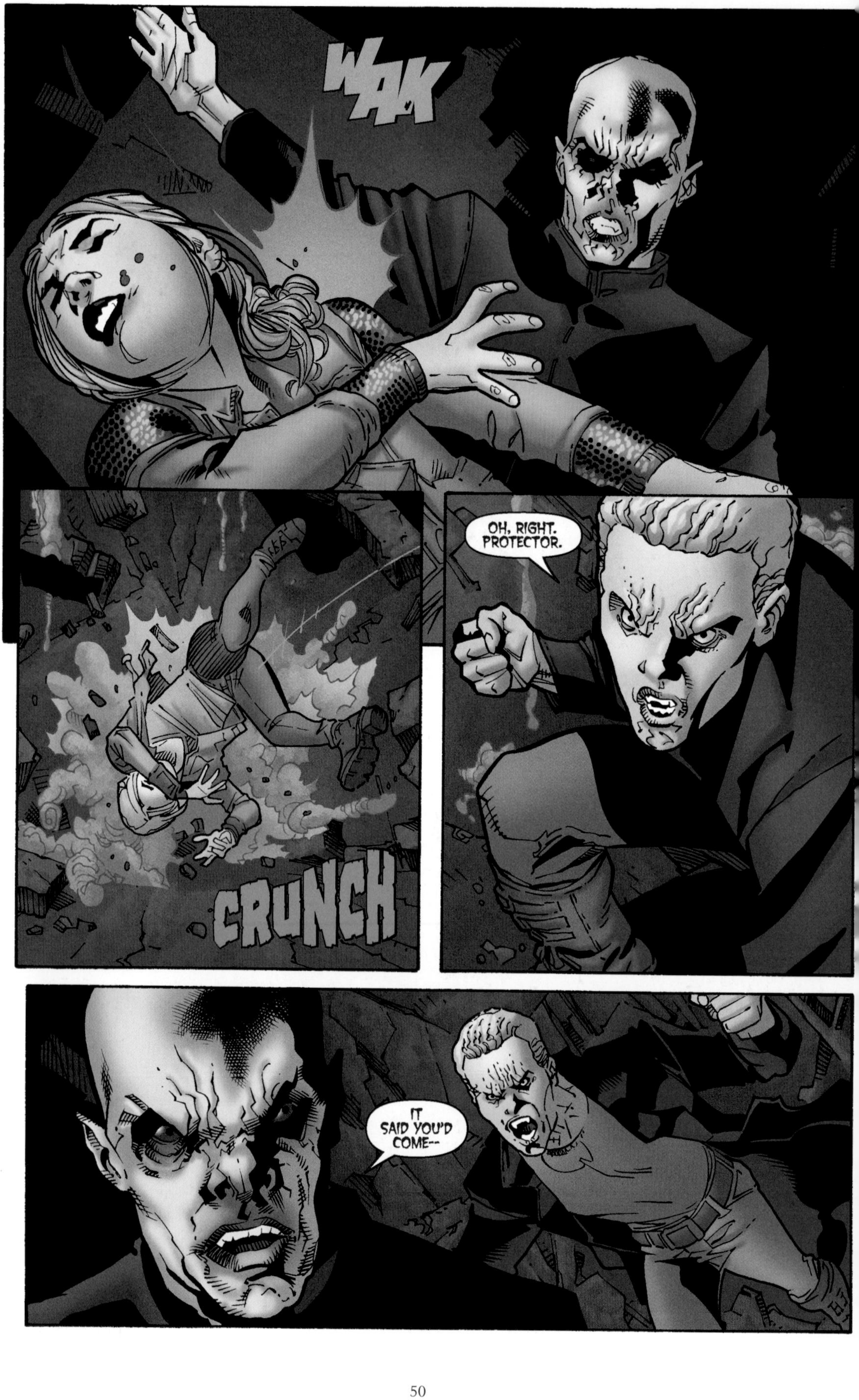
WAK
CRUNCH
OH, RIGHT. PROTECTOR.
IT SAID YOU'D COME--

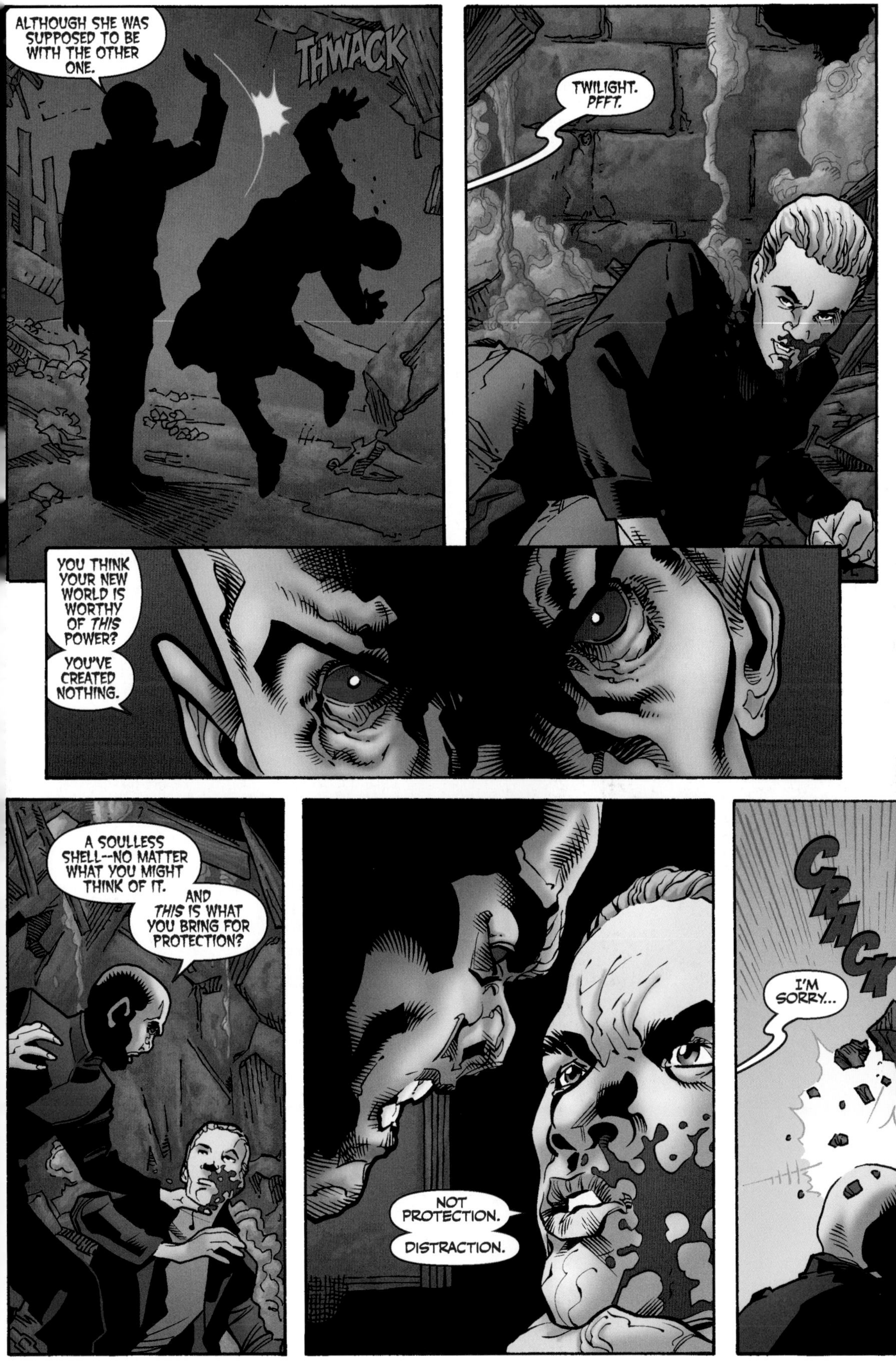
ALTHOUGH SHE WAS SUPPOSED TO BE WITH THE OTHER ONE.
THWACK
TWILIGHT. PFFT.
YOU THINK YOUR NEW WORLD IS WORTHY OF THIS POWER?
YOU'VE CREATED NOTHING.
A SOULLESS SHELL--NO MATTER WHAT YOU MIGHT THINK OF IT.
AND THIS IS WHAT YOU BRING FOR PROTECTION?
NOT PROTECTION.
DISTRACTION.
CRACK
I'M SORRY...

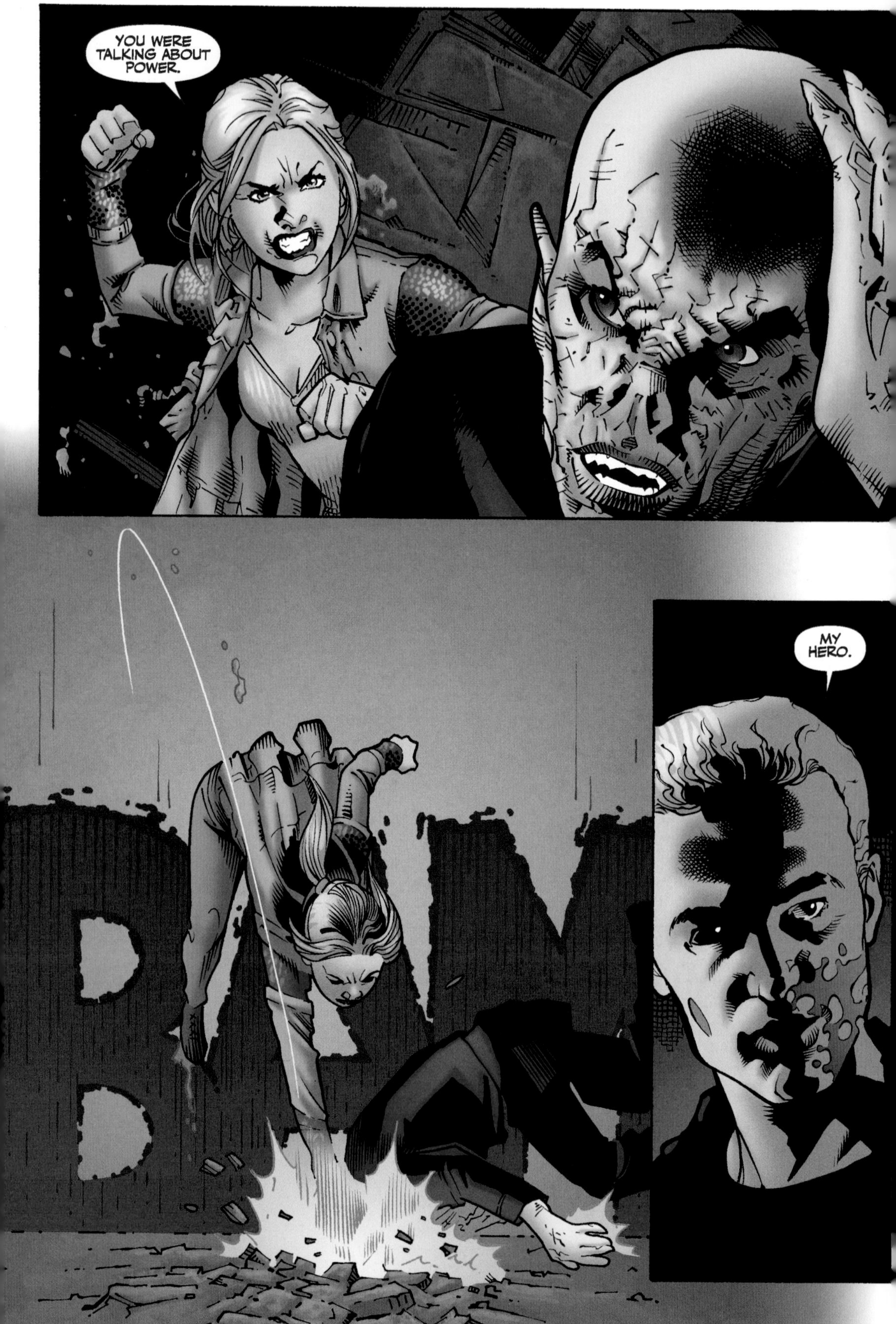
YOU WERE TALKING ABOUT POWER.
MY HERO.

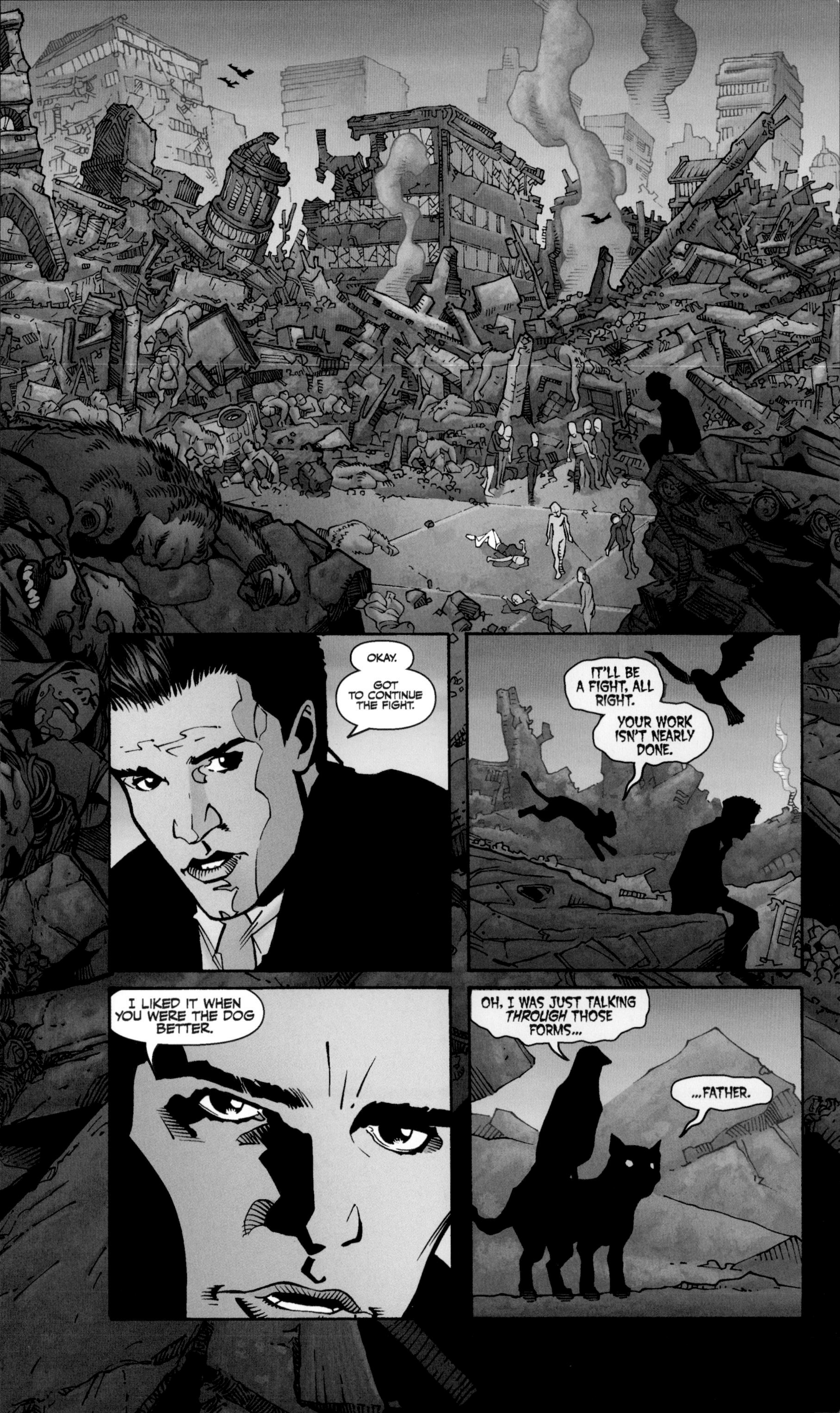
OKAY.
GOT TO CONTINUE THE FIGHT.
IT'LL BE A FIGHT, ALL RIGHT.
YOUR WORK ISN'T NEARLY DONE.
I LIKED IT WHEN YOU WERE THE DOG BETTER.
OH, I WAS JUST TALKING *THROUGH* THOSE FORMS...
...FATHER.

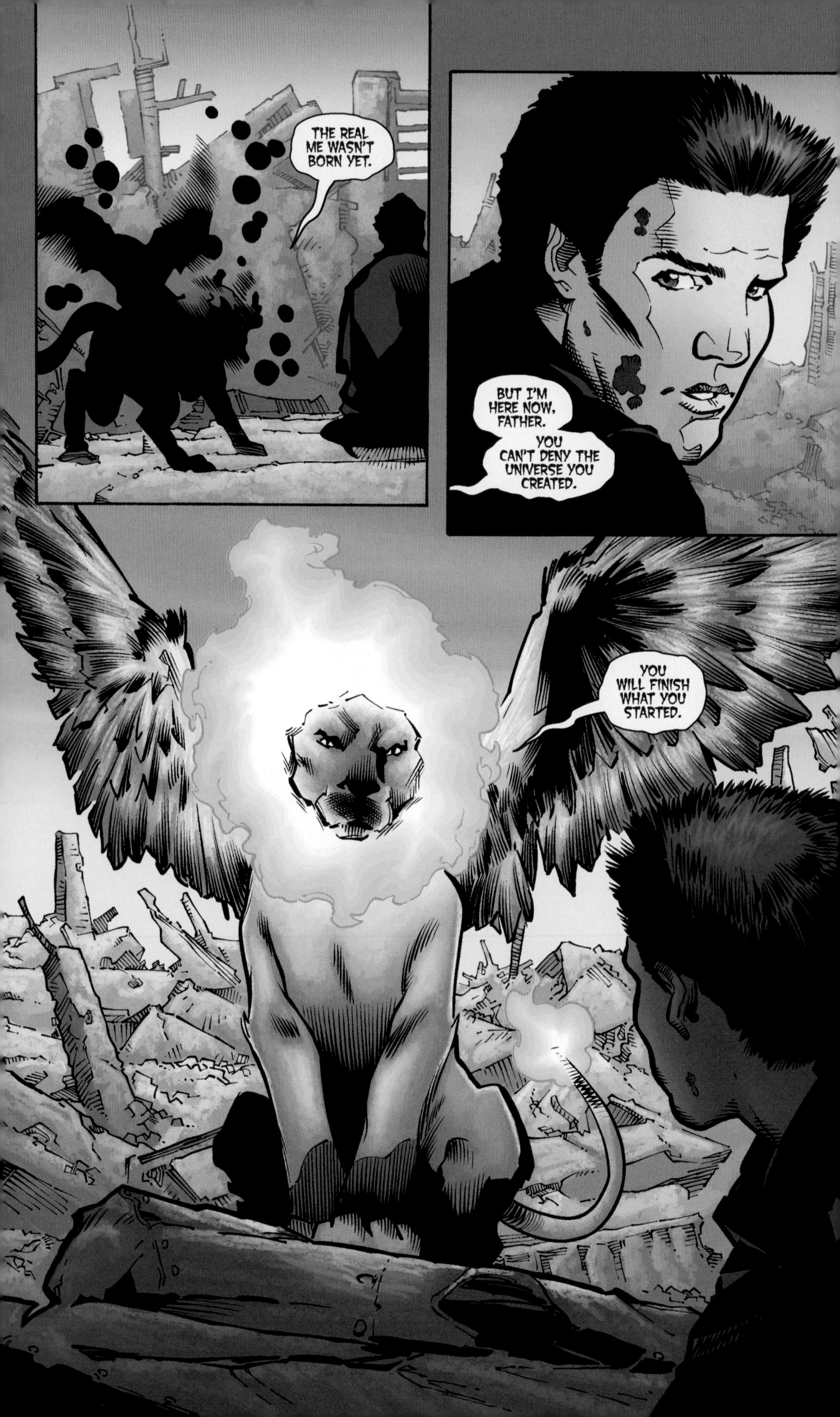
THE REAL ME WASN'T BORN YET.
BUT I'M HERE NOW, FATHER.
YOU CAN'T DENY THE UNIVERSE YOU CREATED.
YOU WILL FINISH WHAT YOU STARTED.

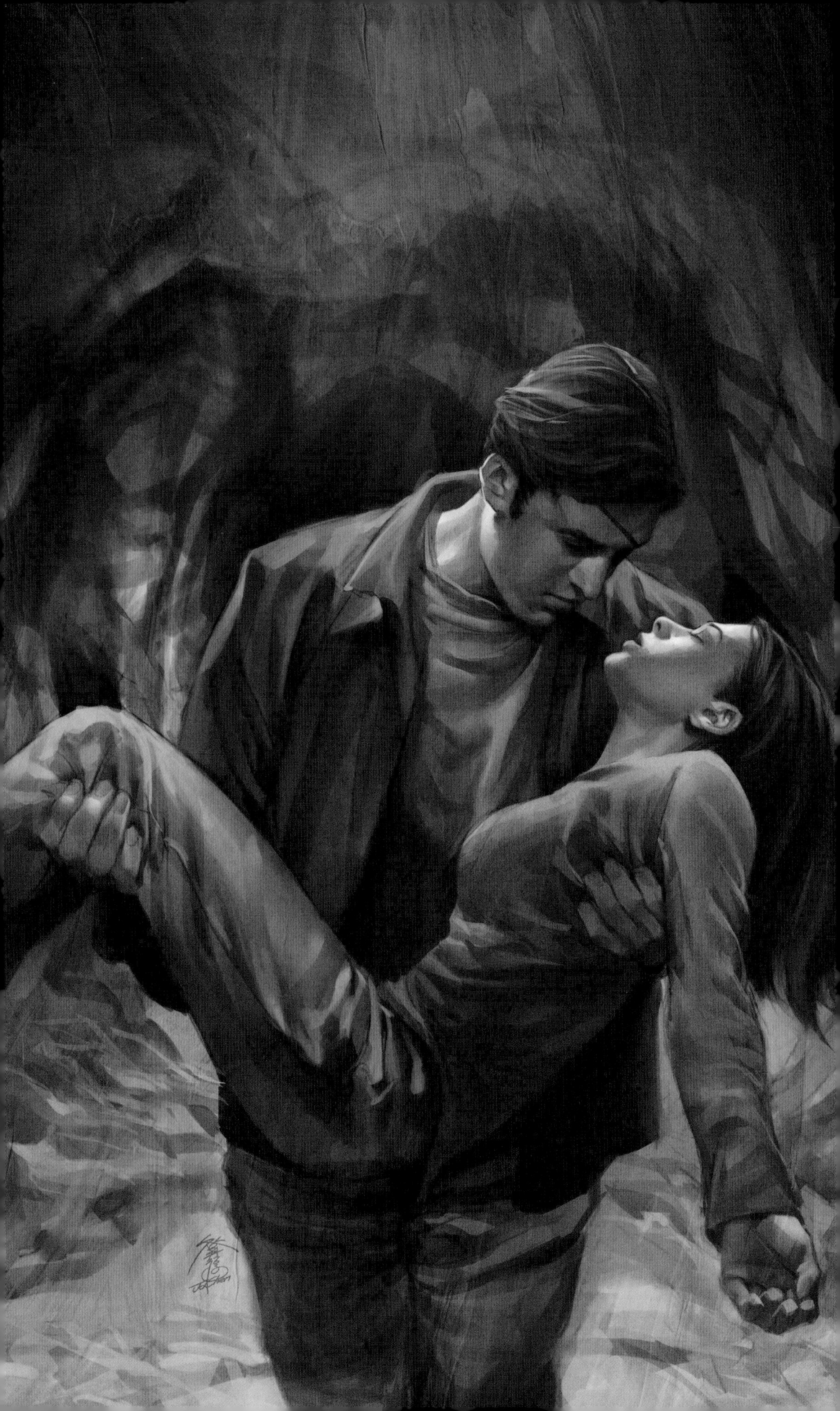

LAST GLEAMING

PART THREE

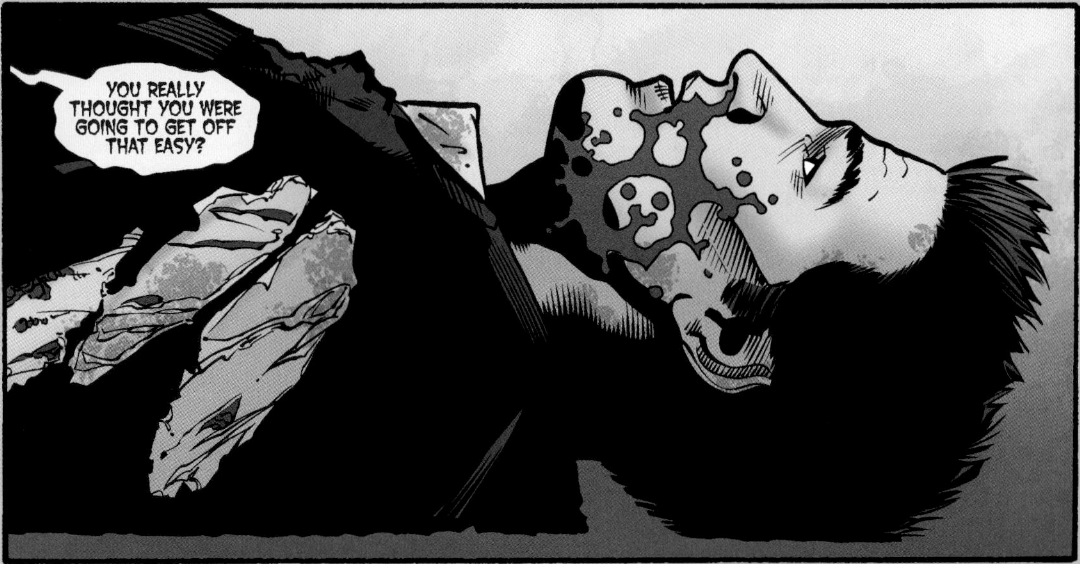
YOU REALLY THOUGHT YOU WERE GOING TO GET OFF THAT EASY?

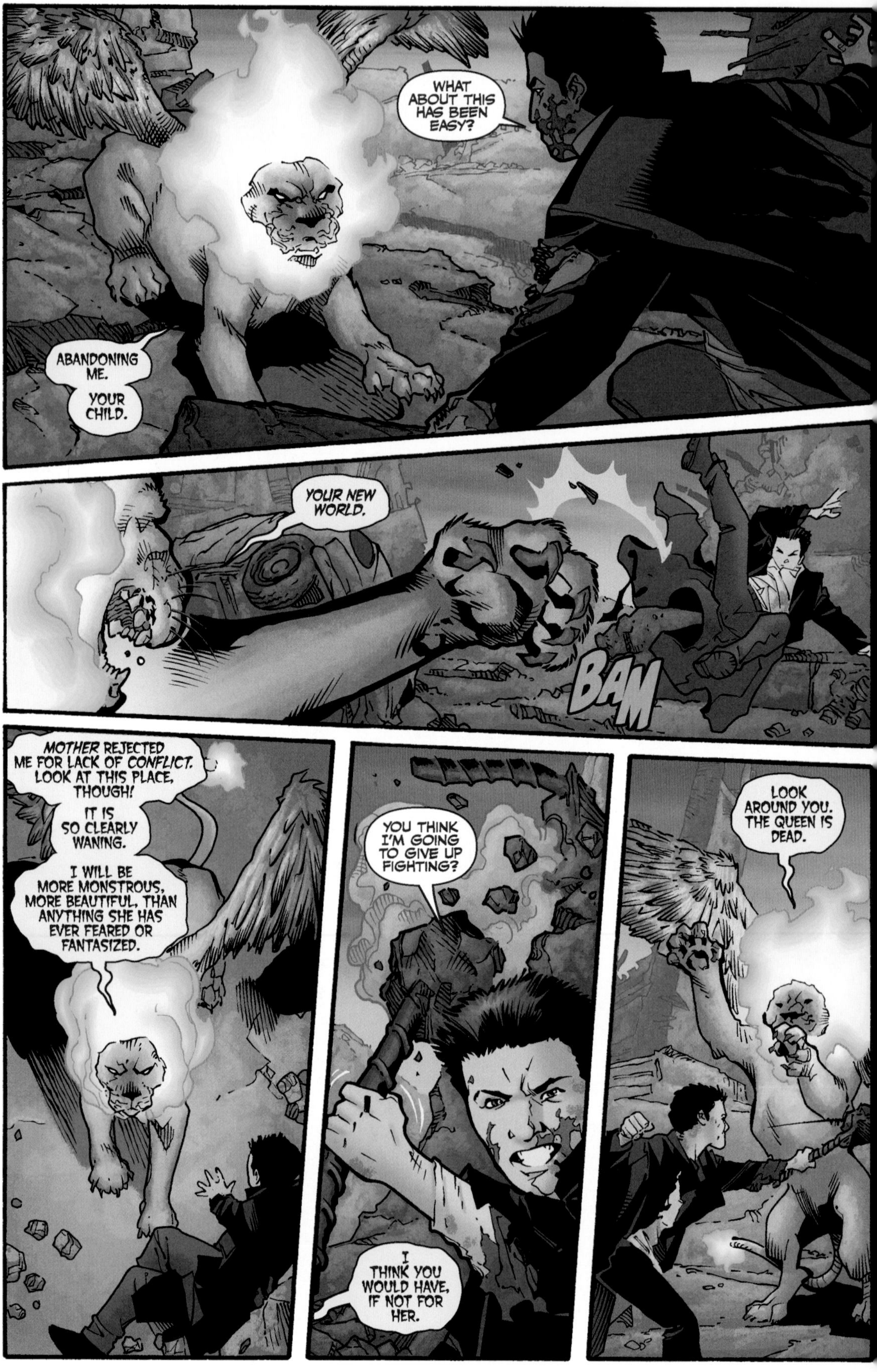
WHAT ABOUT THIS HAS BEEN EASY?
ABANDONING ME.
YOUR CHILD.
YOUR NEW WORLD.
BAM
MOTHER REJECTED ME FOR LACK OF CONFLICT. LOOK AT THIS PLACE, THOUGH!
IT IS SO CLEARLY WANING.
I WILL BE MORE MONSTROUS, MORE BEAUTIFUL, THAN ANYTHING SHE HAS EVER FEARED OR FANTASIZED.
YOU THINK I'M GOING TO GIVE UP FIGHTING?
I THINK YOU WOULD HAVE, IF NOT FOR HER.
LOOK AROUND YOU. THE QUEEN IS DEAD.

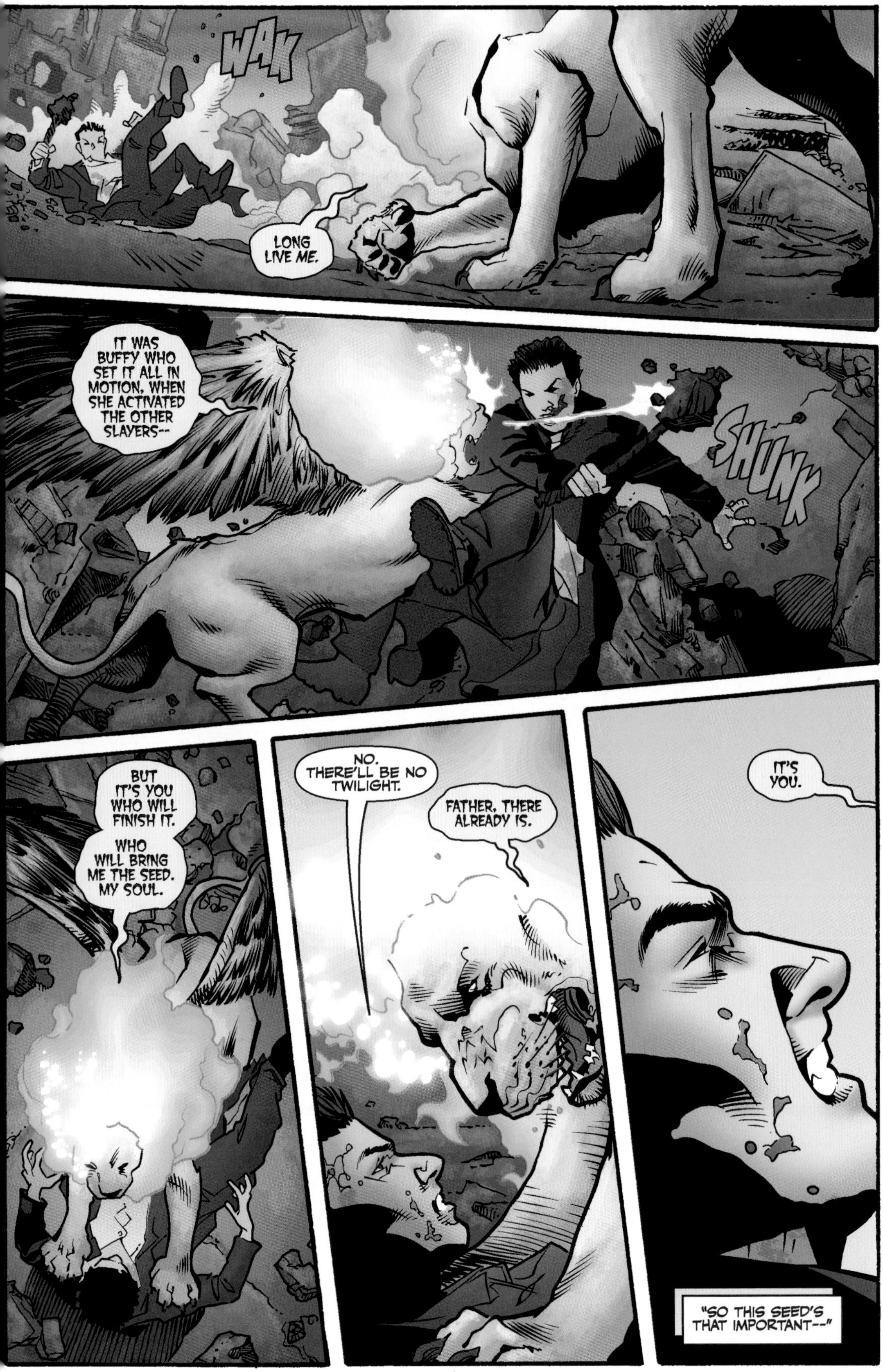

WAK
LONG LIVE ME.
IT WAS BUFFY WHO SET IT ALL IN MOTION, WHEN SHE ACTIVATED THE OTHER SLAYERS--
SHUNK
BUT IT'S YOU WHO WILL FINISH IT.
WHO WILL BRING ME THE SEED. MY SOUL.
NO. THERE'LL BE NO TWILIGHT.
FATHER, THERE ALREADY IS.
IT'S YOU.
"SO THIS SEED'S THAT IMPORTANT--"

--AND IT'S GOT *HIM* DEFENDING IT?

THE WORD IMPORTANT ISN'T *IMPORTANT* ENOUGH FOR HOW IMPORTANT IT IS.

YOU KNEW THE MASTER WAS ALIVE AND YOU DIDN'T TELL ANYONE?

MY SOURCES SAID THE SEED ENSLAVED A POWERFUL VAMPIRE EIGHT HUNDRED YEARS AGO--*YOU* LOT SUPPOSEDLY *KILLED* HIM.

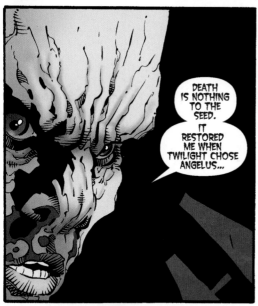

DEATH IS NOTHING TO THE SEED.

IT RESTORED ME WHEN TWILIGHT CHOSE ANGELUS...

I SORT OF THOUGHT HE'D SHOW...

OH, HE'LL BE AROUND LATER TO TAKE CREDIT FOR EVERYTHING, DON'T YOU FRET.

BEFORE TWILIGHT, I HADN'T THOUGHT THE SEED WAS REAL...MUCH LESS UNDER OUR NOSES...

SO IT WAS JUST HIDING BEHIND THE HELLMOUTH, PULLING THE MASTER'S STRINGS ALL THOSE YEARS--ALL THOSE LIVES--WITHOUT HIM KNOWING?

I WOULDN'T WORD IT EXACTLY LIKE THAT...

THAT EXPLAINS THE WEIRD FACE I CAN'T WAIT TO HIT AGAIN...

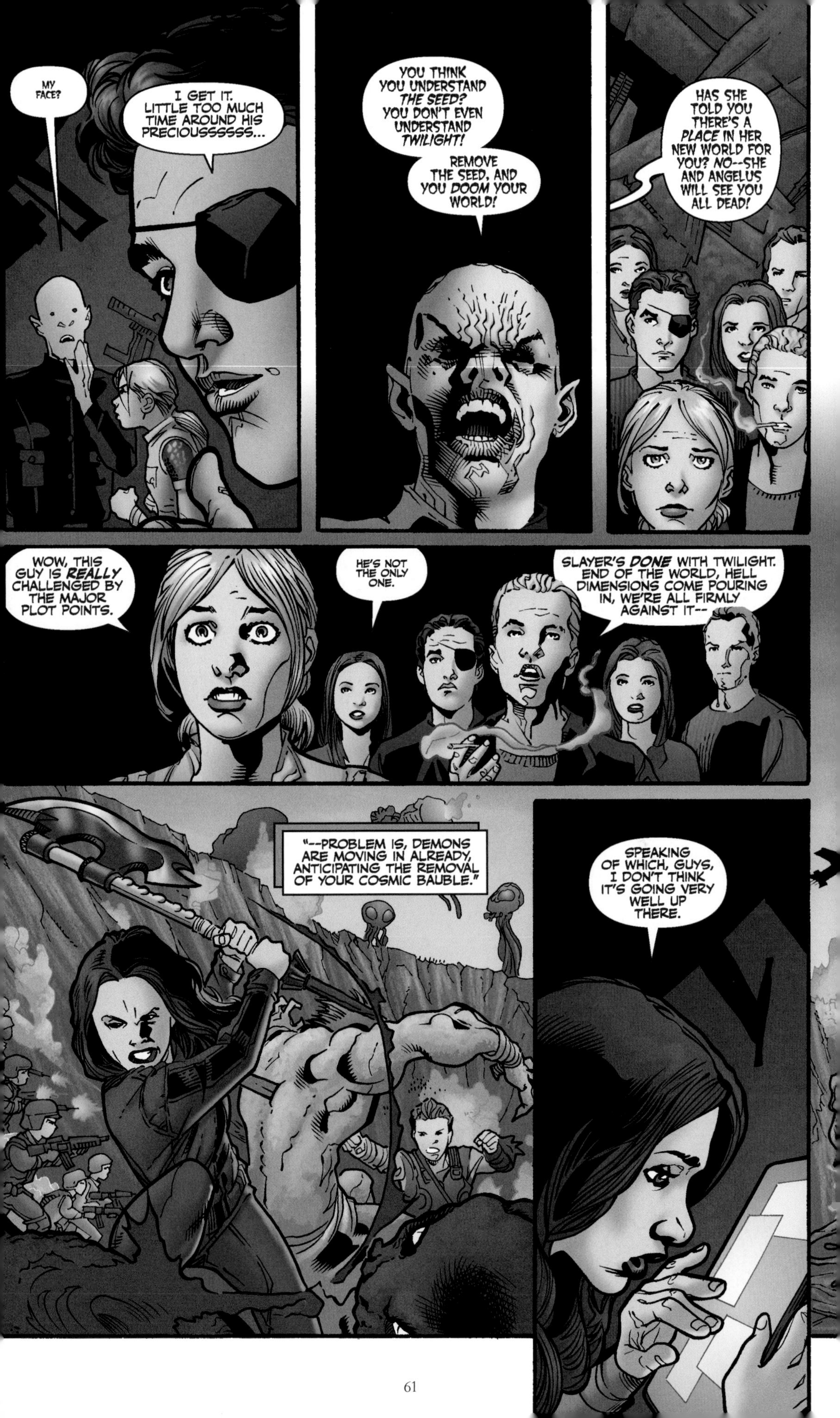

MY FACE?
I GET IT. LITTLE TOO MUCH TIME AROUND HIS PRECIOUSSSSSS...
YOU THINK YOU UNDERSTAND *THE SEED?* YOU DON'T EVEN UNDERSTAND *TWILIGHT!*
REMOVE THE SEED, AND YOU *DOOM* YOUR WORLD!
HAS SHE TOLD YOU THERE'S A *PLACE* IN HER NEW WORLD FOR YOU? *NO*--SHE AND ANGELUS WILL SEE YOU ALL DEAD!
WOW, THIS GUY IS ***REALLY*** CHALLENGED BY THE MAJOR PLOT POINTS.
HE'S NOT THE ONLY ONE.
SLAYER'S ***DONE*** WITH TWILIGHT. END OF THE WORLD, HELL DIMENSIONS COME POURING IN, WE'RE ALL FIRMLY AGAINST IT--
"--PROBLEM IS, DEMONS ARE MOVING IN ALREADY, ANTICIPATING THE REMOVAL OF YOUR COSMIC BAUBLE."
SPEAKING OF WHICH, GUYS, I DON'T THINK IT'S GOING VERY WELL UP THERE.

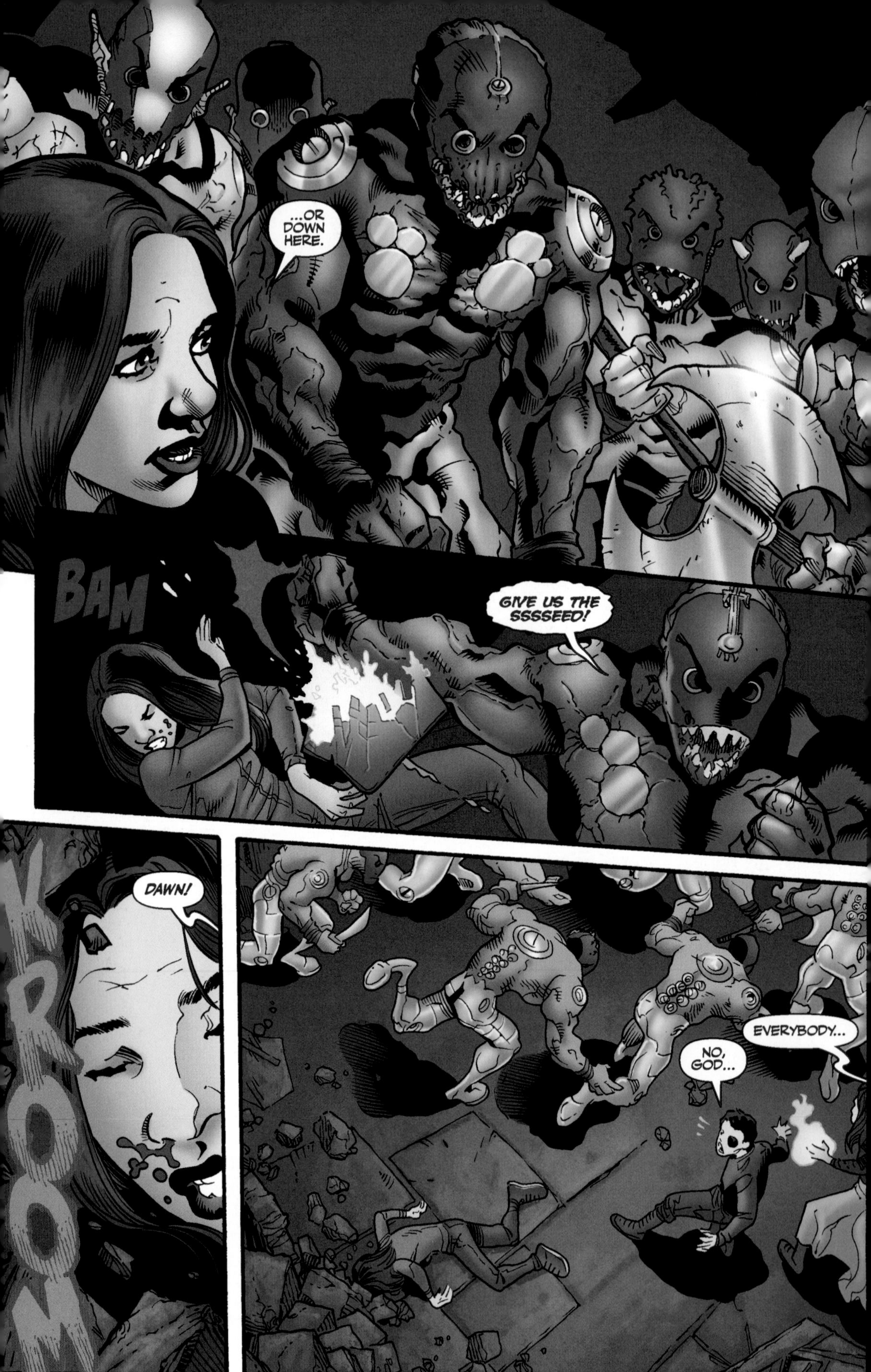
...OR DOWN HERE.
BAM
GIVE US THE SSSSEED!
KRROOOM
DAWN!
EVERYBODY...
NO, GOD...

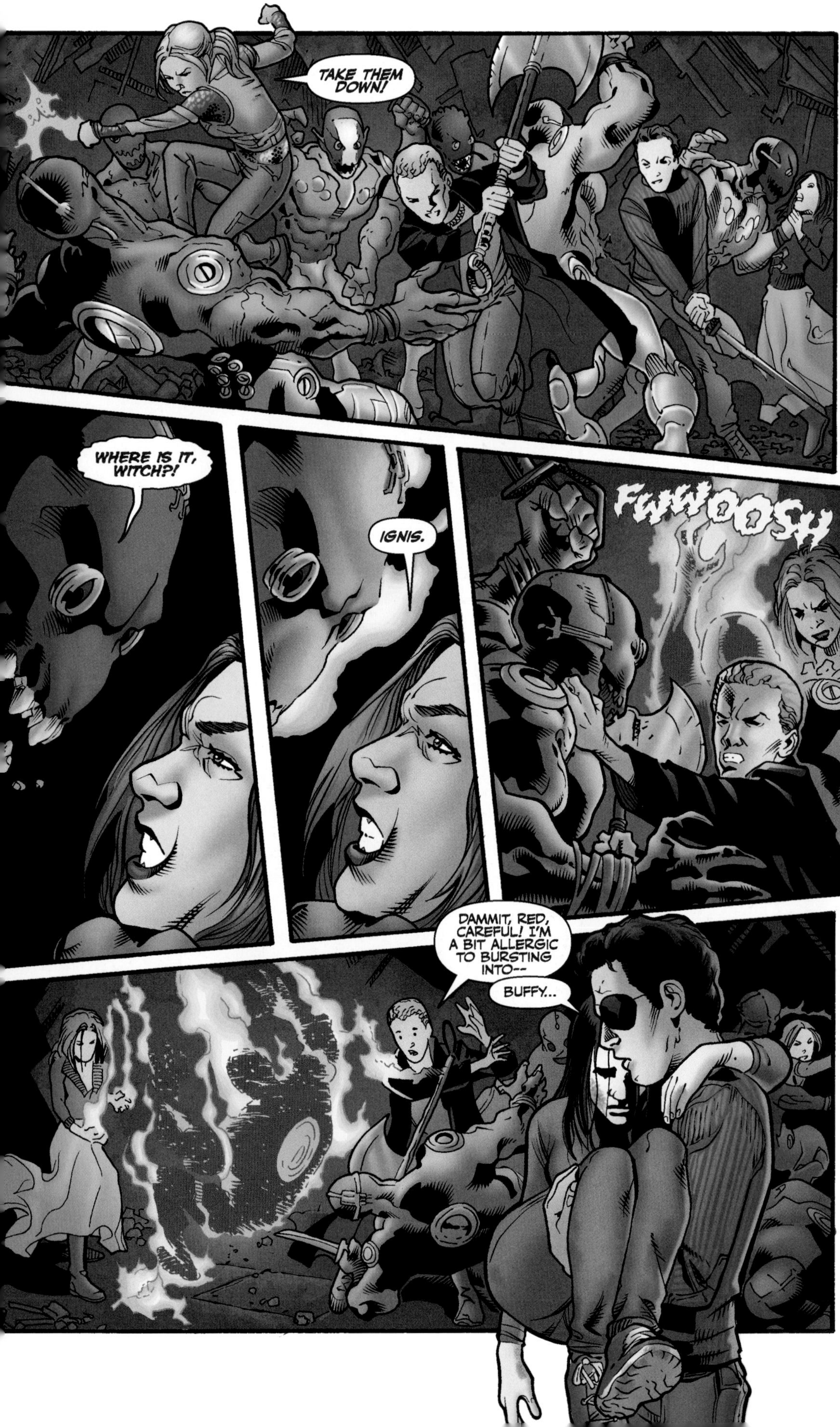
TAKE THEM DOWN!
WHERE IS IT, WITCH?!
IGNIS.
FWWOOSH
DAMMIT, RED, CAREFUL! I'M A BIT ALLERGIC TO BURSTING INTO--
BUFFY...

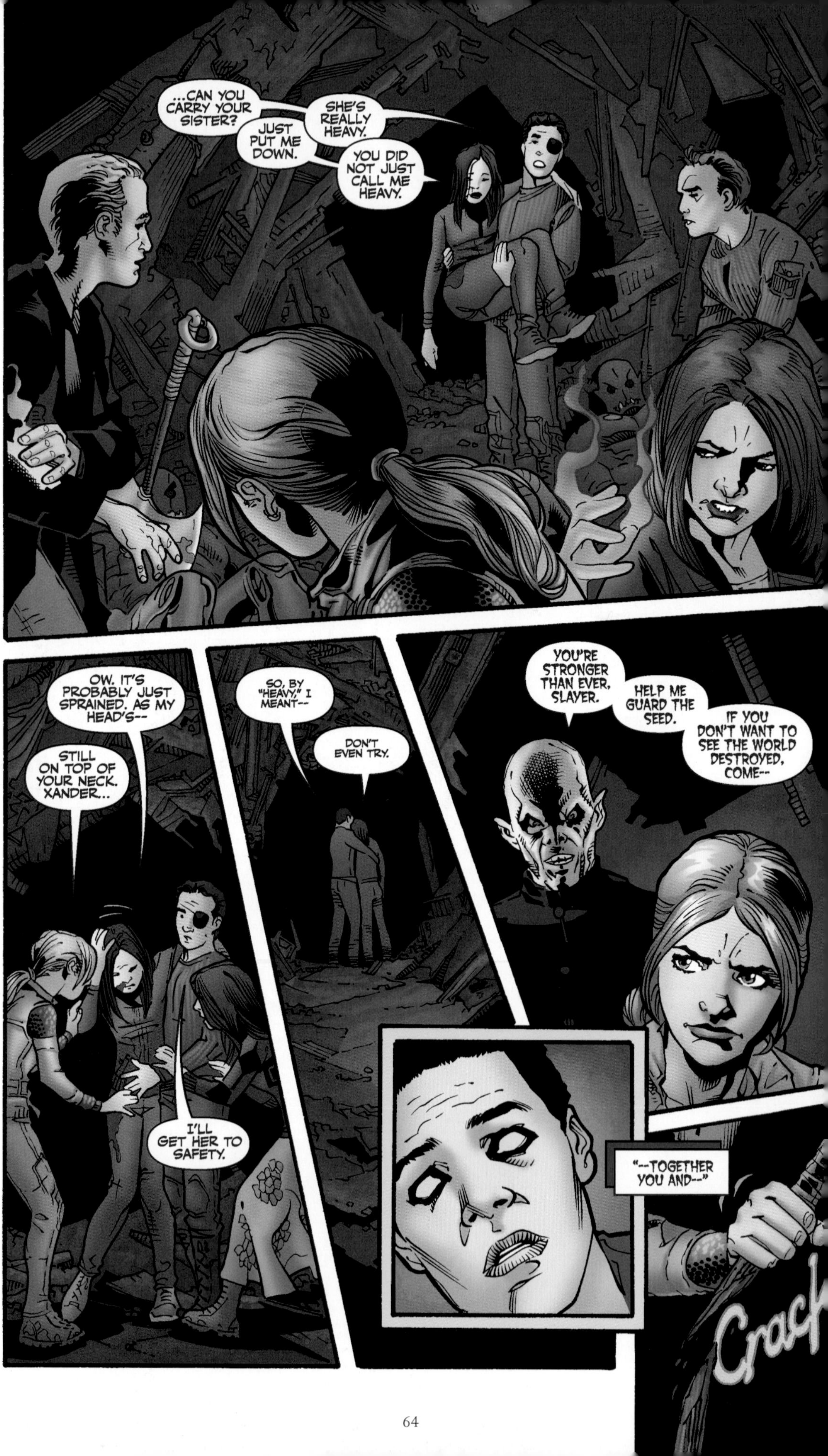
...CAN YOU CARRY YOUR SISTER?
SHE'S REALLY HEAVY.
JUST PUT ME DOWN.
YOU DID NOT JUST CALL ME HEAVY.
OW. IT'S PROBABLY JUST SPRAINED. AS MY HEAD'S--
STILL ON TOP OF YOUR NECK. XANDER...
I'LL GET HER TO SAFETY.
SO, BY "HEAVY," I MEANT--
DON'T EVEN TRY.
YOU'RE STRONGER THAN EVER, SLAYER.
HELP ME GUARD THE SEED.
IF YOU DON'T WANT TO SEE THE WORLD DESTROYED, COME--
"--TOGETHER YOU AND--"
Crack

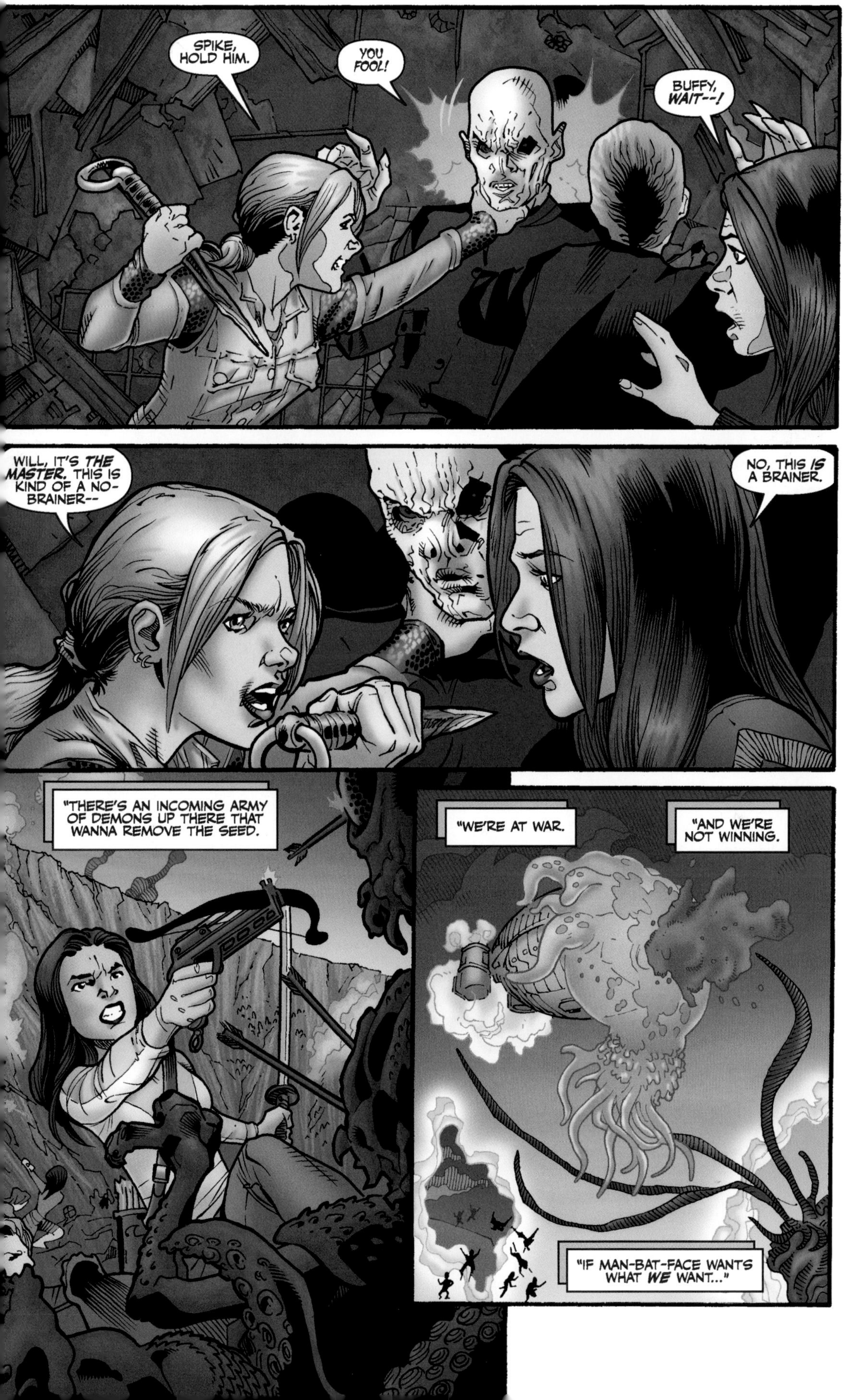
SPIKE, HOLD HIM.
YOU FOOL!
BUFFY, WAIT--!
WILL, IT'S THE MASTER. THIS IS KIND OF A NO-BRAINER--
NO, THIS IS A BRAINER.
"THERE'S AN INCOMING ARMY OF DEMONS UP THERE THAT WANNA REMOVE THE SEED.
"WE'RE AT WAR.
"AND WE'RE NOT WINNING.
"IF MAN-BAT-FACE WANTS WHAT WE WANT..."

HE'S GOTTA BE ON THE TEAM.

IT'S NOT ENOUGH TO SIDE WITH OUR ORIGINAL BIG BAD-- NOW WE'RE WORKING *FOR* HIM.

THIS CRISIS HAS LED TO MANY UNLIKELY ALLIANCES, BUFFY. I DON'T KNOW THAT THE MASTER IS ANY WORSE THAN DRACULA.

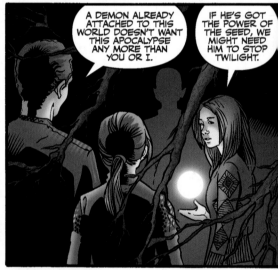

A DEMON ALREADY ATTACHED TO THIS WORLD DOESN'T WANT THIS APOCALYPSE ANY MORE THAN YOU OR I.

IF HE'S GOT THE POWER OF THE SEED, WE MIGHT NEED HIM TO STOP TWILIGHT.

HE'S A MONSTER AND HE KILLED ME.

GRUDGE VALIDATED. MOVE ON.

I MEAN, IT'S NOT LIKE YOU AND SPIKE WERE ALWAYS B.F.F.'S--

THERE'S SOMETHING YOU'RE NOT TELLING US.

WHAT HAPPENED WHEN YOU FAINTED?

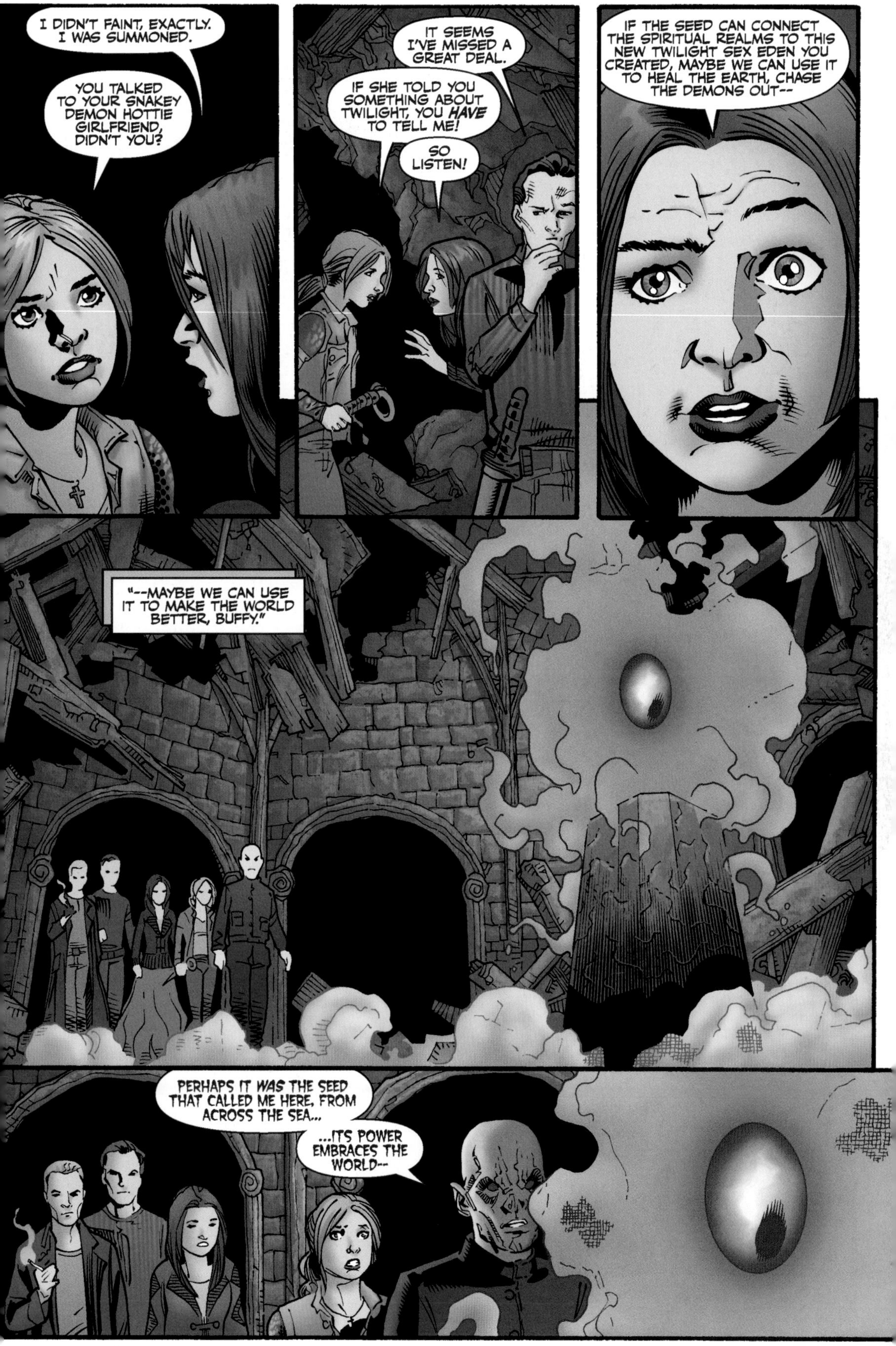

I DIDN'T FAINT, EXACTLY. I WAS SUMMONED.
YOU TALKED TO YOUR SNAKEY DEMON HOTTIE GIRLFRIEND, DIDN'T YOU?
IT SEEMS I'VE MISSED A GREAT DEAL.
IF SHE TOLD YOU SOMETHING ABOUT TWILIGHT, YOU *HAVE* TO TELL ME!
SO LISTEN!
IF THE SEED CAN CONNECT THE SPIRITUAL REALMS TO THIS NEW TWILIGHT SEX EDEN YOU CREATED, MAYBE WE CAN USE IT TO HEAL THE EARTH, CHASE THE DEMONS OUT--
"--MAYBE WE CAN USE IT TO MAKE THE WORLD BETTER, BUFFY."
PERHAPS IT *WAS* THE SEED THAT CALLED ME HERE, FROM ACROSS THE SEA...
...ITS POWER EMBRACES THE WORLD--

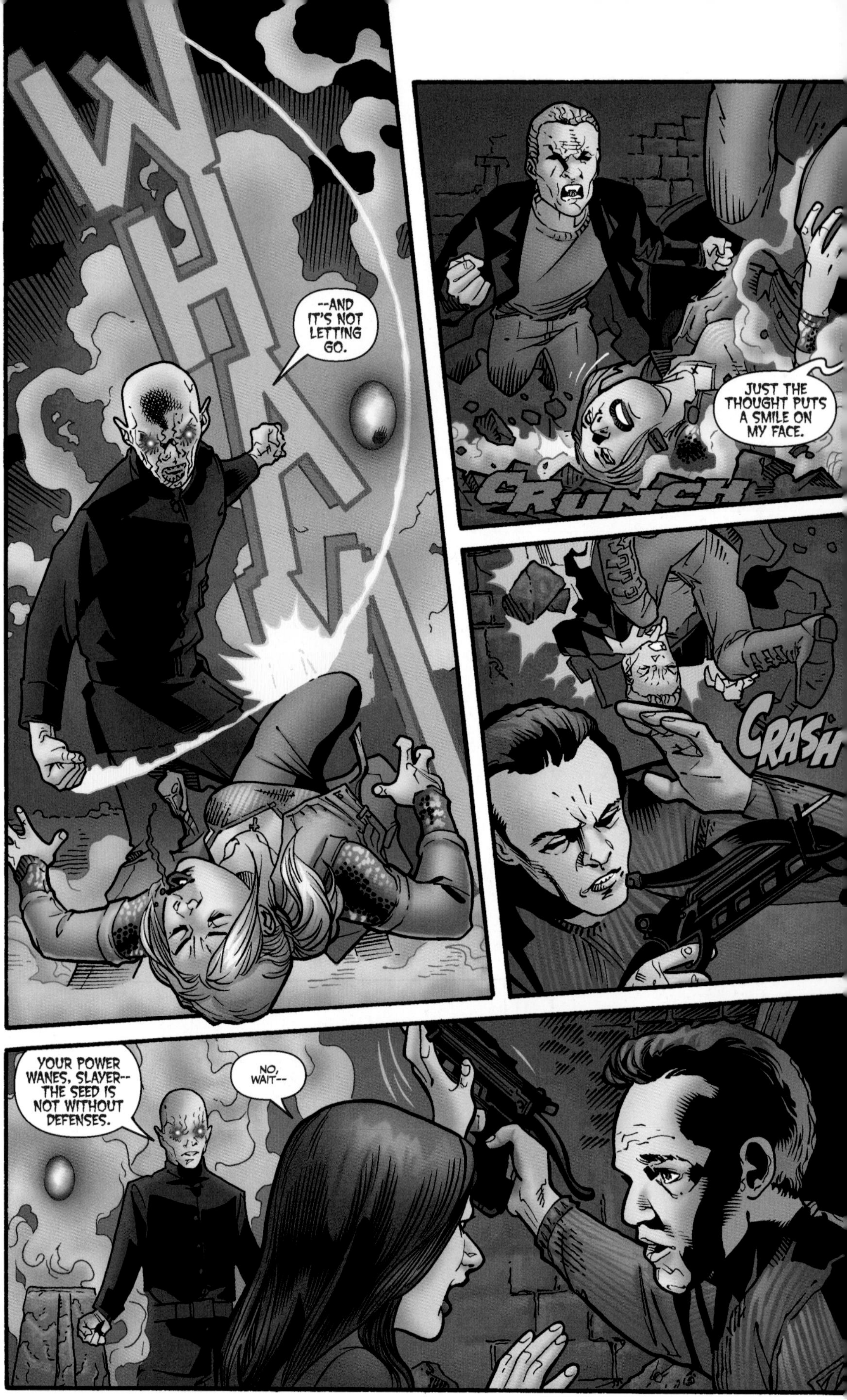
WHAM
--AND IT'S NOT LETTING GO.
JUST THE THOUGHT PUTS A SMILE ON MY FACE.
CRUNCH
CRASH
YOUR POWER WANES, SLAYER-- THE SEED IS NOT WITHOUT DEFENSES.
NO, WAIT--

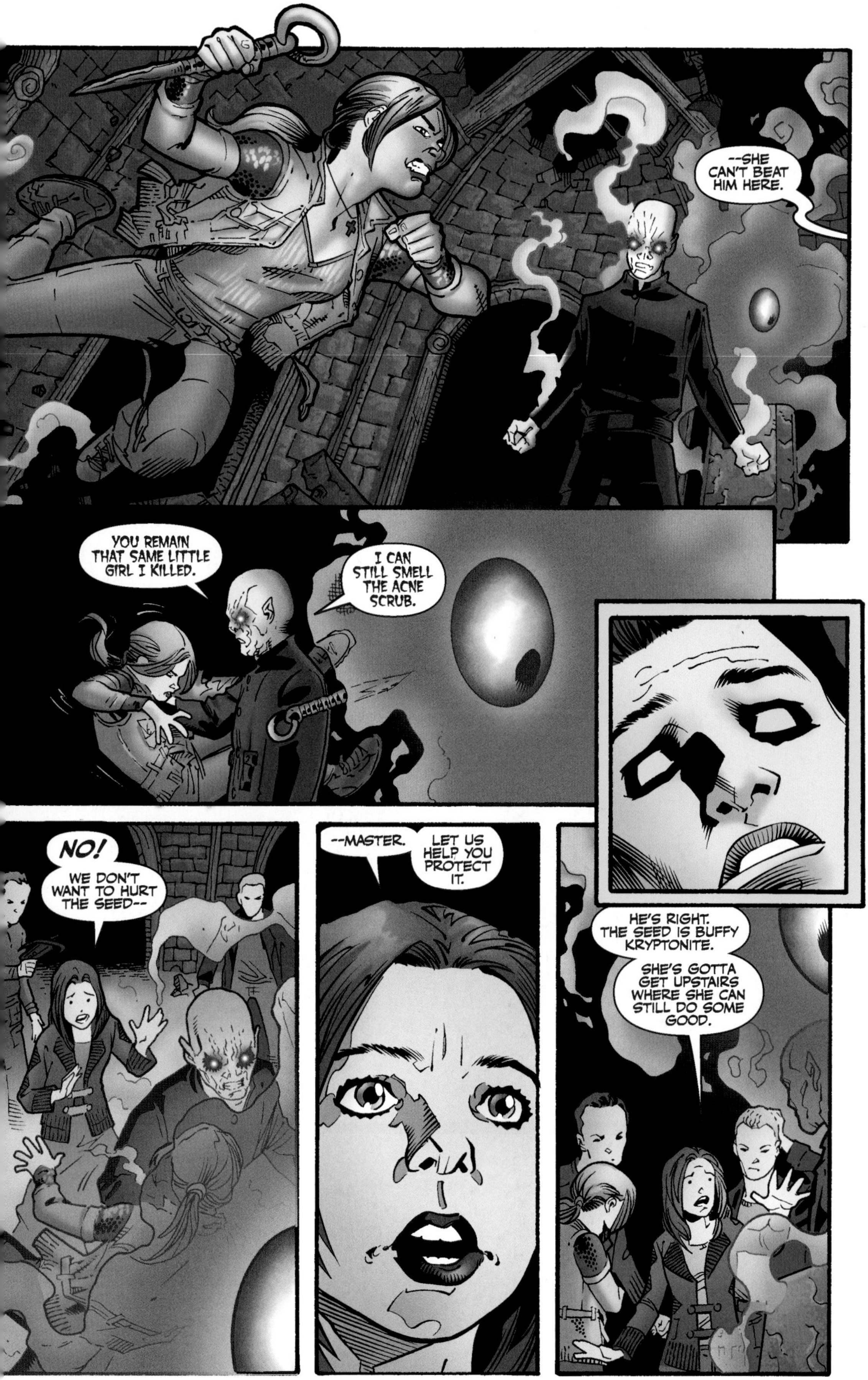
--SHE CAN'T BEAT HIM HERE.
YOU REMAIN THAT SAME LITTLE GIRL I KILLED.
I CAN STILL SMELL THE ACNE SCRUB.
NO!
WE DON'T WANT TO HURT THE SEED--
--MASTER.
LET US HELP YOU PROTECT IT.
HE'S RIGHT. THE SEED IS BUFFY KRYPTONITE.
SHE'S GOTTA GET UPSTAIRS WHERE SHE CAN STILL DO SOME GOOD.

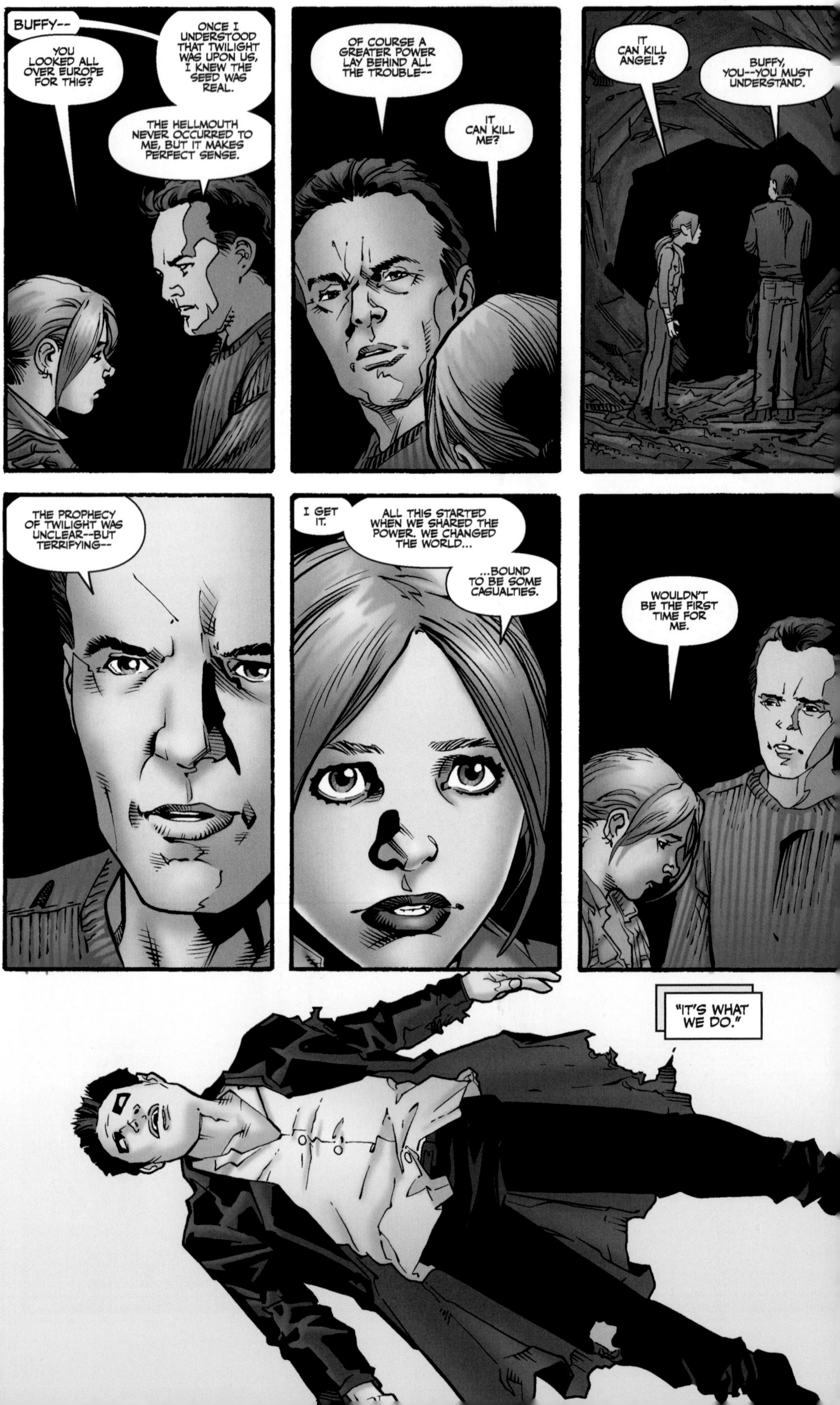

BUFFY--
YOU LOOKED ALL OVER EUROPE FOR THIS?
ONCE I UNDERSTOOD THAT TWILIGHT WAS UPON US, I KNEW THE SEED WAS REAL.
THE HELLMOUTH NEVER OCCURRED TO ME, BUT IT MAKES PERFECT SENSE.
OF COURSE A GREATER POWER LAY BEHIND ALL THE TROUBLE--
IT CAN KILL ME?
IT CAN KILL ANGEL?
BUFFY, YOU--YOU MUST UNDERSTAND.
THE PROPHECY OF TWILIGHT WAS UNCLEAR--BUT TERRIFYING--
I GET IT.
ALL THIS STARTED WHEN WE SHARED THE POWER. WE CHANGED THE WORLD...
...BOUND TO BE SOME CASUALTIES.
WOULDN'T BE THE FIRST TIME FOR ME.
"IT'S WHAT WE DO."

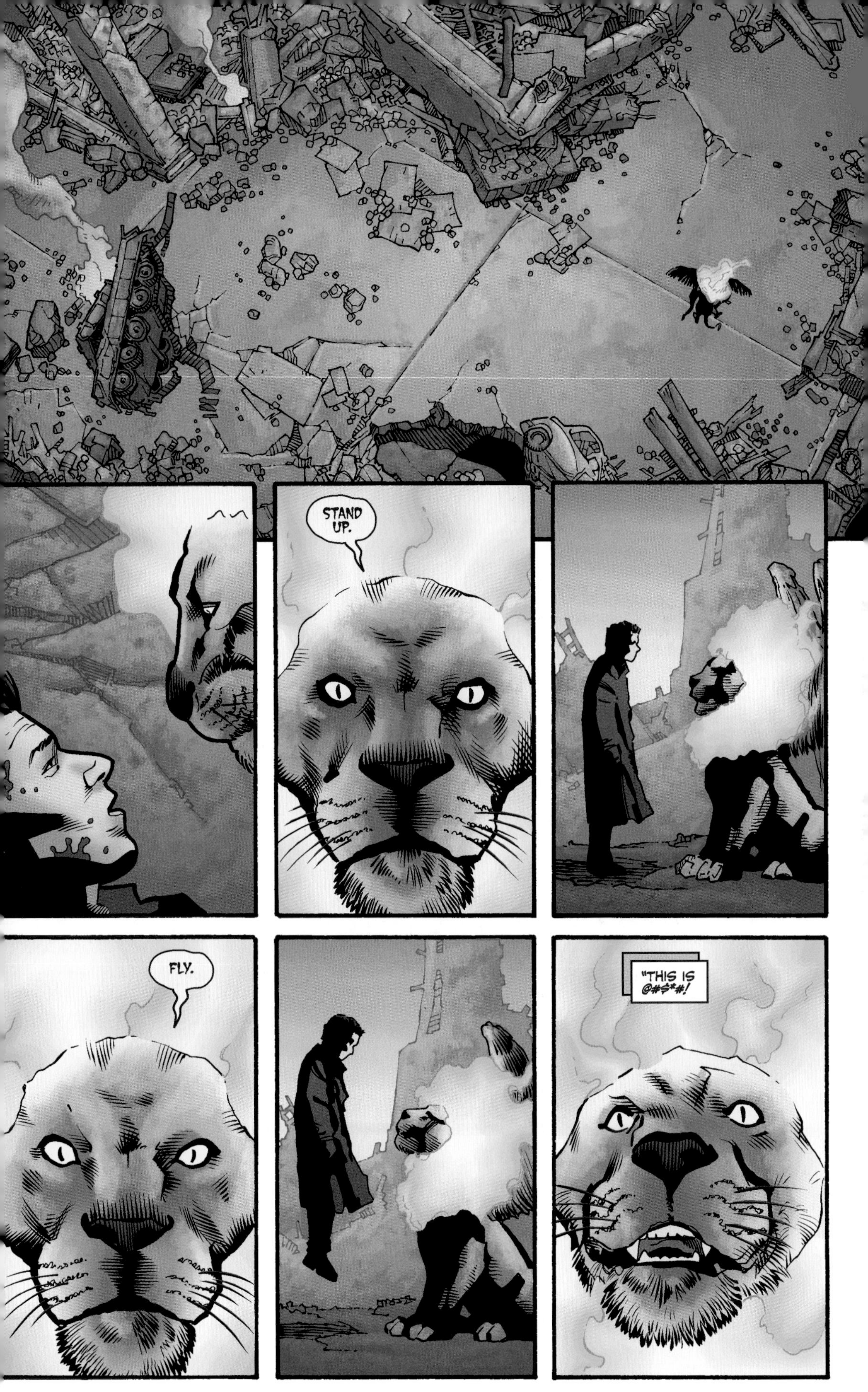
STAND UP.
FLY.
"THIS IS @#$*#!

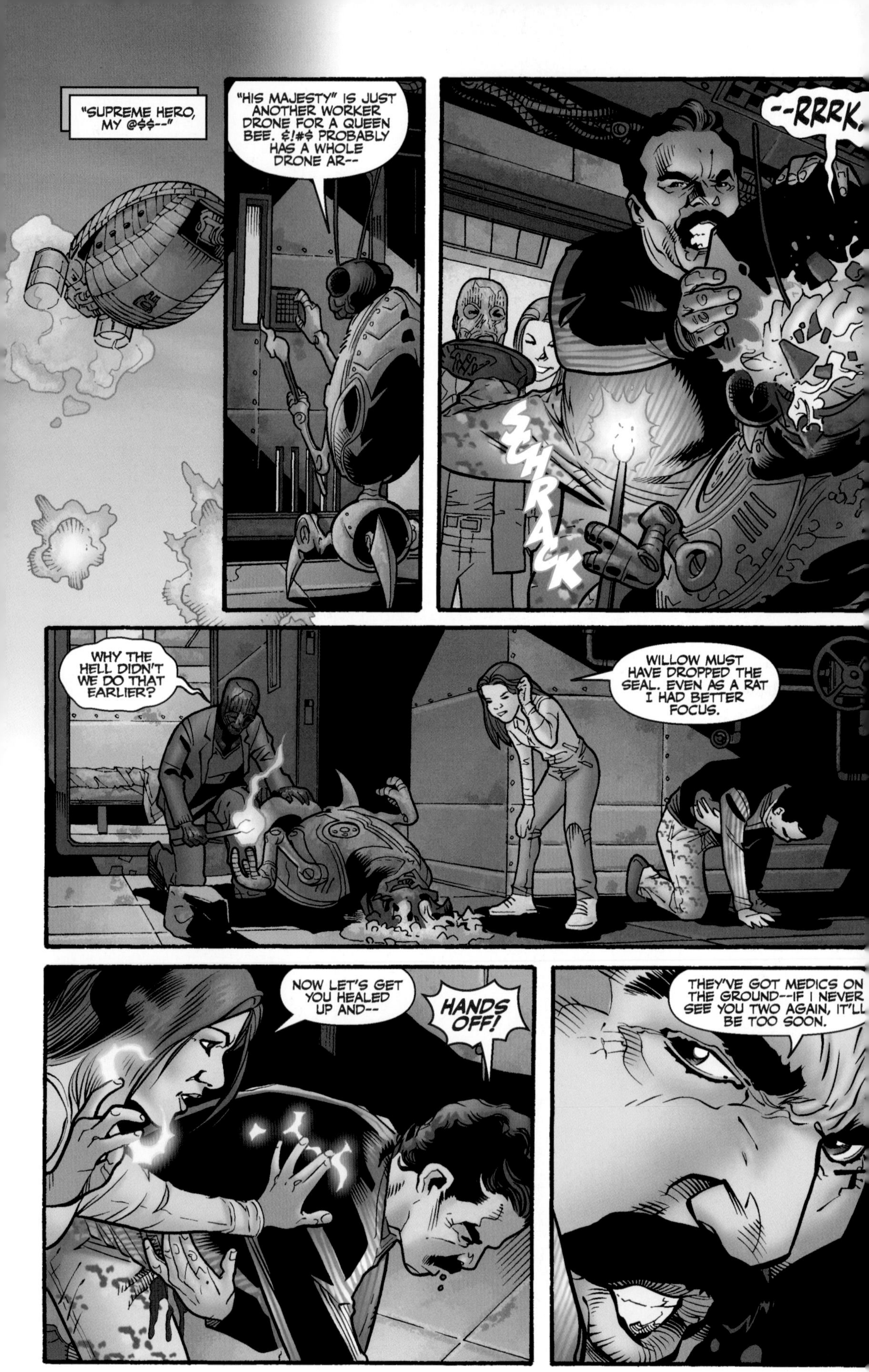

"SUPREME HERO, MY @$$--"
"HIS MAJESTY" IS JUST ANOTHER WORKER DRONE FOR A QUEEN BEE. $!#$ PROBABLY HAS A WHOLE DRONE AR--
--RRRK.
SCHRACK
WHY THE HELL DIDN'T WE DO THAT EARLIER?
WILLOW MUST HAVE DROPPED THE SEAL. EVEN AS A RAT I HAD BETTER FOCUS.
NOW LET'S GET YOU HEALED UP AND--
HANDS OFF!
THEY'VE GOT MEDICS ON THE GROUND--IF I NEVER SEE YOU TWO AGAIN, IT'LL BE TOO SOON.

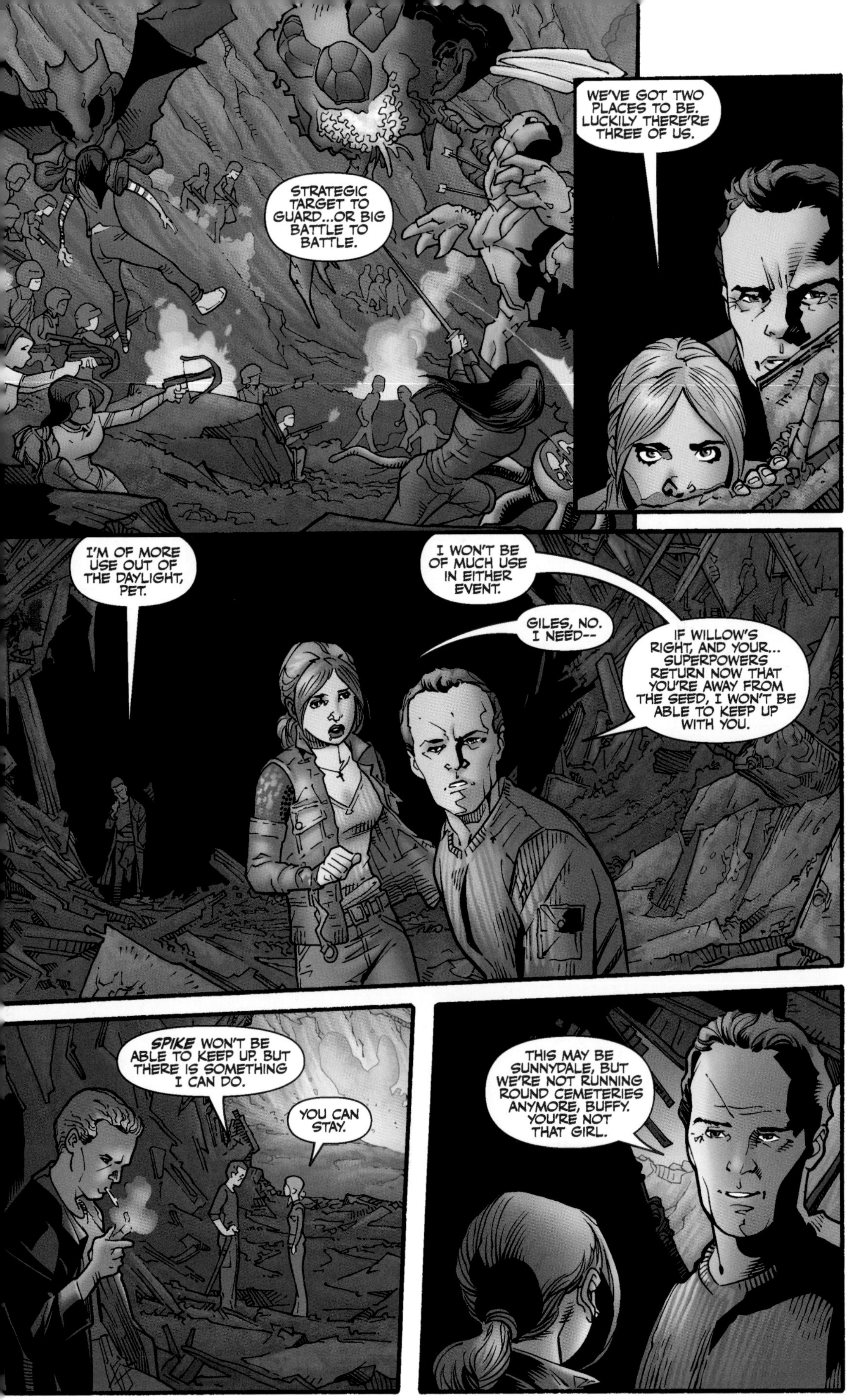
STRATEGIC TARGET TO GUARD...OR BIG BATTLE TO BATTLE.
WE'VE GOT TWO PLACES TO BE. LUCKILY THERE'RE THREE OF US.
I'M OF MORE USE OUT OF THE DAYLIGHT, PET.
I WON'T BE OF MUCH USE IN EITHER EVENT.
GILES, NO. I NEED--
IF WILLOW'S RIGHT, AND YOUR... SUPERPOWERS RETURN NOW THAT YOU'RE AWAY FROM THE SEED, I WON'T BE ABLE TO KEEP UP WITH YOU.
SPIKE WON'T BE ABLE TO KEEP UP. BUT THERE IS SOMETHING I CAN DO.
YOU CAN STAY.
THIS MAY BE SUNNYDALE, BUT WE'RE NOT RUNNING ROUND CEMETERIES ANYMORE, BUFFY. YOU'RE NOT THAT GIRL.

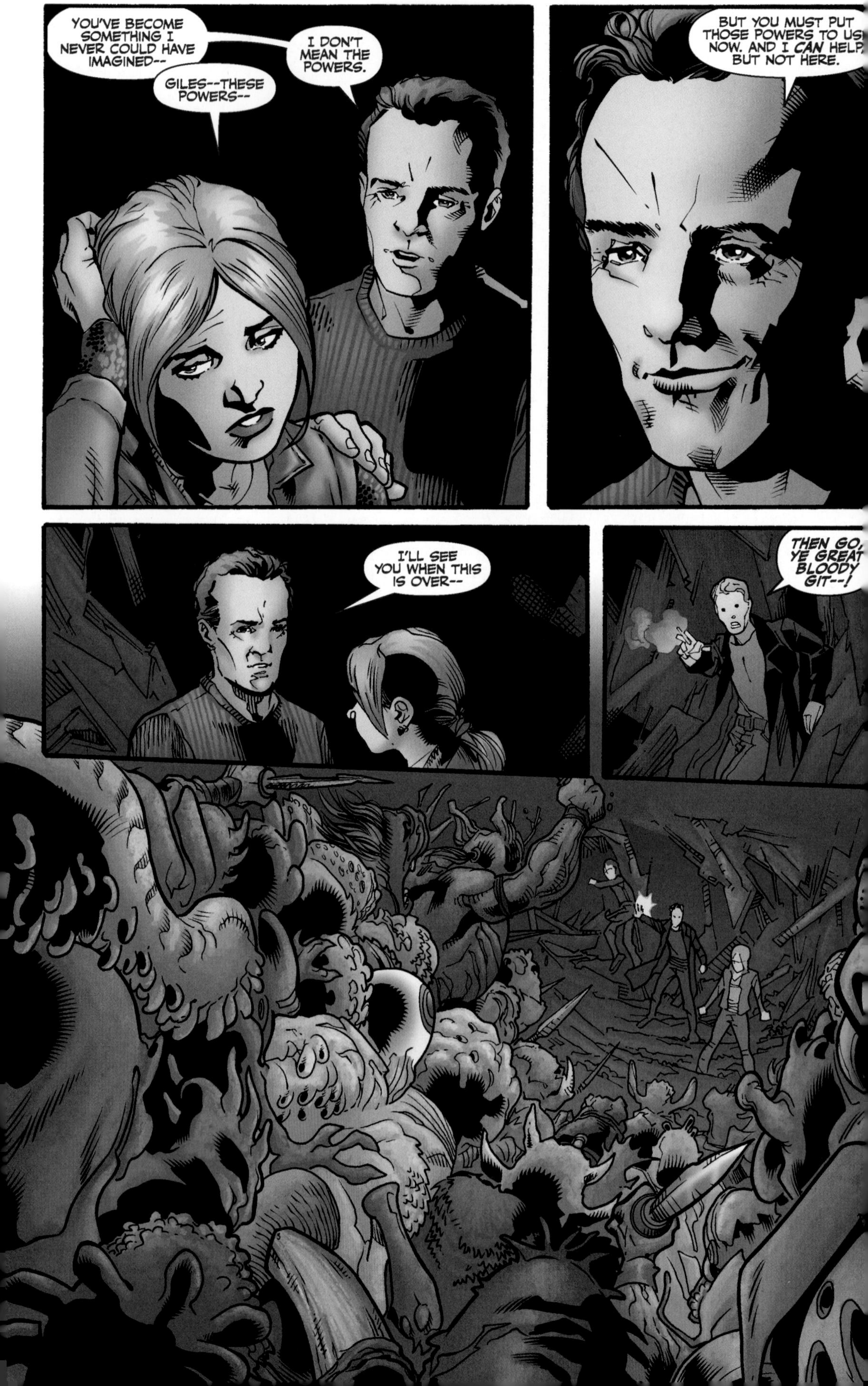
YOU'VE BECOME SOMETHING I NEVER COULD HAVE IMAGINED--
GILES--THESE POWERS--
I DON'T MEAN THE POWERS.
BUT YOU MUST PUT THOSE POWERS TO USE NOW. AND I *CAN* HELP. BUT NOT HERE.
I'LL SEE YOU WHEN THIS IS OVER--
THEN GO, YE GREAT BLOODY GIT--!

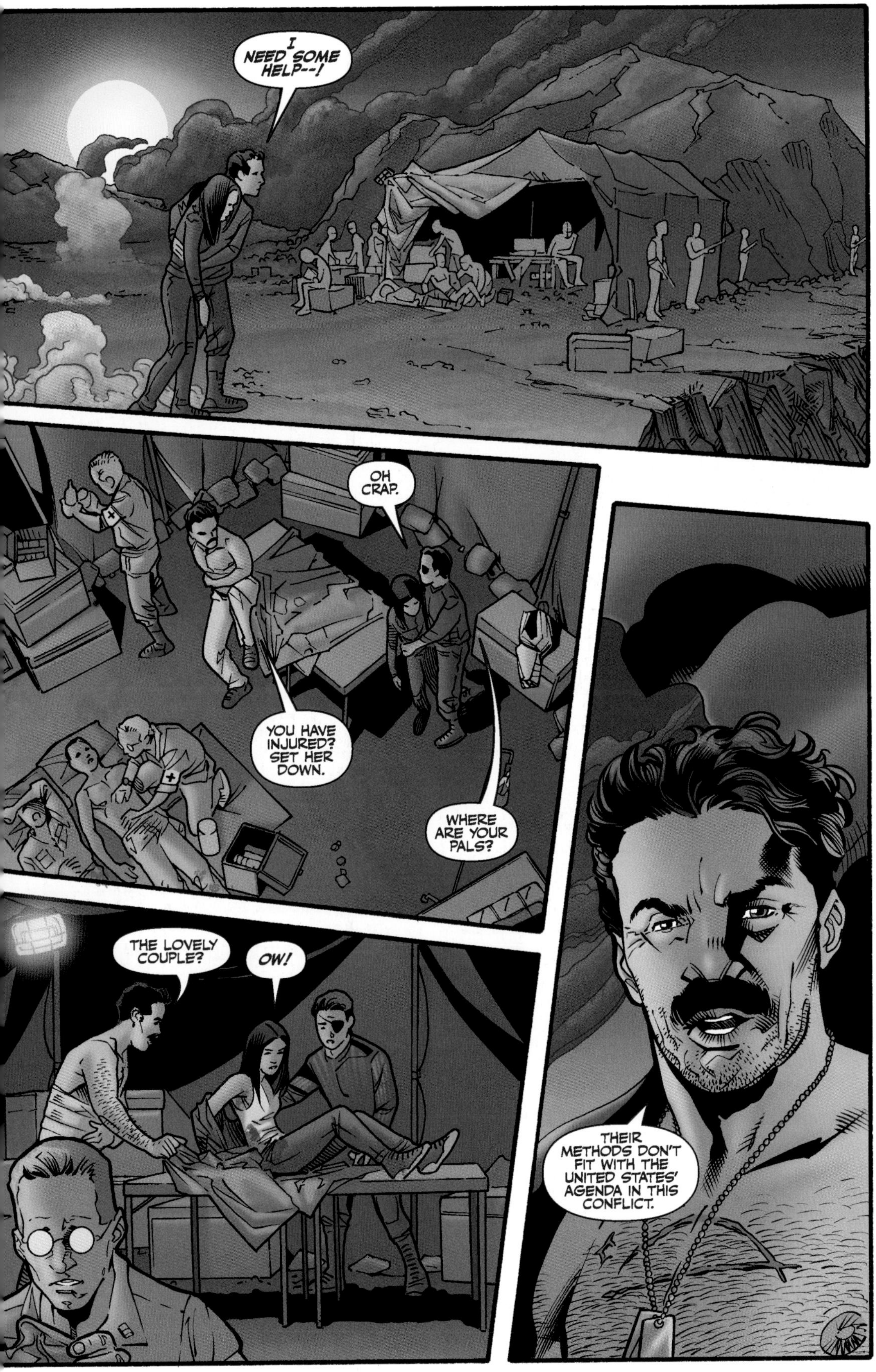

I NEED SOME HELP--!
OH CRAP.
YOU HAVE INJURED? SET HER DOWN.
WHERE ARE YOUR PALS?
THE LOVELY COUPLE?
OW!
THEIR METHODS DON'T FIT WITH THE UNITED STATES' AGENDA IN THIS CONFLICT.

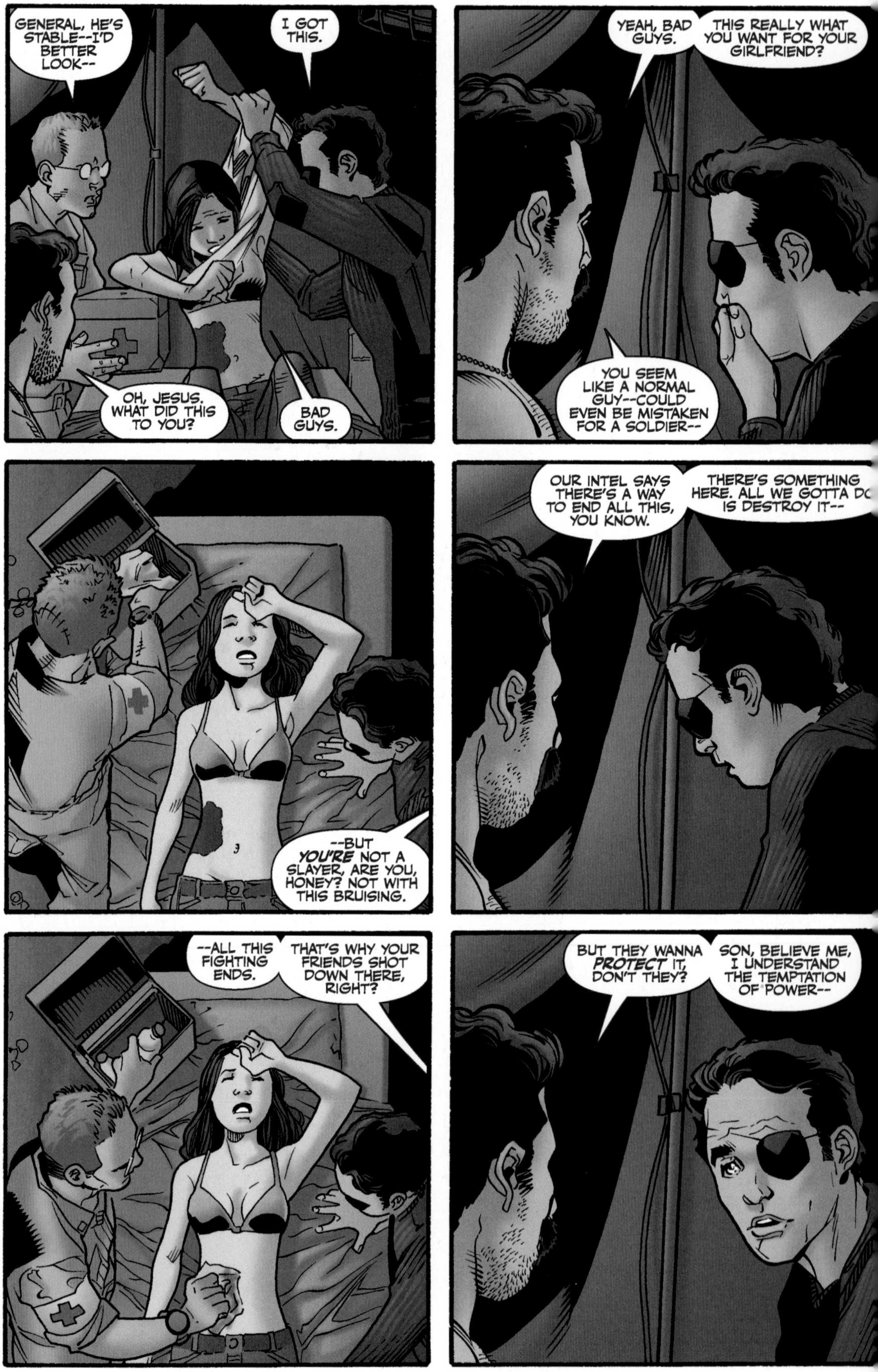
GENERAL, HE'S STABLE--I'D BETTER LOOK--
I GOT THIS.
OH, JESUS. WHAT DID THIS TO YOU?
BAD GUYS.
YEAH, BAD GUYS.
THIS REALLY WHAT YOU WANT FOR YOUR GIRLFRIEND?
YOU SEEM LIKE A NORMAL GUY--COULD EVEN BE MISTAKEN FOR A SOLDIER--
--BUT YOU'RE NOT A SLAYER, ARE YOU, HONEY? NOT WITH THIS BRUISING.
OUR INTEL SAYS THERE'S A WAY TO END ALL THIS, YOU KNOW.
THERE'S SOMETHING HERE. ALL WE GOTTA DO IS DESTROY IT--
--ALL THIS FIGHTING ENDS.
THAT'S WHY YOUR FRIENDS SHOT DOWN THERE, RIGHT?
BUT THEY WANNA PROTECT IT, DON'T THEY?
SON, BELIEVE ME, I UNDERSTAND THE TEMPTATION OF POWER--

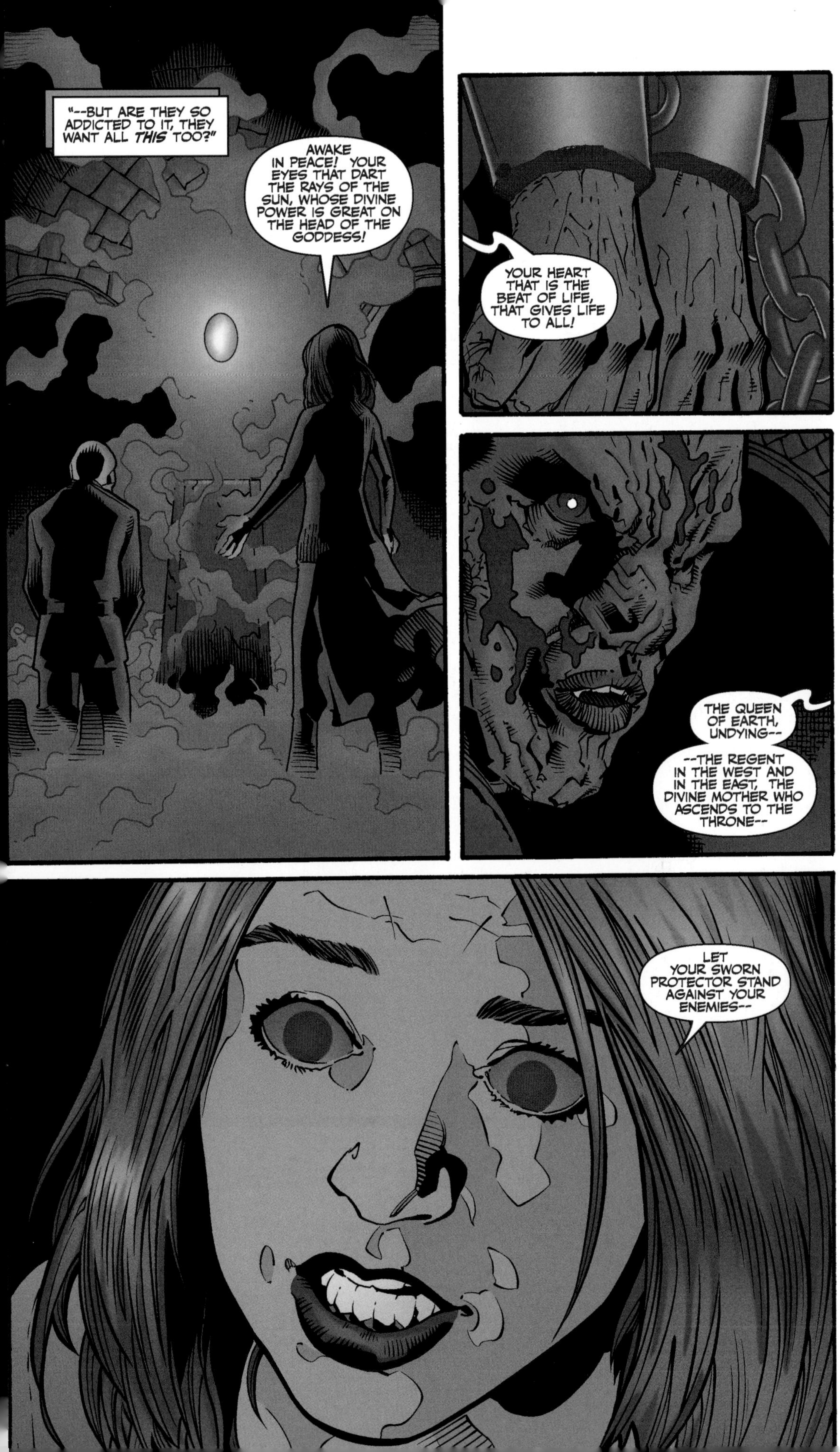
"--BUT ARE THEY SO ADDICTED TO IT, THEY WANT ALL THIS TOO?"
AWAKE IN PEACE! YOUR EYES THAT DART THE RAYS OF THE SUN, WHOSE DIVINE POWER IS GREAT ON THE HEAD OF THE GODDESS!
YOUR HEART THAT IS THE BEAT OF LIFE, THAT GIVES LIFE TO ALL!
THE QUEEN OF EARTH, UNDYING--
--THE REGENT IN THE WEST AND IN THE EAST, THE DIVINE MOTHER WHO ASCENDS TO THE THRONE--
LET YOUR SWORN PROTECTOR STAND AGAINST YOUR ENEMIES--

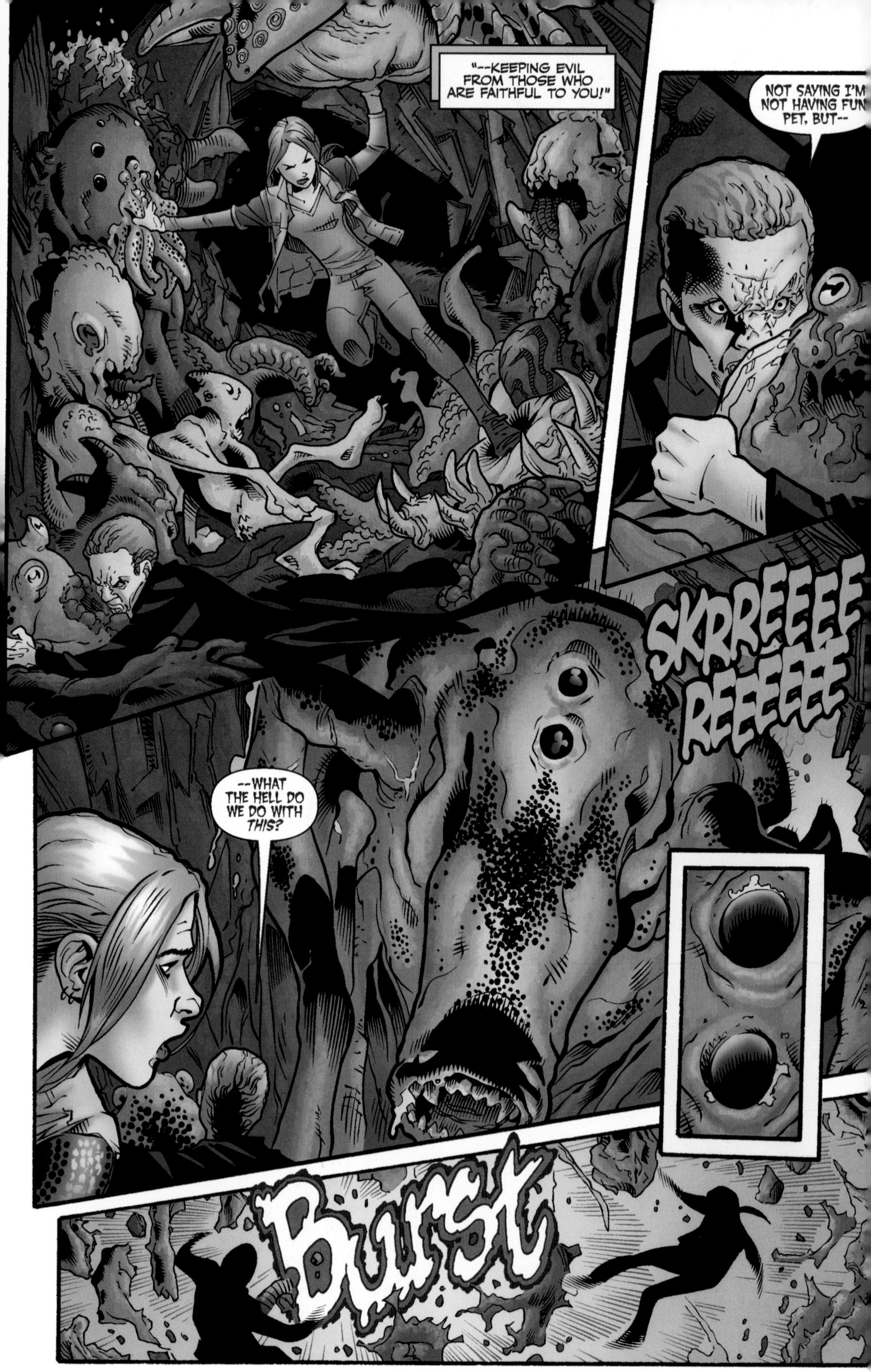
"--KEEPING EVIL FROM THOSE WHO ARE FAITHFUL TO YOU!"
NOT SAYING I'M NOT HAVING FUN PET, BUT--
SKRREEEEE REEEEEE
--WHAT THE HELL DO WE DO WITH THIS?
Burst

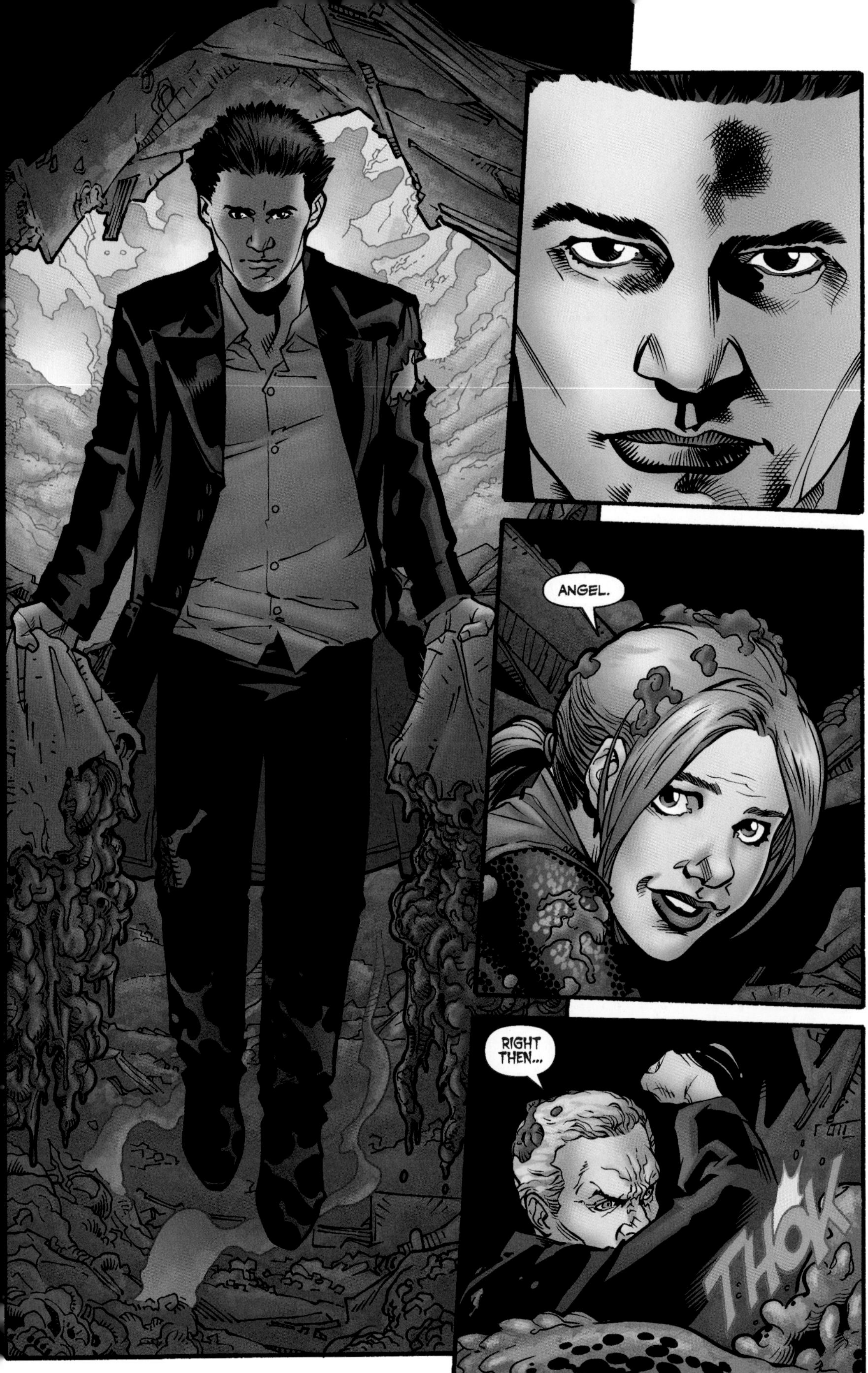
ANGEL.
RIGHT THEN...
THOK

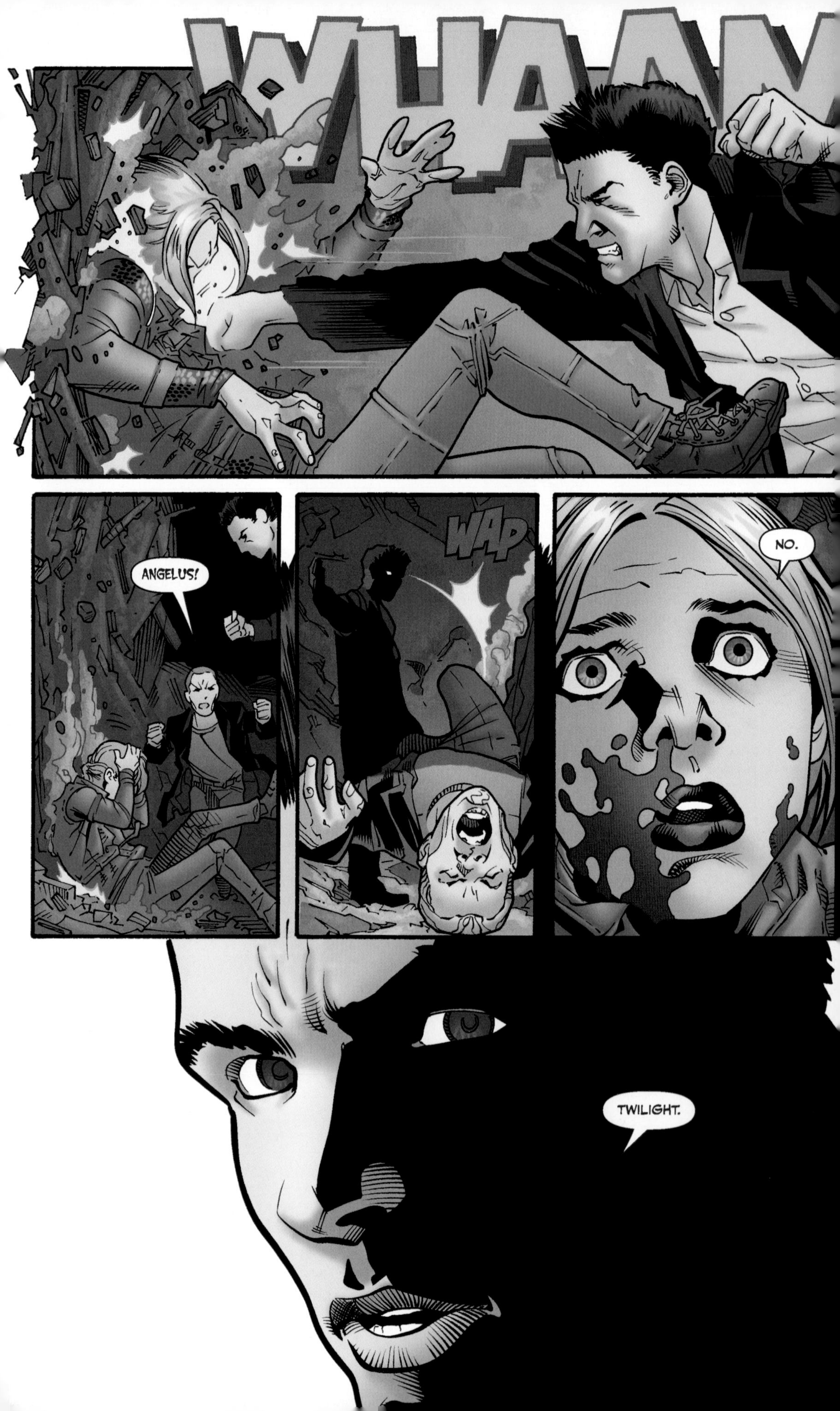

WHAAM
ANGELUS!
WAP
NO.
TWILIGHT.

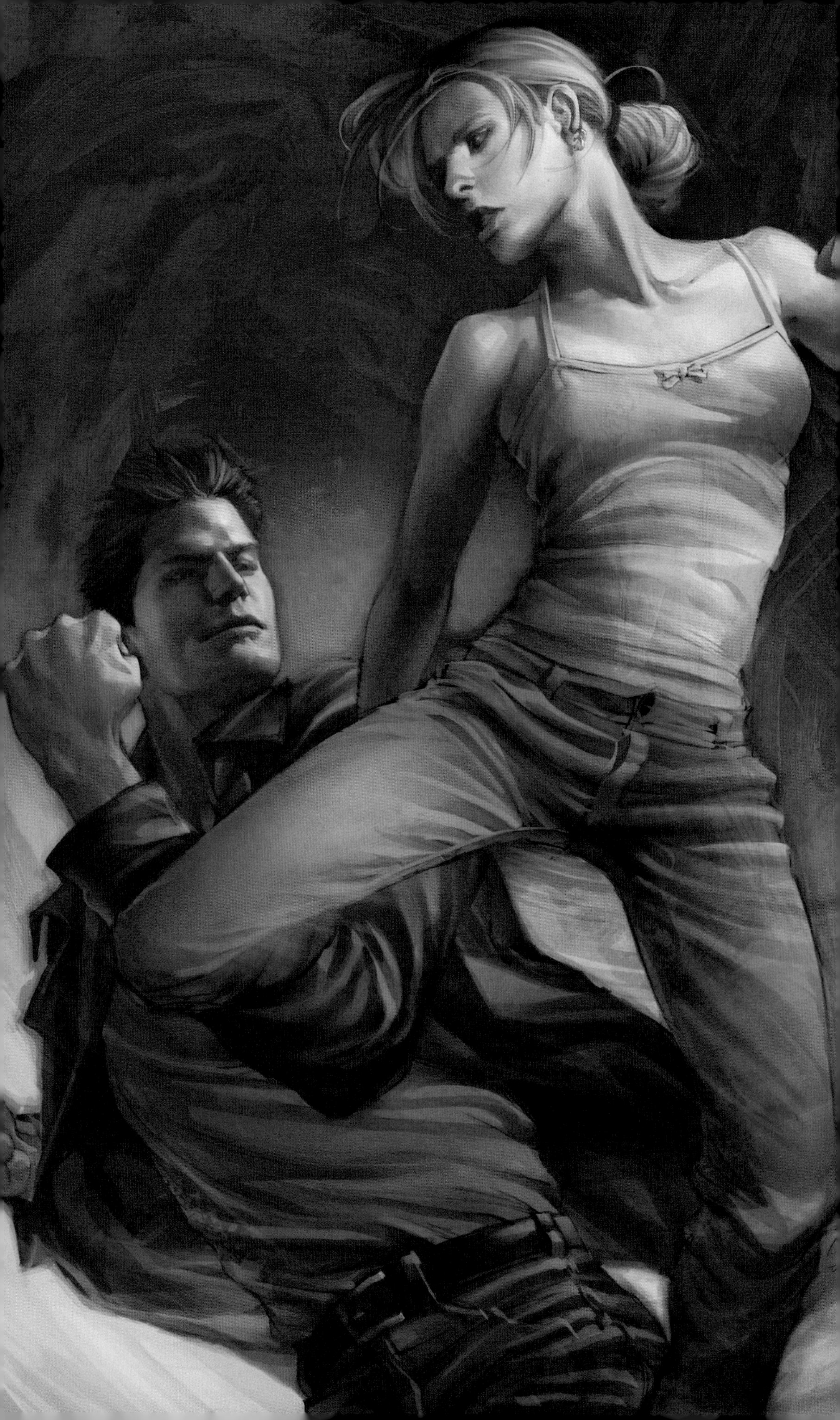

LAST GLEAMING

PART FOUR

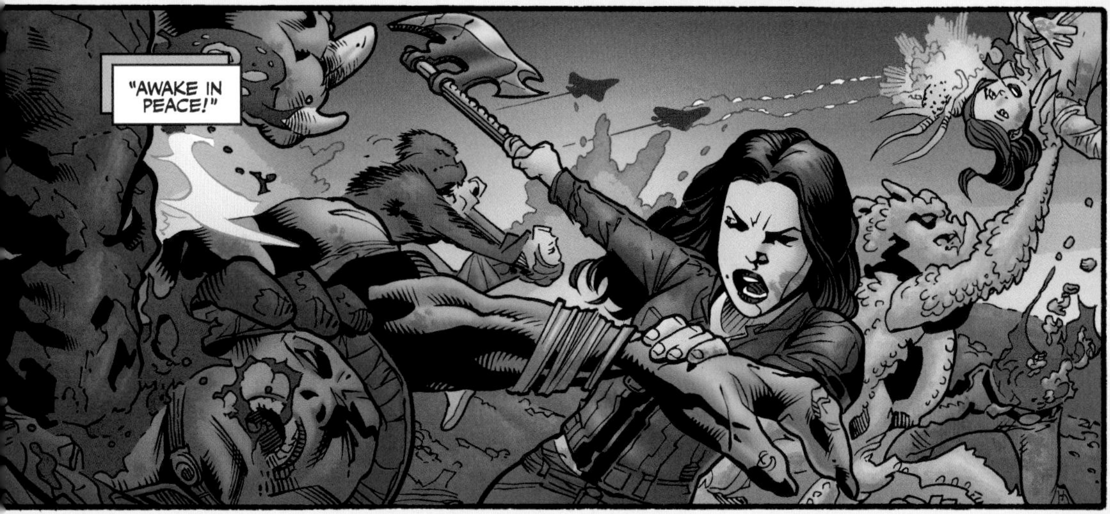
"AWAKE IN PEACE!"

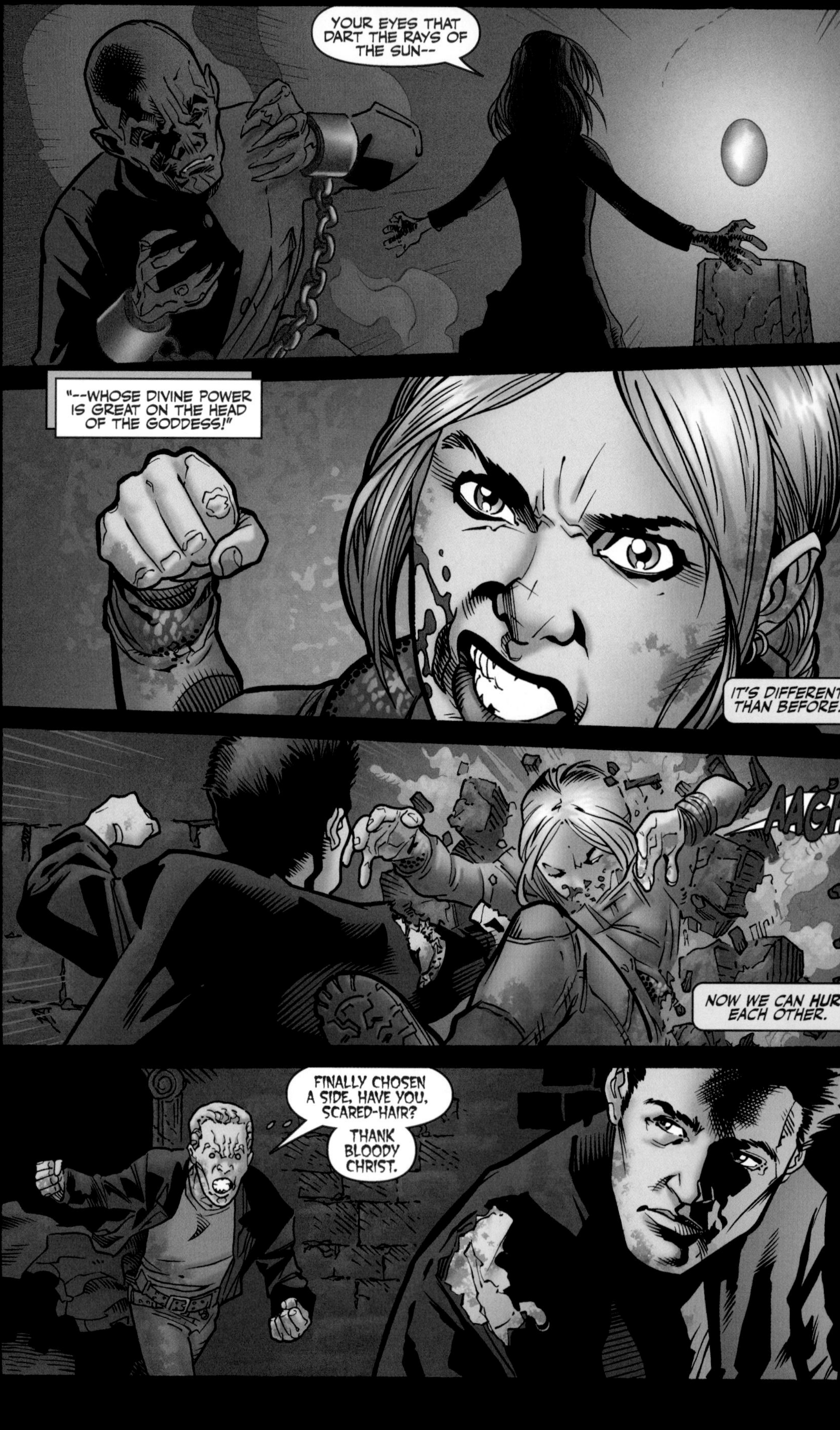
YOUR EYES THAT DART THE RAYS OF THE SUN--
"--WHOSE DIVINE POWER IS GREAT ON THE HEAD OF THE GODDESS!"
IT'S DIFFERENT THAN BEFORE.
AAGH!
NOW WE CAN HURT EACH OTHER.
FINALLY CHOSEN A SIDE, HAVE YOU, SCARED-HAIR?
THANK BLOODY CHRIST.

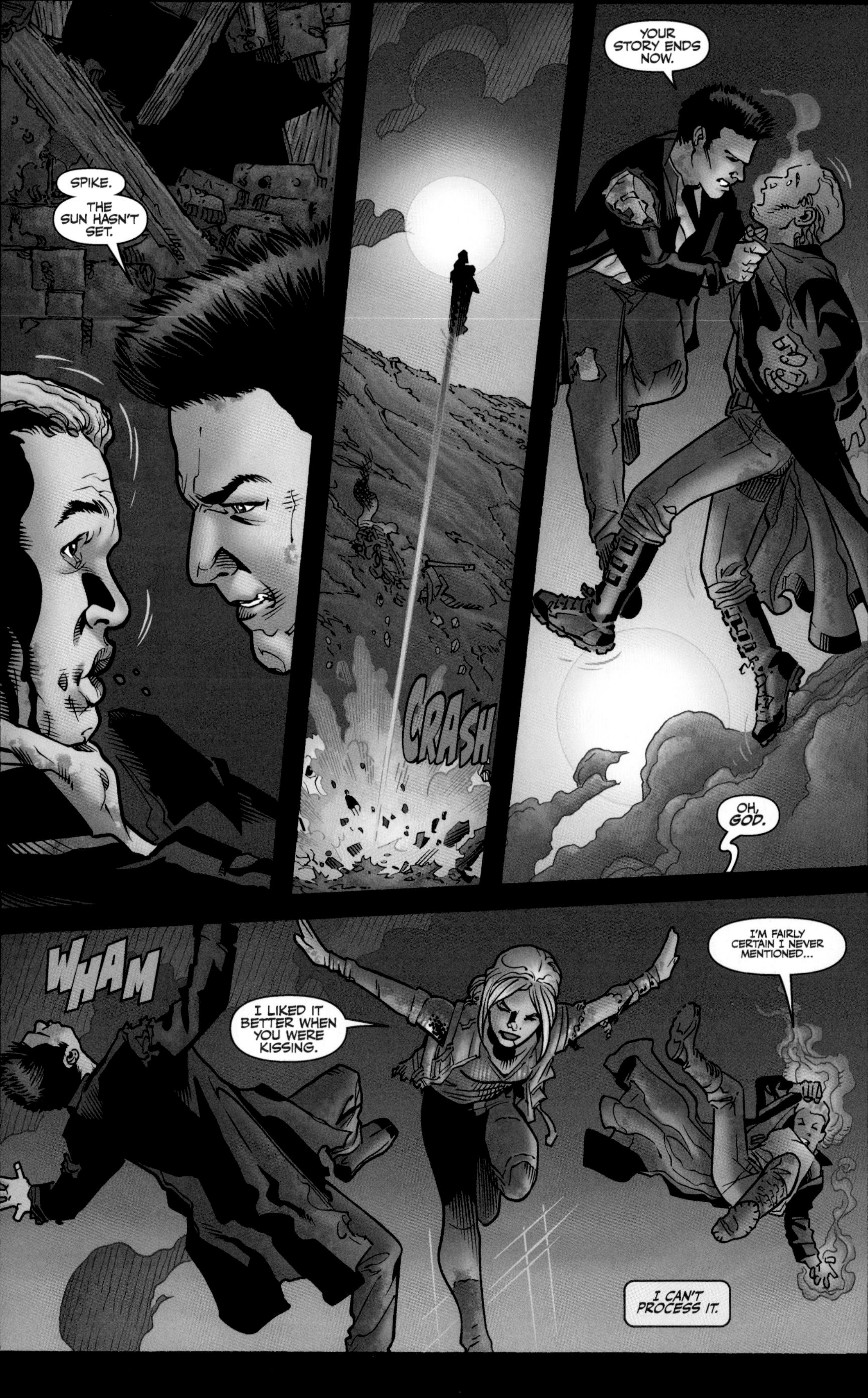
SPIKE.
THE SUN HASN'T SET.
CRASH
YOUR STORY ENDS NOW.
OH, GOD.
WHAM
I LIKED IT BETTER WHEN YOU WERE KISSING.
I'M FAIRLY CERTAIN I NEVER MENTIONED...
I CAN'T PROCESS IT.

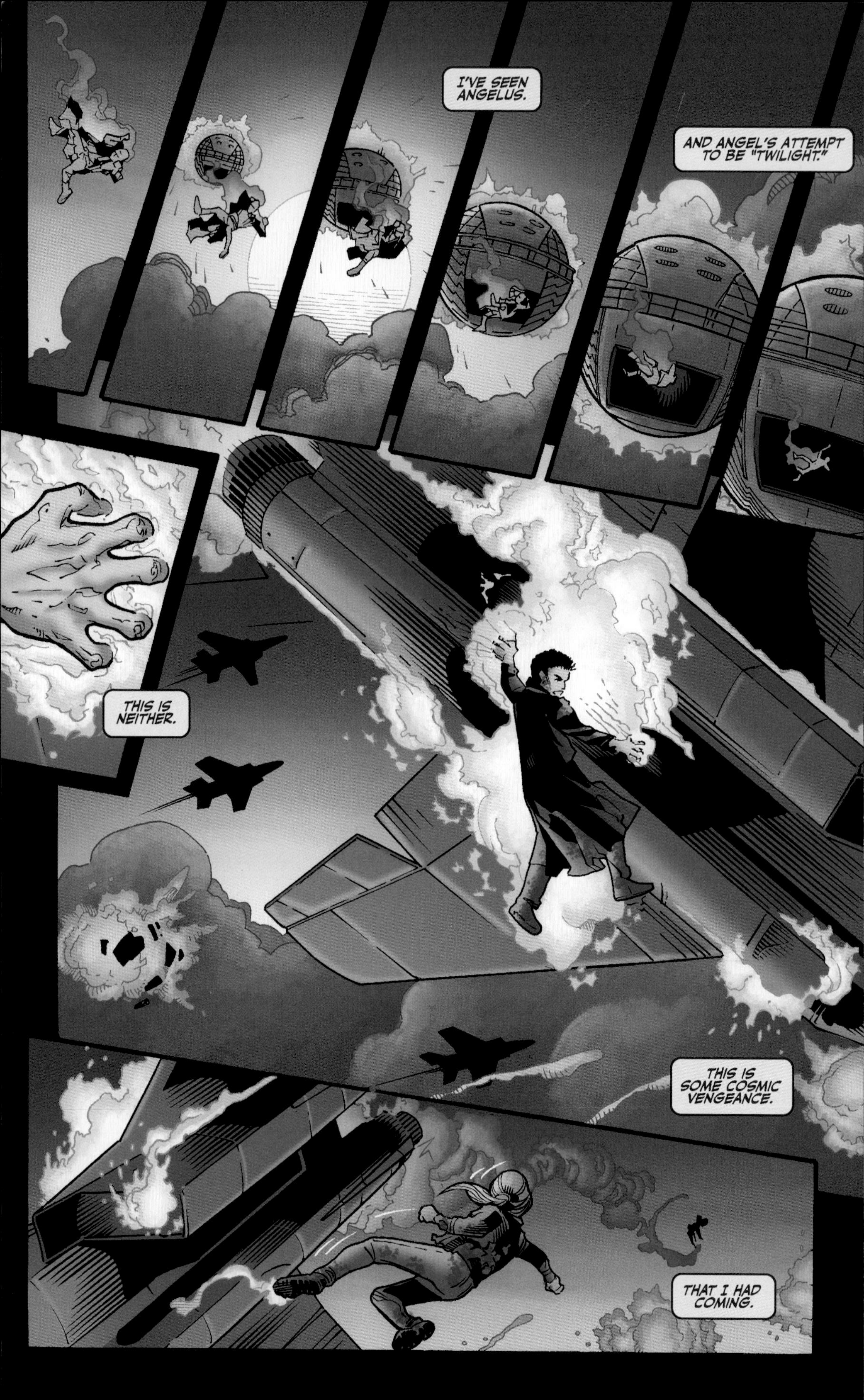
I'VE SEEN ANGELUS.
AND ANGEL'S ATTEMPT TO BE "TWILIGHT."
THIS IS NEITHER.
THIS IS SOME COSMIC VENGEANCE.
THAT I HAD COMING.

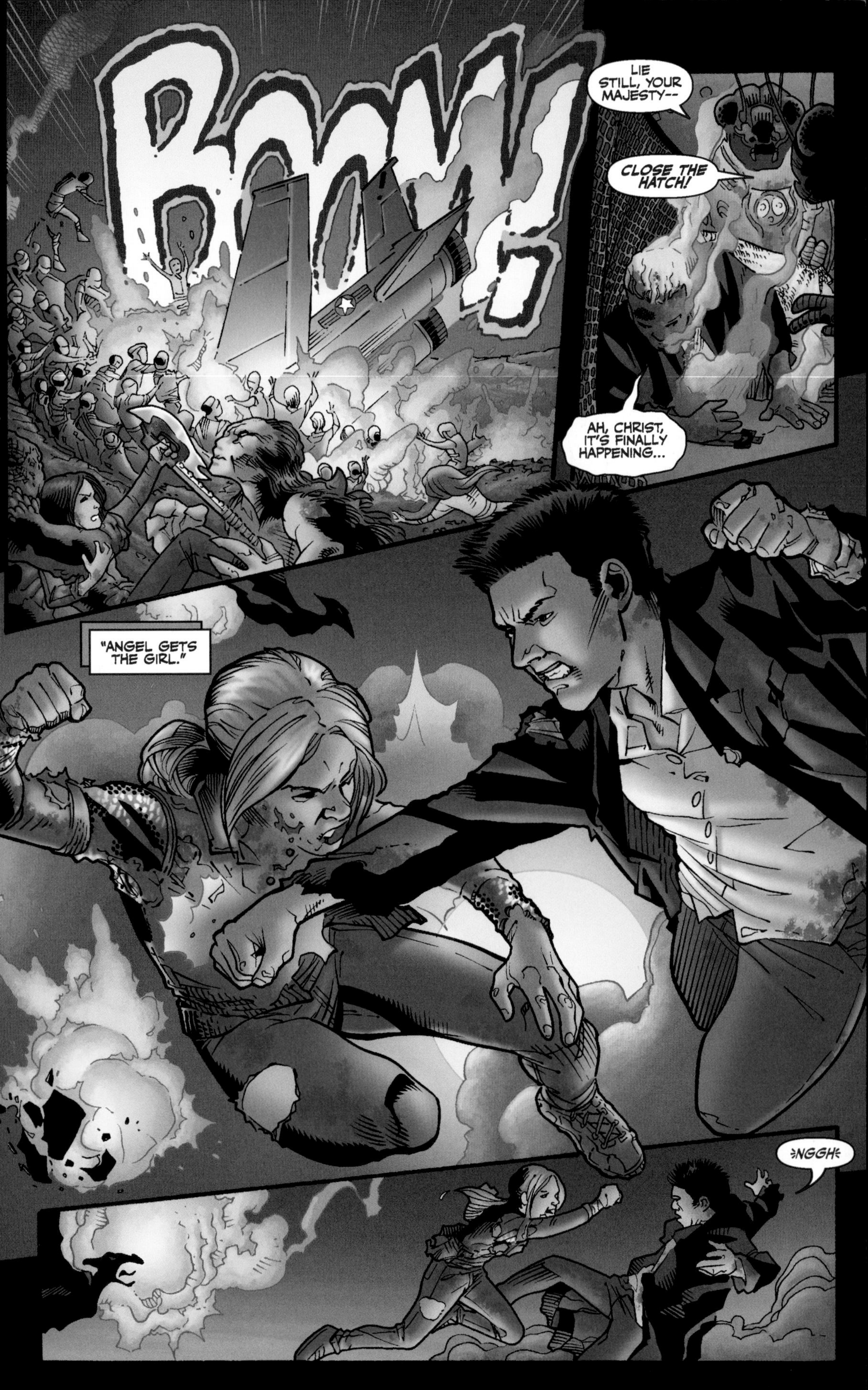
BOOM!
LIE STILL, YOUR MAJESTY--
CLOSE THE HATCH!
AH, CHRIST, IT'S FINALLY HAPPENING...
"ANGEL GETS THE GIRL."
NGGH

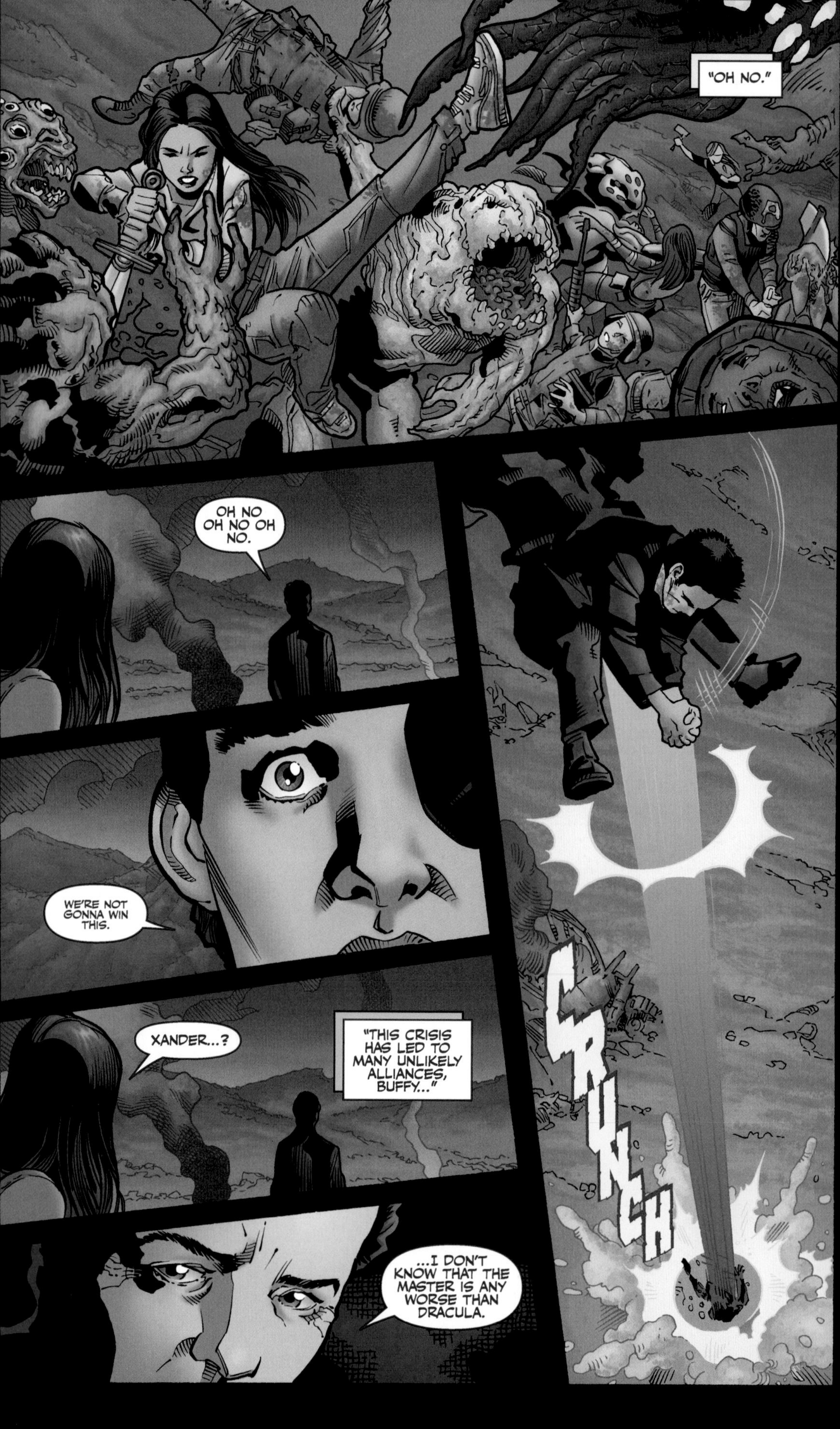
"OH NO."
OH NO OH NO OH NO.
WE'RE NOT GONNA WIN THIS.
XANDER...?
"THIS CRISIS HAS LED TO MANY UNLIKELY ALLIANCES, BUFFY..."
...I DON'T KNOW THAT THE MASTER IS ANY WORSE THAN DRACULA.
CRUNCH

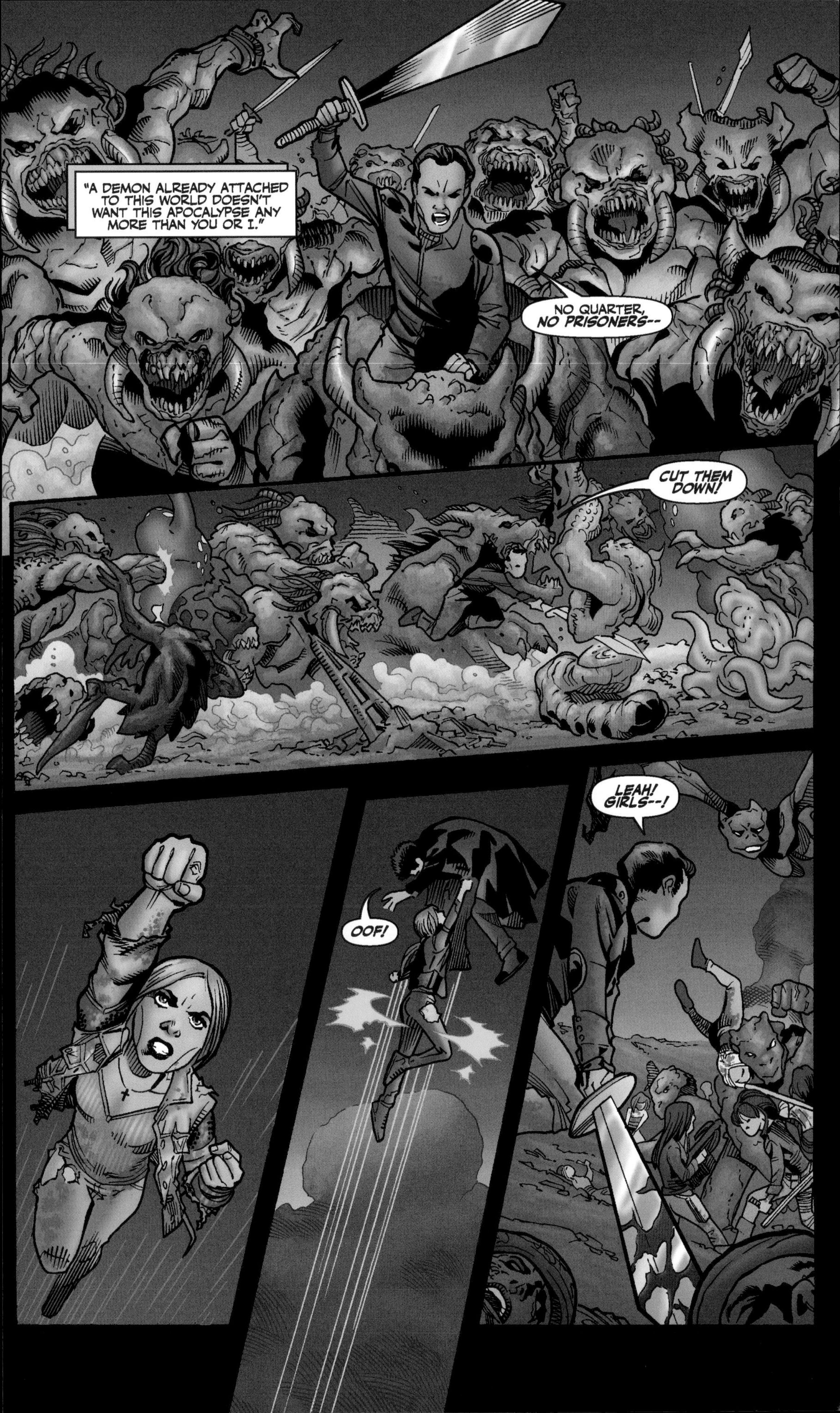
"A DEMON ALREADY ATTACHED TO THIS WORLD DOESN'T WANT THIS APOCALYPSE ANY MORE THAN YOU OR I."
NO QUARTER, NO PRISONERS--
CUT THEM DOWN!
OOF!
LEAH! GIRLS--!

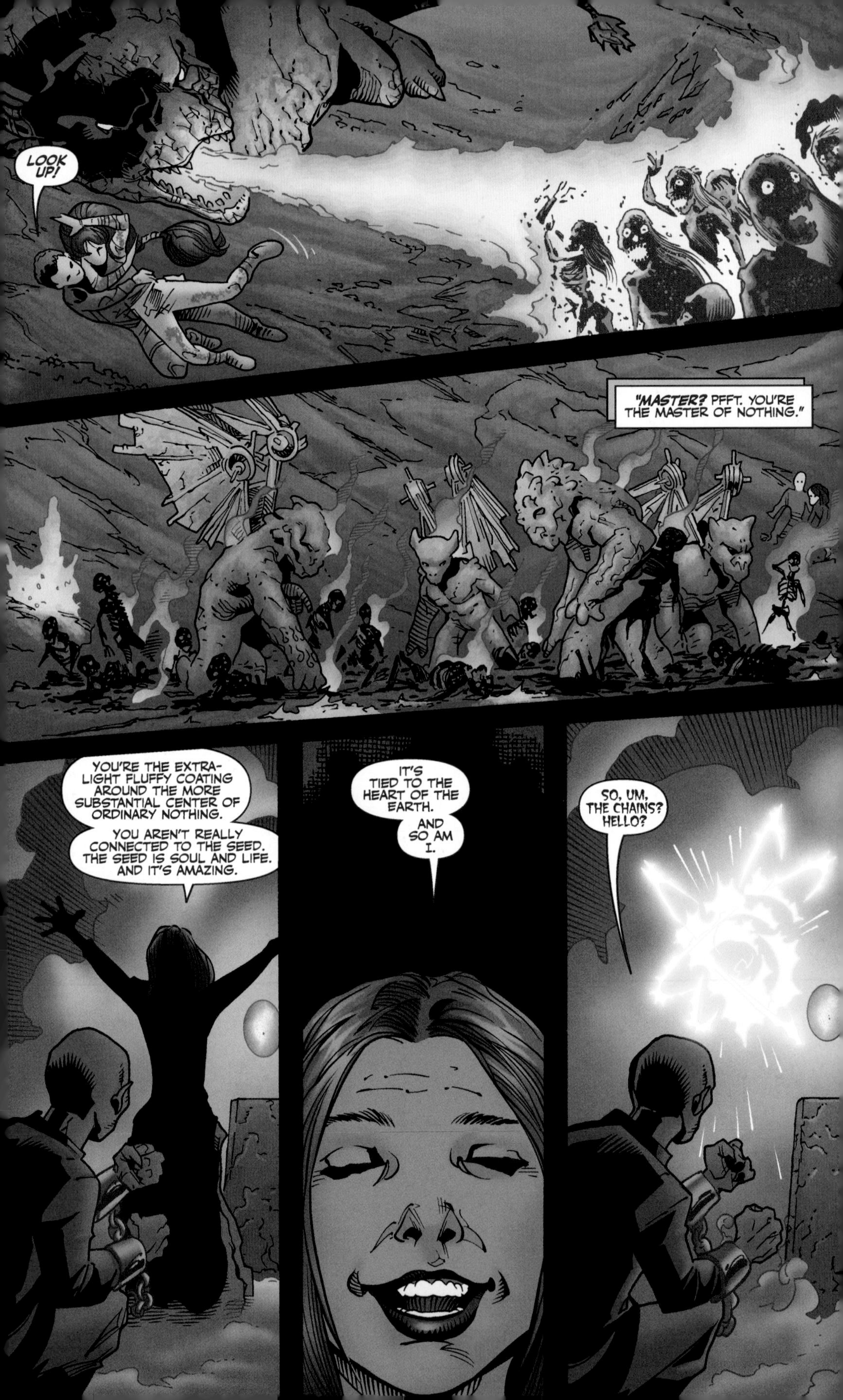
LOOK UP!
"MASTER? PFFT. YOU'RE THE MASTER OF NOTHING."
YOU'RE THE EXTRA-LIGHT FLUFFY COATING AROUND THE MORE SUBSTANTIAL CENTER OF ORDINARY NOTHING.
YOU AREN'T REALLY CONNECTED TO THE SEED. THE SEED IS SOUL AND LIFE. AND IT'S AMAZING.
IT'S TIED TO THE HEART OF THE EARTH.
AND SO AM I.
SO, UM, THE CHAINS? HELLO?

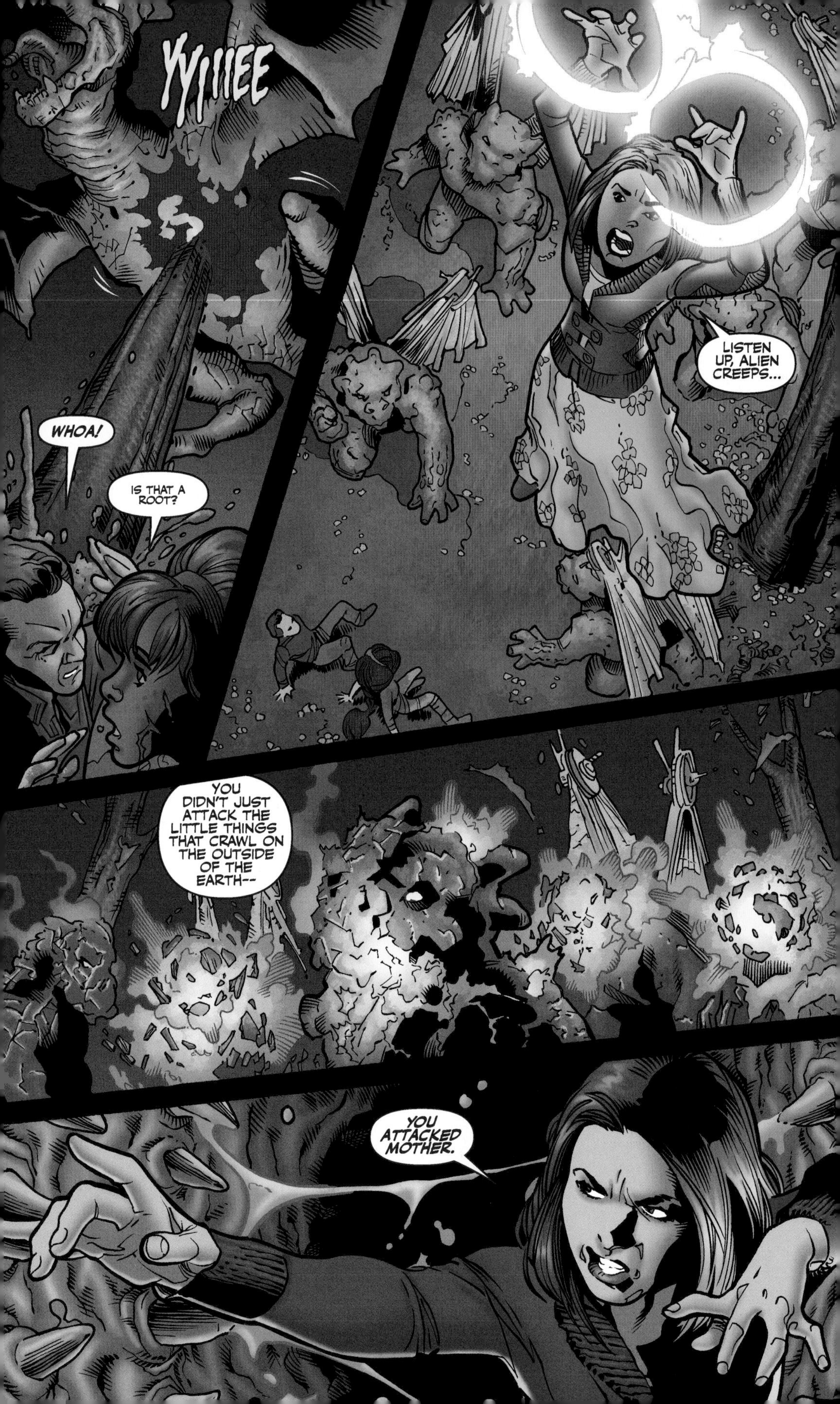
YYIIIEE
WHOA!
IS THAT A ROOT?
LISTEN UP, ALIEN CREEPS...
YOU DIDN'T JUST ATTACK THE LITTLE THINGS THAT CRAWL ON THE OUTSIDE OF THE EARTH--
YOU ATTACKED MOTHER.

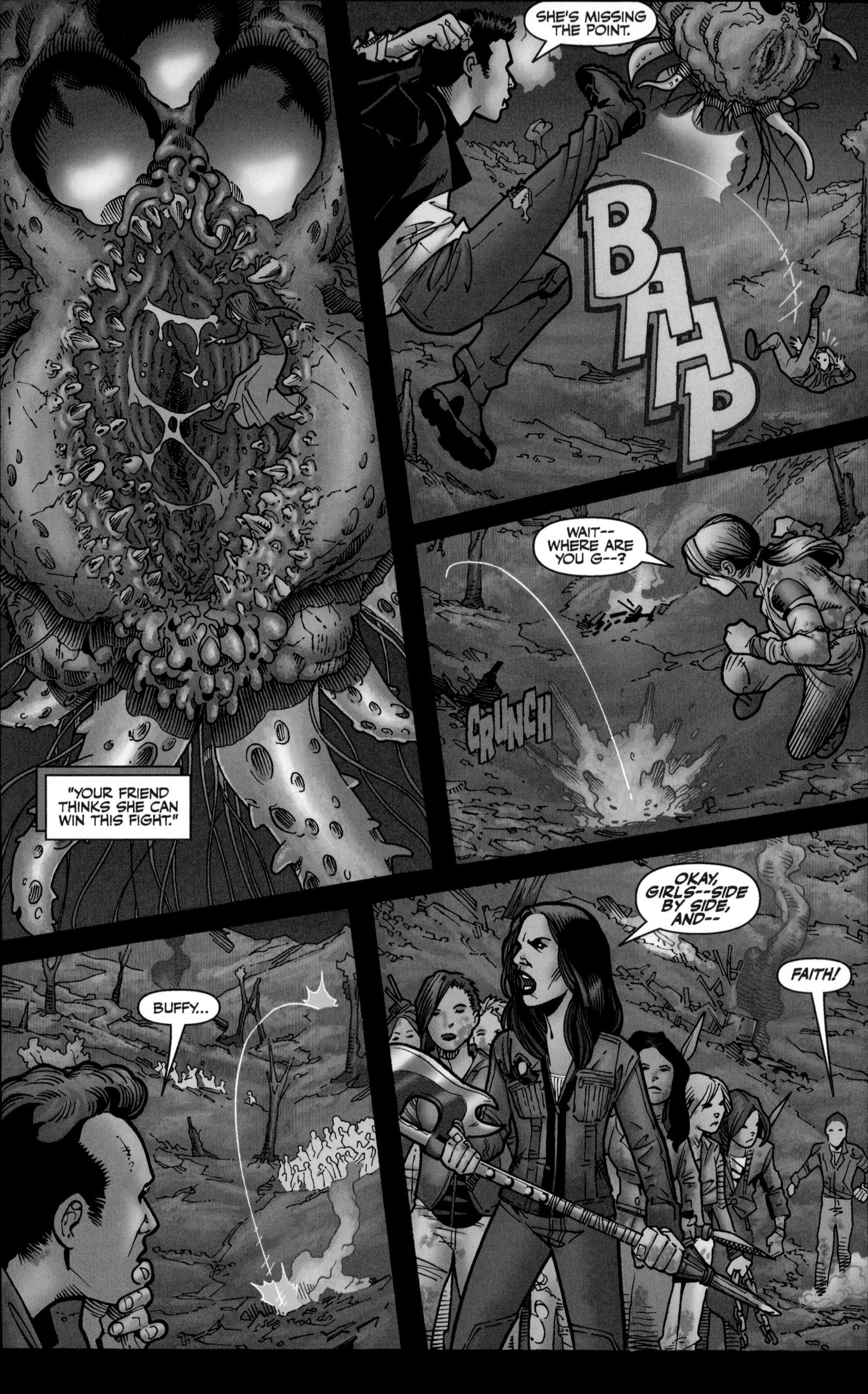
"YOUR FRIEND THINKS SHE CAN WIN THIS FIGHT."
SHE'S MISSING THE POINT.
BAAHP
WAIT-- WHERE ARE YOU G--?
CRUNCH
BUFFY...
OKAY, GIRLS--SIDE BY SIDE, AND--
FAITH!

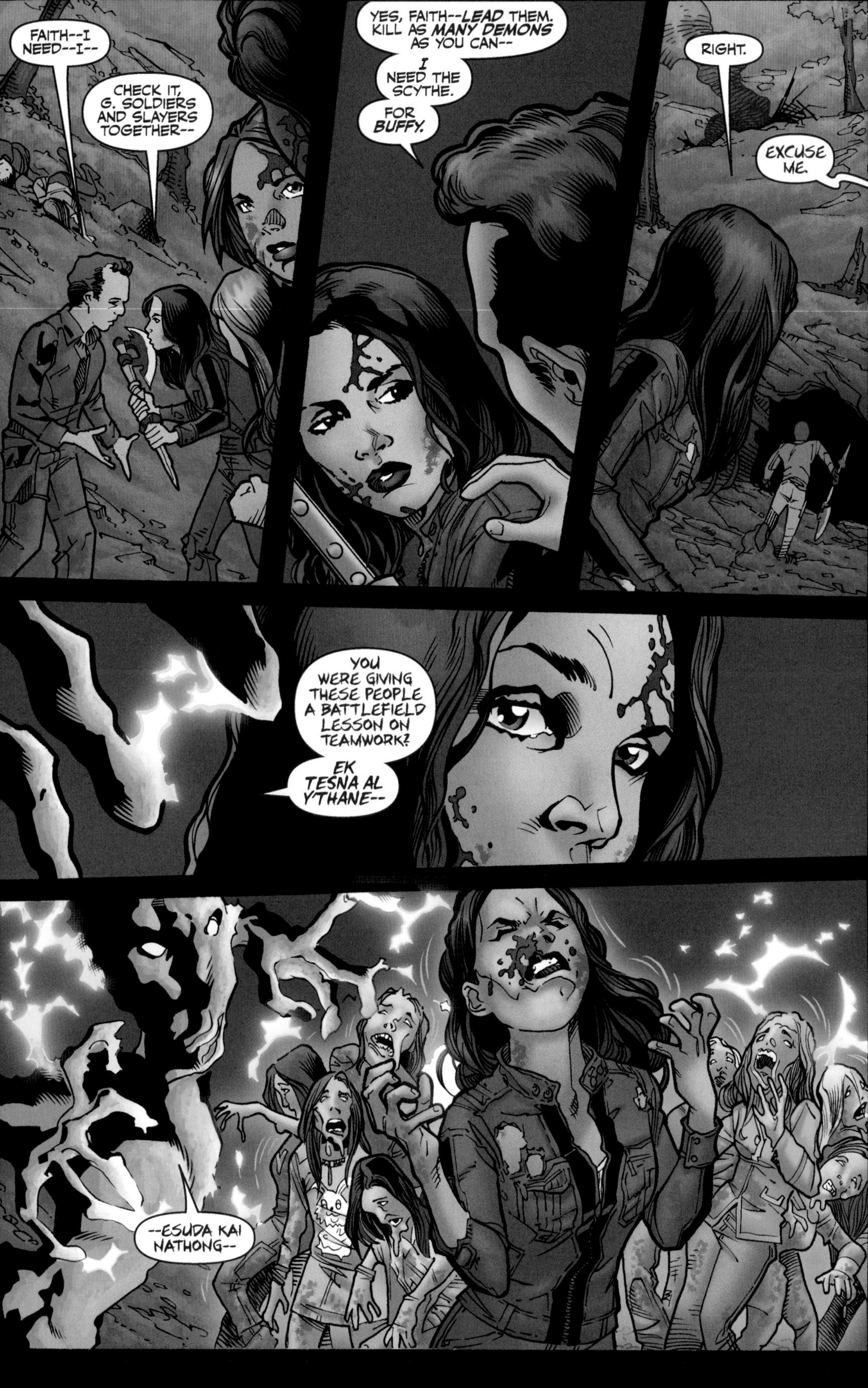
FAITH--I NEED--I--
CHECK IT, G. SOLDIERS AND SLAYERS TOGETHER--
YES, FAITH--LEAD THEM. KILL AS MANY DEMONS AS YOU CAN--
I NEED THE SCYTHE.
FOR BUFFY.
RIGHT.
EXCUSE ME.
YOU WERE GIVING THESE PEOPLE A BATTLEFIELD LESSON ON TEAMWORK?
EK TESNA AL Y'THANE--
--ESUDA KAI NATHONG--

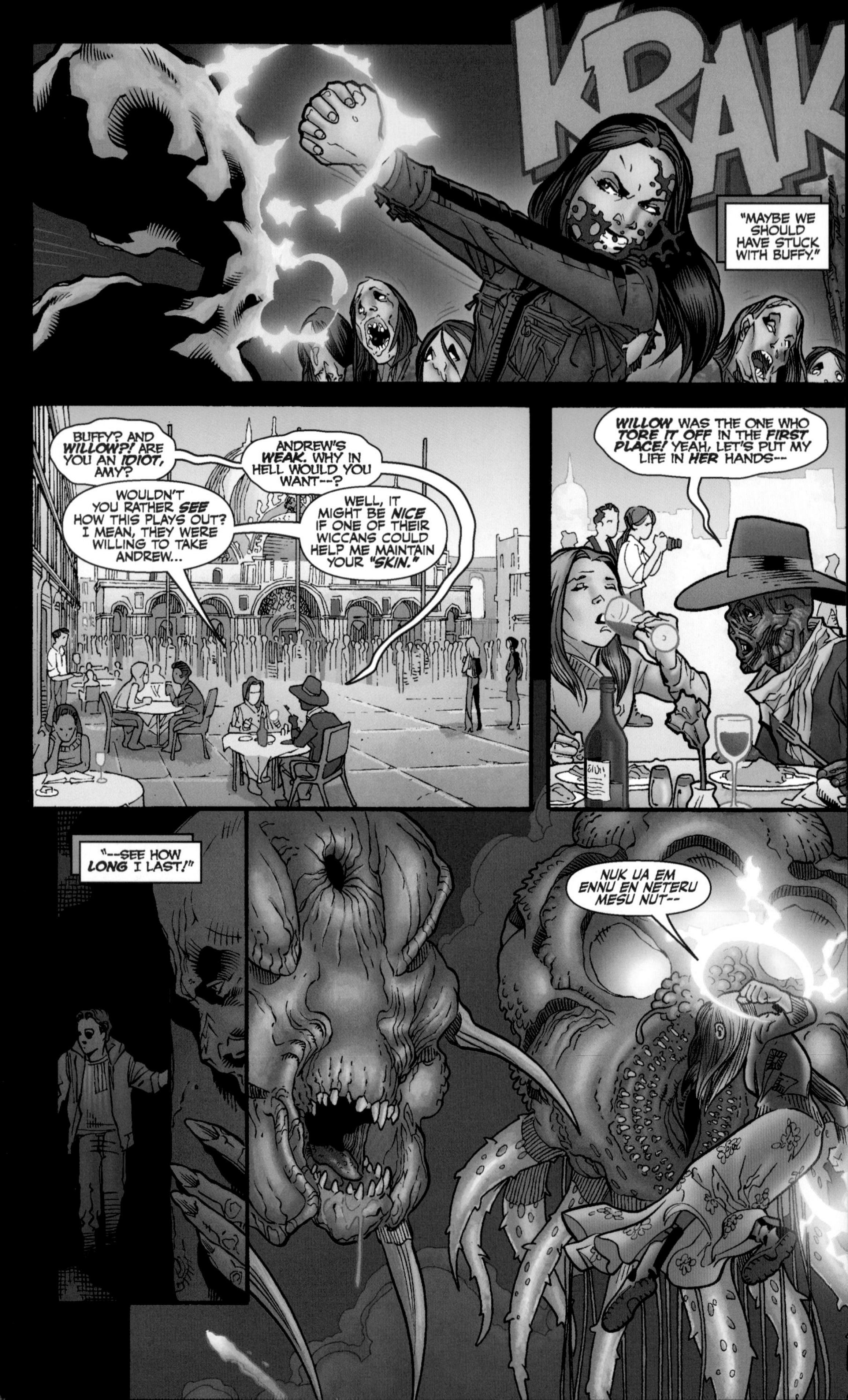

KRAK
"MAYBE WE SHOULD HAVE STUCK WITH BUFFY."
BUFFY? AND WILLOW?! ARE YOU AN IDIOT, AMY?
ANDREW'S WEAK. WHY IN HELL WOULD YOU WANT--?
WOULDN'T YOU RATHER SEE HOW THIS PLAYS OUT? I MEAN, THEY WERE WILLING TO TAKE ANDREW...
WELL, IT MIGHT BE NICE IF ONE OF THEIR WICCANS COULD HELP ME MAINTAIN YOUR "SKIN."
WILLOW WAS THE ONE WHO TORE IT OFF IN THE FIRST PLACE! YEAH, LET'S PUT MY LIFE IN HER HANDS--
"--SEE HOW LONG I LAST!"
NUK UA EM ENNU EN NETERU MESU NUT--

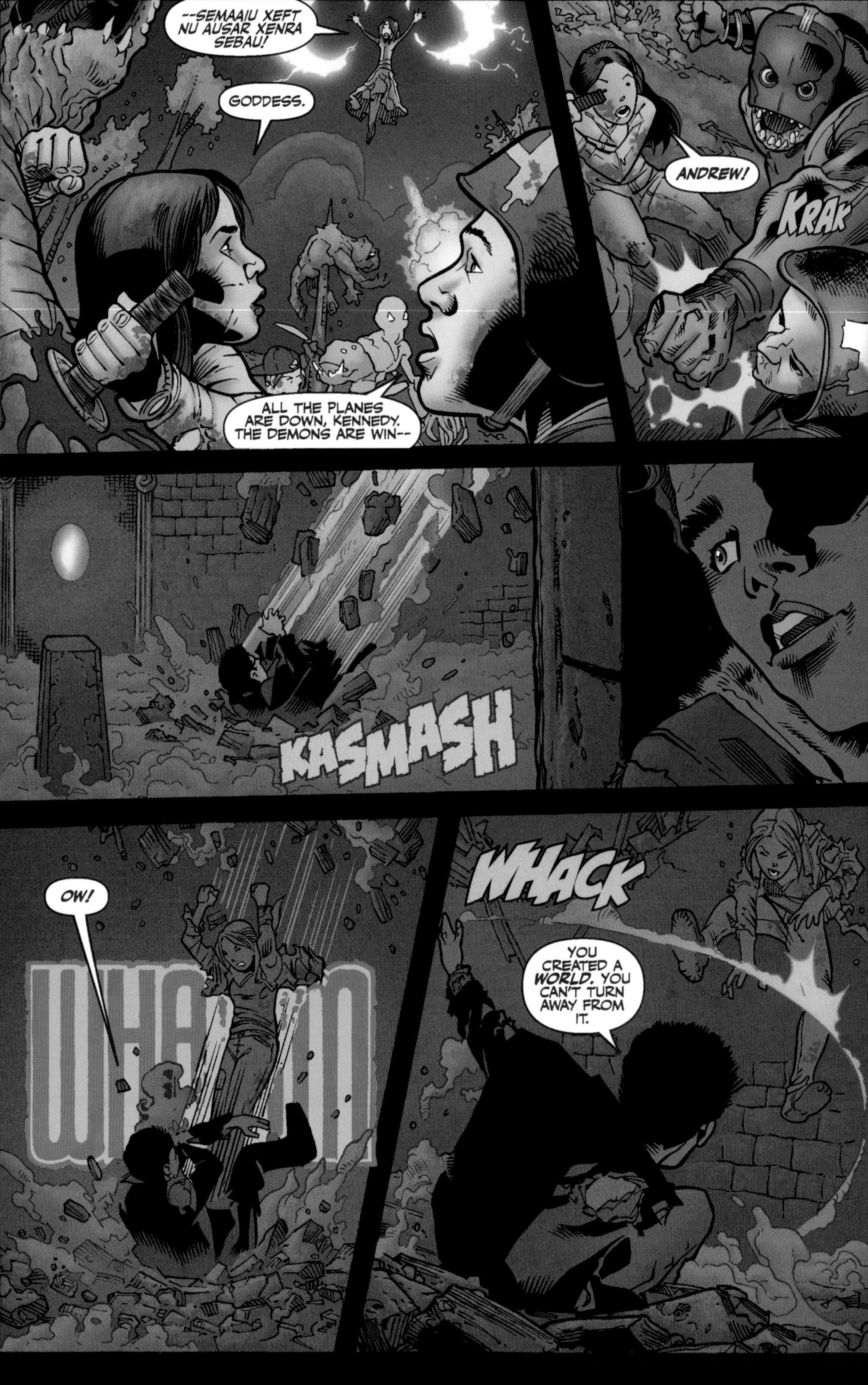
--SEMAAIU XEFT NU AUSAR XENRA SEBAU!
GODDESS.
ALL THE PLANES ARE DOWN, KENNEDY. THE DEMONS ARE WIN--
ANDREW!
KRAK
KASMASH
OW!
WHACK
YOU CREATED A **WORLD.** YOU CAN'T TURN AWAY FROM IT.

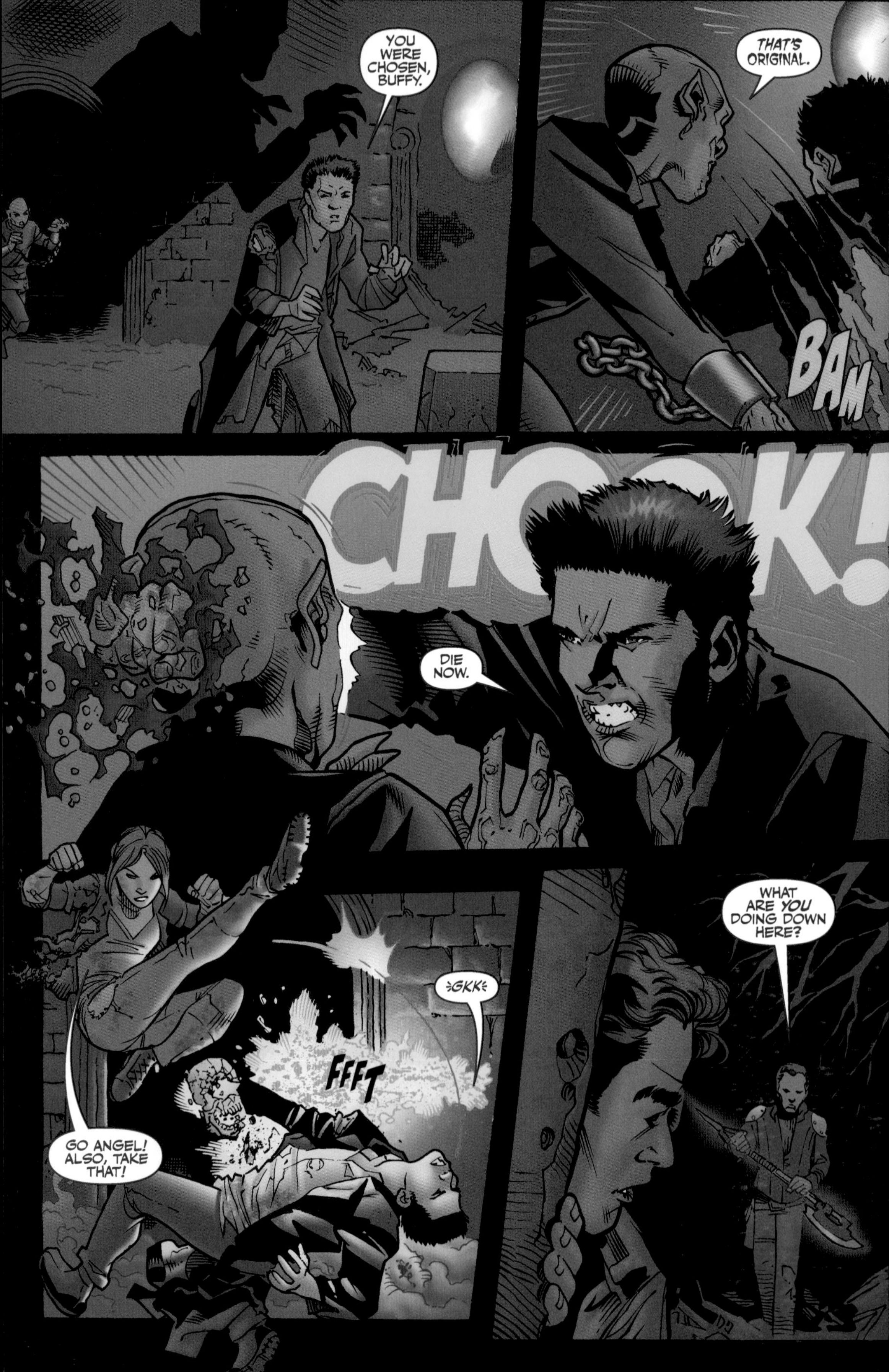
YOU WERE CHOSEN, BUFFY.
THAT'S ORIGINAL.
BAM
CHOOK!
DIE NOW.
GO ANGEL! ALSO, TAKE THAT!
GKK
FFFT
WHAT ARE YOU DOING DOWN HERE?

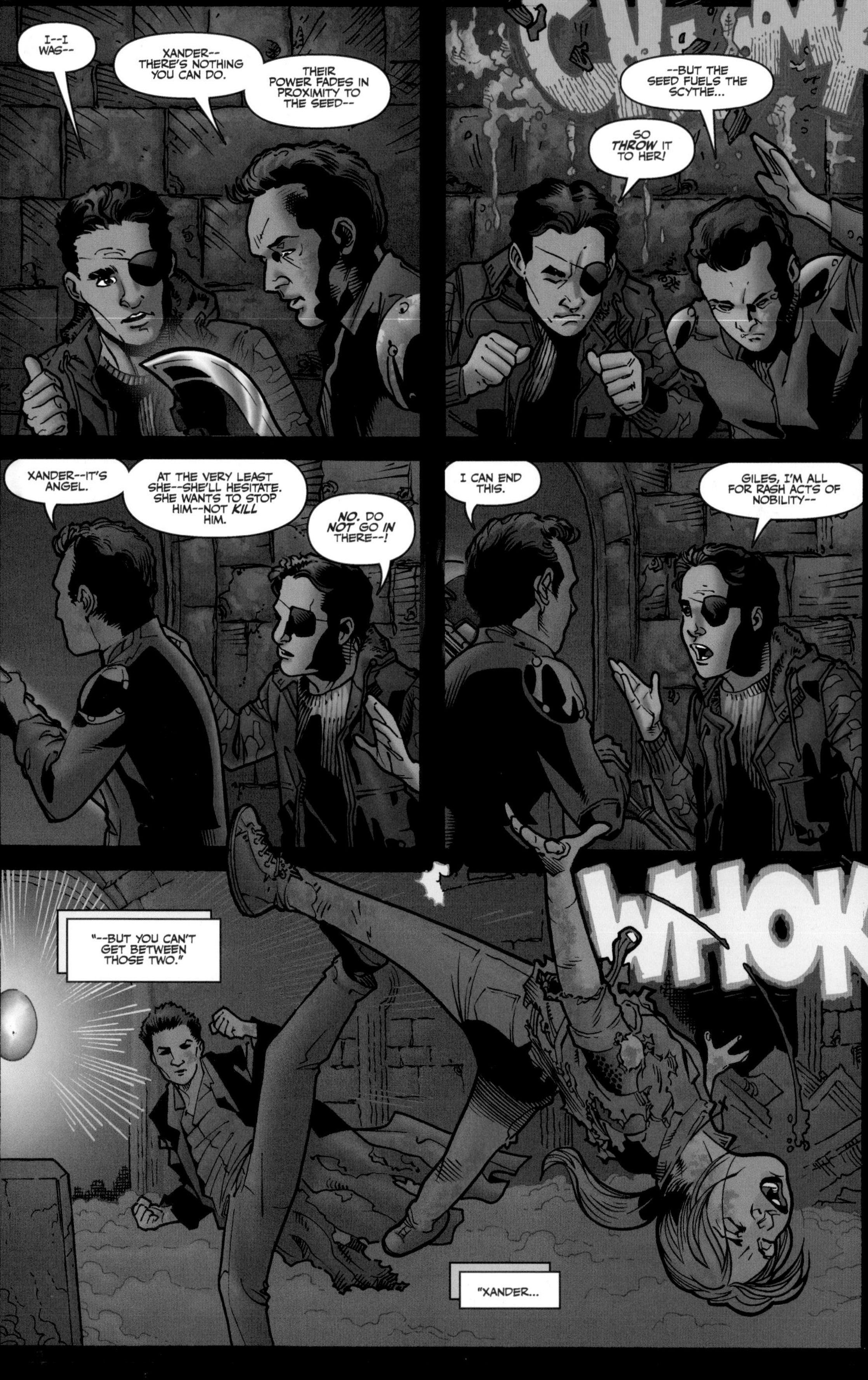
I--I WAS--
XANDER-- THERE'S NOTHING YOU CAN DO.
THEIR POWER FADES IN PROXIMITY TO THE SEED--
CHOMP
--BUT THE SEED FUELS THE SCYTHE...
SO THROW IT TO HER!
XANDER--IT'S ANGEL.
AT THE VERY LEAST SHE--SHE'LL HESITATE. SHE WANTS TO STOP HIM--NOT KILL HIM.
NO. DO NOT GO IN THERE--!
I CAN END THIS.
GILES, I'M ALL FOR RASH ACTS OF NOBILITY--
WHOK
"--BUT YOU CAN'T GET BETWEEN THOSE TWO."
"XANDER...

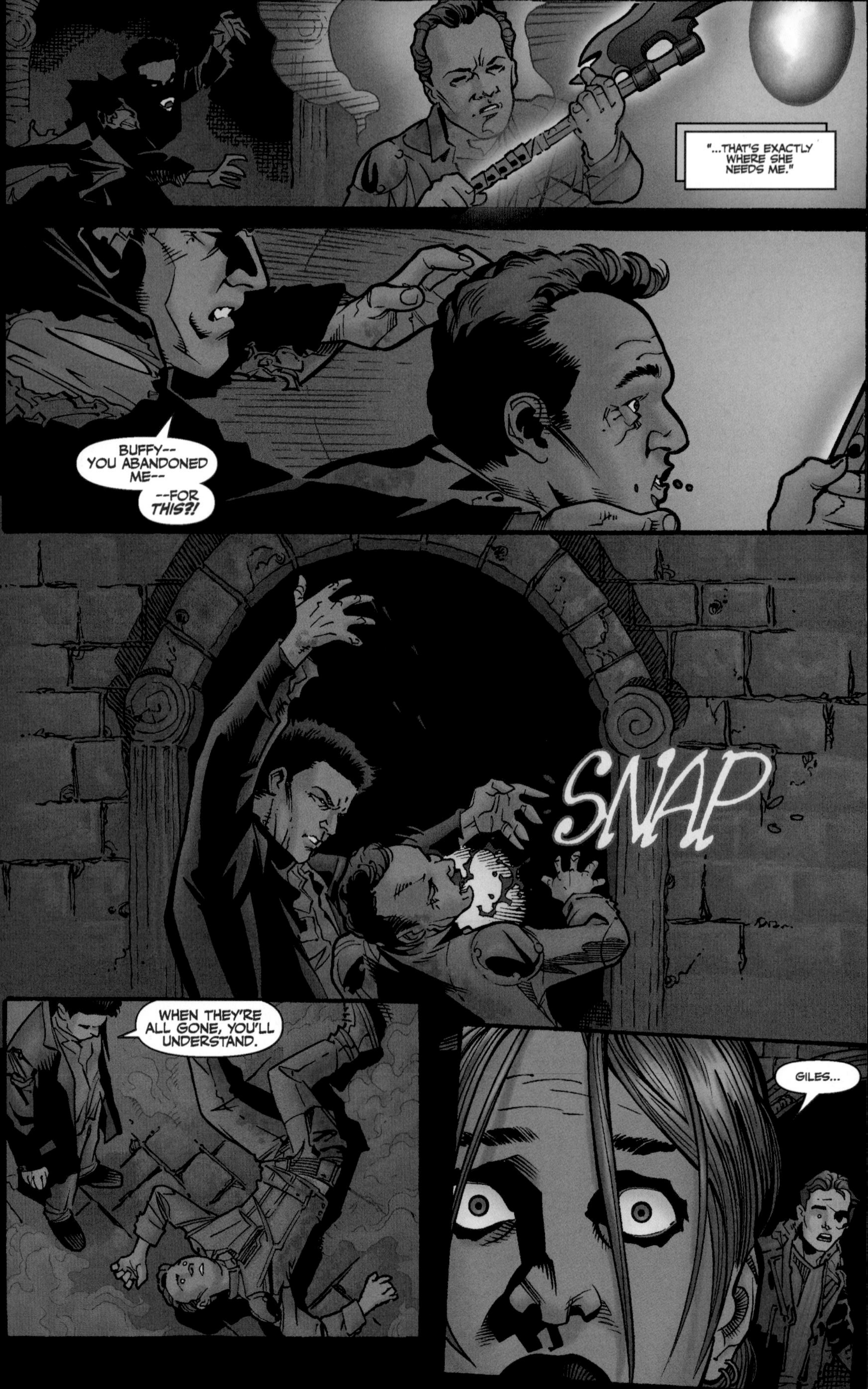
"...THAT'S EXACTLY WHERE SHE NEEDS ME."
BUFFY-- YOU ABANDONED ME--
--FOR *THIS?!*
SNAP
WHEN THEY'RE ALL GONE, YOU'LL UNDERSTAND.
GILES...

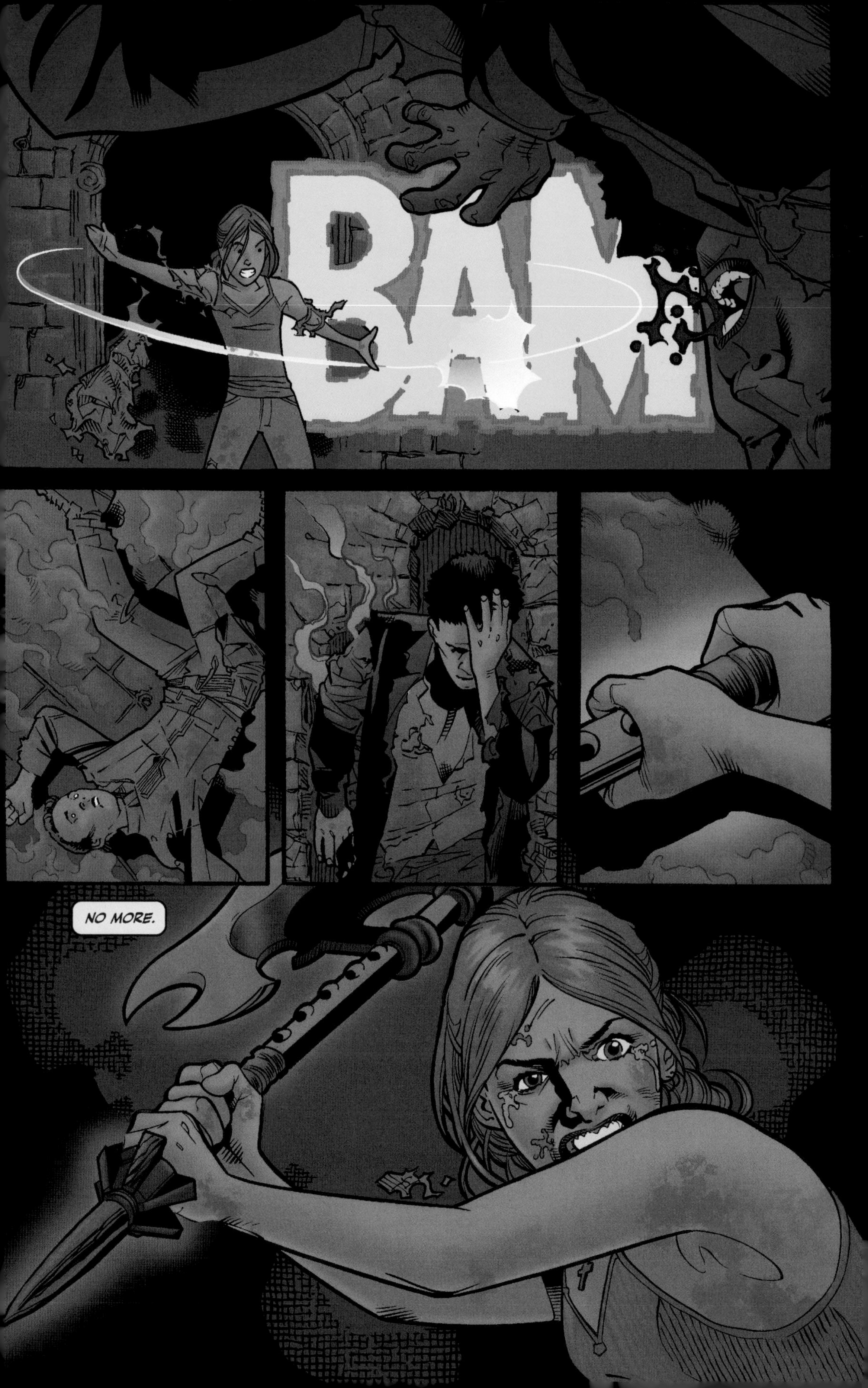
BAM
NO MORE.

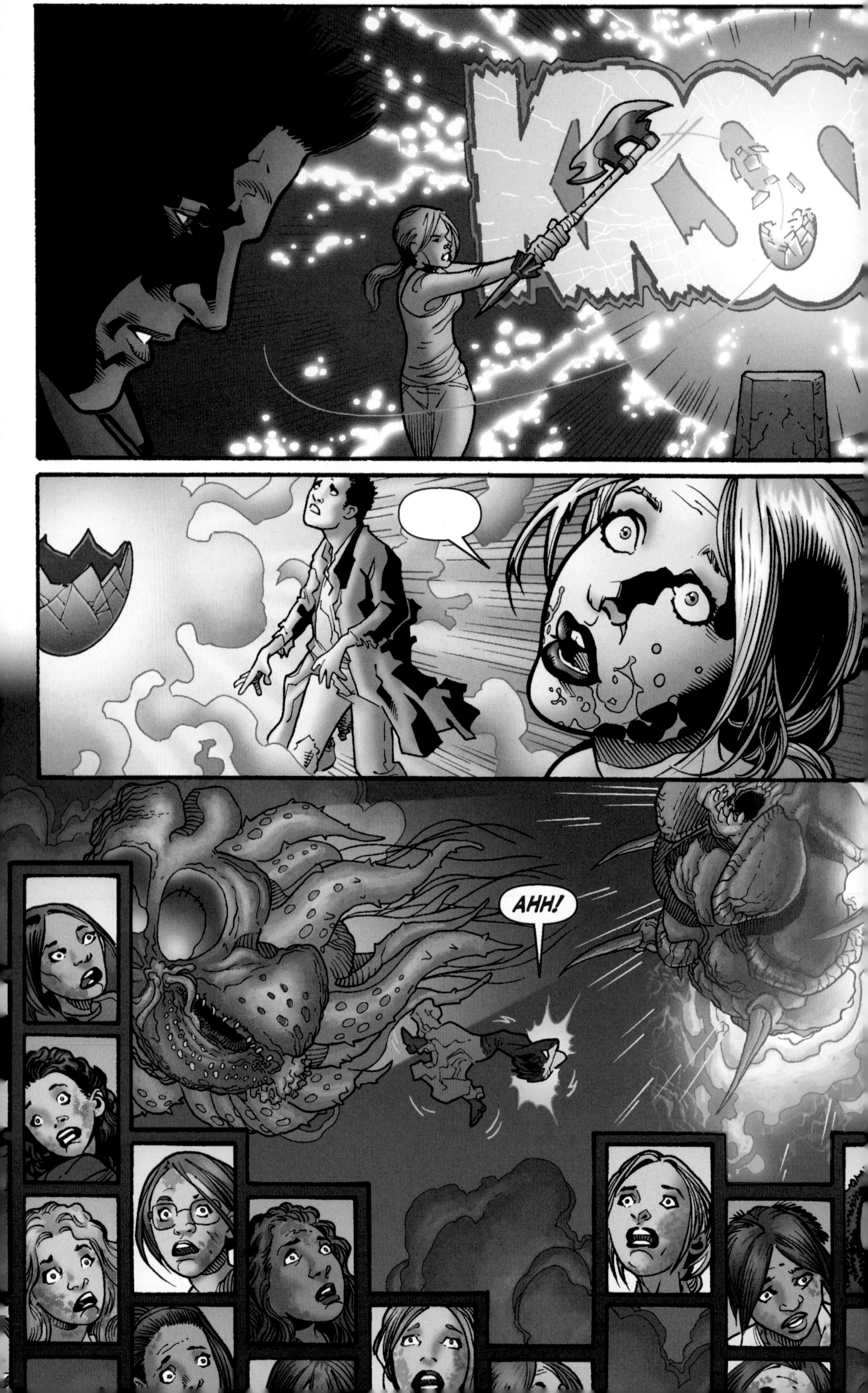
AHH!

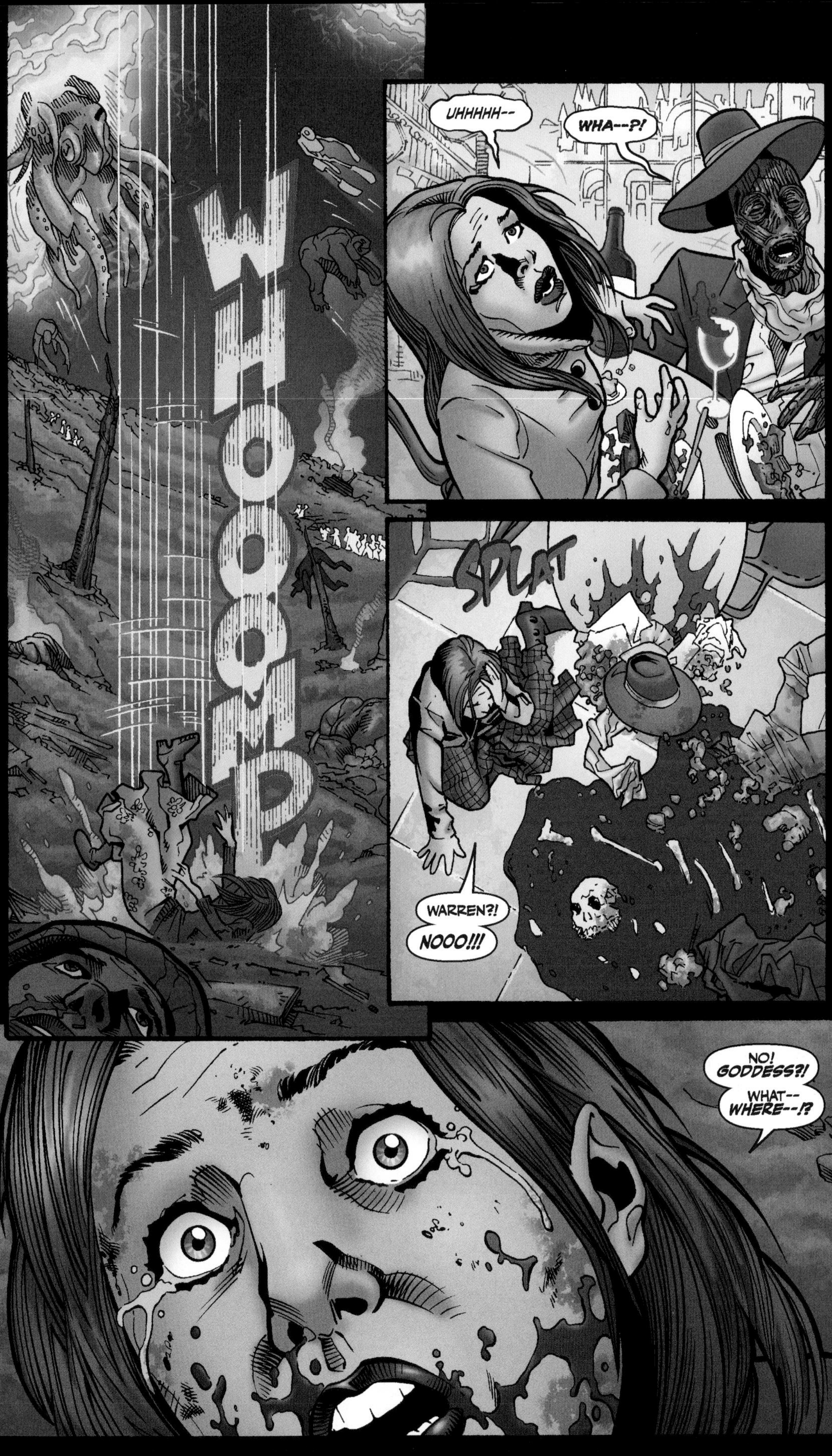
WHOOOOMP
UHHHHH--
WHA--?!
SPLAT
WARREN?!
NOOO!!!
NO! GODDESS?!
WHAT-- WHERE--!?

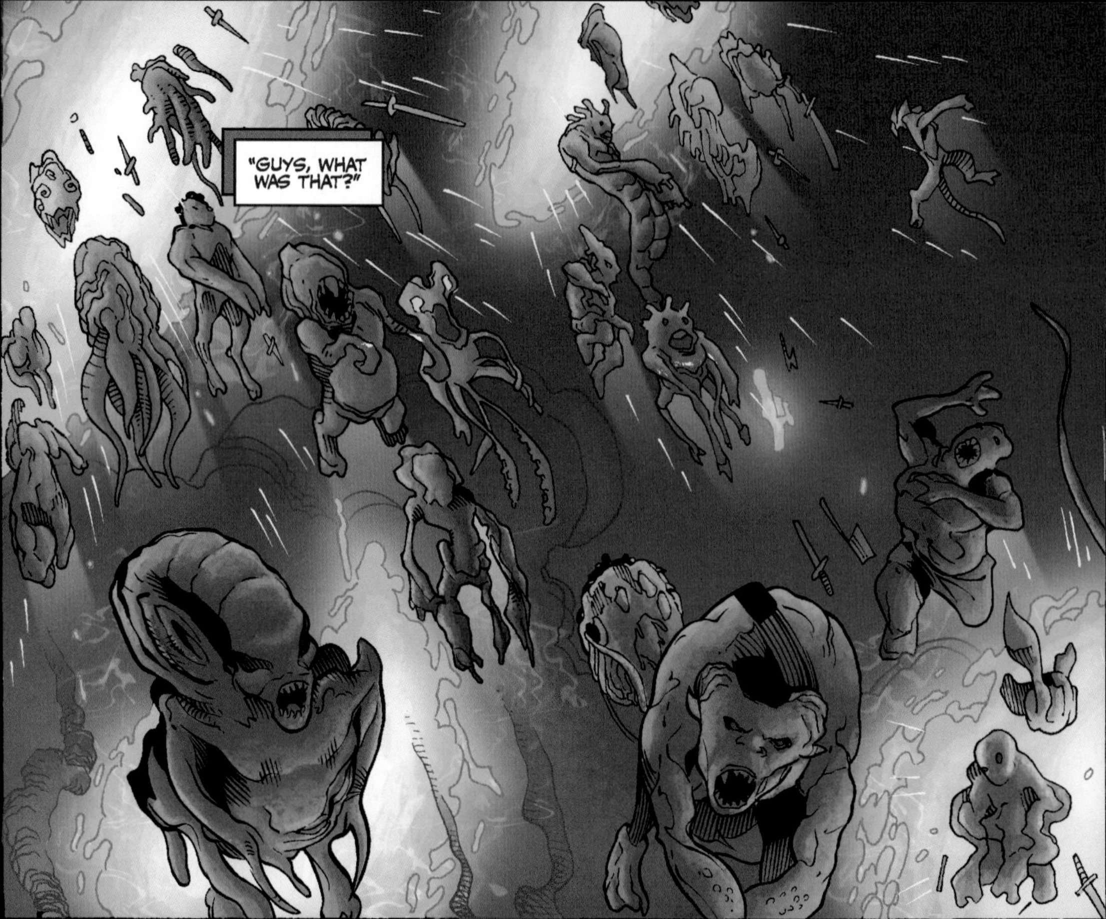
"GUYS, WHAT WAS THAT?"

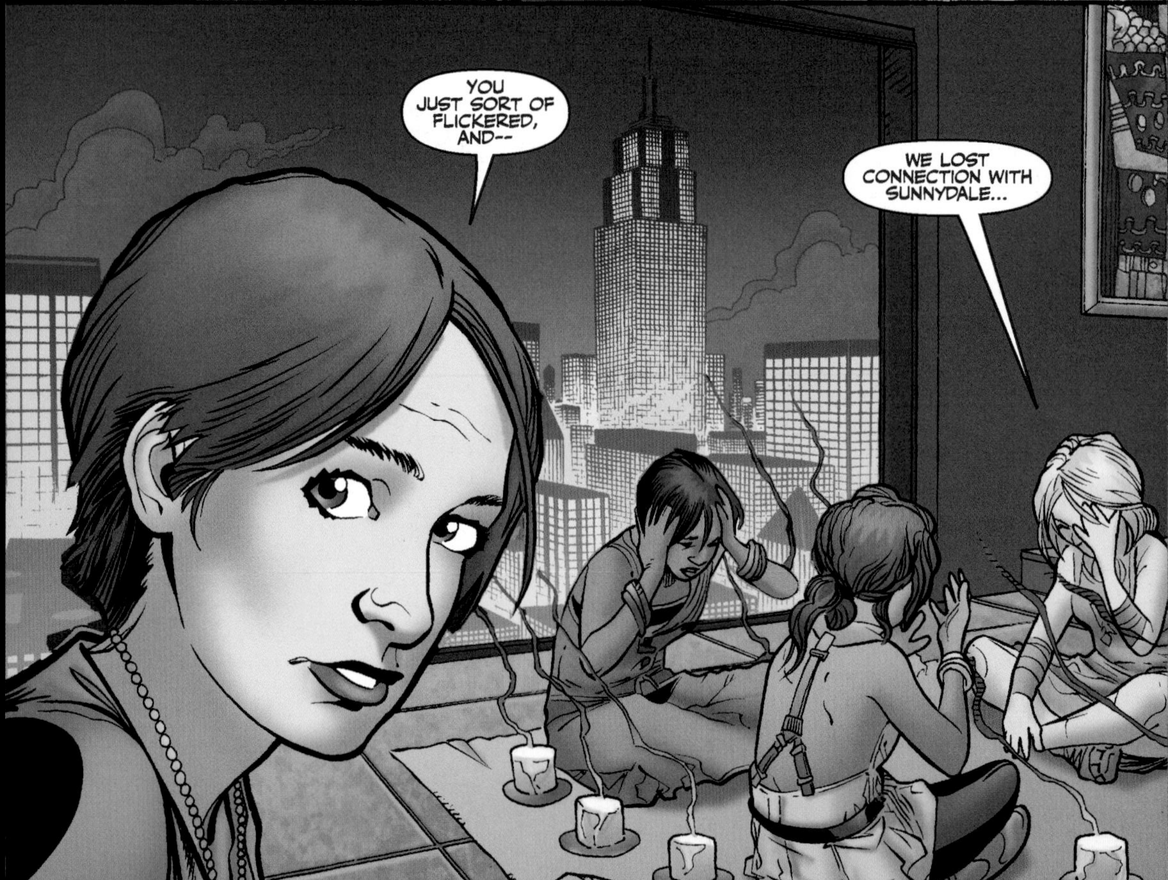
YOU JUST SORT OF FLICKERED, AND--
WE LOST CONNECTION WITH SUNNYDALE...

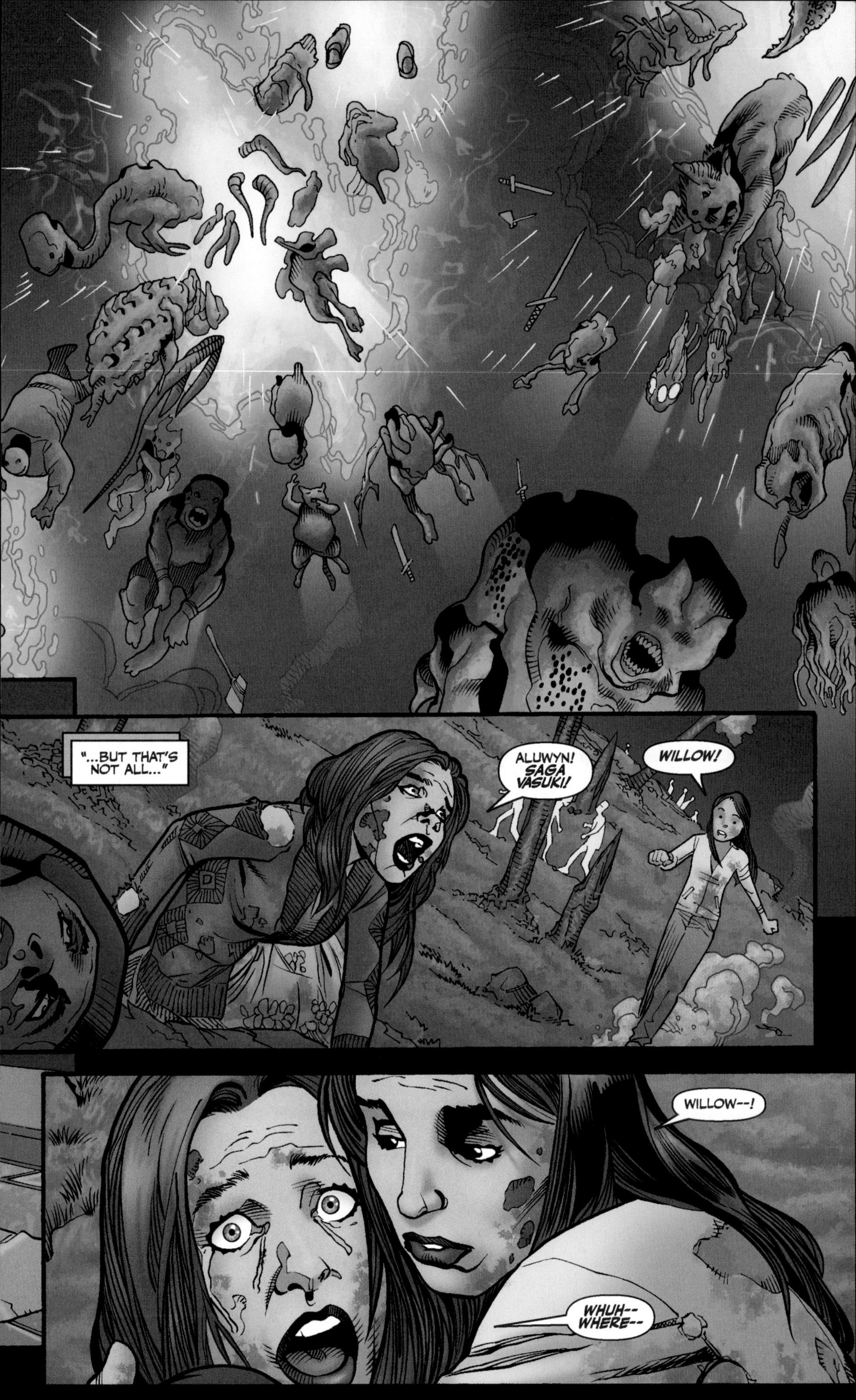
"...BUT THAT'S NOT ALL..."
ALUWYN! SAGA VASUKI!
WILLOW!
WILLOW--!
WHUH-- WHERE--

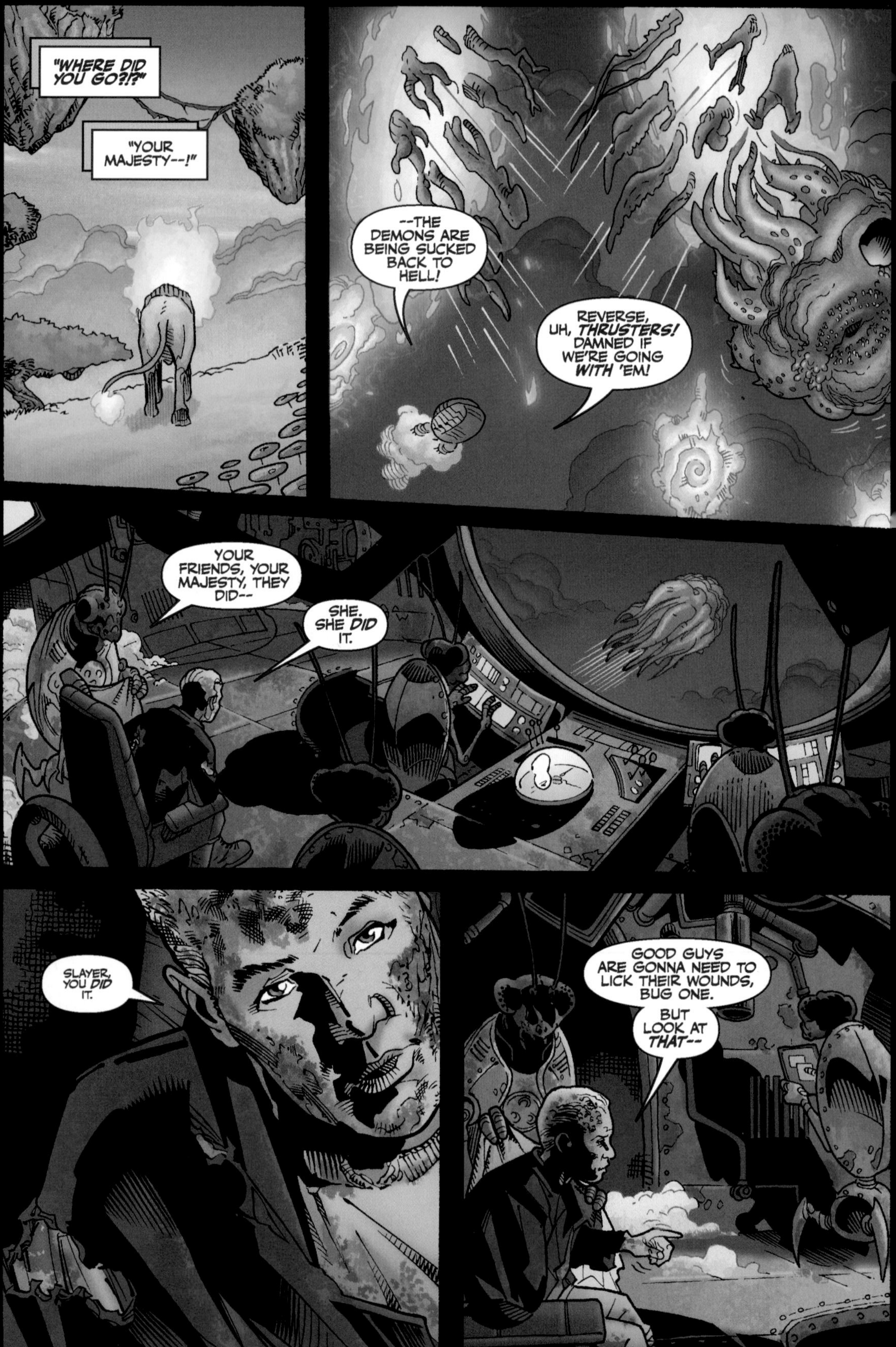
"WHERE DID YOU GO?!?"
"YOUR MAJESTY--!"
--THE DEMONS ARE BEING SUCKED BACK TO HELL!
REVERSE, UH, THRUSTERS! DAMNED IF WE'RE GOING WITH 'EM!
YOUR FRIENDS, YOUR MAJESTY, THEY DID--
SHE. SHE DID IT.
SLAYER, YOU DID IT.
GOOD GUYS ARE GONNA NEED TO LICK THEIR WOUNDS, BUG ONE.
BUT LOOK AT THAT--

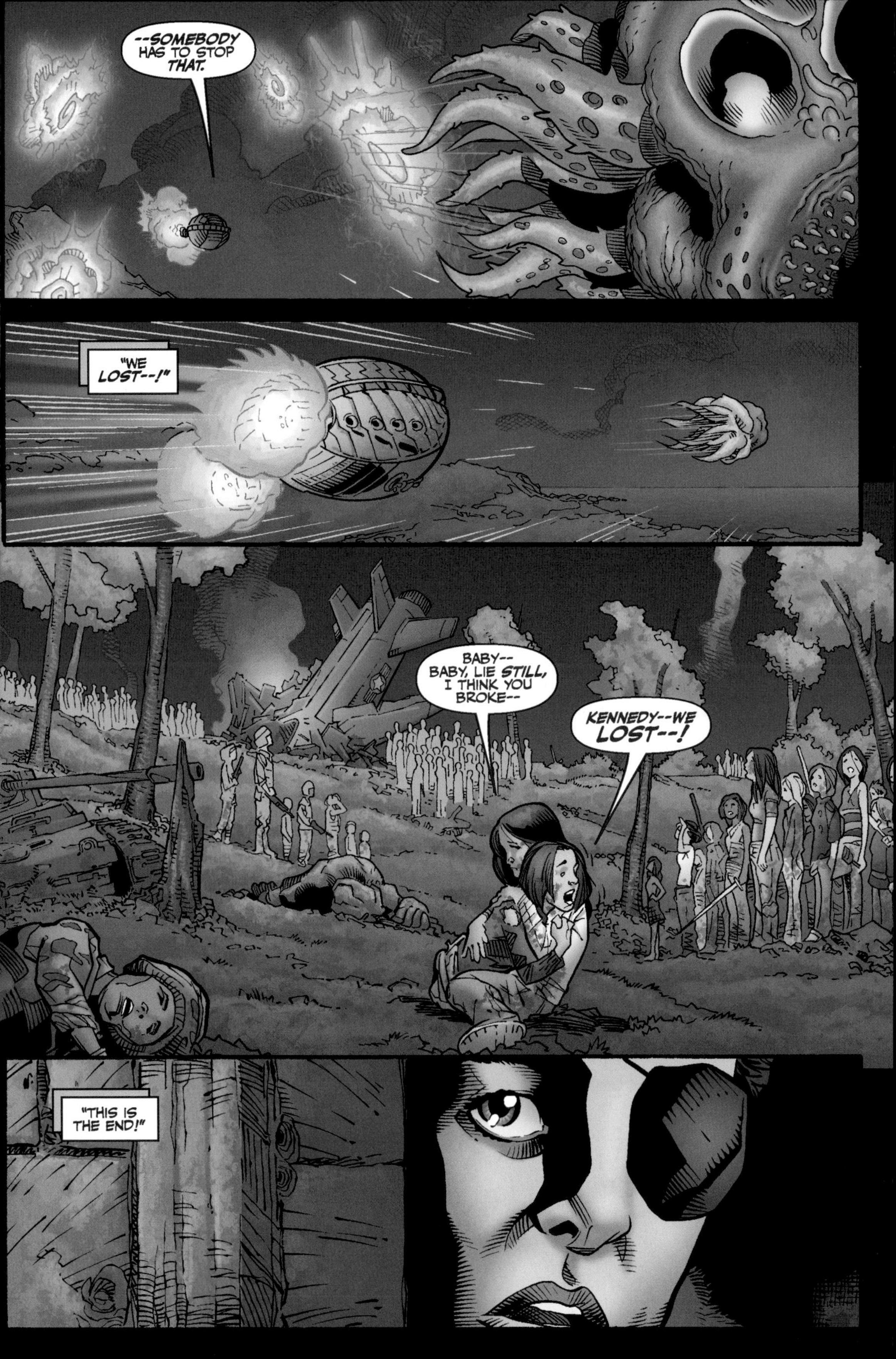
--SOMEBODY HAS TO STOP THAT.
"WE LOST--!"
BABY-- BABY, LIE STILL, I THINK YOU BROKE--
KENNEDY--WE LOST--!
"THIS IS THE END!"

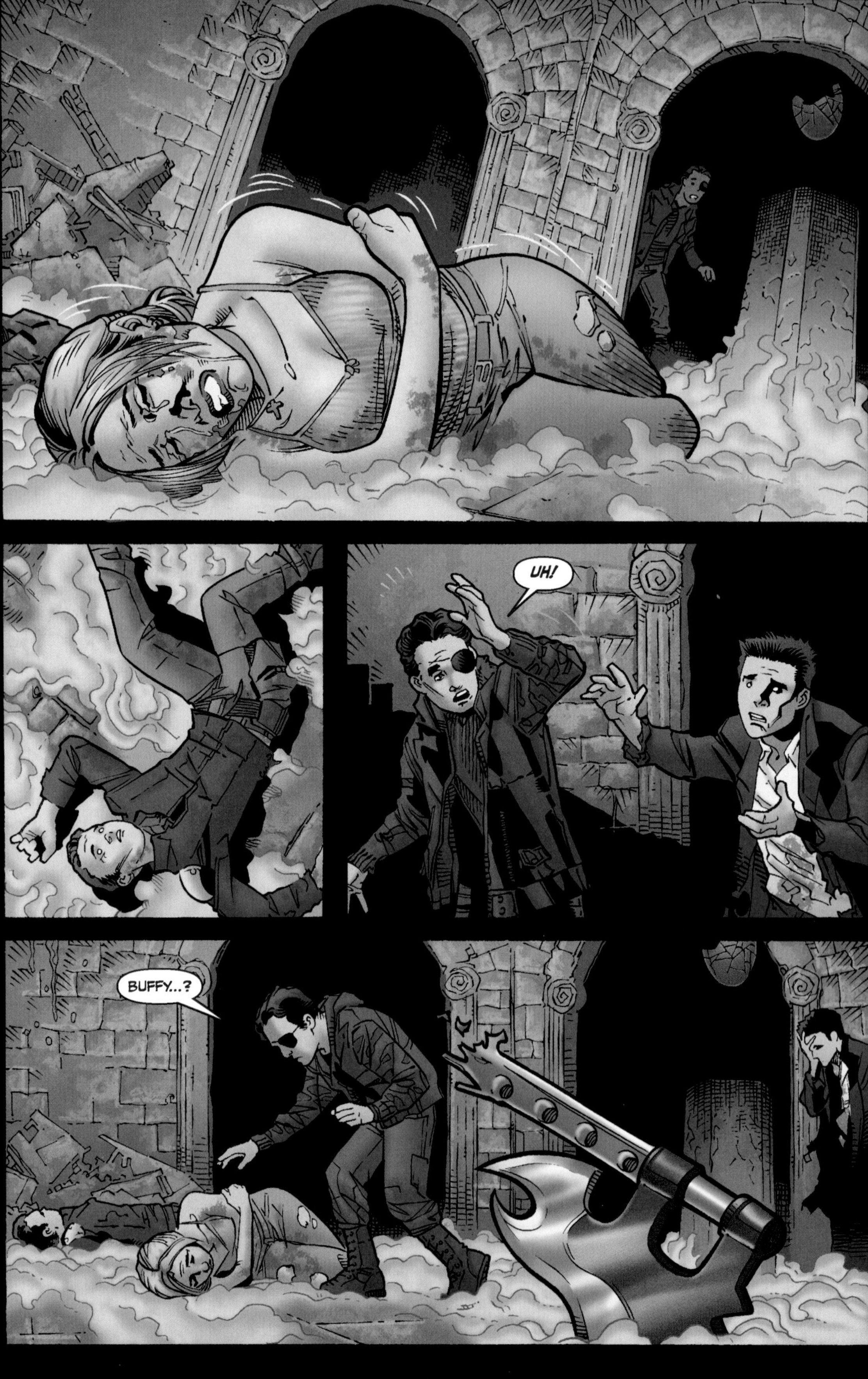
UH!
BUFFY...?

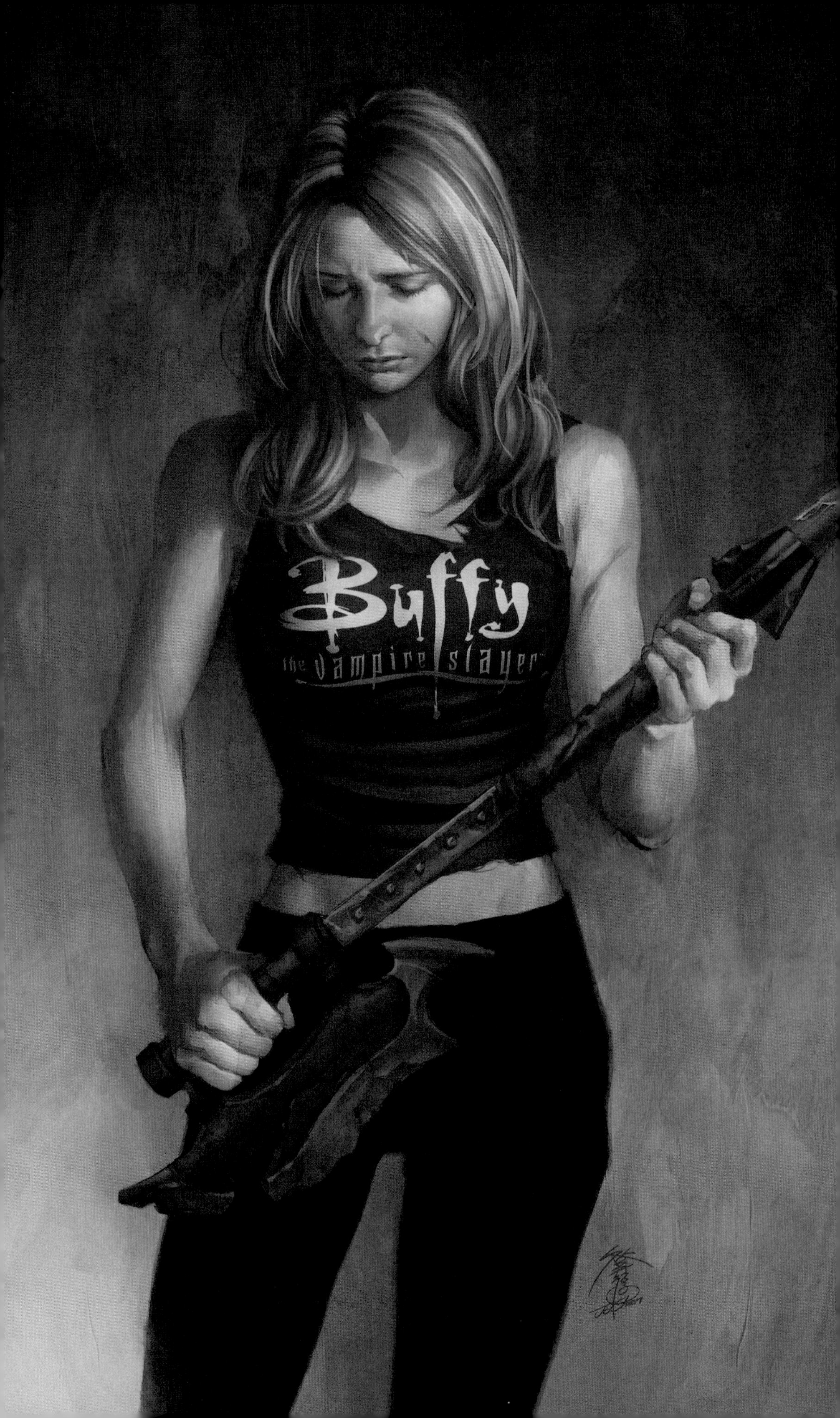
Buffy
the vampire slayer

LAST GLEAMING

PART FIVE

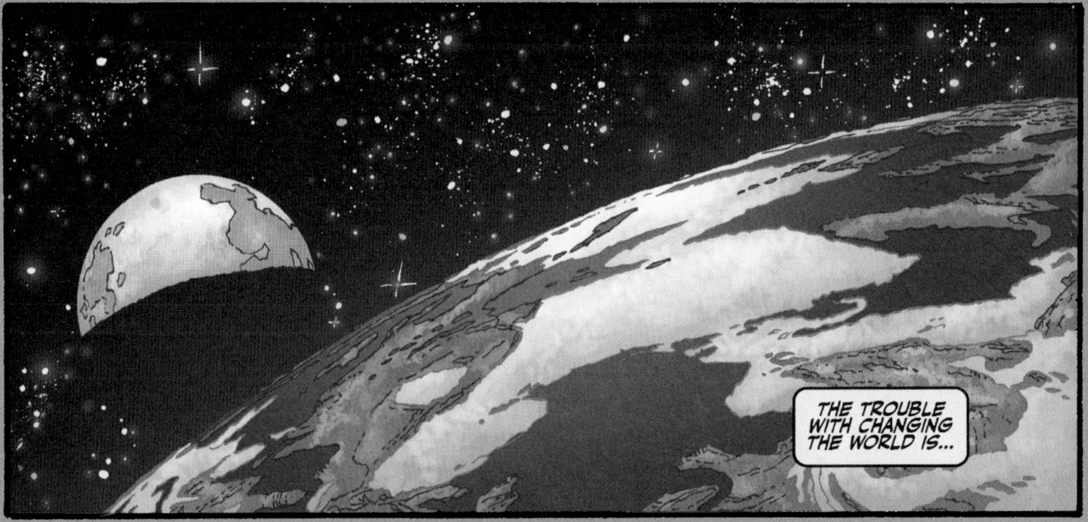
THE TROUBLE WITH CHANGING THE WORLD IS...

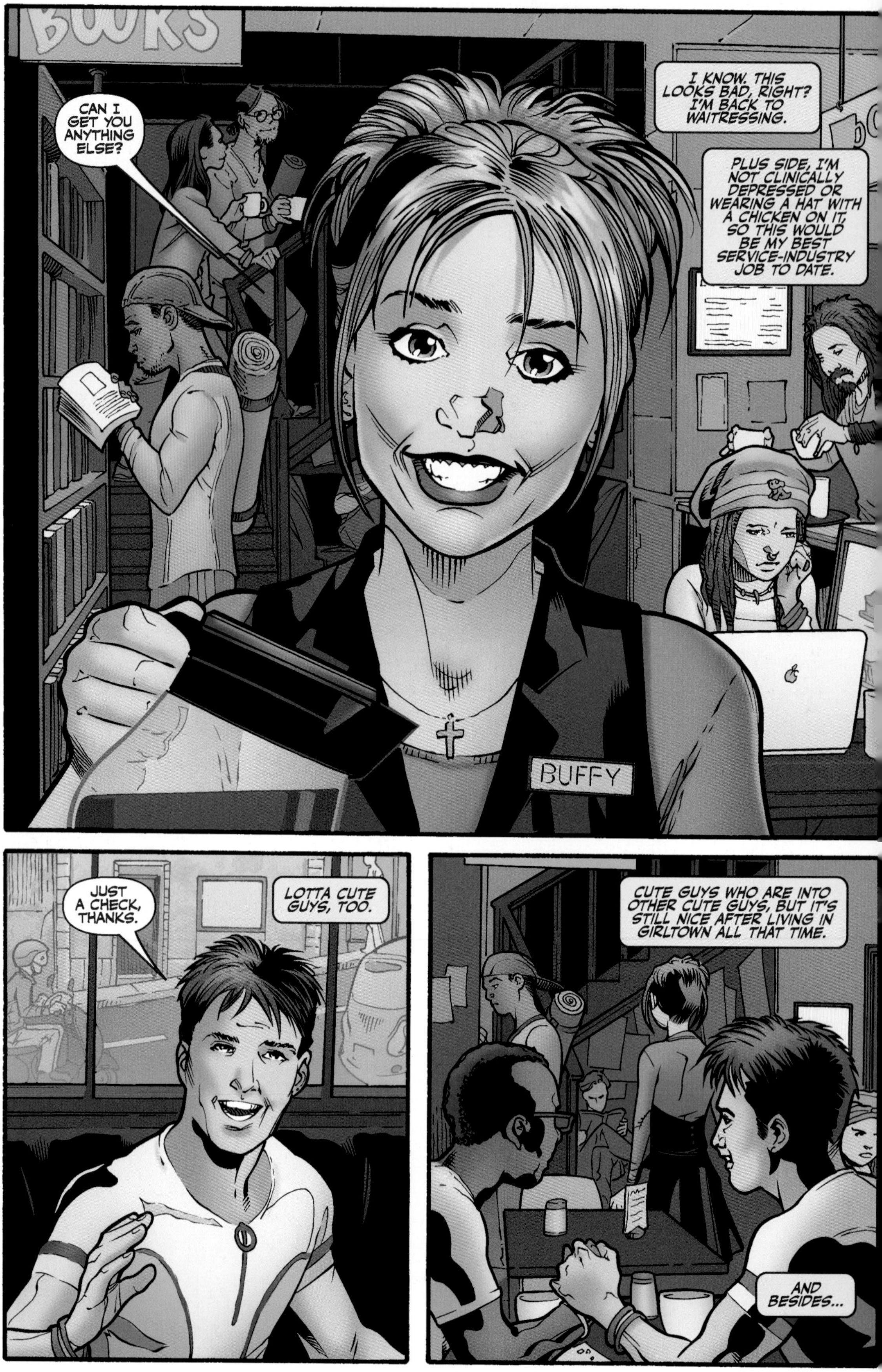
BOOKS
CAN I GET YOU ANYTHING ELSE?
I KNOW. THIS LOOKS BAD, RIGHT? I'M BACK TO WAITRESSING.
PLUS SIDE, I'M NOT CLINICALLY DEPRESSED OR WEARING A HAT WITH A CHICKEN ON IT, SO THIS WOULD BE MY BEST SERVICE-INDUSTRY JOB TO DATE.
BUFFY
JUST A CHECK, THANKS.
LOTTA CUTE GUYS, TOO.
CUTE GUYS WHO ARE INTO OTHER CUTE GUYS, BUT IT'S STILL NICE AFTER LIVING IN GIRLTOWN ALL THAT TIME.
AND BESIDES...

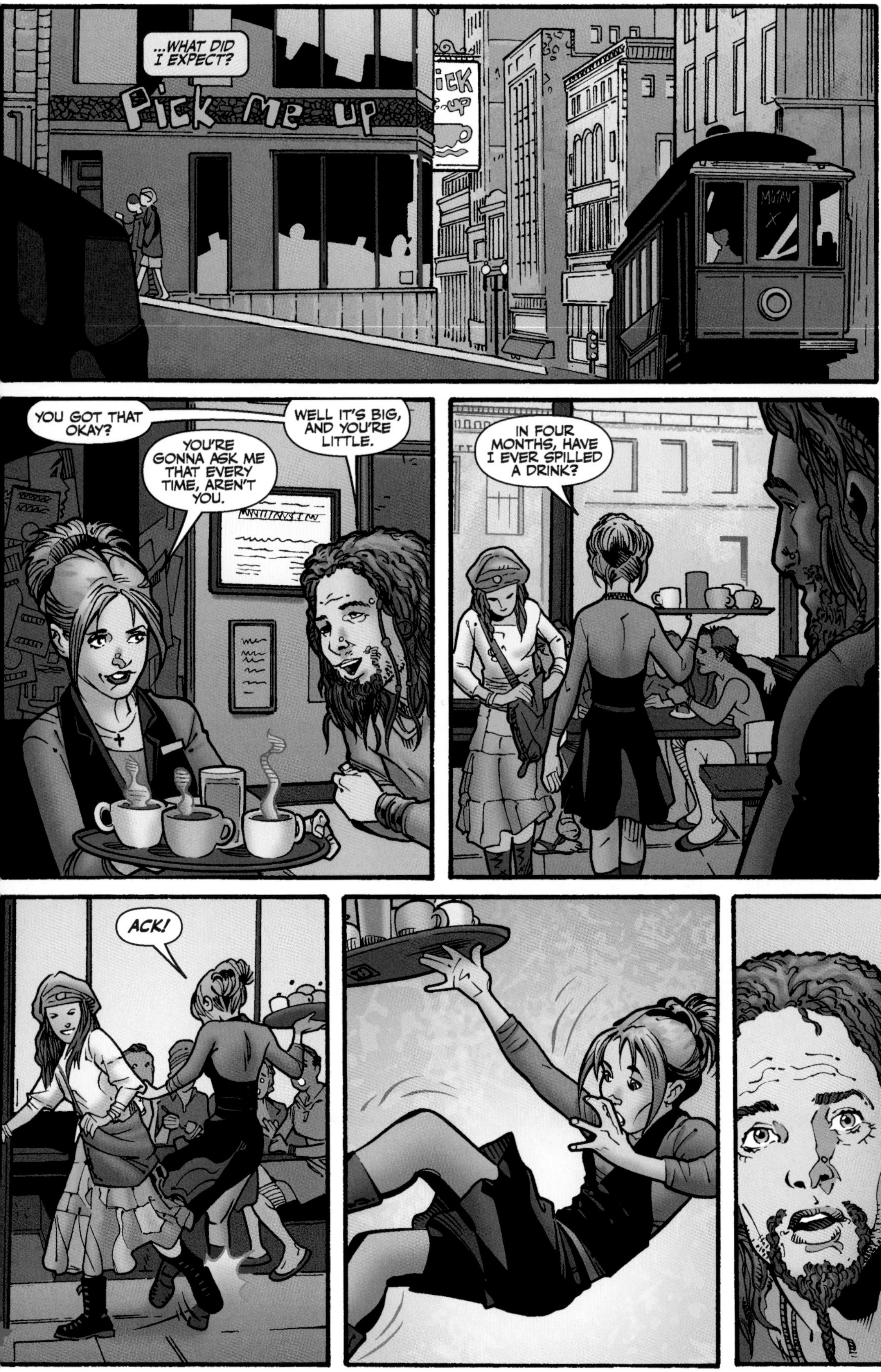
...WHAT DID I EXPECT?
Pick me up
YOU GOT THAT OKAY?
WELL IT'S BIG, AND YOU'RE LITTLE.
YOU'RE GONNA ASK ME THAT EVERY TIME, AREN'T YOU.
IN FOUR MONTHS, HAVE I EVER SPILLED A DRINK?
ACK!

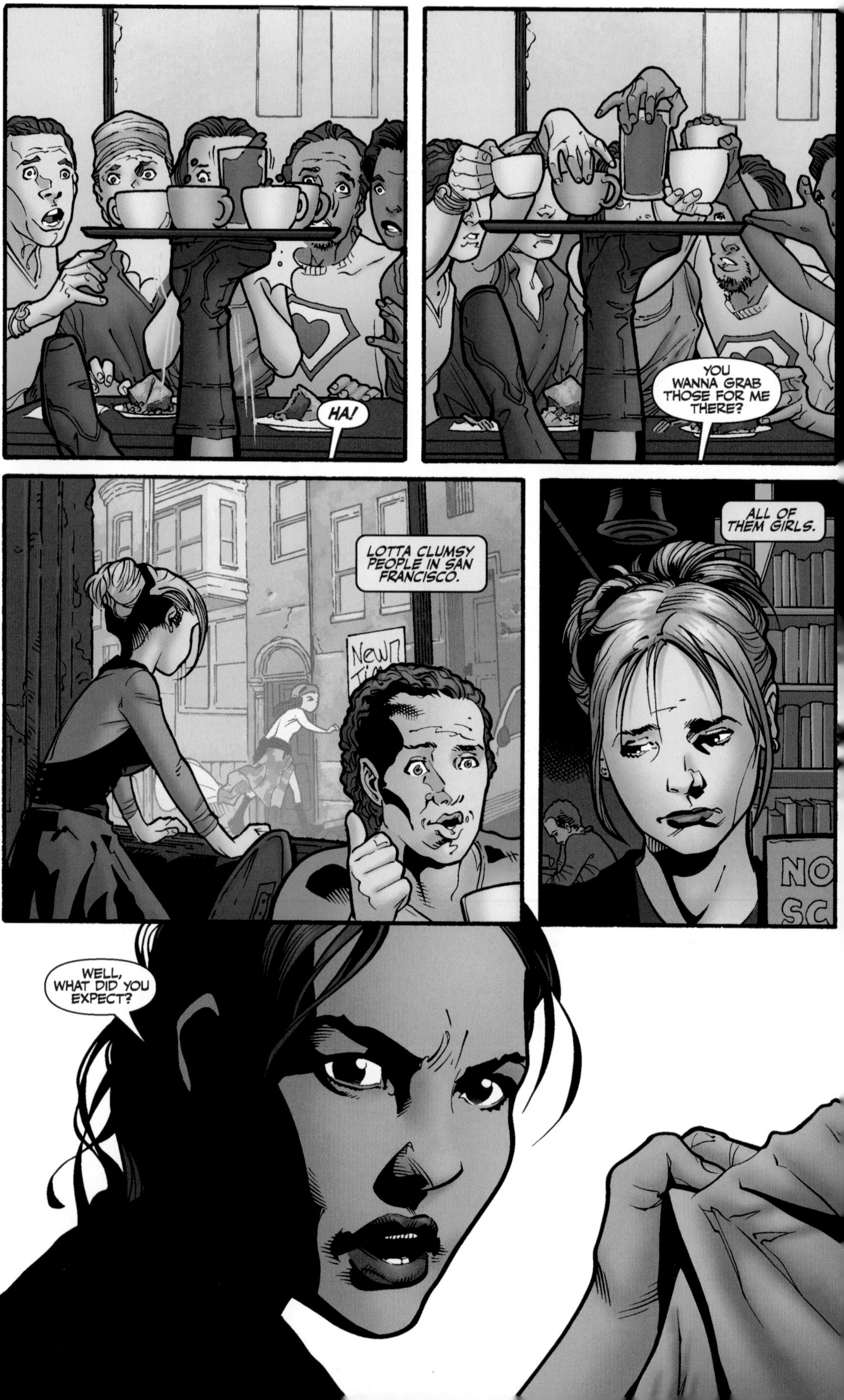
HA!
YOU WANNA GRAB THOSE FOR ME THERE?
LOTTA CLUMSY PEOPLE IN SAN FRANCISCO.
ALL OF THEM GIRLS.
WELL, WHAT DID YOU EXPECT?

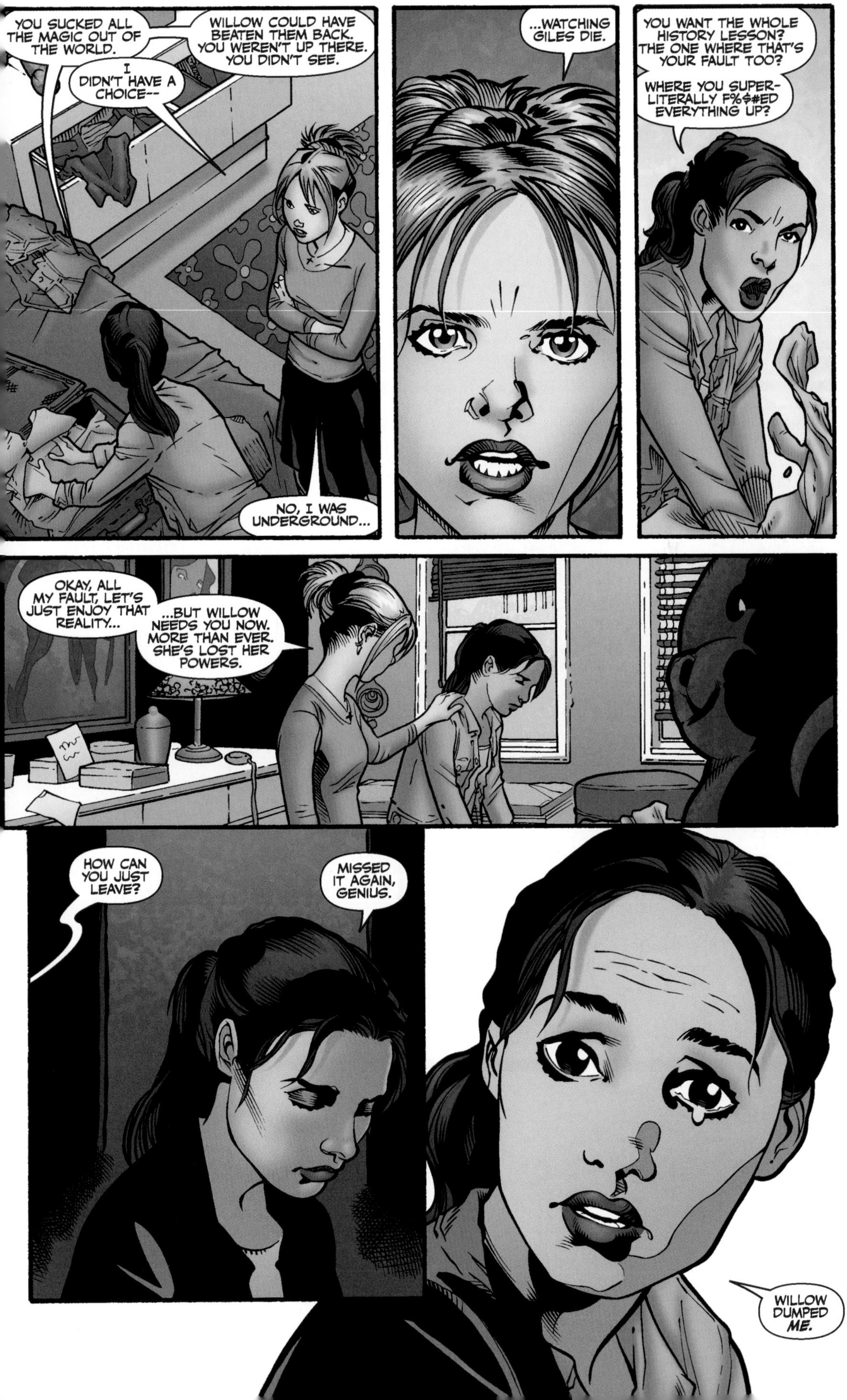
YOU SUCKED ALL THE MAGIC OUT OF THE WORLD.
I DIDN'T HAVE A CHOICE--
WILLOW COULD HAVE BEATEN THEM BACK. YOU WEREN'T UP THERE. YOU DIDN'T SEE.
NO, I WAS UNDERGROUND...
...WATCHING GILES DIE.
YOU WANT THE WHOLE HISTORY LESSON? THE ONE WHERE THAT'S YOUR FAULT TOO?
WHERE YOU SUPER-LITERALLY F%$#ED EVERYTHING UP?
OKAY, ALL MY FAULT, LET'S JUST ENJOY THAT REALITY...
...BUT WILLOW NEEDS YOU NOW. MORE THAN EVER. SHE'S LOST HER POWERS.
HOW CAN YOU JUST LEAVE?
MISSED IT AGAIN, GENIUS.
WILLOW DUMPED *ME.*

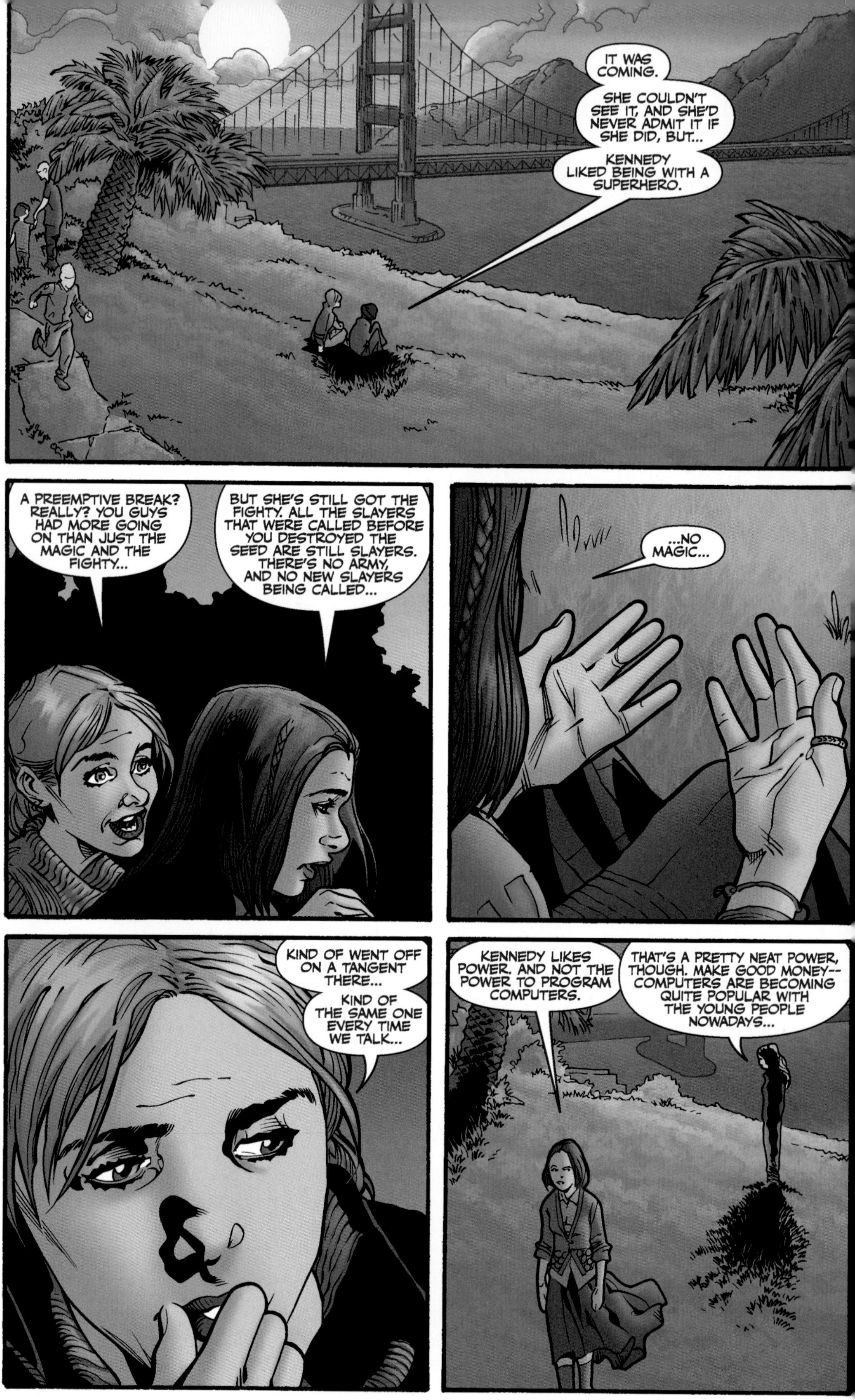
IT WAS COMING.
SHE COULDN'T SEE IT, AND SHE'D NEVER ADMIT IT IF SHE DID, BUT...
KENNEDY LIKED BEING WITH A SUPERHERO.
A PREEMPTIVE BREAK? REALLY? YOU GUYS HAD MORE GOING ON THAN JUST THE MAGIC AND THE FIGHTY...
BUT SHE'S STILL GOT THE FIGHTY. ALL THE SLAYERS THAT WERE CALLED BEFORE YOU DESTROYED THE SEED ARE STILL SLAYERS. THERE'S NO ARMY, AND NO NEW SLAYERS BEING CALLED...
...NO MAGIC...
KIND OF WENT OFF ON A TANGENT THERE...
KIND OF THE SAME ONE EVERY TIME WE TALK...
KENNEDY LIKES POWER. AND NOT THE POWER TO PROGRAM COMPUTERS.
THAT'S A PRETTY NEAT POWER, THOUGH. MAKE GOOD MONEY--COMPUTERS ARE BECOMING QUITE POPULAR WITH THE YOUNG PEOPLE NOWADAYS...

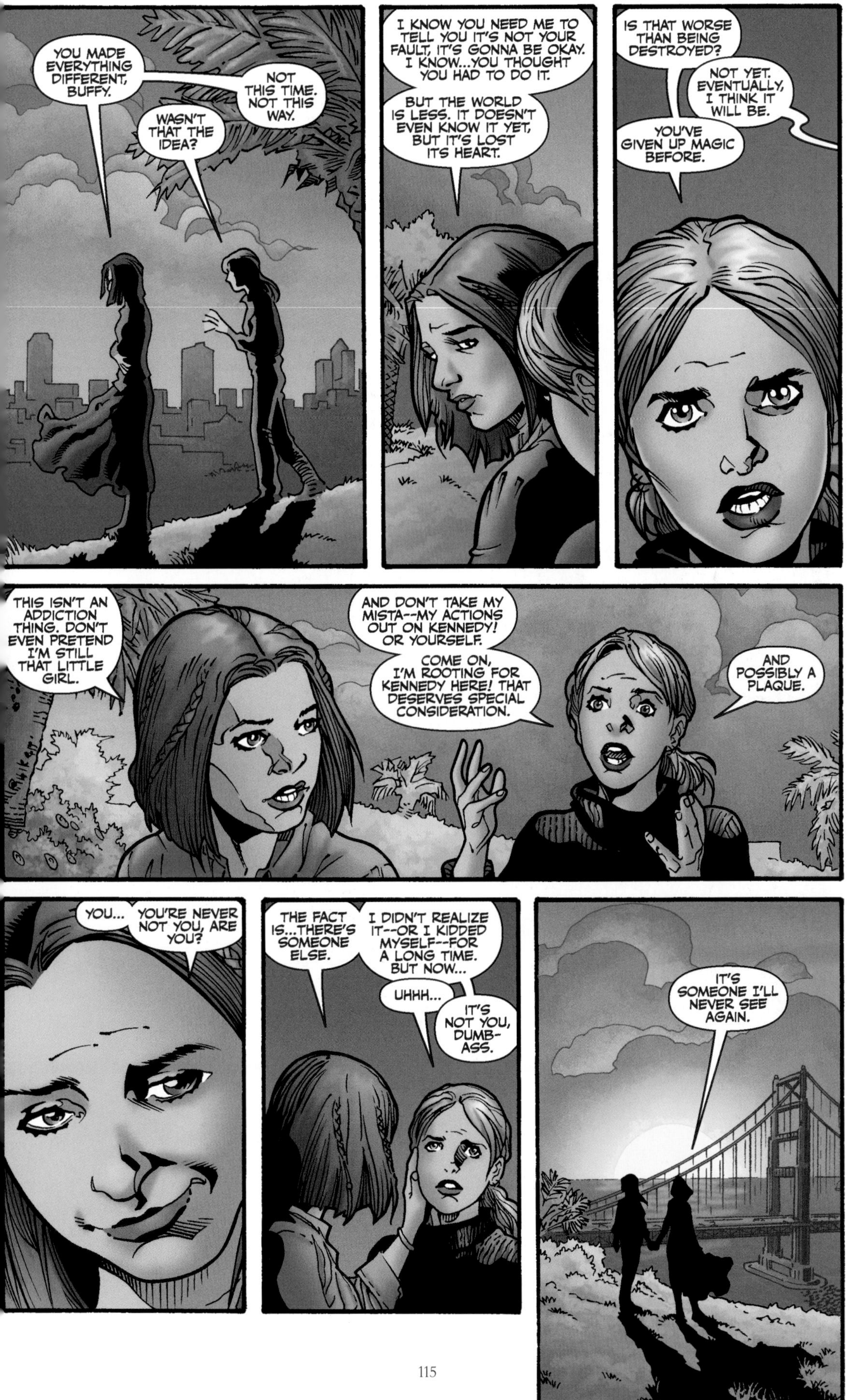
YOU MADE EVERYTHING DIFFERENT, BUFFY.
NOT THIS TIME. NOT THIS WAY.
WASN'T THAT THE IDEA?
I KNOW YOU NEED ME TO TELL YOU IT'S NOT YOUR FAULT, IT'S GONNA BE OKAY. I KNOW...YOU THOUGHT YOU HAD TO DO IT.
BUT THE WORLD IS LESS. IT DOESN'T EVEN KNOW IT YET, BUT IT'S LOST ITS HEART.
IS THAT WORSE THAN BEING DESTROYED?
NOT YET. EVENTUALLY, I THINK IT WILL BE.
YOU'VE GIVEN UP MAGIC BEFORE.
THIS ISN'T AN ADDICTION THING. DON'T EVEN PRETEND I'M STILL THAT LITTLE GIRL.
AND DON'T TAKE MY MISTA--MY ACTIONS OUT ON KENNEDY! OR YOURSELF.
COME ON, I'M ROOTING FOR KENNEDY HERE! THAT DESERVES SPECIAL CONSIDERATION.
AND POSSIBLY A PLAQUE.
YOU...
YOU'RE NEVER NOT YOU, ARE YOU?
THE FACT IS...THERE'S SOMEONE ELSE.
I DIDN'T REALIZE IT--OR I KIDDED MYSELF--FOR A LONG TIME. BUT NOW...
UHHH...
IT'S NOT YOU, DUMB-ASS.
IT'S SOMEONE I'LL NEVER SEE AGAIN.

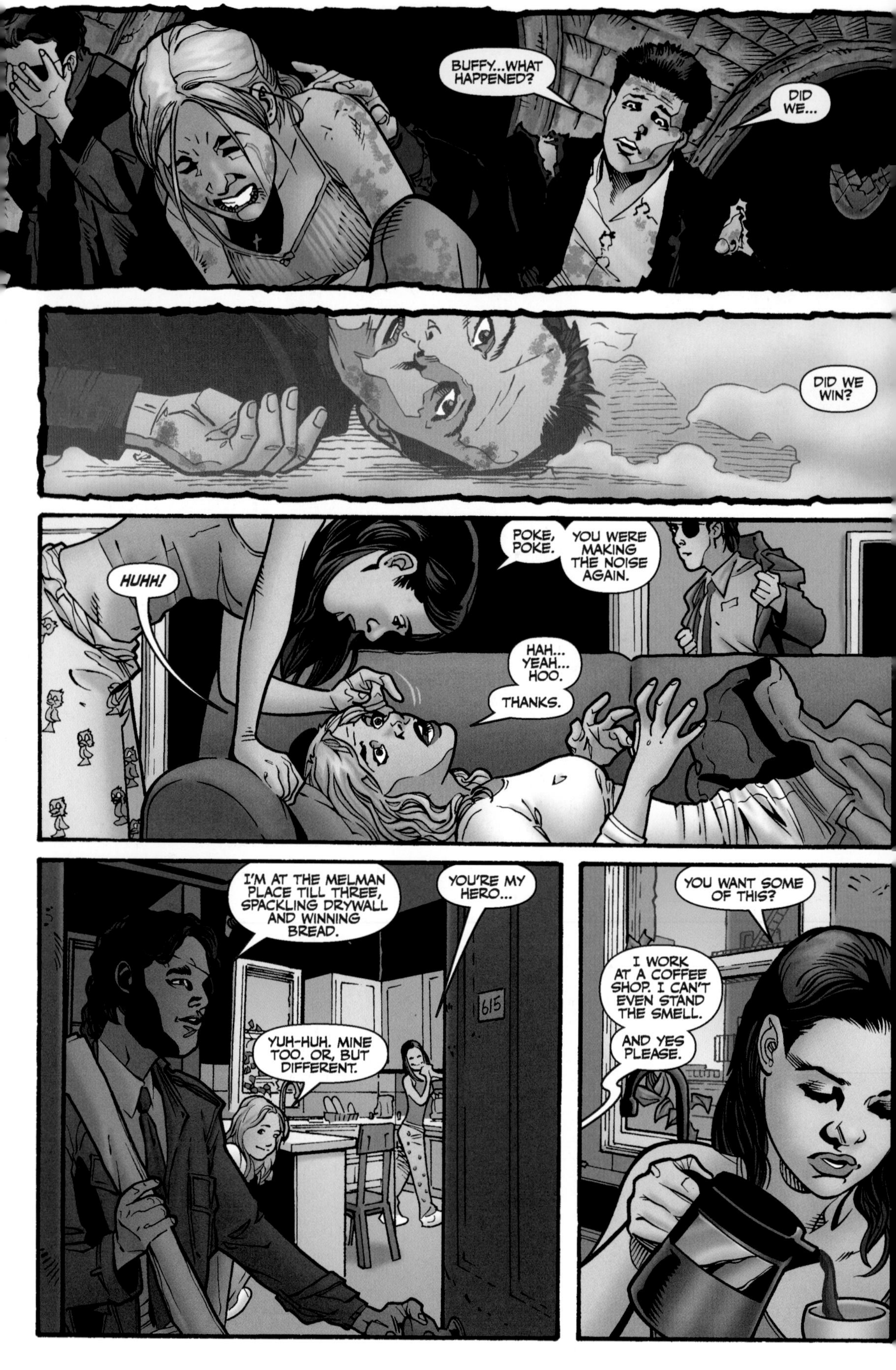
BUFFY...WHAT HAPPENED?
DID WE...
DID WE WIN?
HUHH!
POKE, POKE.
YOU WERE MAKING THE NOISE AGAIN.
HAH... YEAH... HOO.
THANKS.
I'M AT THE MELMAN PLACE TILL THREE, SPACKLING DRYWALL AND WINNING BREAD.
YOU'RE MY HERO...
YUH-HUH. MINE TOO. OR, BUT DIFFERENT.
615
YOU WANT SOME OF THIS?
I WORK AT A COFFEE SHOP. I CAN'T EVEN STAND THE SMELL.
AND YES PLEASE.

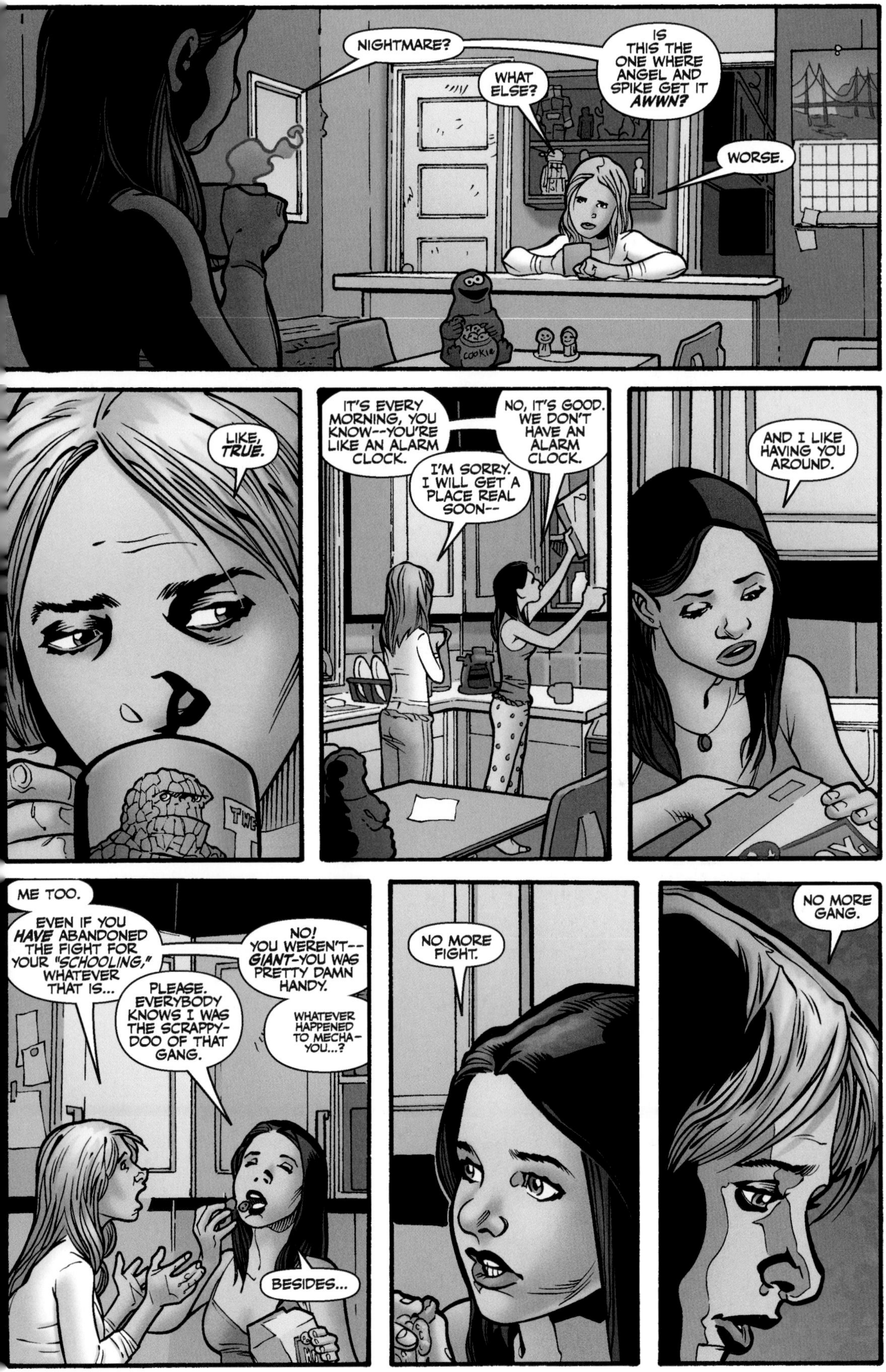
NIGHTMARE?
IS THIS THE ONE WHERE ANGEL AND SPIKE GET IT AWWN?
WHAT ELSE?
WORSE.
LIKE, TRUE.
IT'S EVERY MORNING, YOU KNOW--YOU'RE LIKE AN ALARM CLOCK.
I'M SORRY. I WILL GET A PLACE REAL SOON--
NO, IT'S GOOD. WE DON'T HAVE AN ALARM CLOCK.
AND I LIKE HAVING YOU AROUND.
ME TOO.
EVEN IF YOU HAVE ABANDONED THE FIGHT FOR YOUR "SCHOOLING," WHATEVER THAT IS...
PLEASE. EVERYBODY KNOWS I WAS THE SCRAPPY-DOO OF THAT GANG.
NO! YOU WEREN'T--GIANT-YOU WAS PRETTY DAMN HANDY.
WHATEVER HAPPENED TO MECHA-YOU...?
BESIDES...
NO MORE FIGHT.
NO MORE GANG.

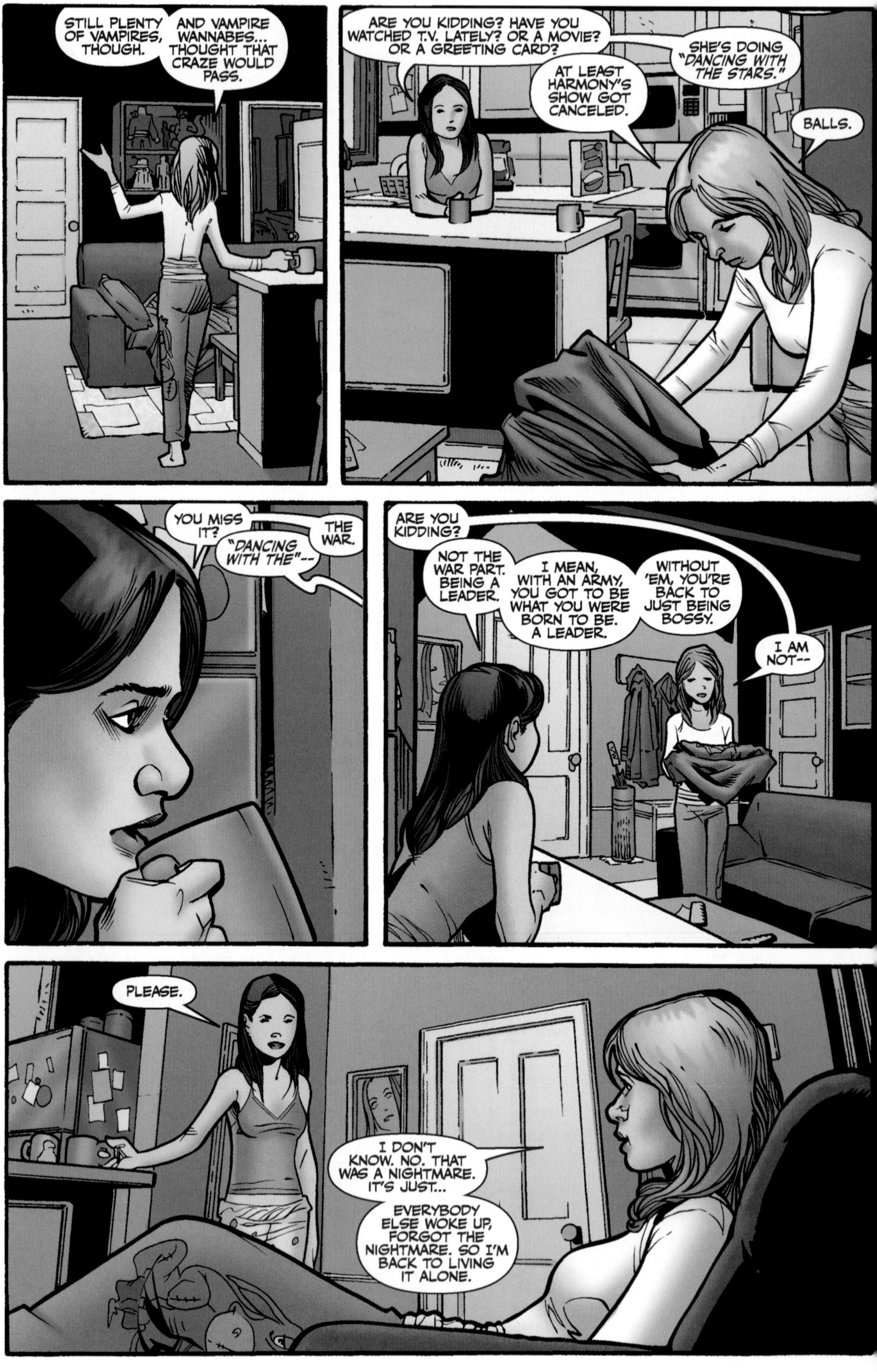
STILL PLENTY OF VAMPIRES, THOUGH.
AND VAMPIRE WANNABES... THOUGHT THAT CRAZE WOULD PASS.
ARE YOU KIDDING? HAVE YOU WATCHED T.V. LATELY? OR A MOVIE? OR A GREETING CARD?
AT LEAST HARMONY'S SHOW GOT CANCELED.
SHE'S DOING "DANCING WITH THE STARS."
BALLS.
YOU MISS IT?
"DANCING WITH THE"--
THE WAR.
ARE YOU KIDDING?
NOT THE WAR PART. BEING A LEADER.
I MEAN, WITH AN ARMY, YOU GOT TO BE WHAT YOU WERE BORN TO BE. A LEADER.
WITHOUT 'EM, YOU'RE BACK TO JUST BEING BOSSY.
I AM NOT--
PLEASE.
I DON'T KNOW. NO. THAT WAS A NIGHTMARE. IT'S JUST...
EVERYBODY ELSE WOKE UP, FORGOT THE NIGHTMARE. SO I'M BACK TO LIVING IT ALONE.

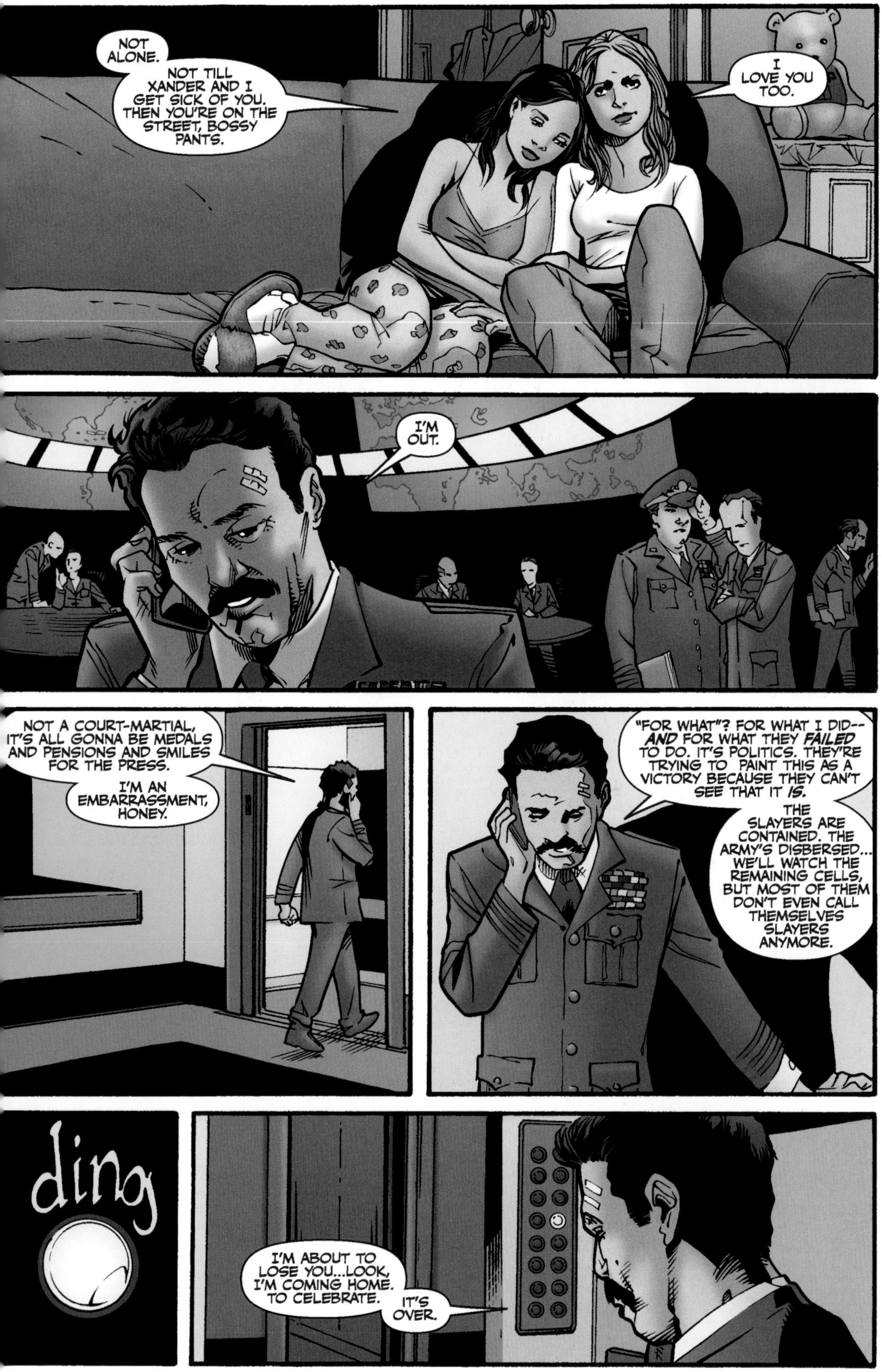

NOT ALONE.
NOT TILL XANDER AND I GET SICK OF YOU. THEN YOU'RE ON THE STREET, BOSSY PANTS.
I LOVE YOU TOO.
I'M OUT.
NOT A COURT-MARTIAL, IT'S ALL GONNA BE MEDALS AND PENSIONS AND SMILES FOR THE PRESS.
I'M AN EMBARRASSMENT, HONEY.
"FOR WHAT"? FOR WHAT I DID-- AND FOR WHAT THEY FAILED TO DO. IT'S POLITICS. THEY'RE TRYING TO PAINT THIS AS A VICTORY BECAUSE THEY CAN'T SEE THAT IT IS.
THE SLAYERS ARE CONTAINED. THE ARMY'S DISBERSED... WE'LL WATCH THE REMAINING CELLS, BUT MOST OF THEM DON'T EVEN CALL THEMSELVES SLAYERS ANYMORE.
ding
I'M ABOUT TO LOSE YOU...LOOK, I'M COMING HOME. TO CELEBRATE.
IT'S OVER.

PFFT

IT'S OVER FOR *SOME* PEOPLE.

"AND SO I, RUPERT EDMUND GILES, DO HEREBY BEQUEATH ALL OF MY BELONGINGS--SAVE THOSE LISTED ABOVE-- AND ALL MY SAVINGS AND PROPERTIES, INCLUDING THE LONDON FLAT...

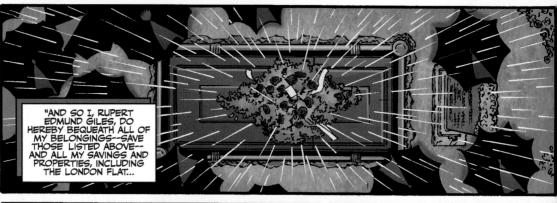

"...TO FAITH LEHANE."

"I'M JUST AS FREAKED AS YOU, B."

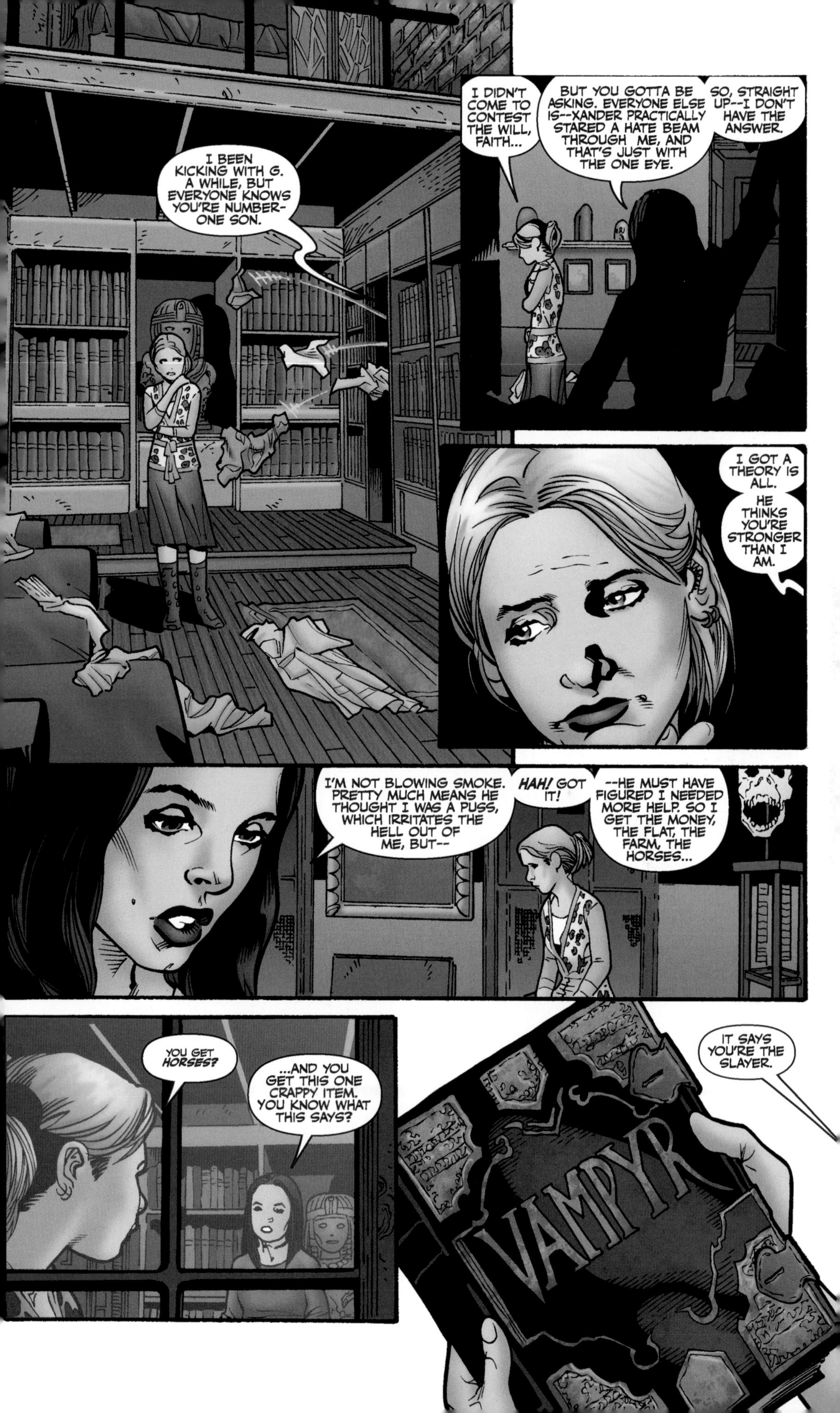
I BEEN KICKING WITH G. A WHILE, BUT EVERYONE KNOWS YOU'RE NUMBER-ONE SON.
I DIDN'T COME TO CONTEST THE WILL, FAITH...
BUT YOU GOTTA BE ASKING. EVERYONE ELSE IS--XANDER PRACTICALLY STARED A HATE BEAM THROUGH ME, AND THAT'S JUST WITH THE ONE EYE.
SO, STRAIGHT UP--I DON'T HAVE THE ANSWER.
I GOT A THEORY IS ALL.
HE THINKS YOU'RE STRONGER THAN I AM.
I'M NOT BLOWING SMOKE. PRETTY MUCH MEANS HE THOUGHT I WAS A PUSS, WHICH IRRITATES THE HELL OUT OF ME, BUT--
HAH! GOT IT!
--HE MUST HAVE FIGURED I NEEDED MORE HELP. SO I GET THE MONEY, THE FLAT, THE FARM, THE HORSES...
YOU GET HORSES?
...AND YOU GET THIS ONE CRAPPY ITEM. YOU KNOW WHAT THIS SAYS?
VAMPYR
IT SAYS YOU'RE THE SLAYER.

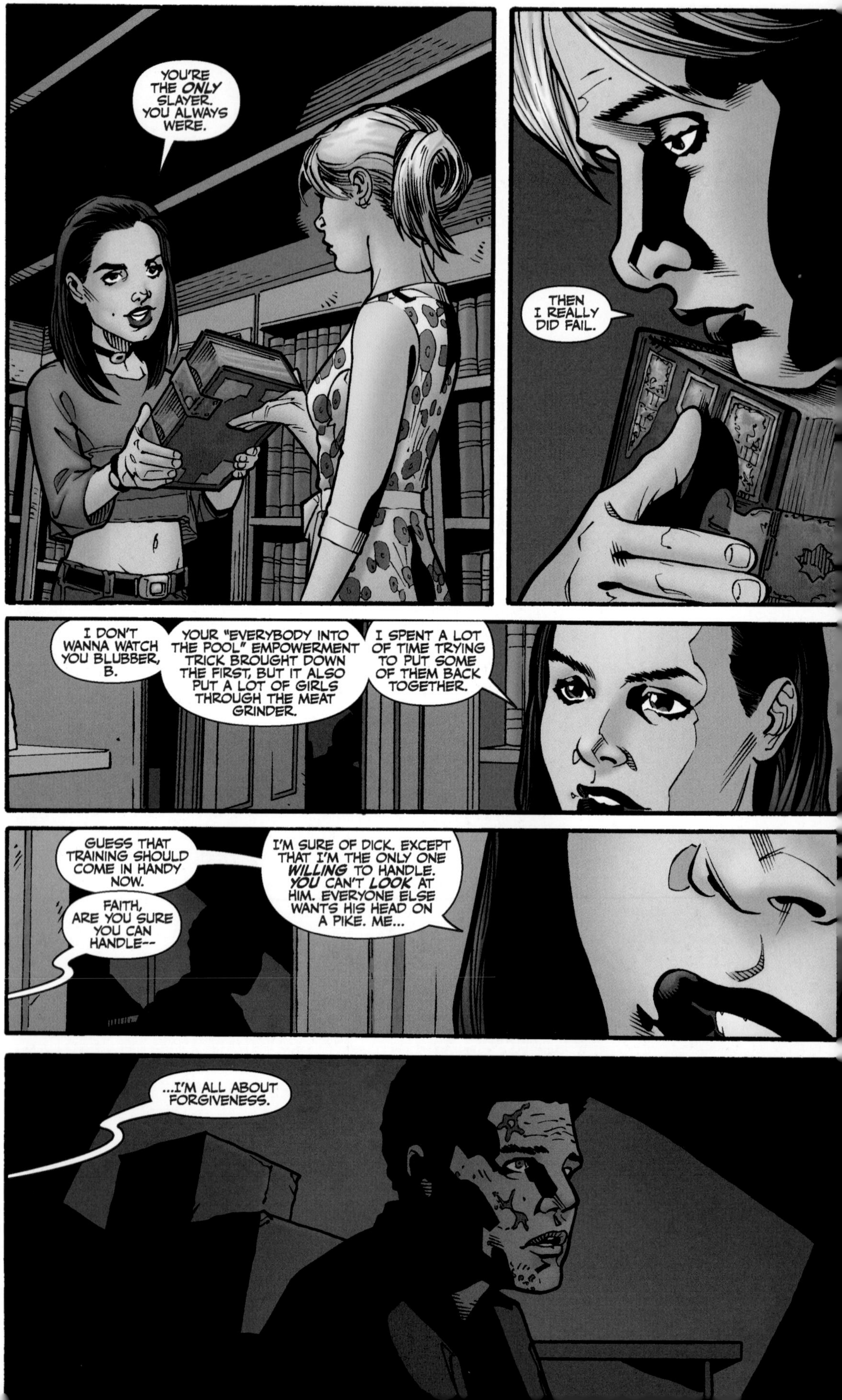
YOU'RE THE *ONLY* SLAYER. YOU ALWAYS WERE.
THEN I REALLY DID FAIL.
I DON'T WANNA WATCH YOU BLUBBER, B.
YOUR "EVERYBODY INTO THE POOL" EMPOWERMENT TRICK BROUGHT DOWN THE FIRST, BUT IT ALSO PUT A LOT OF GIRLS THROUGH THE MEAT GRINDER.
I SPENT A LOT OF TIME TRYING TO PUT SOME OF THEM BACK TOGETHER.
GUESS THAT TRAINING SHOULD COME IN HANDY NOW.
FAITH, ARE YOU SURE YOU CAN HANDLE--
I'M SURE OF DICK. EXCEPT THAT I'M THE ONLY ONE *WILLING* TO HANDLE. *YOU* CAN'T *LOOK* AT HIM. EVERYONE ELSE WANTS HIS HEAD ON A PIKE. ME...
...I'M ALL ABOUT FORGIVENESS.

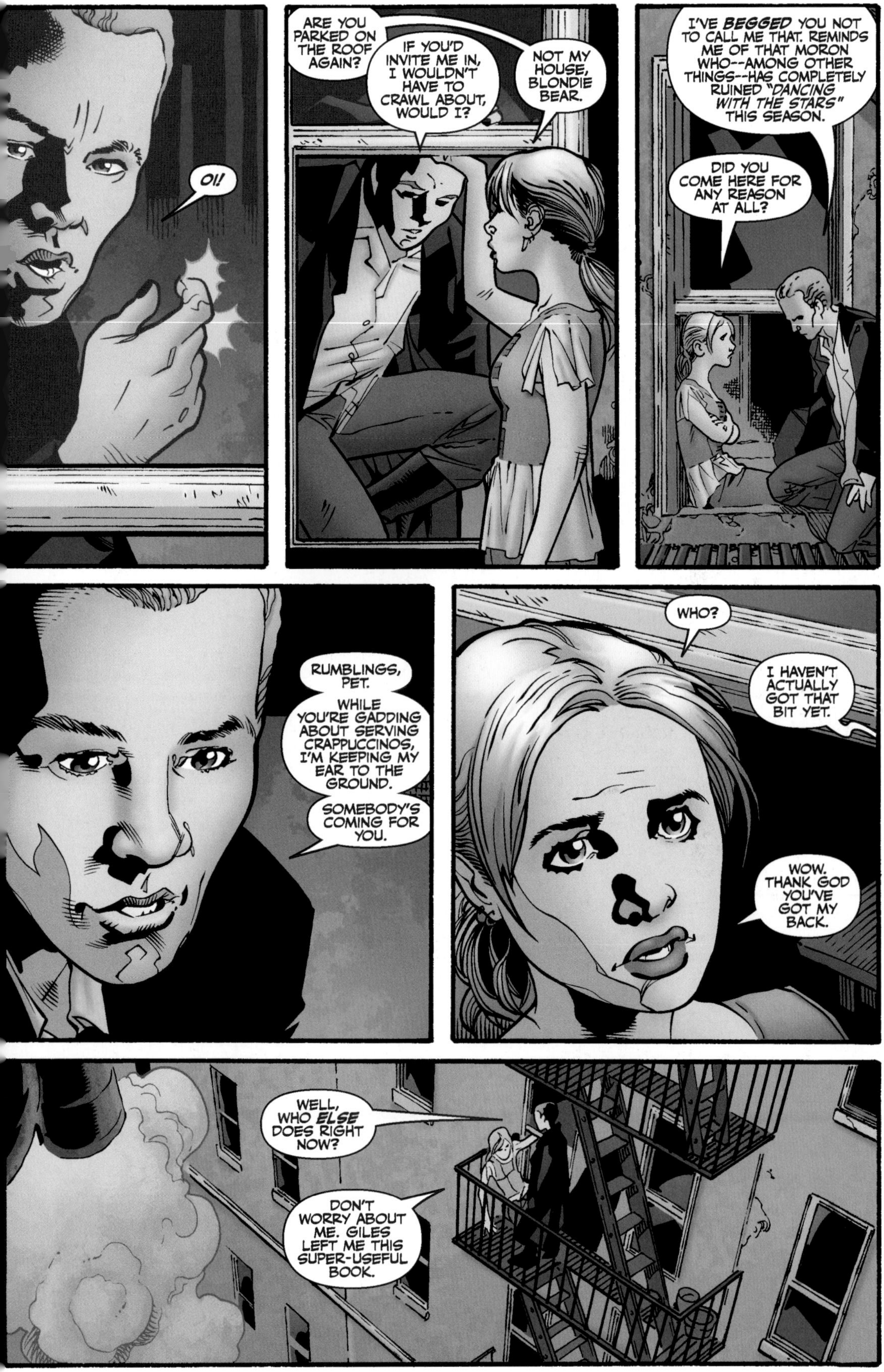
OI!
ARE YOU PARKED ON THE ROOF AGAIN?
IF YOU'D INVITE ME IN, I WOULDN'T HAVE TO CRAWL ABOUT, WOULD I?
NOT MY HOUSE, BLONDIE BEAR.
I'VE BEGGED YOU NOT TO CALL ME THAT. REMINDS ME OF THAT MORON WHO--AMONG OTHER THINGS--HAS COMPLETELY RUINED "DANCING WITH THE STARS" THIS SEASON.
DID YOU COME HERE FOR ANY REASON AT ALL?
RUMBLINGS, PET.
WHILE YOU'RE GADDING ABOUT SERVING CRAPPUCCINOS, I'M KEEPING MY EAR TO THE GROUND.
SOMEBODY'S COMING FOR YOU.
WHO?
I HAVEN'T ACTUALLY GOT THAT BIT YET.
WOW. THANK GOD YOU'VE GOT MY BACK.
WELL, WHO ELSE DOES RIGHT NOW?
DON'T WORRY ABOUT ME. GILES LEFT ME THIS SUPER-USEFUL BOOK.

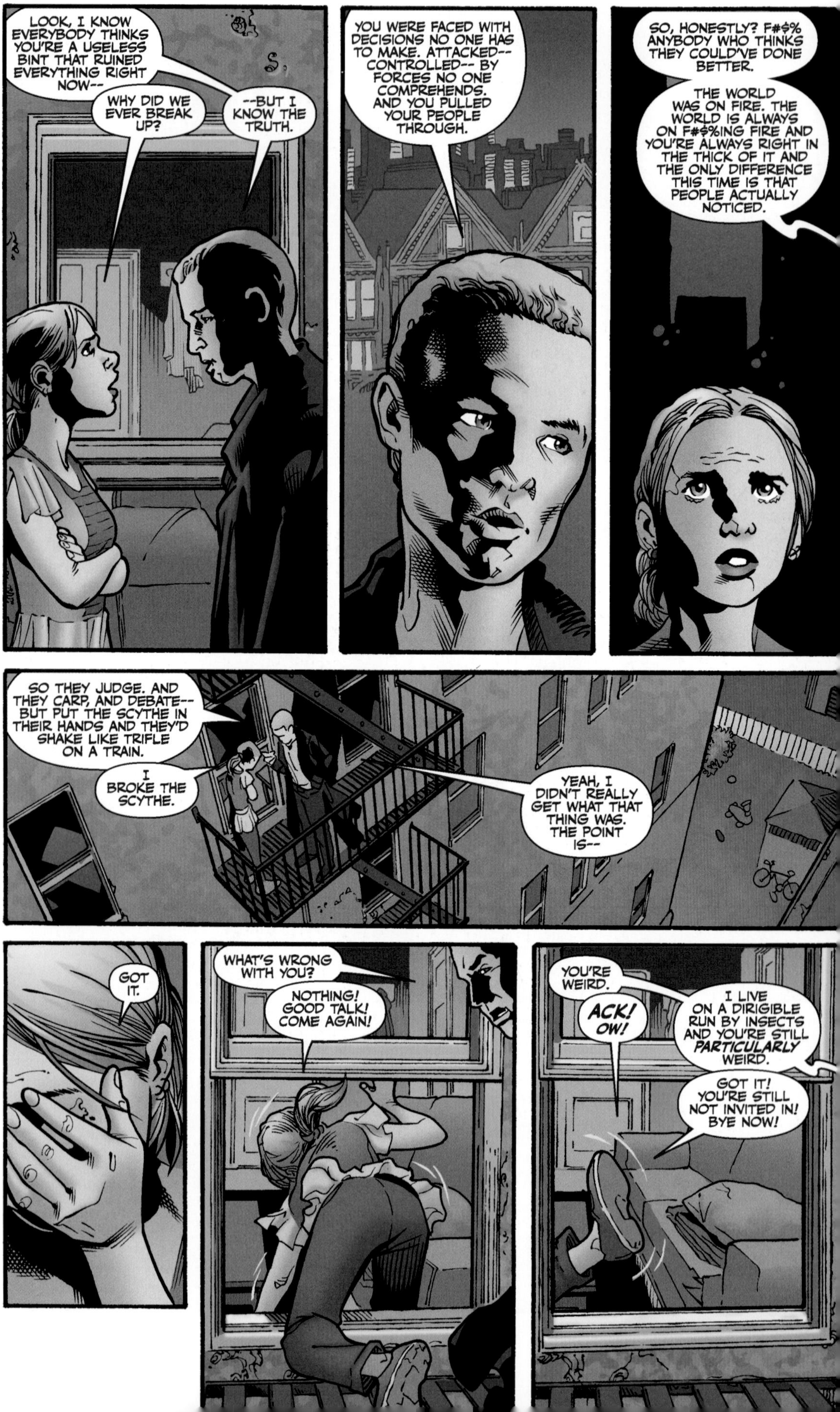
LOOK, I KNOW EVERYBODY THINKS YOU'RE A USELESS BINT THAT RUINED EVERYTHING RIGHT NOW--
WHY DID WE EVER BREAK UP?
--BUT I KNOW THE TRUTH.
YOU WERE FACED WITH DECISIONS NO ONE HAS TO MAKE. ATTACKED-- CONTROLLED-- BY FORCES NO ONE COMPREHENDS. AND YOU PULLED YOUR PEOPLE THROUGH.
SO, HONESTLY? F#$% ANYBODY WHO THINKS THEY COULD'VE DONE BETTER.
THE WORLD WAS ON FIRE. THE WORLD IS ALWAYS ON F#$%ING FIRE AND YOU'RE ALWAYS RIGHT IN THE THICK OF IT AND THE ONLY DIFFERENCE THIS TIME IS THAT PEOPLE ACTUALLY NOTICED.
SO THEY JUDGE. AND THEY CARP, AND DEBATE-- BUT PUT THE SCYTHE IN THEIR HANDS AND THEY'D SHAKE LIKE TRIFLE ON A TRAIN.
I BROKE THE SCYTHE.
YEAH, I DIDN'T REALLY GET WHAT THAT THING WAS. THE POINT IS--
GOT IT.
WHAT'S WRONG WITH YOU?
NOTHING! GOOD TALK! COME AGAIN!
YOU'RE WEIRD.
ACK! OW!
I LIVE ON A DIRIGIBLE RUN BY INSECTS AND YOU'RE STILL *PARTICULARLY* WEIRD.
GOT IT! YOU'RE STILL NOT INVITED IN! BYE NOW!

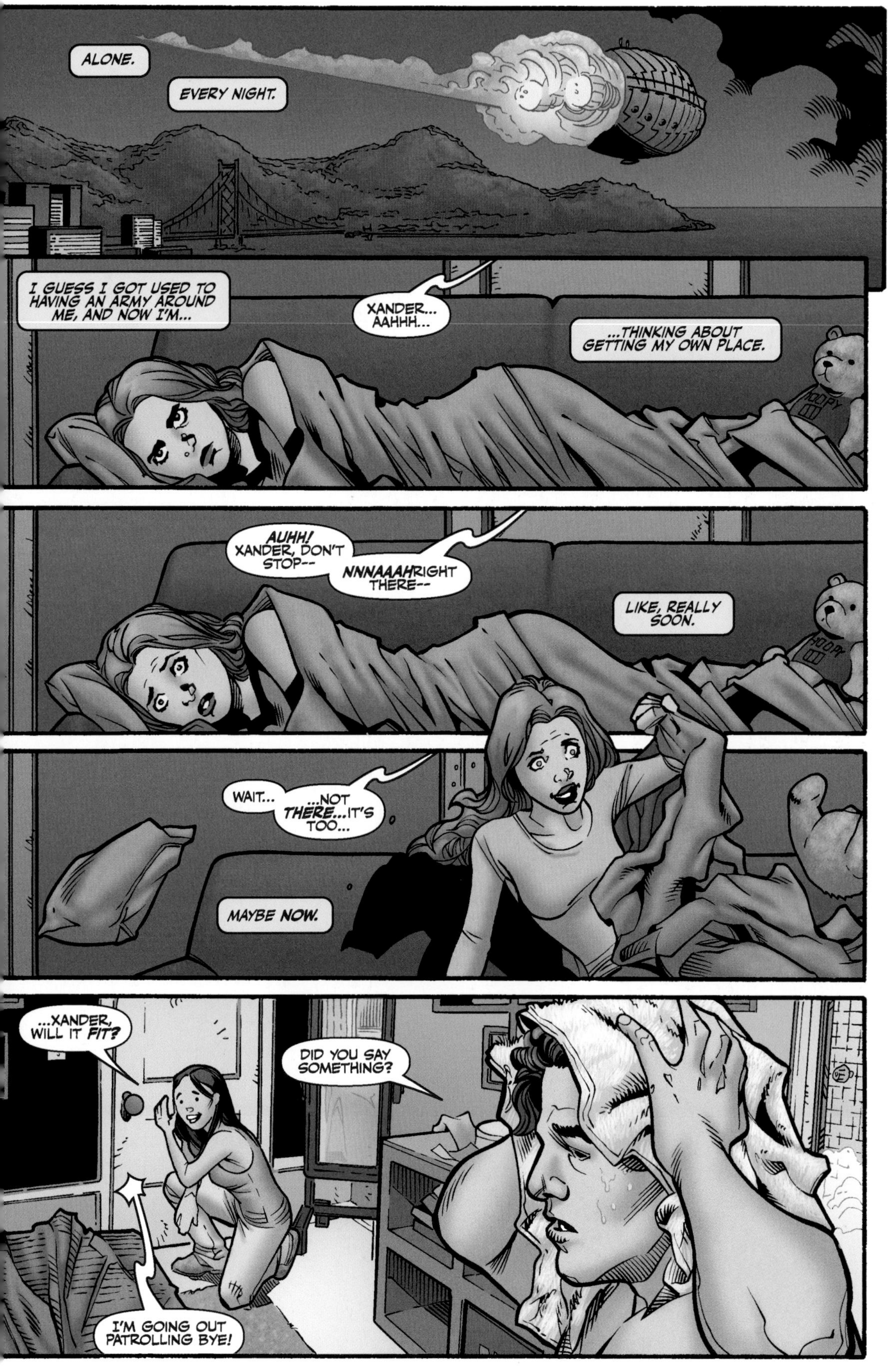
ALONE.
EVERY NIGHT.
I GUESS I GOT USED TO HAVING AN ARMY AROUND ME, AND NOW I'M...
XANDER... AAHHH...
...THINKING ABOUT GETTING MY OWN PLACE.
AUHH! XANDER, DON'T STOP--
NNNAAAHRIGHT THERE--
LIKE, REALLY SOON.
WAIT...
...NOT THERE...IT'S TOO...
MAYBE NOW.
...XANDER, WILL IT FIT?
DID YOU SAY SOMETHING?
I'M GOING OUT PATROLLING BYE!

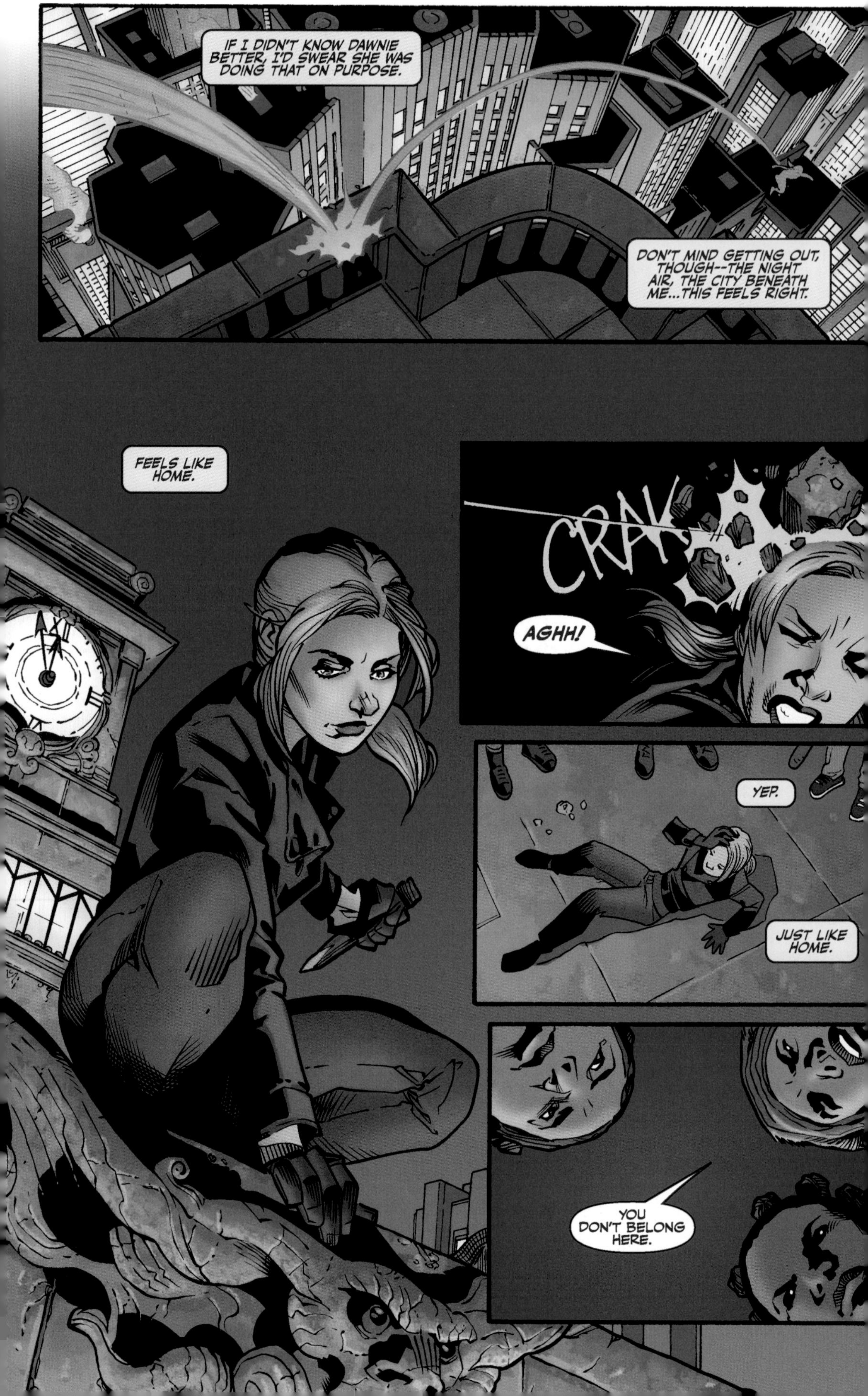
IF I DIDN'T KNOW DAWNIE BETTER, I'D SWEAR SHE WAS DOING THAT ON PURPOSE.
DON'T MIND GETTING OUT, THOUGH--THE NIGHT AIR, THE CITY BENEATH ME...THIS FEELS RIGHT.
FEELS LIKE HOME.
CRAK
AGHH!
YEP.
JUST LIKE HOME.
YOU DON'T BELONG HERE.

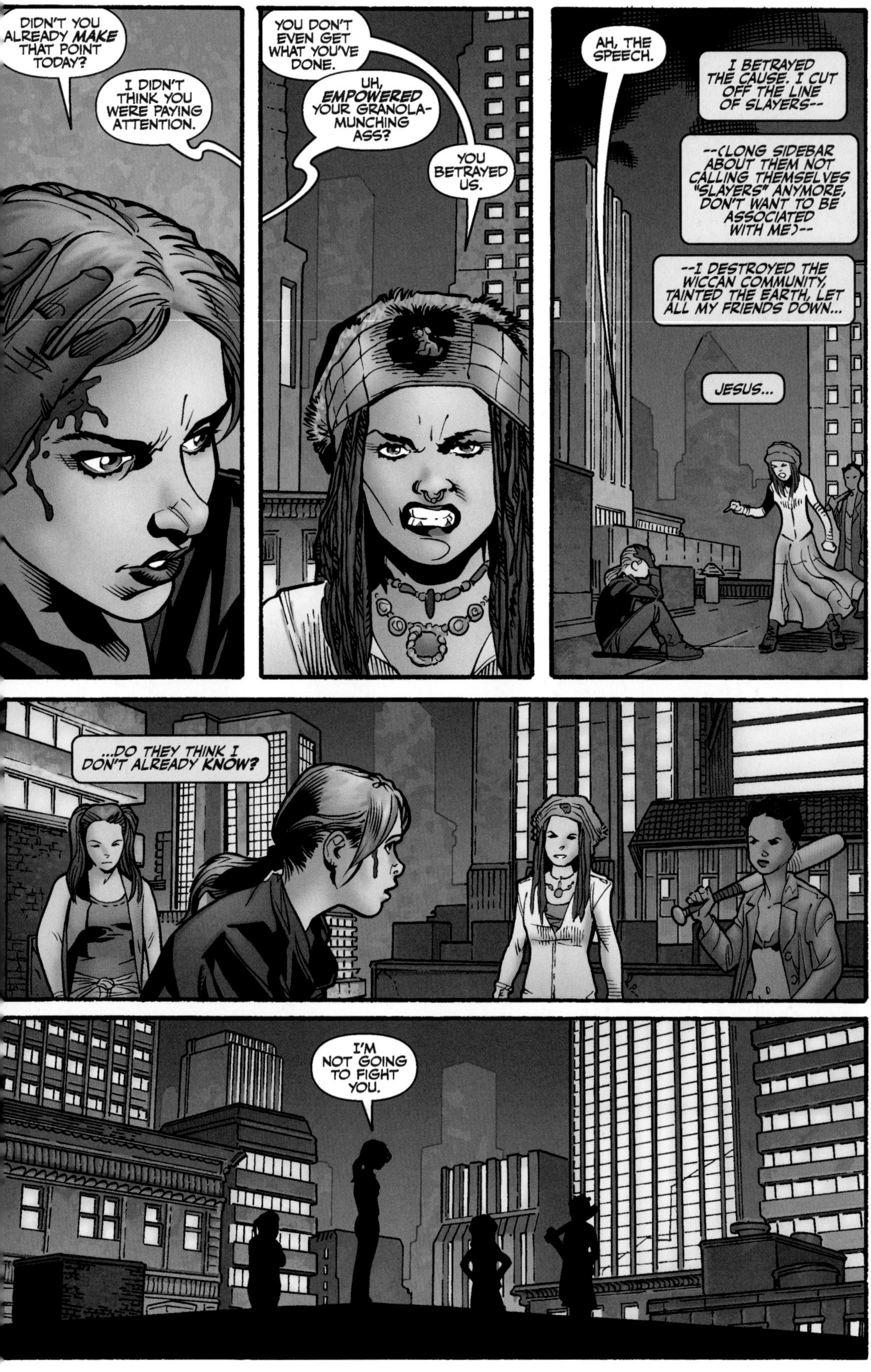

DIDN'T YOU ALREADY MAKE THAT POINT TODAY?
I DIDN'T THINK YOU WERE PAYING ATTENTION.
YOU DON'T EVEN GET WHAT YOU'VE DONE.
UH, EMPOWERED YOUR GRANOLA-MUNCHING ASS?
YOU BETRAYED US.
AH, THE SPEECH.
I BETRAYED THE CAUSE. I CUT OFF THE LINE OF SLAYERS--
--(LONG SIDEBAR ABOUT THEM NOT CALLING THEMSELVES "SLAYERS" ANYMORE, DON'T WANT TO BE ASSOCIATED WITH ME)--
--I DESTROYED THE WICCAN COMMUNITY, TAINTED THE EARTH, LET ALL MY FRIENDS DOWN...
JESUS...
...DO THEY THINK I DON'T ALREADY KNOW?
I'M NOT GOING TO FIGHT YOU.

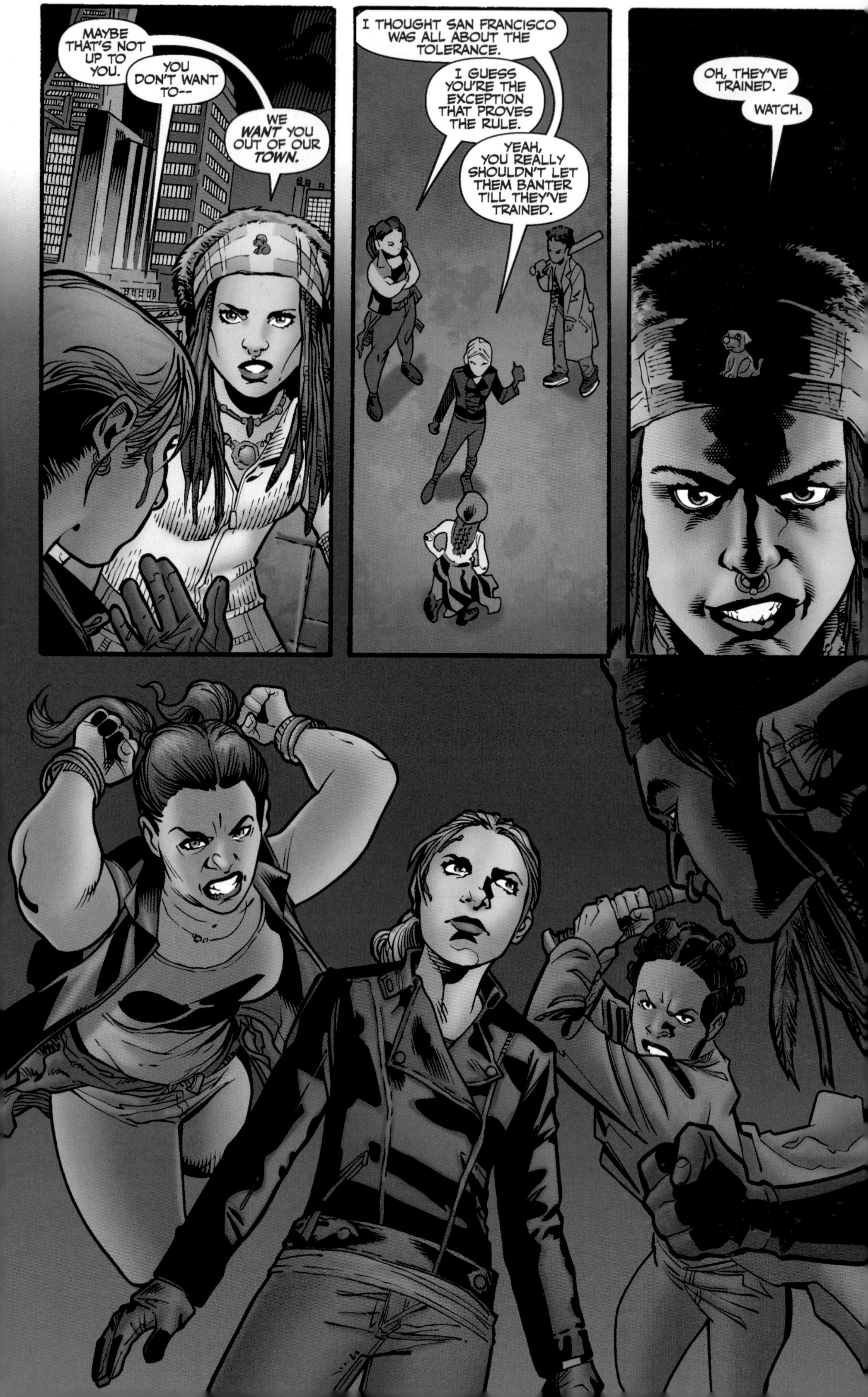
MAYBE THAT'S NOT UP TO YOU.
YOU DON'T WANT TO--
WE *WANT* YOU OUT OF OUR *TOWN.*
I THOUGHT SAN FRANCISCO WAS ALL ABOUT THE TOLERANCE.
I GUESS YOU'RE THE EXCEPTION THAT PROVES THE RULE.
YEAH, YOU REALLY SHOULDN'T LET THEM BANTER TILL THEY'VE TRAINED.
OH, THEY'VE TRAINED.
WATCH.

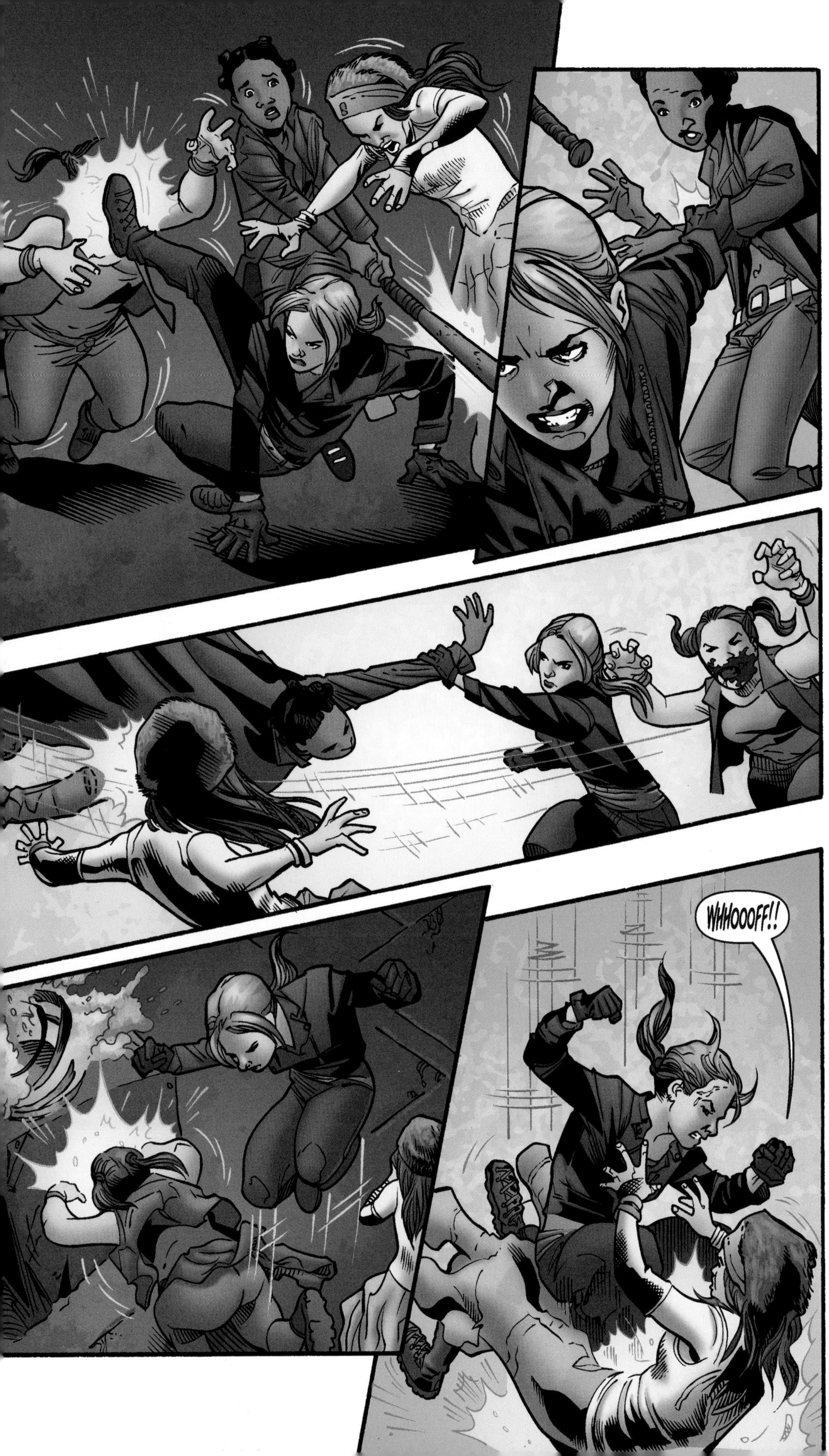
WHHOOOFF!!

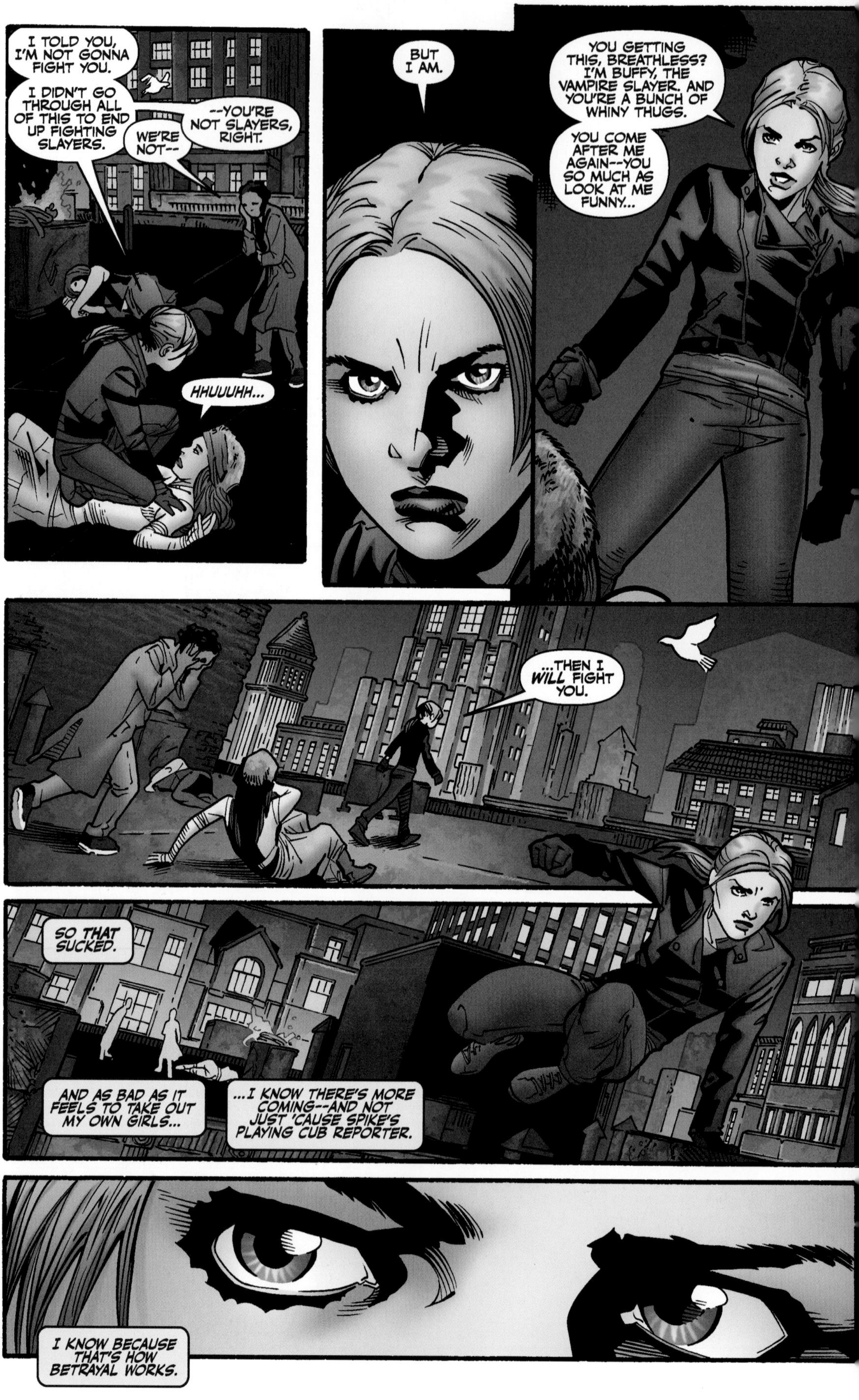
I TOLD YOU, I'M NOT GONNA FIGHT YOU.
I DIDN'T GO THROUGH ALL OF THIS TO END UP FIGHTING SLAYERS.
WE'RE NOT--
--YOU'RE NOT SLAYERS, RIGHT.
HHUUUHH...
BUT I AM.
YOU GETTING THIS, BREATHLESS? I'M BUFFY, THE VAMPIRE SLAYER. AND YOU'RE A BUNCH OF WHINY THUGS.
YOU COME AFTER ME AGAIN--YOU SO MUCH AS LOOK AT ME FUNNY...
...THEN I WILL FIGHT YOU.
SO THAT SUCKED.
AND AS BAD AS IT FEELS TO TAKE OUT MY OWN GIRLS...
...I KNOW THERE'S MORE COMING--AND NOT JUST 'CAUSE SPIKE'S PLAYING CUB REPORTER.
I KNOW BECAUSE THAT'S HOW BETRAYAL WORKS.

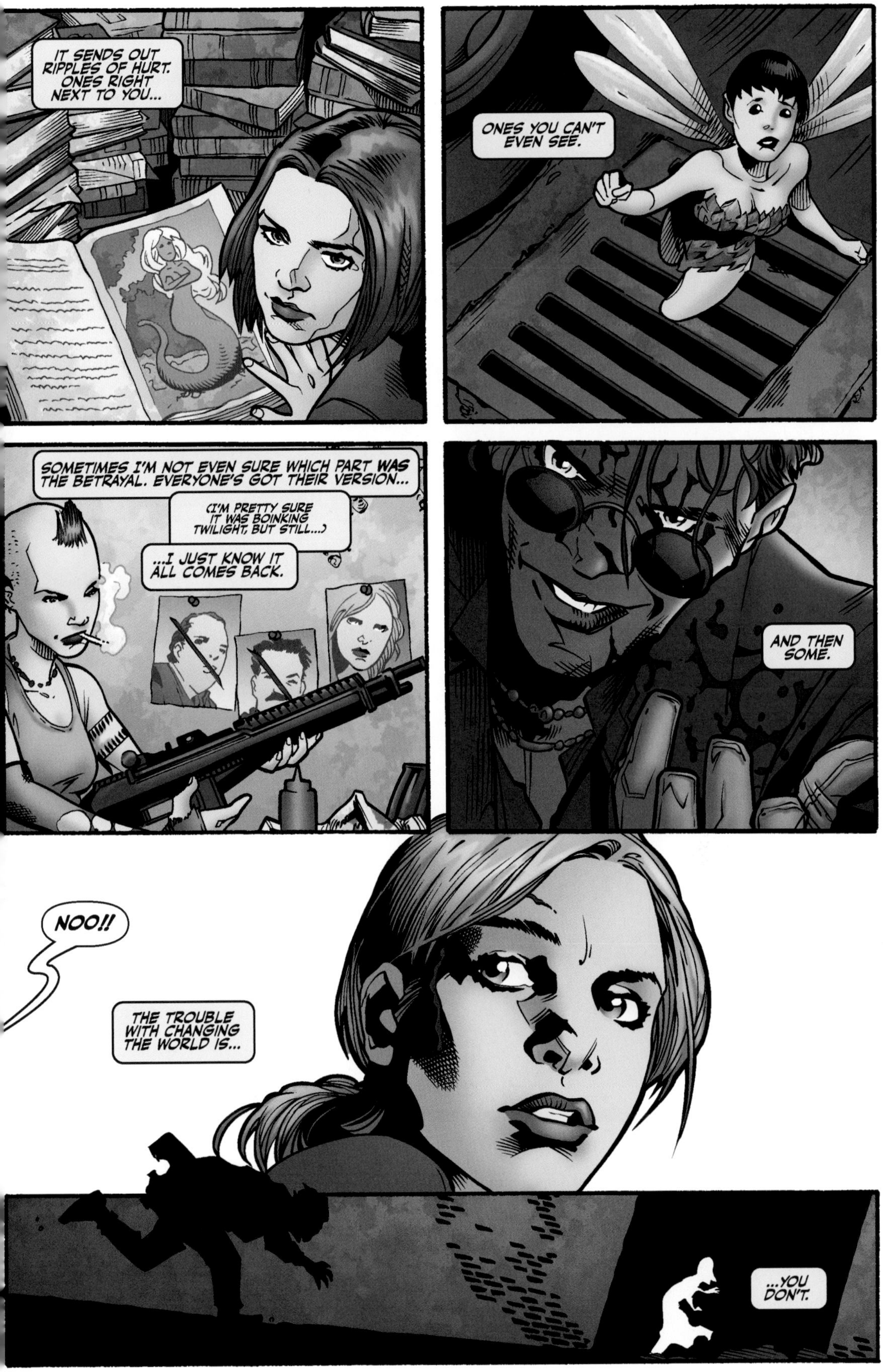
IT SENDS OUT RIPPLES OF HURT. ONES RIGHT NEXT TO YOU...
ONES YOU CAN'T EVEN SEE.
SOMETIMES I'M NOT EVEN SURE WHICH PART WAS THE BETRAYAL. EVERYONE'S GOT THEIR VERSION...
(I'M PRETTY SURE IT WAS BOINKING TWILIGHT, BUT STILL...)
...I JUST KNOW IT ALL COMES BACK.
AND THEN SOME.
NOO!!
THE TROUBLE WITH CHANGING THE WORLD IS...
...YOU DON'T.

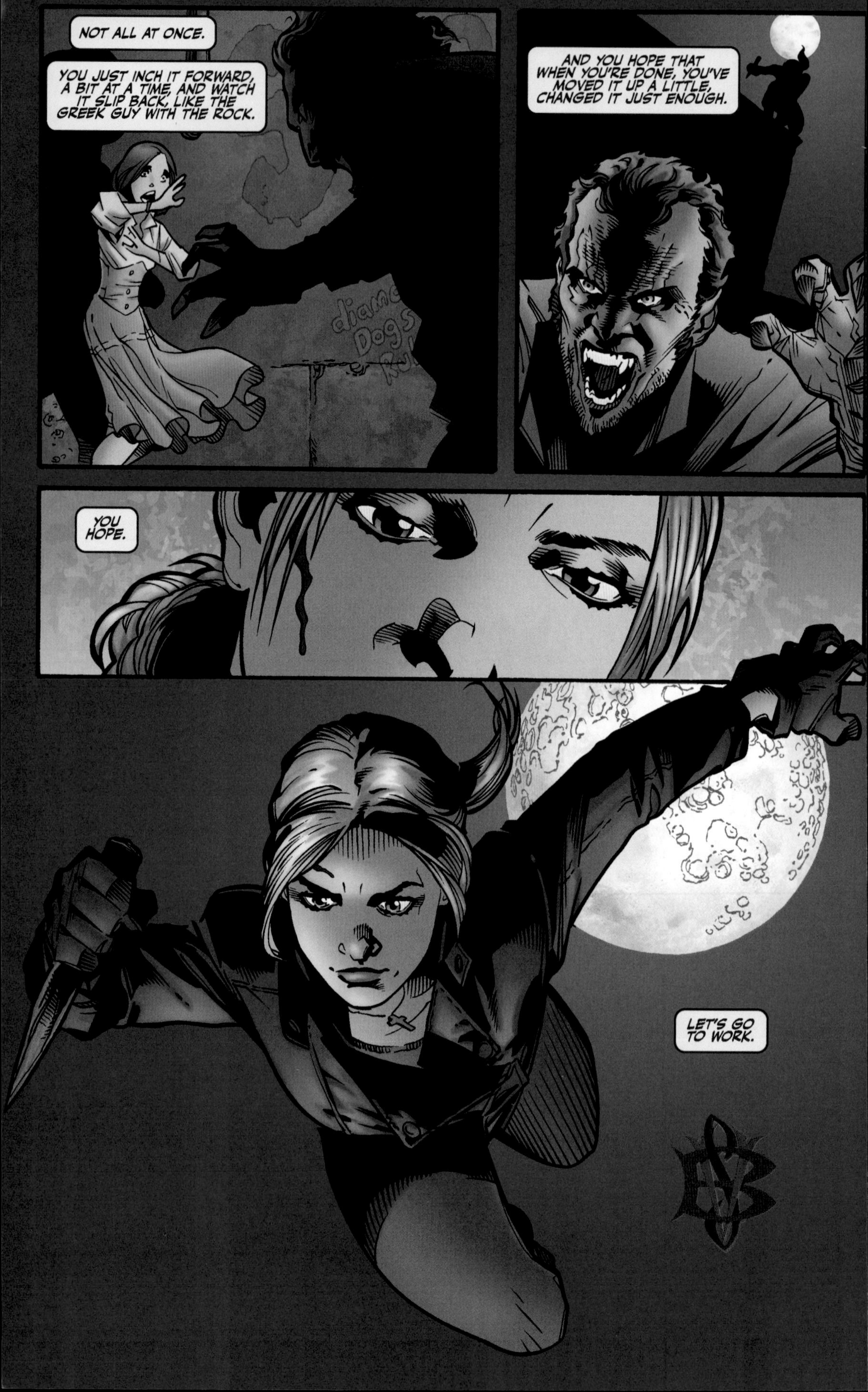
NOT ALL AT ONCE.
YOU JUST INCH IT FORWARD, A BIT AT A TIME, AND WATCH IT SLIP BACK, LIKE THE GREEK GUY WITH THE ROCK.
AND YOU HOPE THAT WHEN YOU'RE DONE, YOU'VE MOVED IT UP A LITTLE, CHANGED IT JUST ENOUGH.
YOU HOPE.
LET'S GO TO WORK.

SO, OUR ENDLESS SEASON ENDS. We've laughed, we've cried, we've thrown up a little in our mouths, but most of all we've learned. Not you guys—us. We've learned what you like, what you don't, how this TV show translated to the world of comics, and how it didn't quite. We've lost a few fans along the way and, hopefully, gained a few. I can't say exactly how much has changed, in our lives or our work. The only thing that's certain is this: all of us involved in this venture, without exception, have weirder-looking hair.

If you've read this volume, you've got a sense of where we're heading for Season 9. Back, a bit, to the everyday trials that made Buffy more than a superhero. That made her us. I was so excited to finally have an unlimited budget that I wanted to make the book an epic, but I realized along the way that the things I loved the best were the things you loved the best: the peeps. The down-to-earth, recognizable people. And Mecha-Dawn. (She has a *tail*!) So that's what we'll try to evoke next season—along with the usual perils, and a few new ones, of course.

Every season of *Buffy* had a different intent, and a different set of challenges, from which to build. The biggest challenge in Season 8 was that many years ago I wrote a Slayer comic and set it in the far future so that it could *never affect Buffy's life*. I was so young. But the challenge of reconciling the optimistic, empowering message of the final episode with the dystopian, Slayerless vision of Fray's future gave Season 8 a genuine weight. There is never progress without hateful, reactionary blowback. That's never been more apparent than in today's political scene in America. The mission was to deal with the consequences of Buffy and Willow's empowering spell (the good and the terrible), steer toward a possible *Fray* future without undoing all the good Buffy had done (the girls still have their power), and tee us up for a very different Season 9. Some adjustments had to be made along the way, particularly when I completely changed my plan for Season 9. I changed it for the reasons stated above. No matter how interesting the world stage or mystical dimensions can be, Buffy's best when she's walking that alley, dusting vamps, and nursing a pouty heart. We're not going back to

square one, but our square will definitely have a oneishness to it. It should be nice, after the wild ride that was Season 8—not always perfect, but made with love and delight that I think shine through.

The people who need to be thanked really deserve more than just thanks—but we're all too scattered for the inappropriate touching required to convey my gratitude and occasional awe. Scott Allie is why there are editors. Smart, patient, pushy when it's time to be pushy—straddling the minutiae and the Big Picture in a way any show runner would envy. Georges—no book without Georges. If I didn't make the smoothest transition from TV to comics, he sure as hell did. He drew wonderful likenesses that never felt like portraits, and panels that were dynamic, funny, and emotional. . . . No one could have evoked the ethos of the show better. Jo Chen's covers make me cry. I won't say more, or I'll cry.

If I start listing the writers, this will be longer than the comic. But Drew Goddard writes the stuff I wish I had. Brad Meltzer writes like he was on the staff for all seven years (and is a nut for structure, which helped more than I like admitting). Jane Espenson, Brian K. Vaughan. . . . Wait, didn't I just promise not to do this? Everyone brought such love and talent to the table, writers and artists and inkers and colorists and letterers and editors I've left in the cold (sorry, Sierra) in order to wrap this up. . . . The point is, this has been a long, strange trip, but it worked (when it did) because so many overqualified souls poured themselves into it. I'm grateful.

I'm grateful to the guys at IDW, particularly Chris Ryall and Brian Lynch, for handling the *Angel* series with such passion and hilarity, and for being kind and cooperative when I decided the two universes needed to be under one roof.

And I'm grateful to you guys, for coming on the ride. I promise it won't get smoother. We've got a lot of new—and old—friends along, some new titles, and a bunch of limited series. . . . It's nuts; I'm exhausted by the end of Season 8. So why am I so giddy about Season 9?

Maybe I'm a fan.

—joss

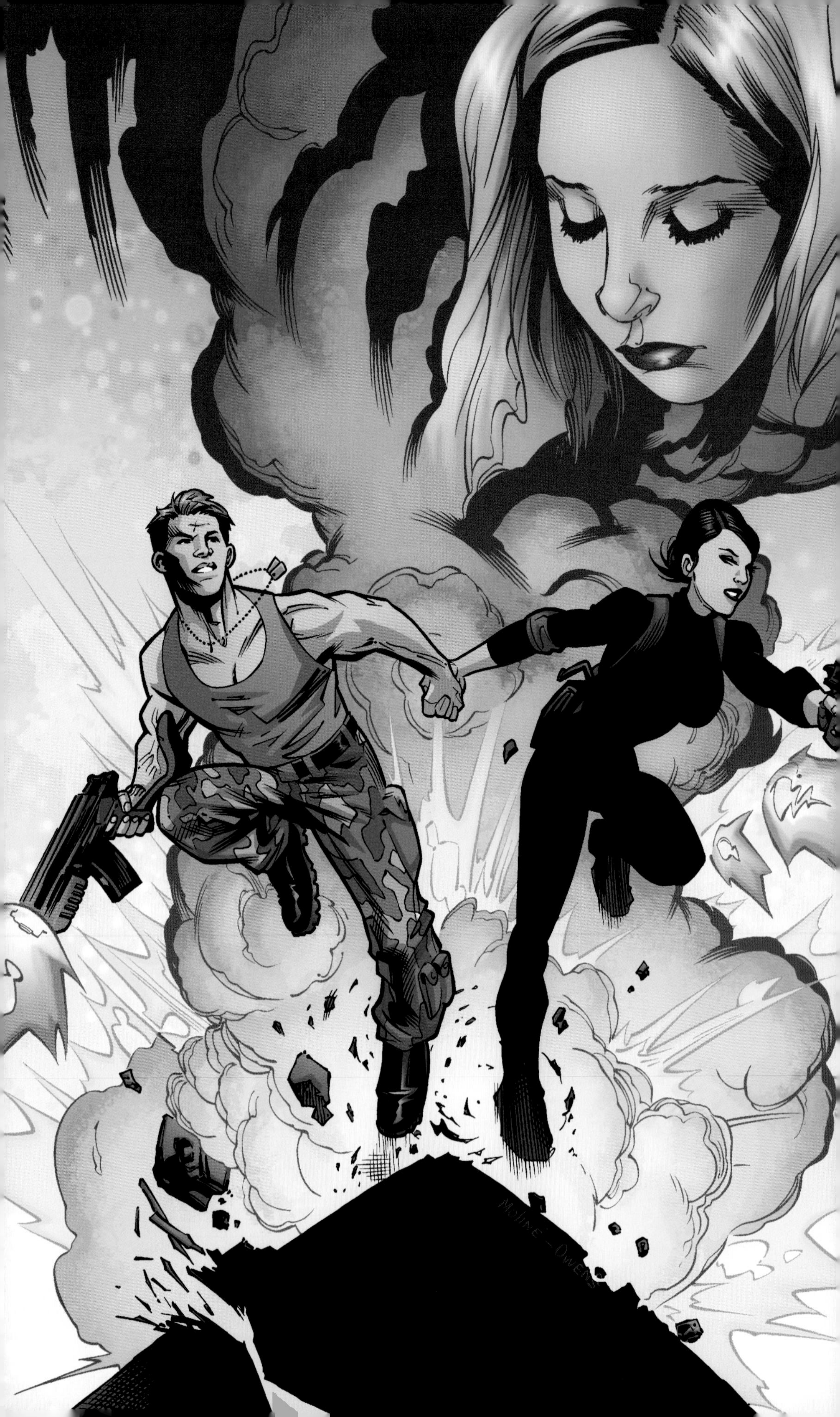

COMMITMENT THROUGH DISTANCE, VIRTUE THROUGH SIN

Script JANE ESPENSON

Pencils KARL MOLINE

Inks ANDY OWENS

Colors MICHELLE MADSEN

Letters RICHARD STARKINGS &
COMICRAFT'S JIMMY BETANCOURT

This story takes place before the events of
Buffy the Vampire Slayer *Season 8.*

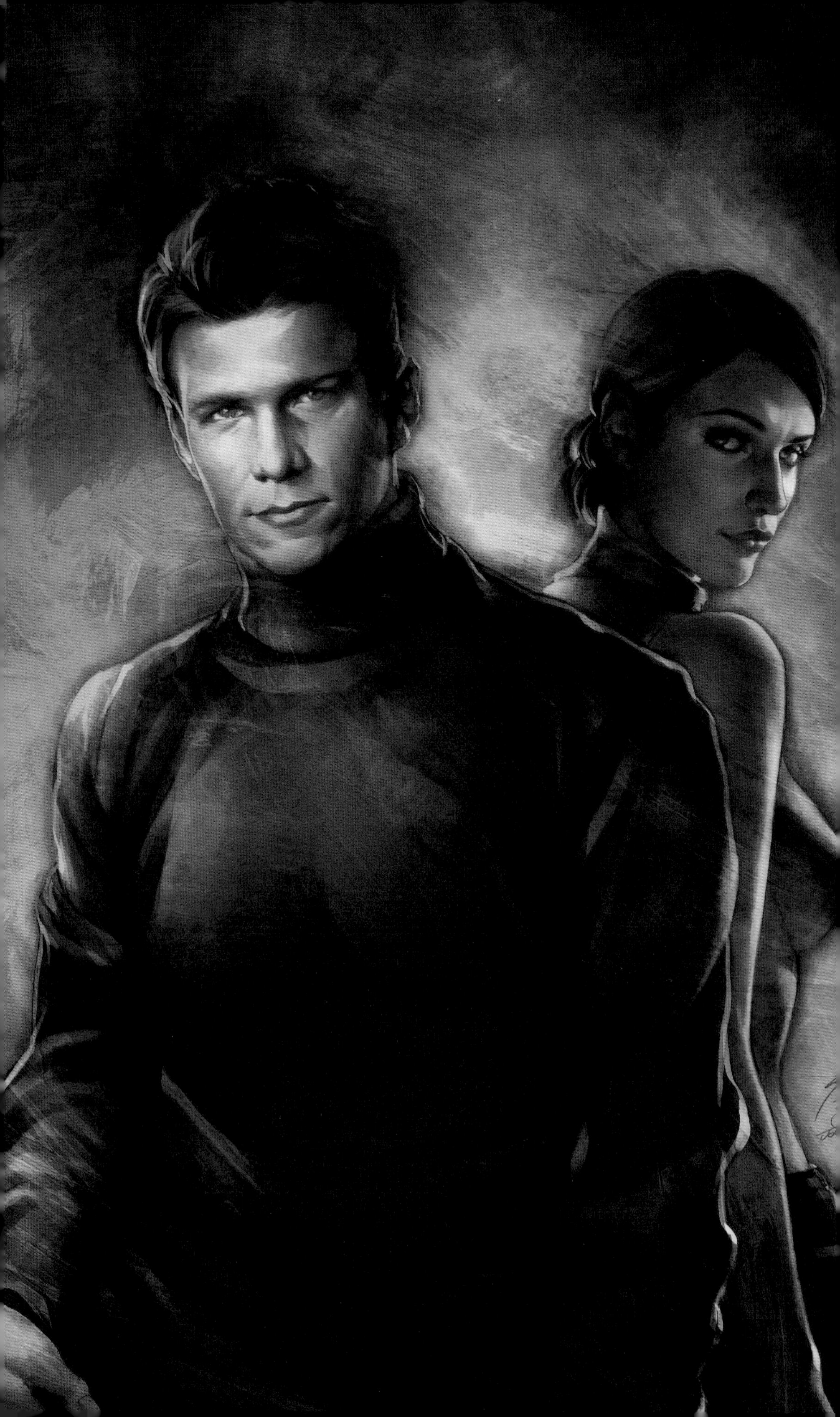

COMMITMENT THROUGH DISTANCE
VIRTUE THROUGH SIN

"GREAT DINNER, MOM! SAM AND I ARE GONNA TAKE THE TRUCK... BE BACK IN A BIT!"

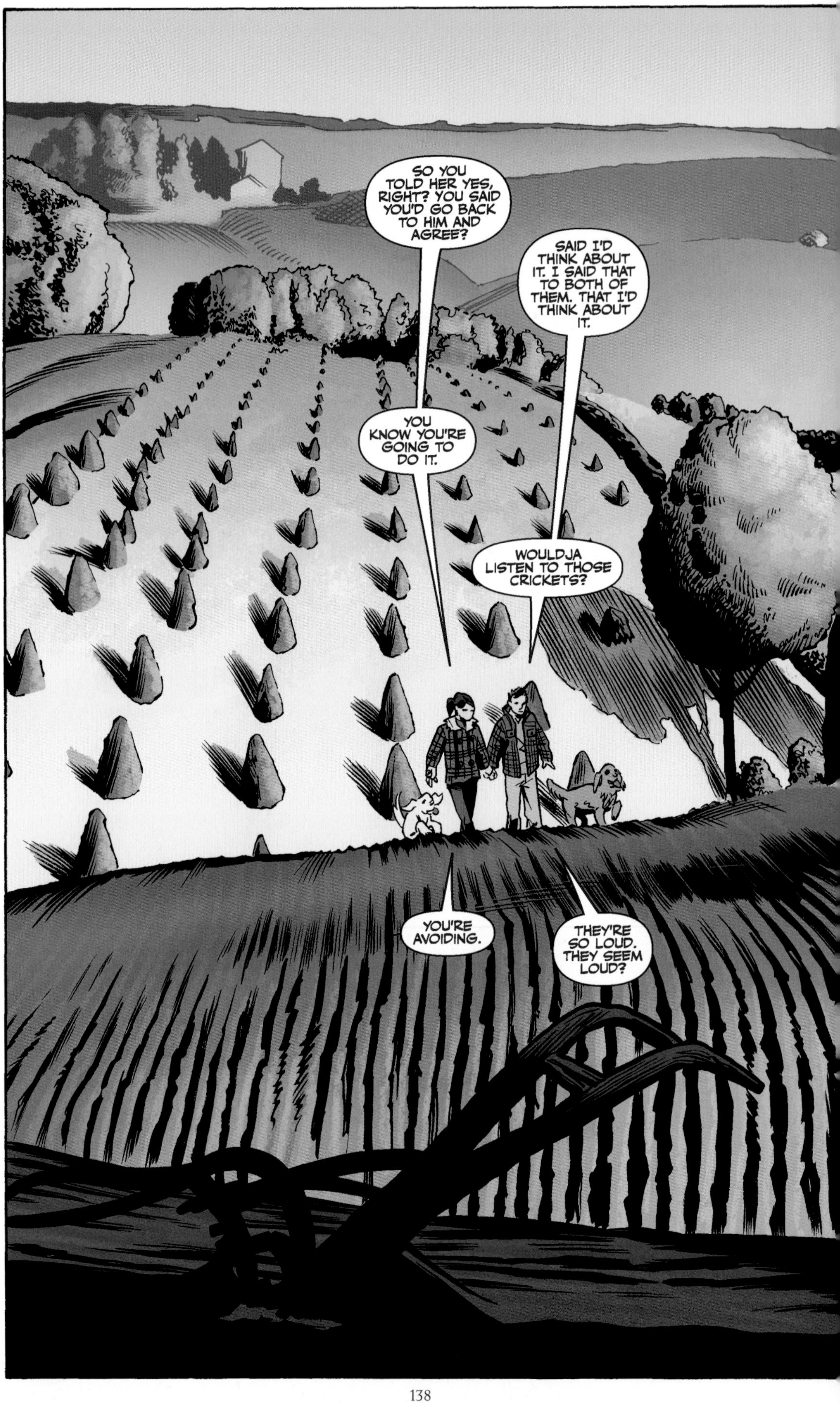
SO YOU TOLD HER YES, RIGHT? YOU SAID YOU'D GO BACK TO HIM AND AGREE?
SAID I'D THINK ABOUT IT. I SAID THAT TO BOTH OF THEM. THAT I'D THINK ABOUT IT.
YOU KNOW YOU'RE GOING TO DO IT.
WOULDJA LISTEN TO THOSE CRICKETS?
YOU'RE AVOIDING.
THEY'RE SO LOUD. THEY SEEM LOUD?

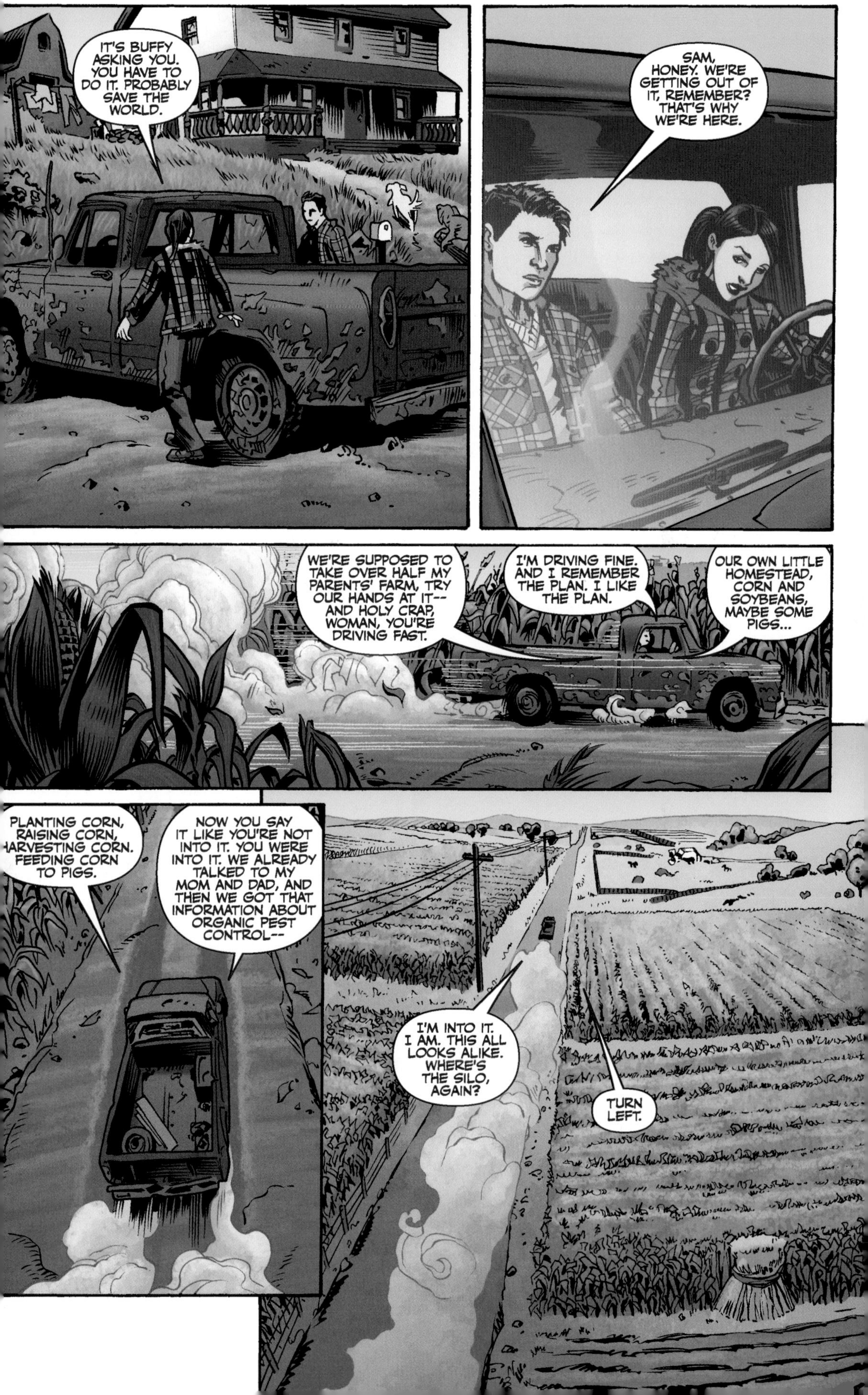
IT'S BUFFY ASKING YOU. YOU HAVE TO DO IT. PROBABLY SAVE THE WORLD.
SAM, HONEY. WE'RE GETTING OUT OF IT, REMEMBER? THAT'S WHY WE'RE HERE.
WE'RE SUPPOSED TO TAKE OVER HALF MY PARENTS' FARM, TRY OUR HANDS AT IT-- AND HOLY CRAP, WOMAN, YOU'RE DRIVING FAST.
I'M DRIVING FINE. AND I REMEMBER THE PLAN. I LIKE THE PLAN.
OUR OWN LITTLE HOMESTEAD, CORN AND SOYBEANS, MAYBE SOME PIGS...
PLANTING CORN, RAISING CORN, HARVESTING CORN. FEEDING CORN TO PIGS.
NOW YOU SAY IT LIKE YOU'RE NOT INTO IT. YOU WERE INTO IT. WE ALREADY TALKED TO MY MOM AND DAD, AND THEN WE GOT THAT INFORMATION ABOUT ORGANIC PEST CONTROL--
I'M INTO IT. I AM. THIS ALL LOOKS ALIKE. WHERE'S THE SILO, AGAIN?
TURN LEFT.

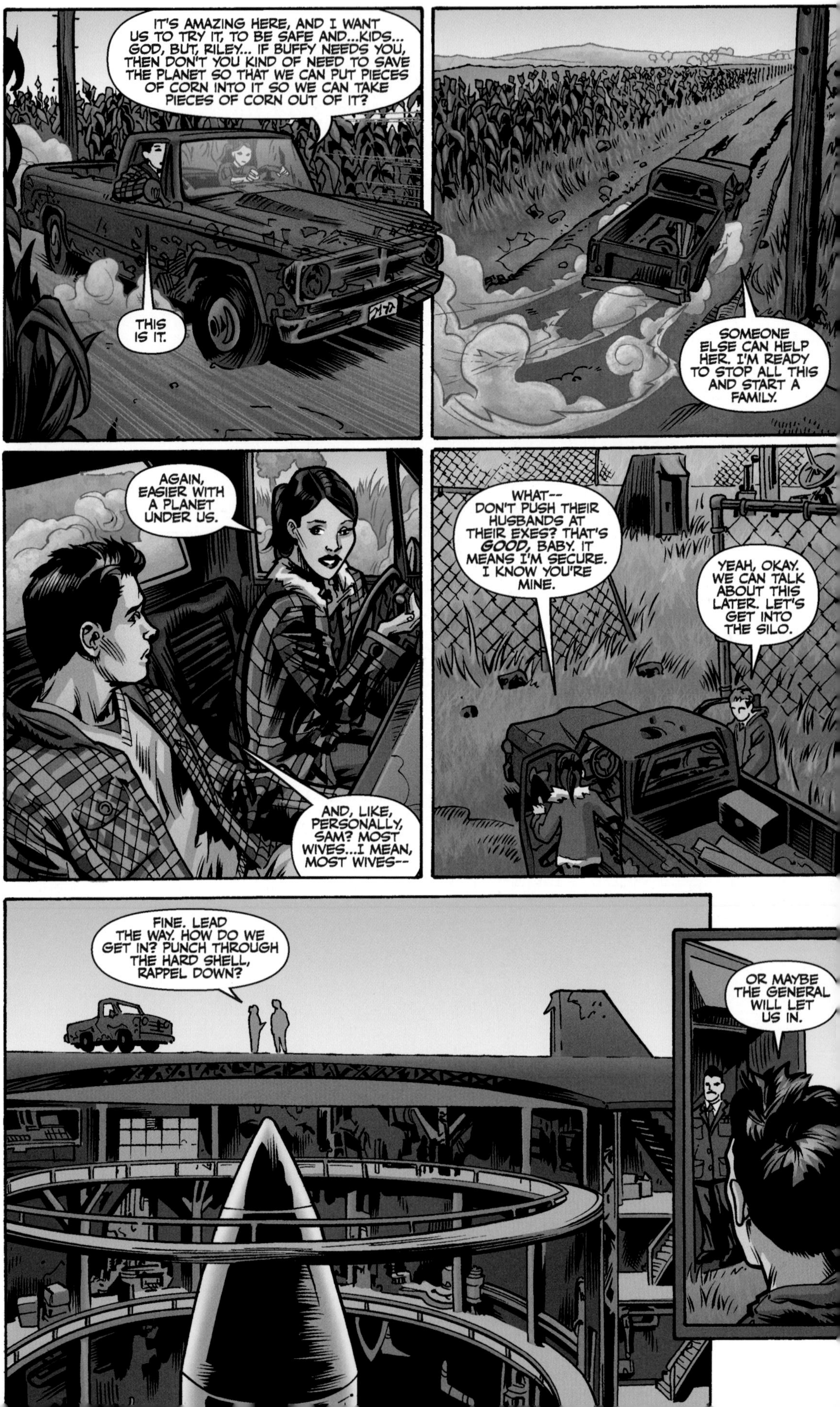
IT'S AMAZING HERE, AND I WANT US TO TRY IT, TO BE SAFE AND...KIDS... GOD, BUT, RILEY... IF BUFFY NEEDS YOU, THEN DON'T YOU KIND OF NEED TO SAVE THE PLANET SO THAT WE CAN PUT PIECES OF CORN INTO IT SO WE CAN TAKE PIECES OF CORN OUT OF IT?
THIS IS IT.
SOMEONE ELSE CAN HELP HER. I'M READY TO STOP ALL THIS AND START A FAMILY.
AGAIN, EASIER WITH A PLANET UNDER US.
AND, LIKE, PERSONALLY, SAM? MOST WIVES...I MEAN, MOST WIVES--
WHAT-- DON'T PUSH THEIR HUSBANDS AT THEIR EXES? THAT'S GOOD, BABY. IT MEANS I'M SECURE. I KNOW YOU'RE MINE.
YEAH, OKAY. WE CAN TALK ABOUT THIS LATER. LET'S GET INTO THE SILO.
FINE. LEAD THE WAY. HOW DO WE GET IN? PUNCH THROUGH THE HARD SHELL, RAPPEL DOWN?
OR MAYBE THE GENERAL WILL LET US IN.

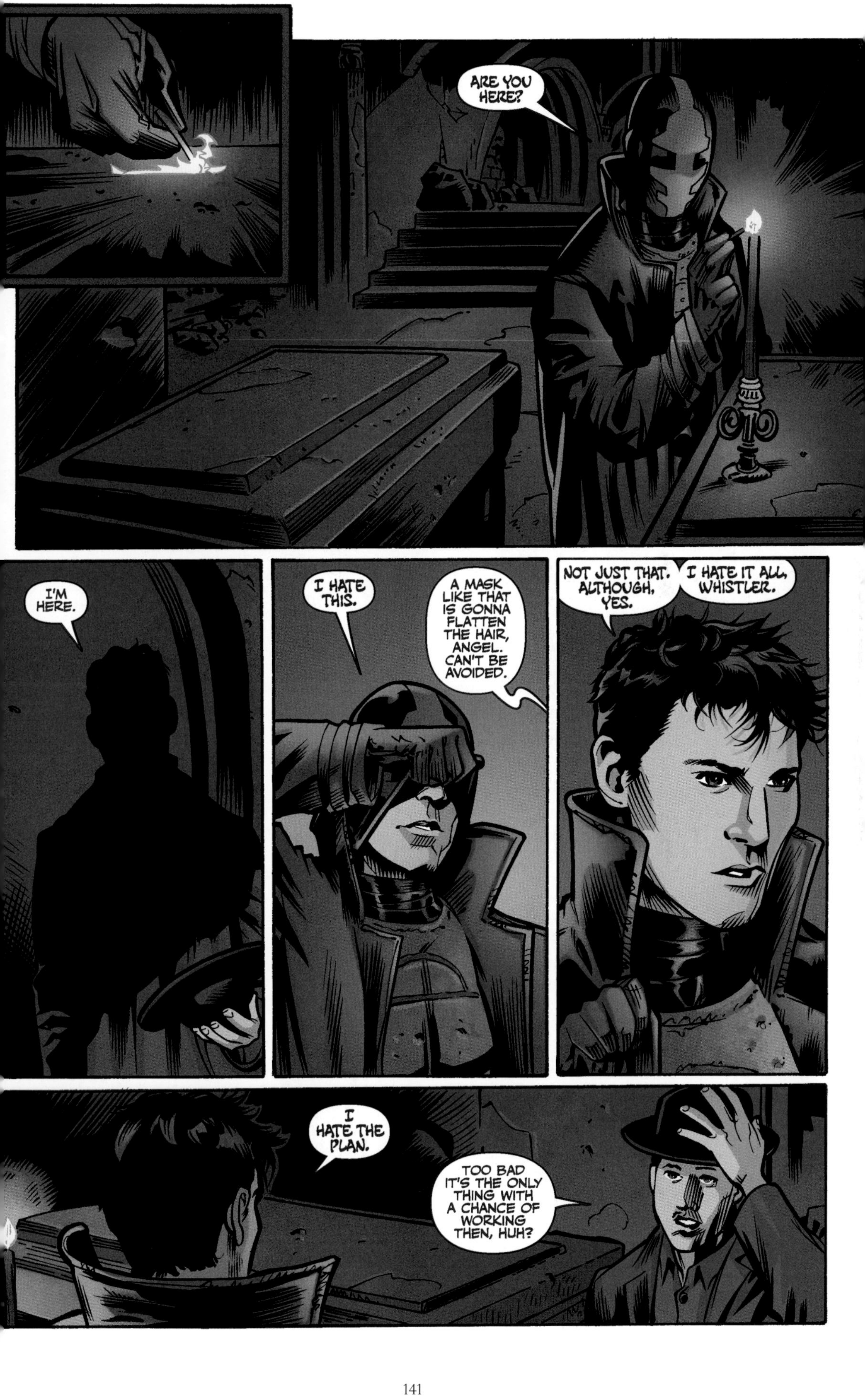
ARE YOU HERE?
I'M HERE.
I HATE THIS.
A MASK LIKE THAT IS GONNA FLATTEN THE HAIR, ANGEL. CAN'T BE AVOIDED.
NOT JUST THAT. ALTHOUGH, YES.
I HATE IT ALL, WHISTLER.
I HATE THE PLAN.
TOO BAD IT'S THE ONLY THING WITH A CHANCE OF WORKING THEN, HUH?

WE DIDN'T REALLY HAVE A PLAN FOR THIS. SO WE JUST CLEARED EVERYONE OUT WHEN IT STARTED ACTING UP.

GOOD POLICY FOR MISSILES, SIR.

AT FIRST WE JUST NOTICED THAT THE MISSILE WAS SHOWING MORE ACTIVE TIME THAN THE MAIN CONTROLLER WAS.

SO YOU FIGURED SOME OTHER COMPUTER WAS IN CONTACT WITH THE MISSILE.

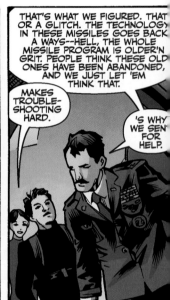

THAT'S WHAT WE FIGURED. THAT OR A GLITCH. THE TECHNOLOGY IN THESE MISSILES GOES BACK A WAYS--HELL, THE WHOLE MISSILE PROGRAM IS OLDER'N GRIT. PEOPLE THINK THESE OLD ONES HAVE BEEN ABANDONED, AND WE JUST LET 'EM THINK THAT.

MAKES TROUBLE-SHOOTING HARD.

'S WHY WE SENT FOR HELP.

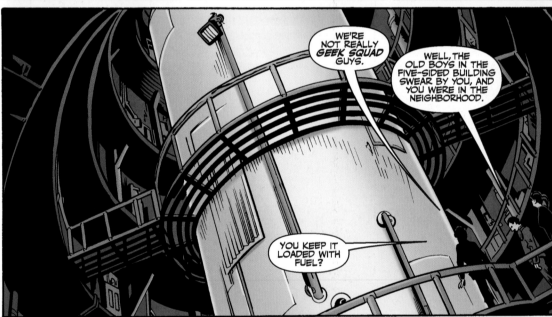

WE'RE NOT REALLY GEEK SQUAD GUYS.

WELL, THE OLD BOYS IN THE FIVE-SIDED BUILDING SWEAR BY YOU, AND YOU WERE IN THE NEIGHBORHOOD.

YOU KEEP IT LOADED WITH FUEL?

HELL, NO. IT TAKES A CRYOGENIC LIQUID FUEL. IT'S AUTOMATICALLY TRIGGERED TO FUEL UP BEFORE A LAUNCH. PUT THE FUEL IN EARLY AND THE WHOLE THING WOULD BE...

REALLY REALLY COLD?

IT'S FUELED ITSELF UP. WHAT THE HECK IS GOING ON?

I SUGGEST YOU LEAVE, SIR. MY WIFE AND I WILL TAKE IT FROM HERE.

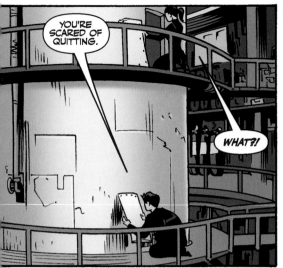

YOU'RE SCARED OF QUITTING.

WHAT?!

YOU'RE SCARED OF QUITTING.

QUITTING THIS, THE EXCITEMENT OF BEING THE OPERATIVES WHO GET CALLED WHEN A MISSILE ACTS UP.

OH. I THOUGHT YOU SAID SOMETHING ELSE.

WHAT DID YOU THINK I SAID?

I THOUGHT YOU SAID I WAS SCARED OF *QUILTING*.

I GUESS IT'S SORT OF THE SAME TH--

HUH.

YOU GOT THE ANSWER?

NO, BUT I KNOW WHAT THE QUESTION IS...

WHY ARE THERE TARGET COORDINATES SET?

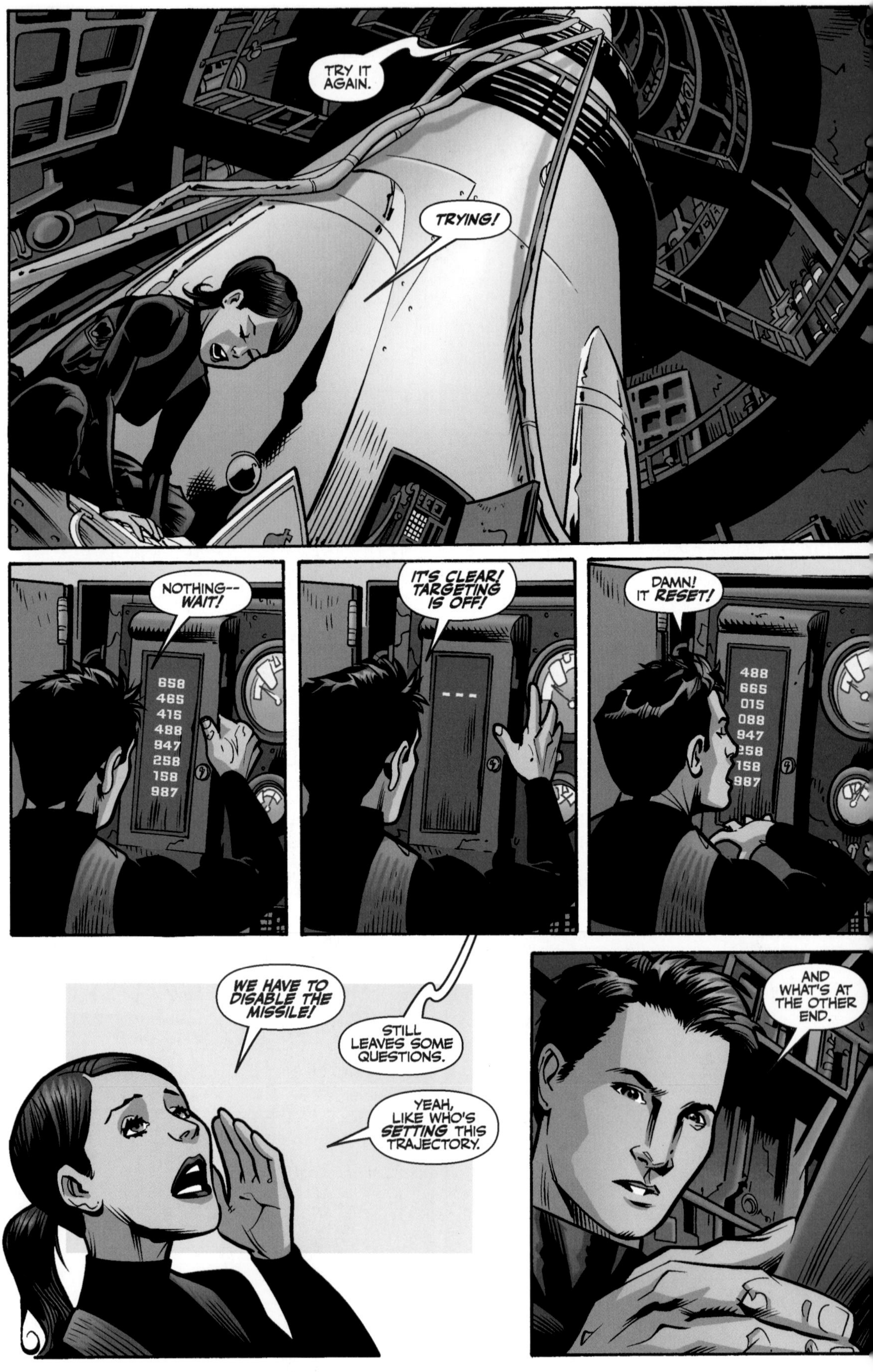
TRY IT AGAIN.
TRYING!
NOTHING-- WAIT!
658
465
415
488
947
258
158
987
IT'S CLEAR! TARGETING IS OFF!
DAMN! IT RESET!
488
665
015
088
947
258
158
987
WE HAVE TO DISABLE THE MISSILE!
STILL LEAVES SOME QUESTIONS.
YEAH, LIKE WHO'S SETTING THIS TRAJECTORY.
AND WHAT'S AT THE OTHER END.

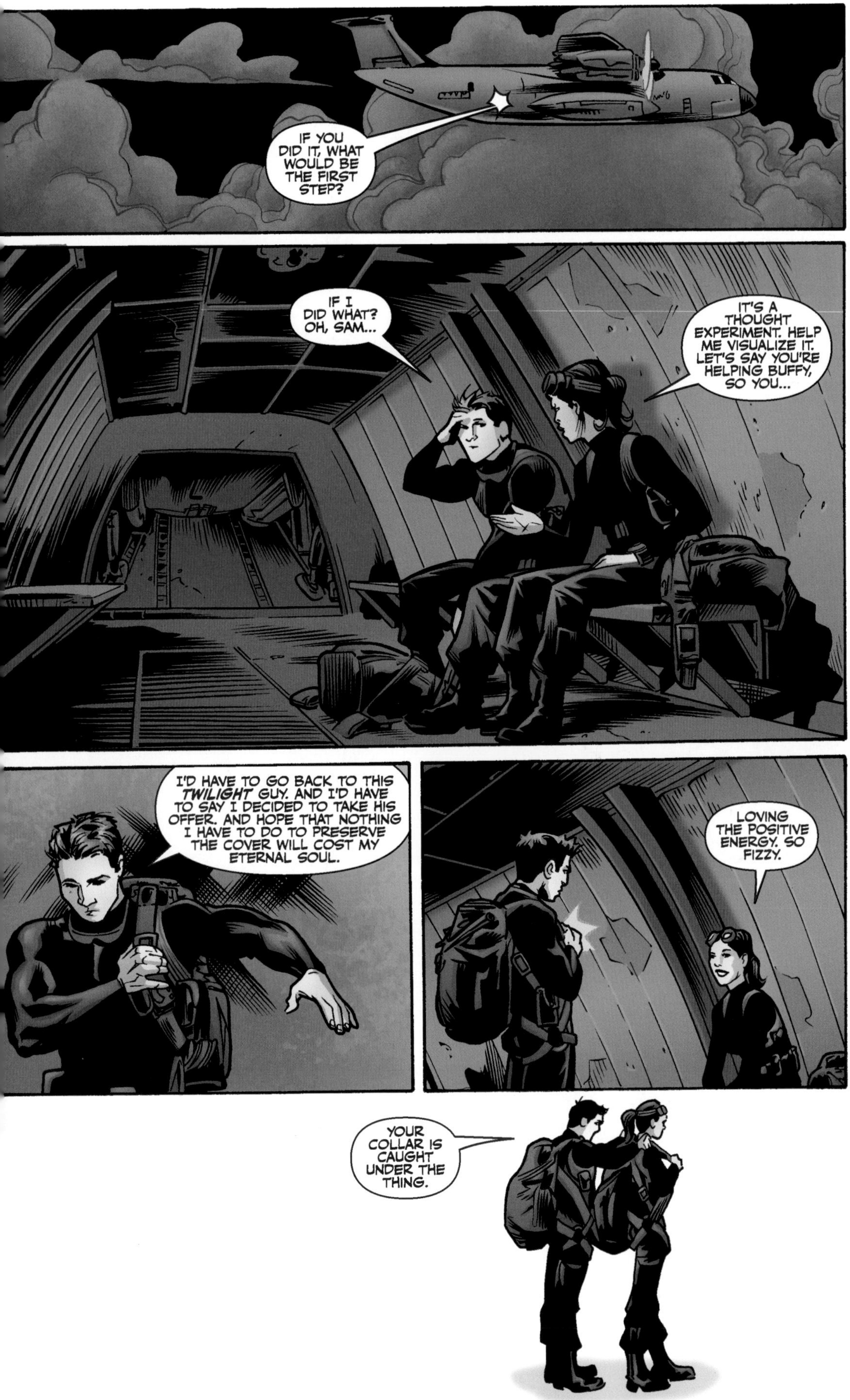
IF YOU DID IT, WHAT WOULD BE THE FIRST STEP?
IF I DID WHAT? OH, SAM...
IT'S A THOUGHT EXPERIMENT. HELP ME VISUALIZE IT. LET'S SAY YOU'RE HELPING BUFFY, SO YOU...
I'D HAVE TO GO BACK TO THIS *TWILIGHT* GUY. AND I'D HAVE TO SAY I DECIDED TO TAKE HIS OFFER. AND HOPE THAT NOTHING I HAVE TO DO TO PRESERVE THE COVER WILL COST MY ETERNAL SOUL.
LOVING THE POSITIVE ENERGY. SO FIZZY.
YOUR COLLAR IS CAUGHT UNDER THE THING.

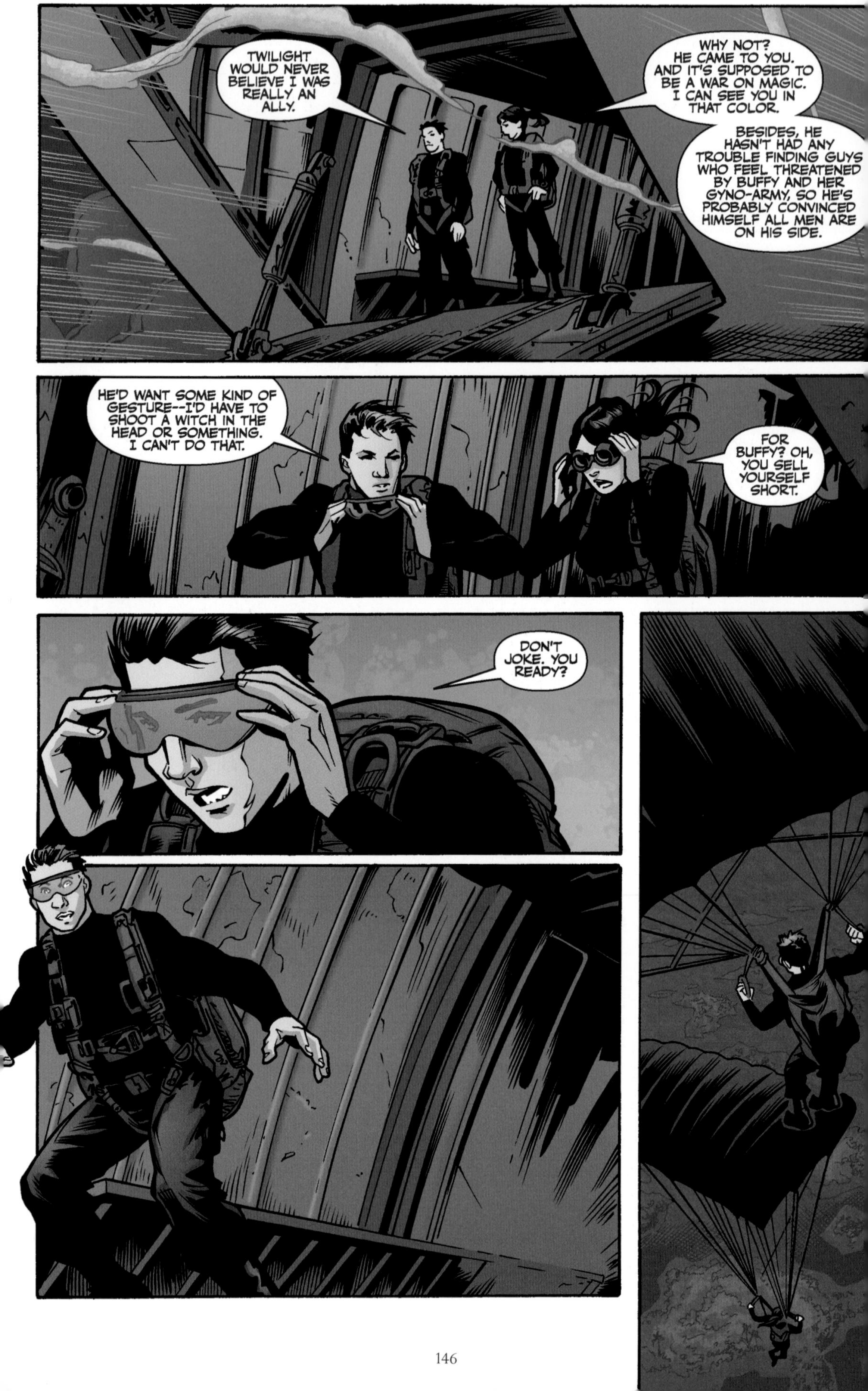
TWILIGHT WOULD NEVER BELIEVE I WAS REALLY AN ALLY.
WHY NOT? HE CAME TO YOU. AND IT'S SUPPOSED TO BE A WAR ON MAGIC. I CAN SEE YOU IN THAT COLOR.
BESIDES, HE HASN'T HAD ANY TROUBLE FINDING GUYS WHO FEEL THREATENED BY BUFFY AND HER GYNO-ARMY, SO HE'S PROBABLY CONVINCED HIMSELF ALL MEN ARE ON HIS SIDE.
HE'D WANT SOME KIND OF GESTURE--I'D HAVE TO SHOOT A WITCH IN THE HEAD OR SOMETHING. I CAN'T DO THAT.
FOR BUFFY? OH, YOU SELL YOURSELF SHORT.
DON'T JOKE. YOU READY?

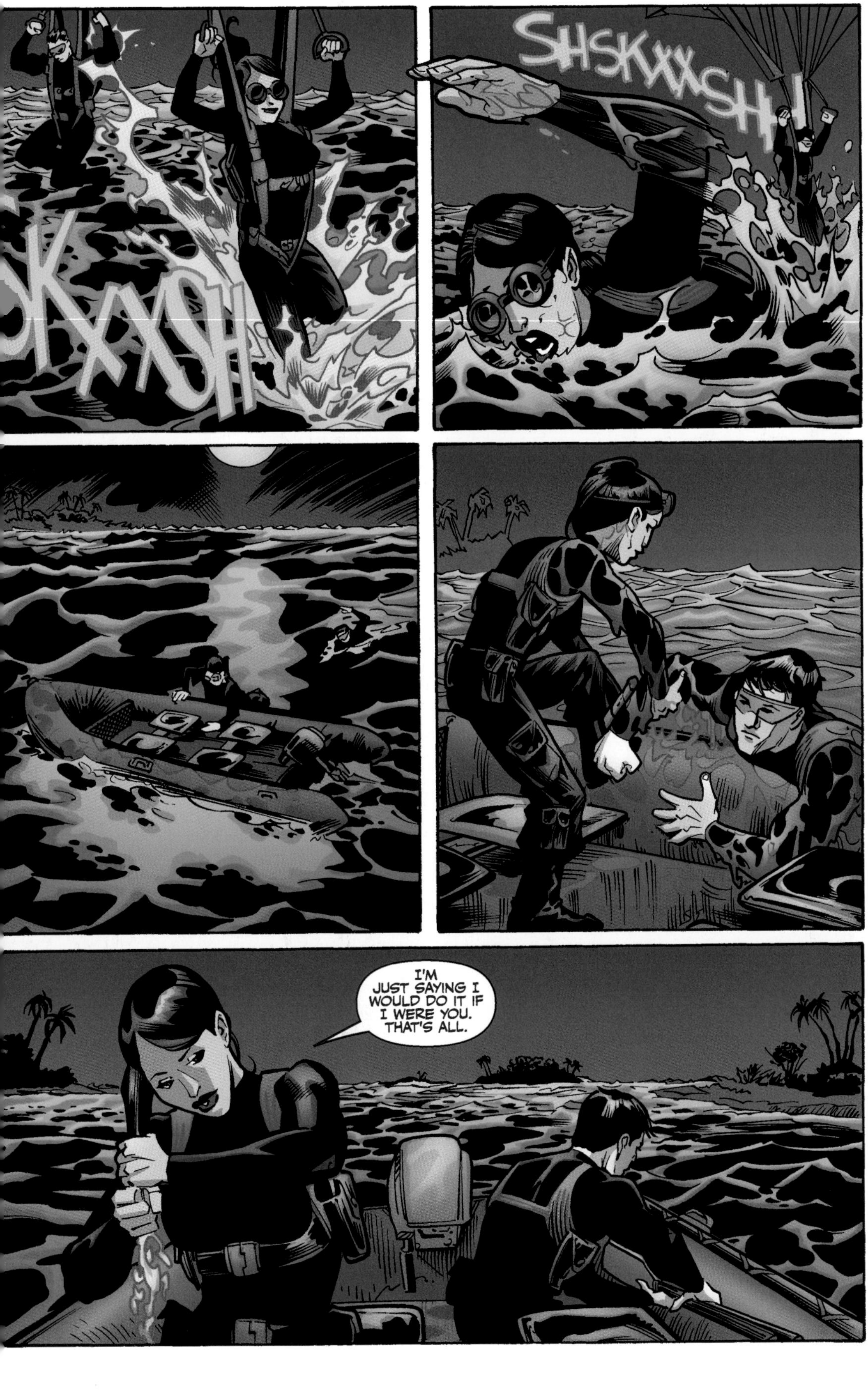
KXXSH
SHSKXXXSHH
I'M JUST SAYING I WOULD DO IT IF I WERE YOU. THAT'S ALL.

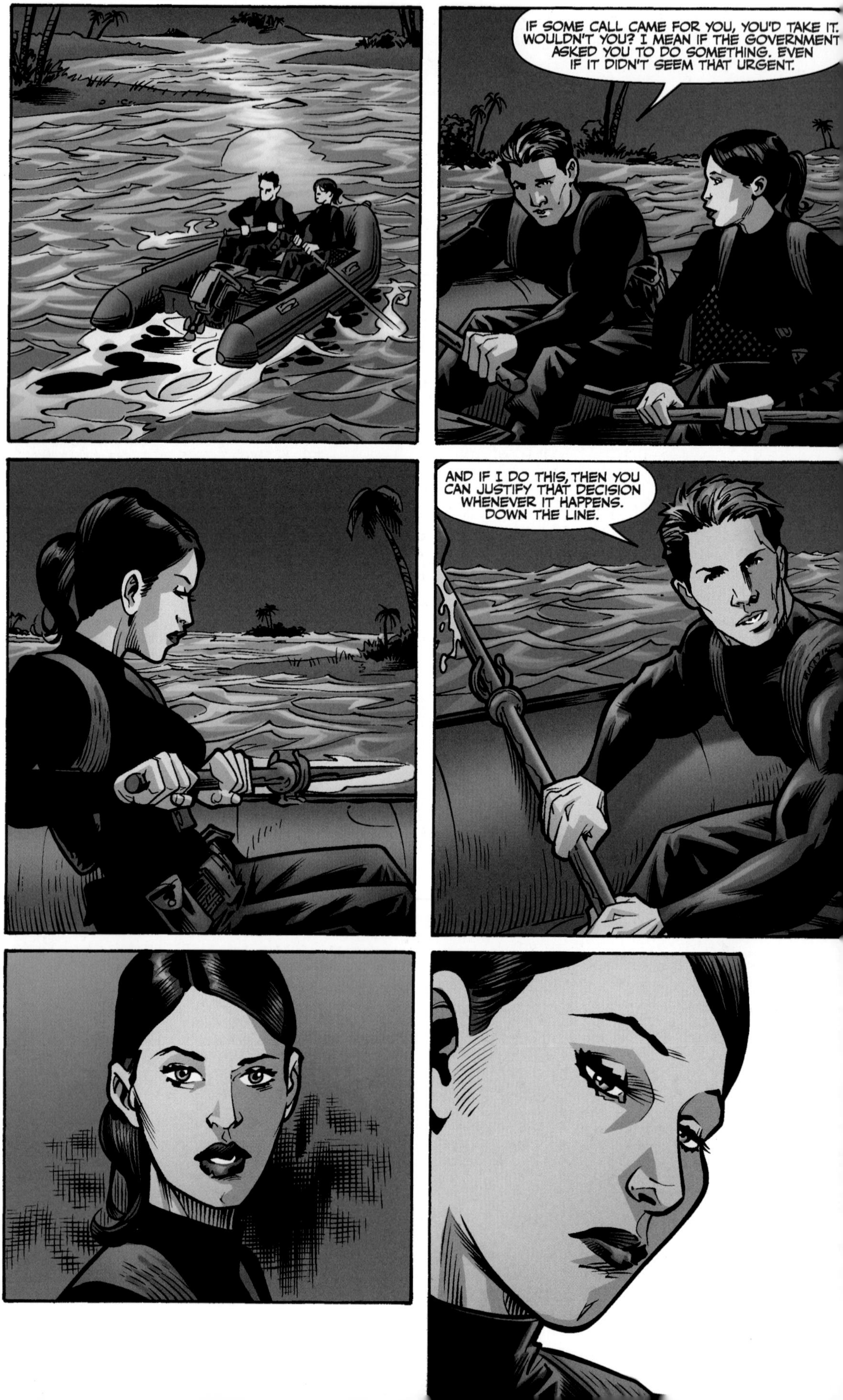
IF SOME CALL CAME FOR YOU, YOU'D TAKE IT. WOULDN'T YOU? I MEAN IF THE GOVERNMENT ASKED YOU TO DO SOMETHING. EVEN IF IT DIDN'T SEEM THAT URGENT.
AND IF I DO THIS, THEN YOU CAN JUSTIFY THAT DECISION WHENEVER IT HAPPENS. DOWN THE LINE.

TELL ME WHAT YOU NEED.

I NEED TO FIND ANOTHER PATH.

YOU'RE PRETTY FAR DOWN THIS ONE, YEAH? BOUGHT THE COSTUME? THE ARMY? WORKING HER EX? HER *OTHER* EX?

SHE SHOULD BE THE MOST POWERFUL PLAYER IN THE GAME, NOT A PIECE ON THE BOARD. THIS IS WRONG.

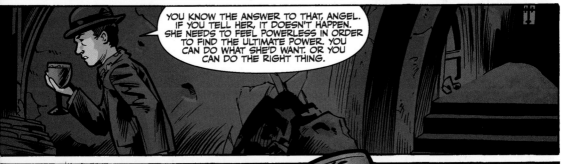

YOU KNOW THE ANSWER TO THAT, ANGEL. IF YOU TELL HER, IT DOESN'T HAPPEN. SHE NEEDS TO FEEL POWERLESS IN ORDER TO FIND THE ULTIMATE POWER. YOU CAN DO WHAT SHE'D WANT. OR YOU CAN DO THE RIGHT THING.

TORTURE THE FORMER CHEERLEADER, SAVE THE WORLD.

IS HE GONNA SIGN UP?

RILEY FINN? MAYBE. HE'S NO FAN OF MAGIC. VERY "HUMANS FIRST."

I DON'T GET WHAT SHE SAW IN HIM.

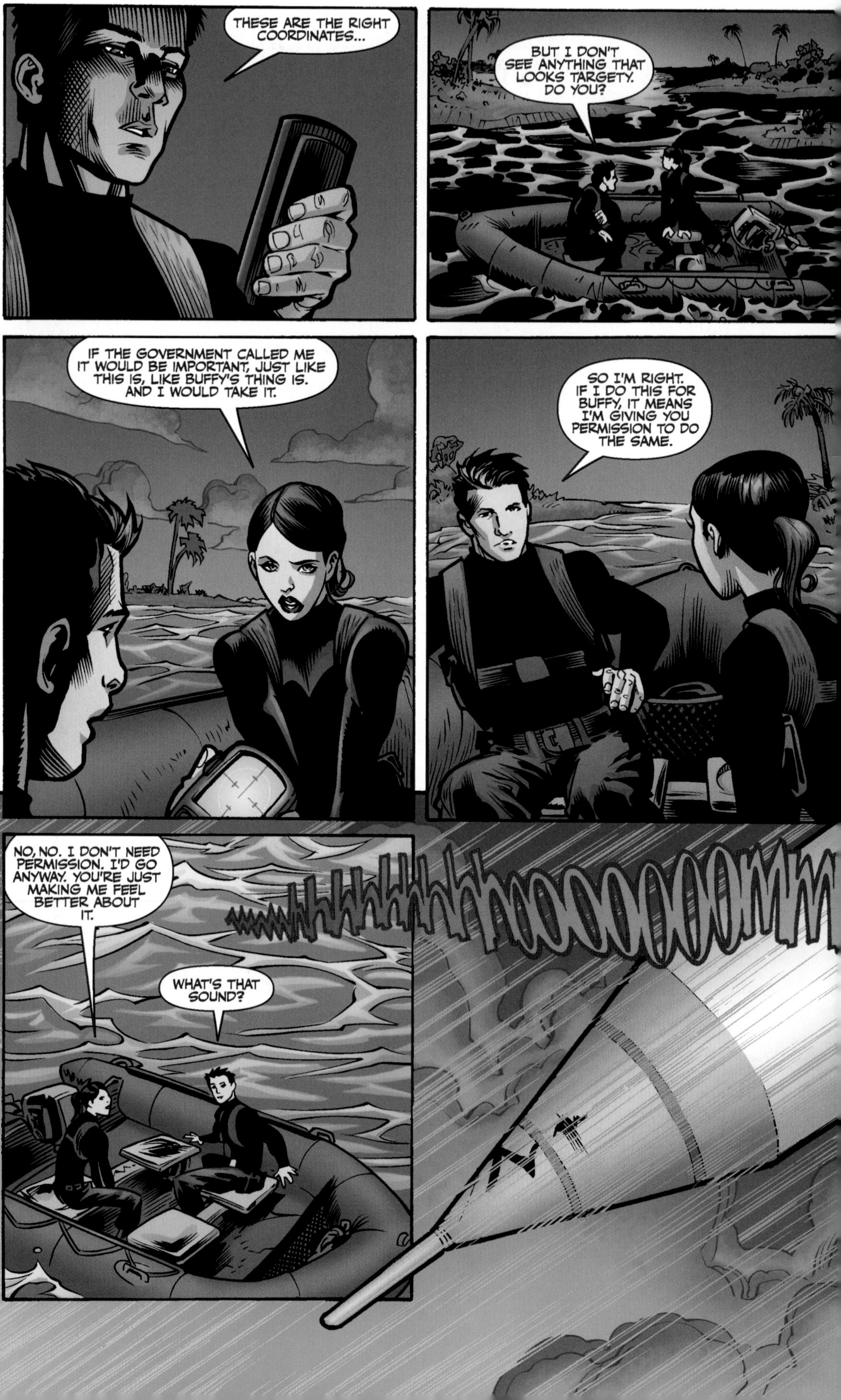
THESE ARE THE RIGHT COORDINATES...
BUT I DON'T SEE ANYTHING THAT LOOKS TARGETY. DO YOU?
IF THE GOVERNMENT CALLED ME IT WOULD BE IMPORTANT, JUST LIKE THIS IS, LIKE BUFFY'S THING IS. AND I WOULD TAKE IT.
SO I'M RIGHT. IF I DO THIS FOR BUFFY, IT MEANS I'M GIVING YOU PERMISSION TO DO THE SAME.
NO, NO. I DON'T NEED PERMISSION. I'D GO ANYWAY. YOU'RE JUST MAKING ME FEEL BETTER ABOUT IT.
WHAT'S THAT SOUND?
WWWHHHHHHHOOOOOOOMMM

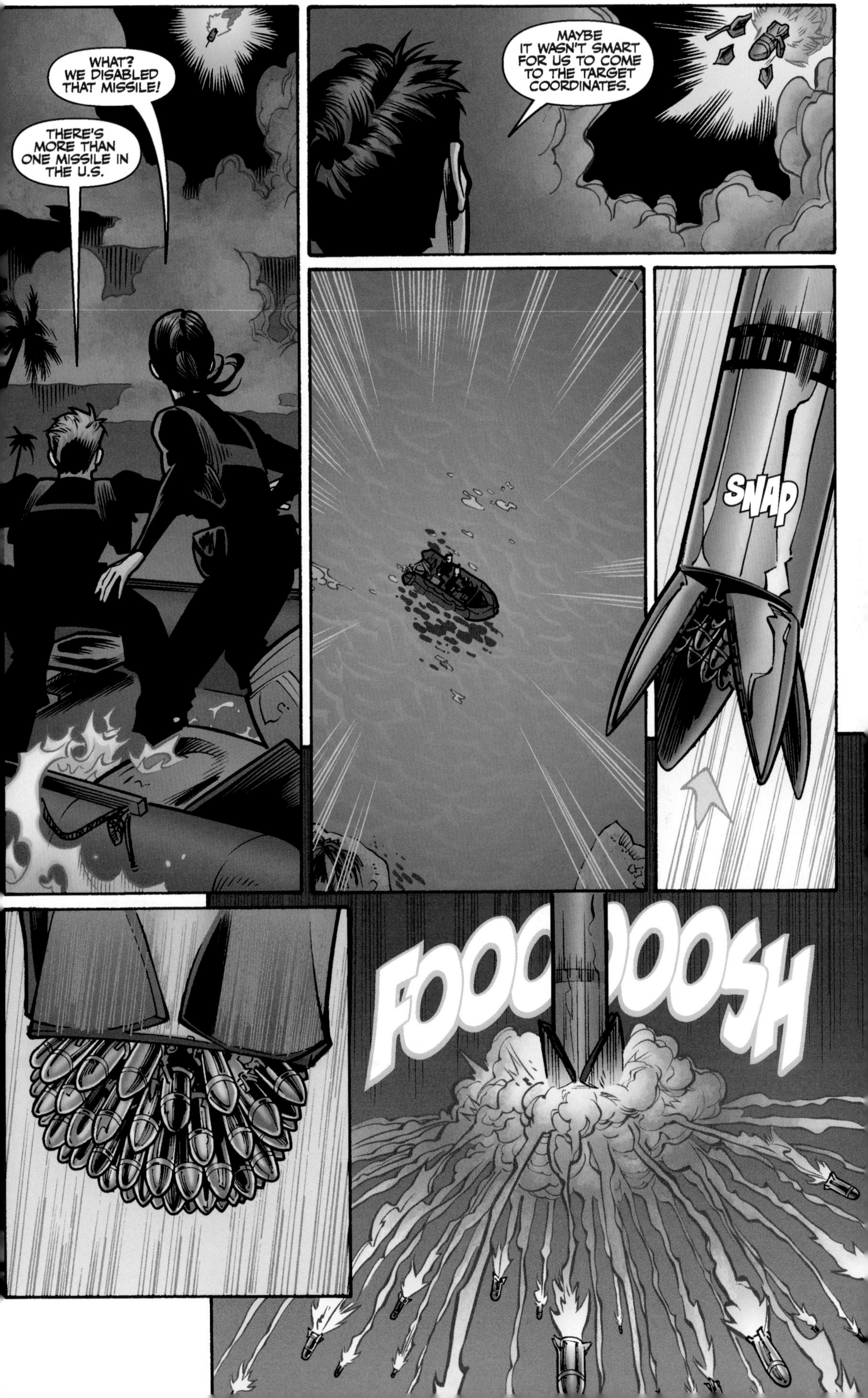
WHAT? WE DISABLED THAT MISSILE!
THERE'S MORE THAN ONE MISSILE IN THE U.S.
MAYBE IT WASN'T SMART FOR US TO COME TO THE TARGET COORDINATES.
SNAP
FOOOOOOOSH

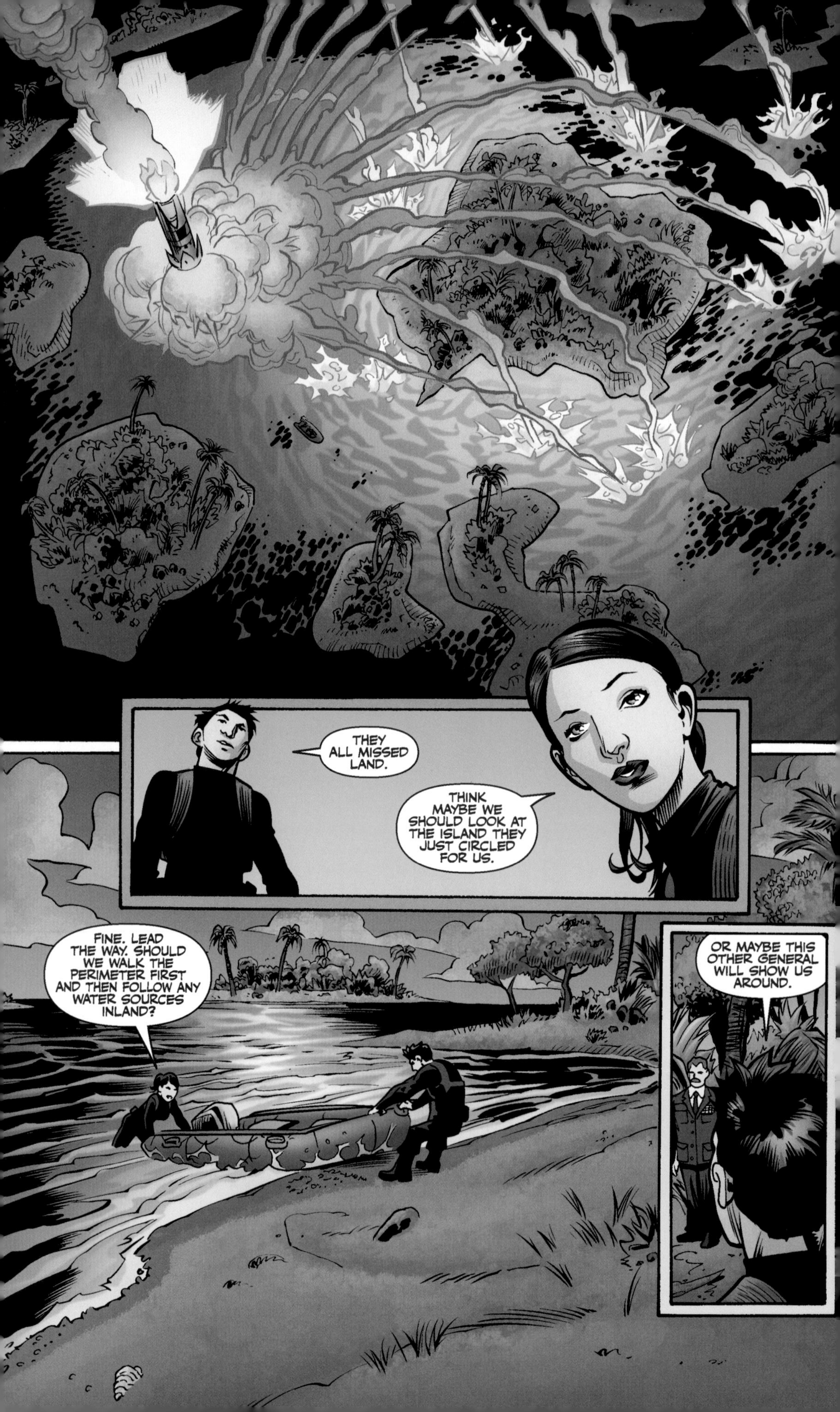
THEY ALL MISSED LAND.
THINK MAYBE WE SHOULD LOOK AT THE ISLAND THEY JUST CIRCLED FOR US.
FINE. LEAD THE WAY. SHOULD WE WALK THE PERIMETER FIRST AND THEN FOLLOW ANY WATER SOURCES INLAND?
OR MAYBE THIS OTHER GENERAL WILL SHOW US AROUND.

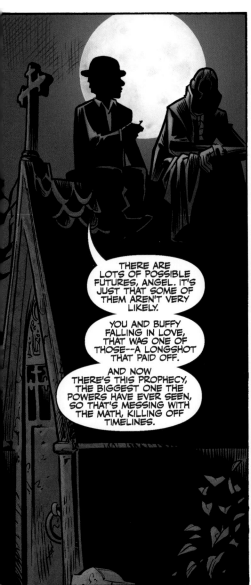

ANYWAY, I'VE SEEN SOME OF THE FUTURES. IN SOME OF THEM, RIGHT EXACTLY AT THIS POINT, YOU TELL HER WHAT'S GOING ON. YOU WORK AS A TEAM, FIGHT SIDE BY SIDE.

REALLY? YOU'VE SEEN THIS?

THERE ARE LOTS OF POSSIBLE FUTURES, ANGEL. IT'S JUST THAT SOME OF THEM AREN'T VERY LIKELY.

YOU AND BUFFY FALLING IN LOVE, THAT WAS ONE OF THOSE--A LONGSHOT THAT PAID OFF.

AND NOW THERE'S THIS PROPHECY, THE BIGGEST ONE THE POWERS HAVE EVER SEEN, SO THAT'S MESSING WITH THE MATH, KILLING OFF TIMELINES.

YOU LOSE THE WAR SIDE BY SIDE. VERY ROMANTIC.

YOU CAN SAVE THE WORLD TOGETHER, BUT ONLY IF YOU'RE *NOT* TOGETHER.

YOU HAVE TO DECIDE WHERE YOUR LOYALTY LIES...

...WITH THE GIRL OR WITH THE WORLD.

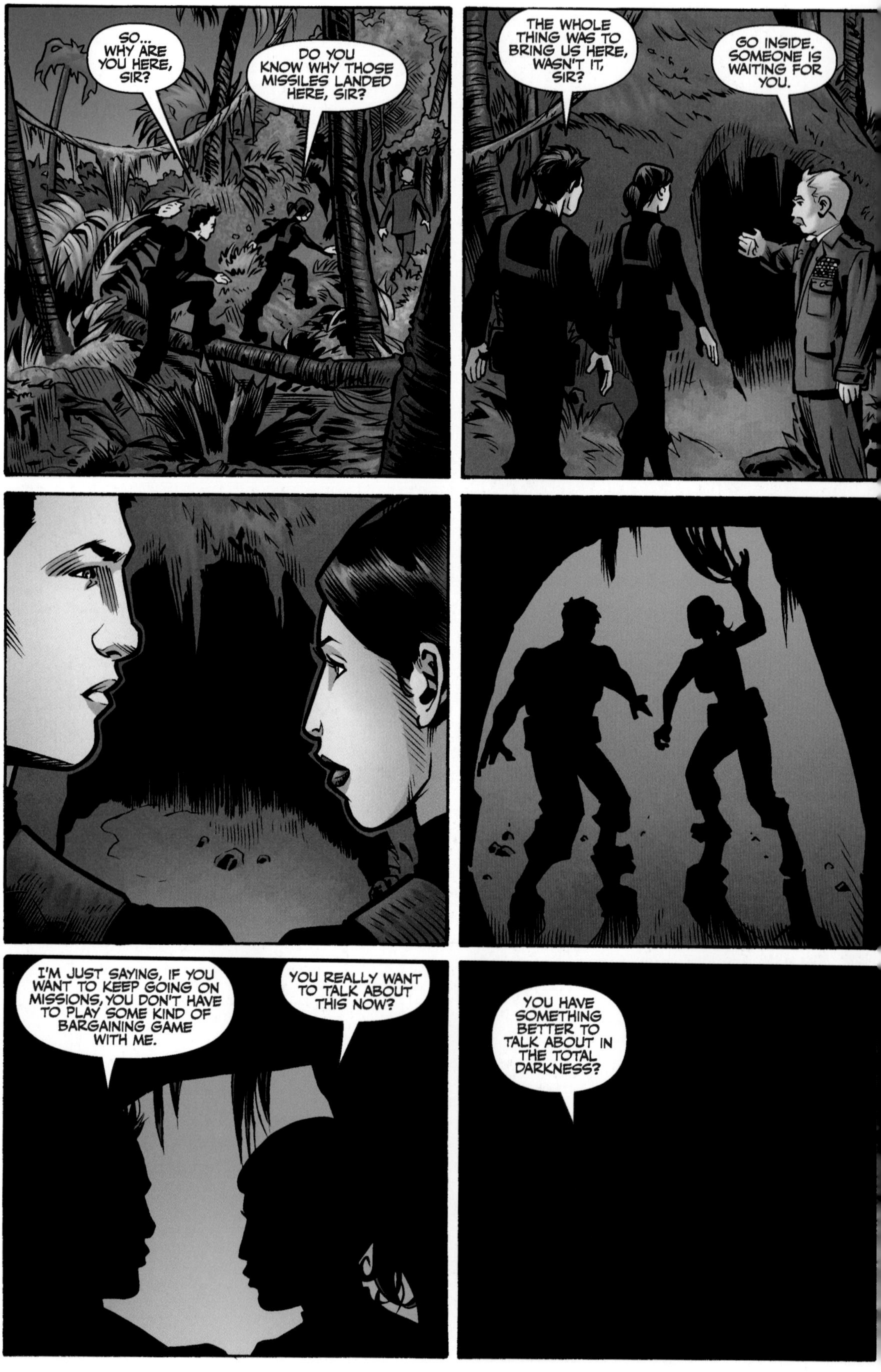
SO... WHY ARE YOU HERE, SIR?
DO YOU KNOW WHY THOSE MISSILES LANDED HERE, SIR?
THE WHOLE THING WAS TO BRING US HERE, WASN'T IT, SIR?
GO INSIDE. SOMEONE IS WAITING FOR YOU.
I'M JUST SAYING, IF YOU WANT TO KEEP GOING ON MISSIONS, YOU DON'T HAVE TO PLAY SOME KIND OF BARGAINING GAME WITH ME.
YOU REALLY WANT TO TALK ABOUT THIS NOW?
YOU HAVE SOMETHING BETTER TO TALK ABOUT IN THE TOTAL DARKNESS?

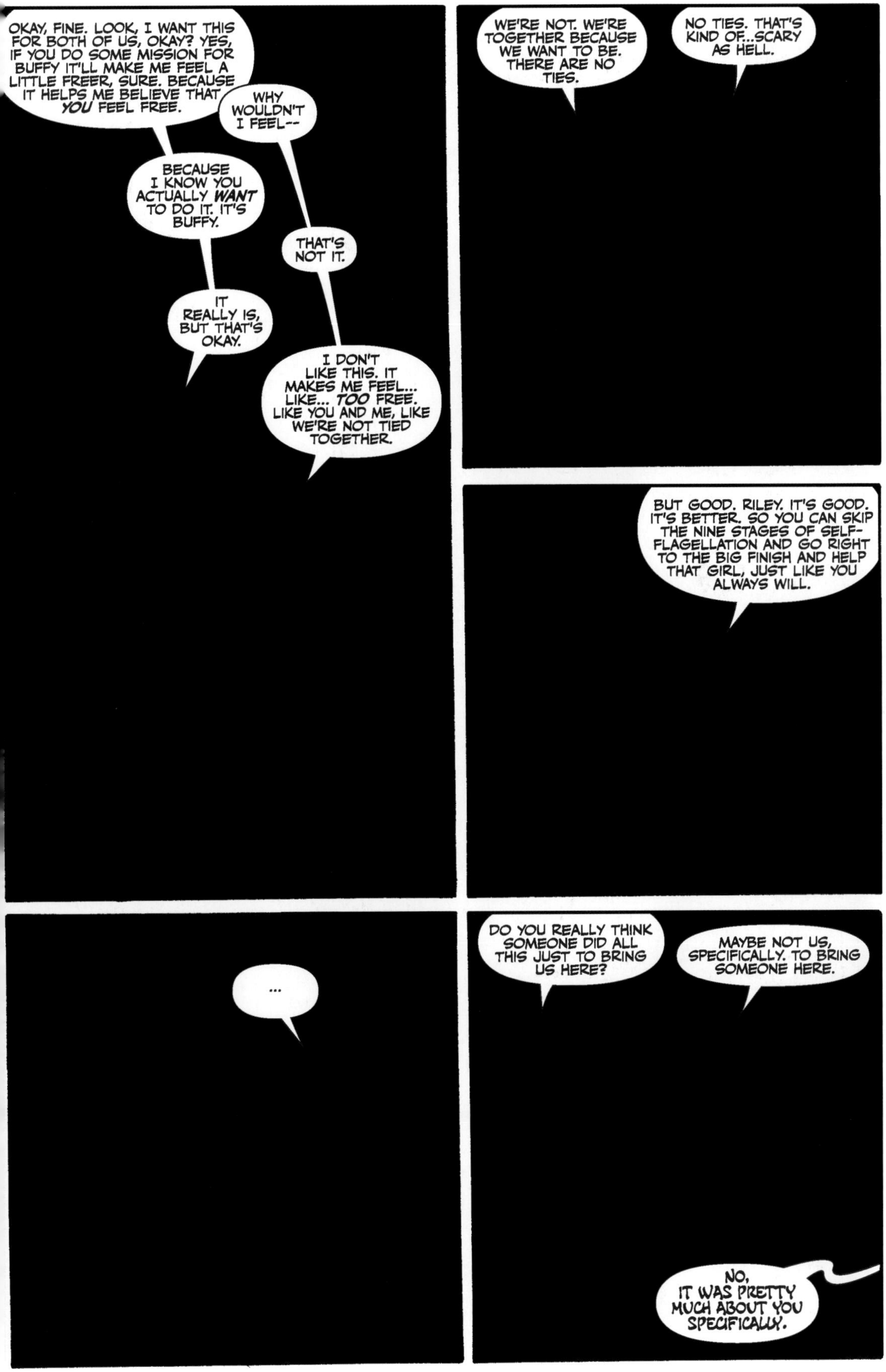
OKAY, FINE. LOOK, I WANT THIS FOR BOTH OF US, OKAY? YES, IF YOU DO SOME MISSION FOR BUFFY IT'LL MAKE ME FEEL A LITTLE FREER, SURE. BECAUSE IT HELPS ME BELIEVE THAT *YOU* FEEL FREE.
WHY WOULDN'T I FEEL--
BECAUSE I KNOW YOU ACTUALLY *WANT* TO DO IT. IT'S BUFFY.
THAT'S NOT IT.
IT REALLY IS, BUT THAT'S OKAY.
I DON'T LIKE THIS. IT MAKES ME FEEL... LIKE... *TOO* FREE. LIKE YOU AND ME, LIKE WE'RE NOT TIED TOGETHER.
WE'RE NOT. WE'RE TOGETHER BECAUSE WE WANT TO BE. THERE ARE NO TIES.
NO TIES. THAT'S KIND OF...SCARY AS HELL.
BUT GOOD. RILEY. IT'S GOOD. IT'S BETTER. SO YOU CAN SKIP THE NINE STAGES OF SELF-FLAGELLATION AND GO RIGHT TO THE BIG FINISH AND HELP THAT GIRL, JUST LIKE YOU ALWAYS WILL.
...
DO YOU REALLY THINK SOMEONE DID ALL THIS JUST TO BRING US HERE?
MAYBE NOT US, SPECIFICALLY. TO BRING SOMEONE HERE.
NO, IT WAS PRETTY MUCH ABOUT YOU SPECIFICALLY.

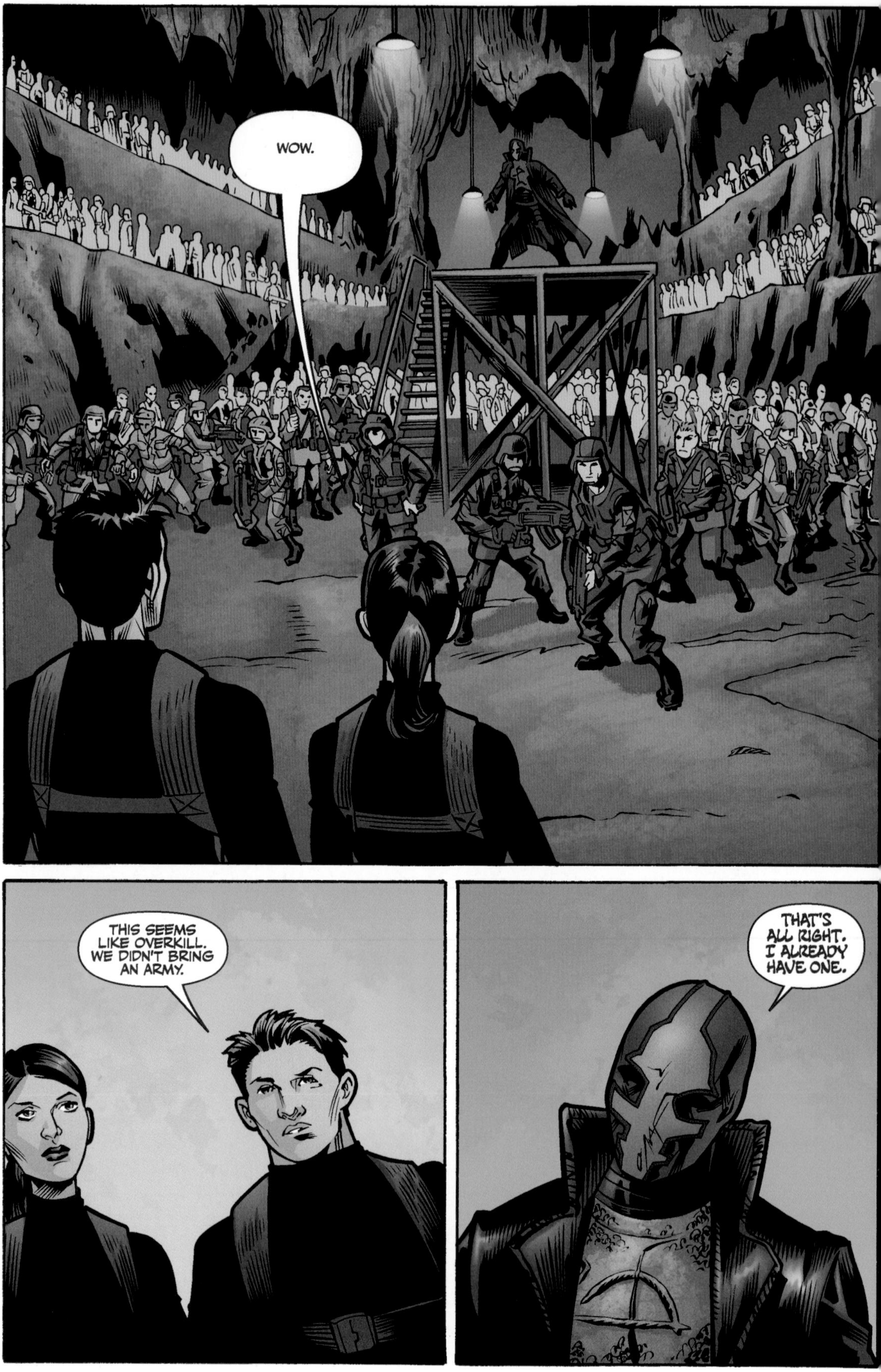
WOW.
THIS SEEMS LIKE OVERKILL. WE DIDN'T BRING AN ARMY.
THAT'S ALL RIGHT. I ALREADY HAVE ONE.

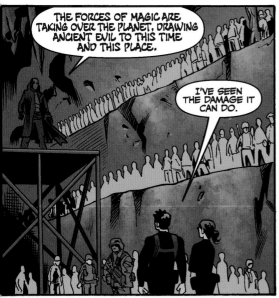

THE FORCES OF MAGIC ARE TAKING OVER THE PLANET, DRAWING ANCIENT EVIL TO THIS TIME AND THIS PLACE.

I'VE SEEN THE DAMAGE IT CAN DO.

WILL YOU STAND AT MY SIDE? FIGHT FOR HUMANKIND?

DO YOU NEED HER PERMISSION TO BE PARTED?

NO. IT'S OKAY. WE'RE TOGETHER EVEN WHEN WE'RE NOT.

AND I'M IN.

GOOD.

I JUST NEED A TOKEN OF YOUR FAITH.

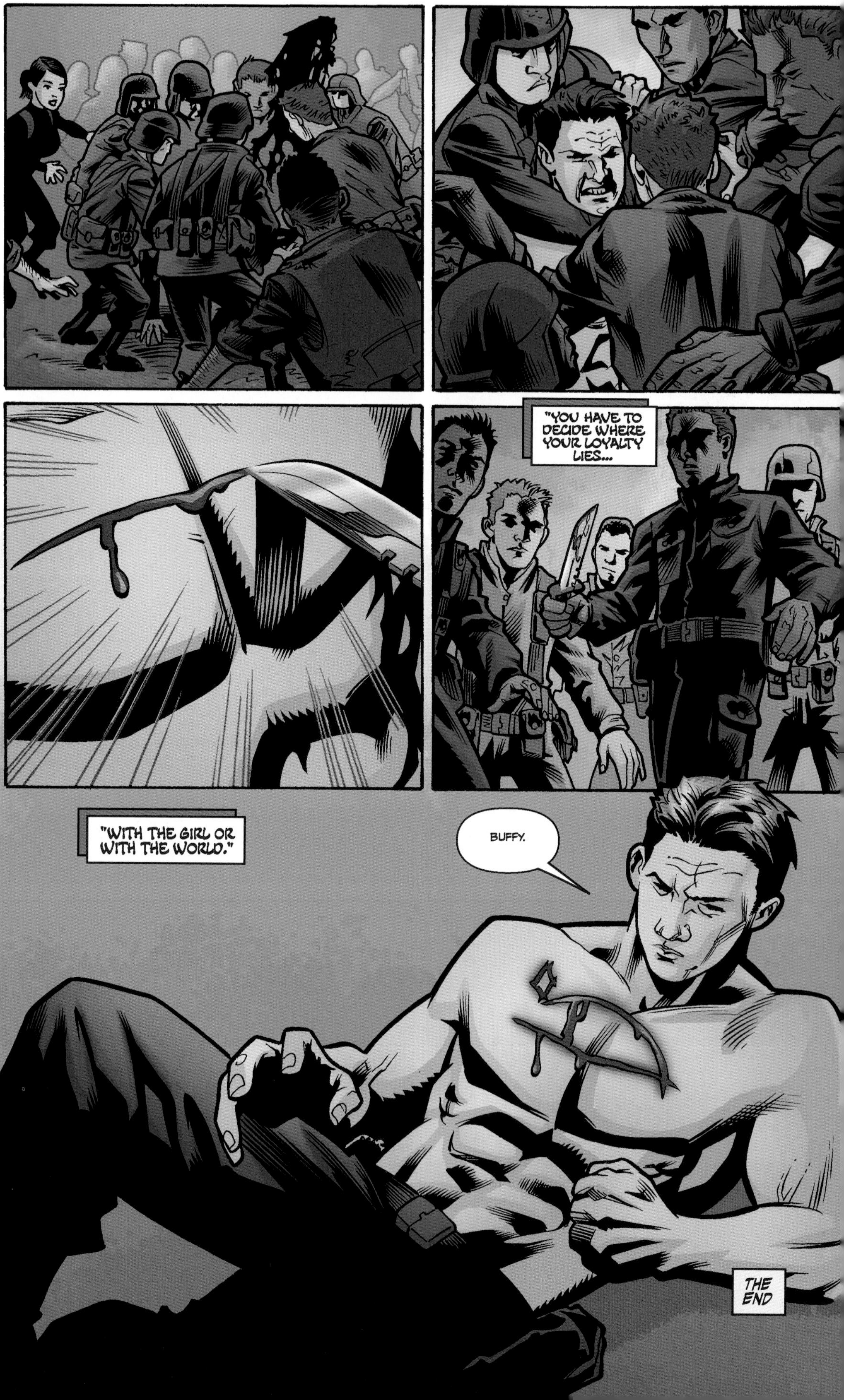
"YOU HAVE TO DECIDE WHERE YOUR LOYALTY LIES...
"WITH THE GIRL OR WITH THE WORLD."
BUFFY.
THE END

COVERS FROM
BUFFY THE VAMPIRE SLAYER
ISSUES #36–#39

By

GEORGES JEANTY

with

DEXTER VINES & MICHELLE MADSEN

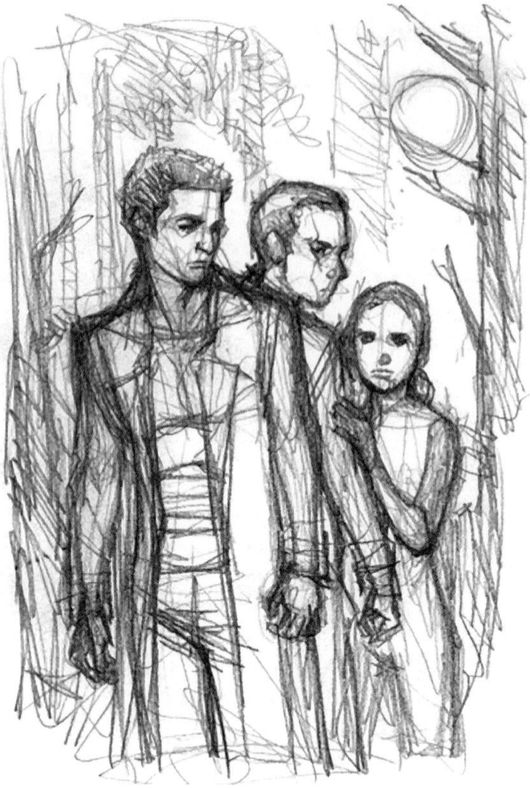

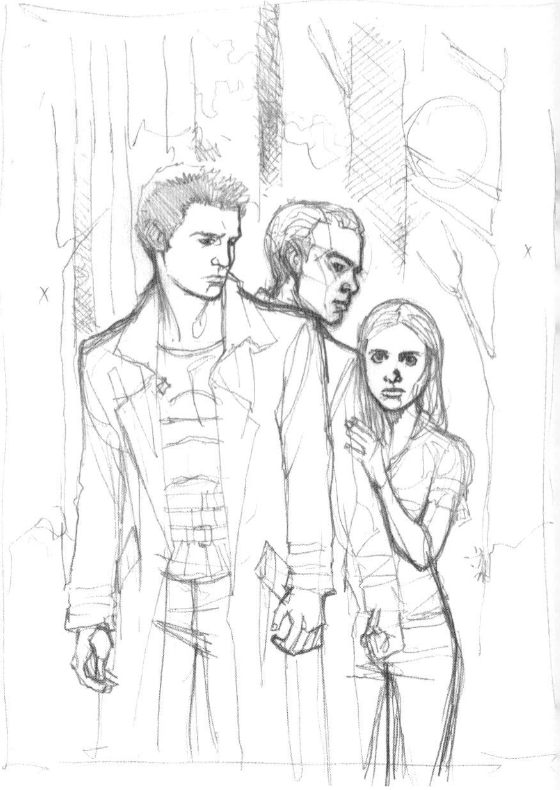

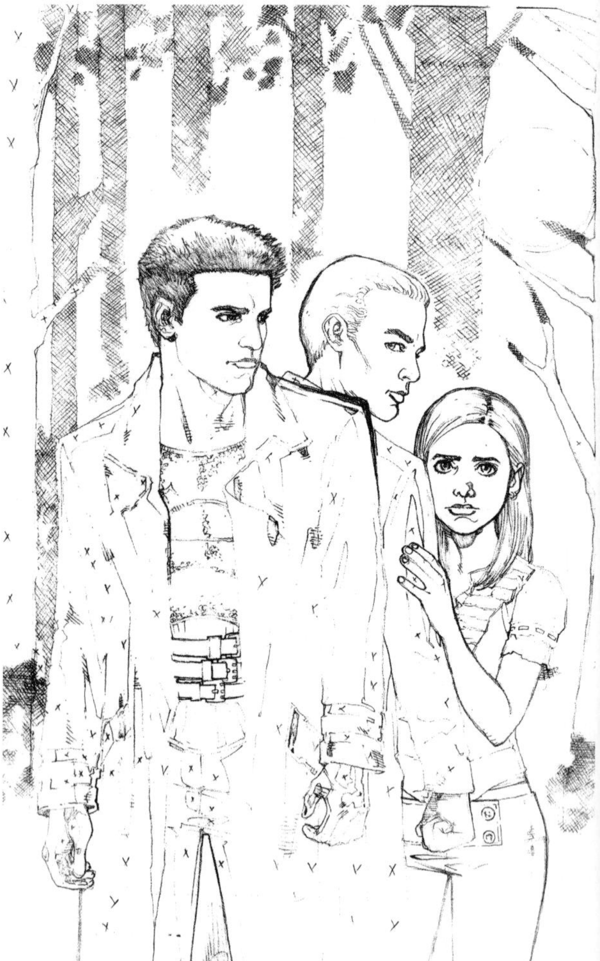

So there's this really popular series of books called the Twilight Saga that then became a really popular series of movies called the Twilight Saga. It's about a beautiful young lady caught in a love triangle between two hunky dudes (one's a vampire, and the other, a wolf). Some people might say that the complexity of that relationship is vaguely similar to Buffy's own love triangle with Angel and Spike. Furthermore—our Big Bad is coincidentally (I swear) named Twilight! We couldn't resist spoofing the poster for the *Twilight* film *Eclipse*.

FAR RIGHT: *Buffy* #36 cover

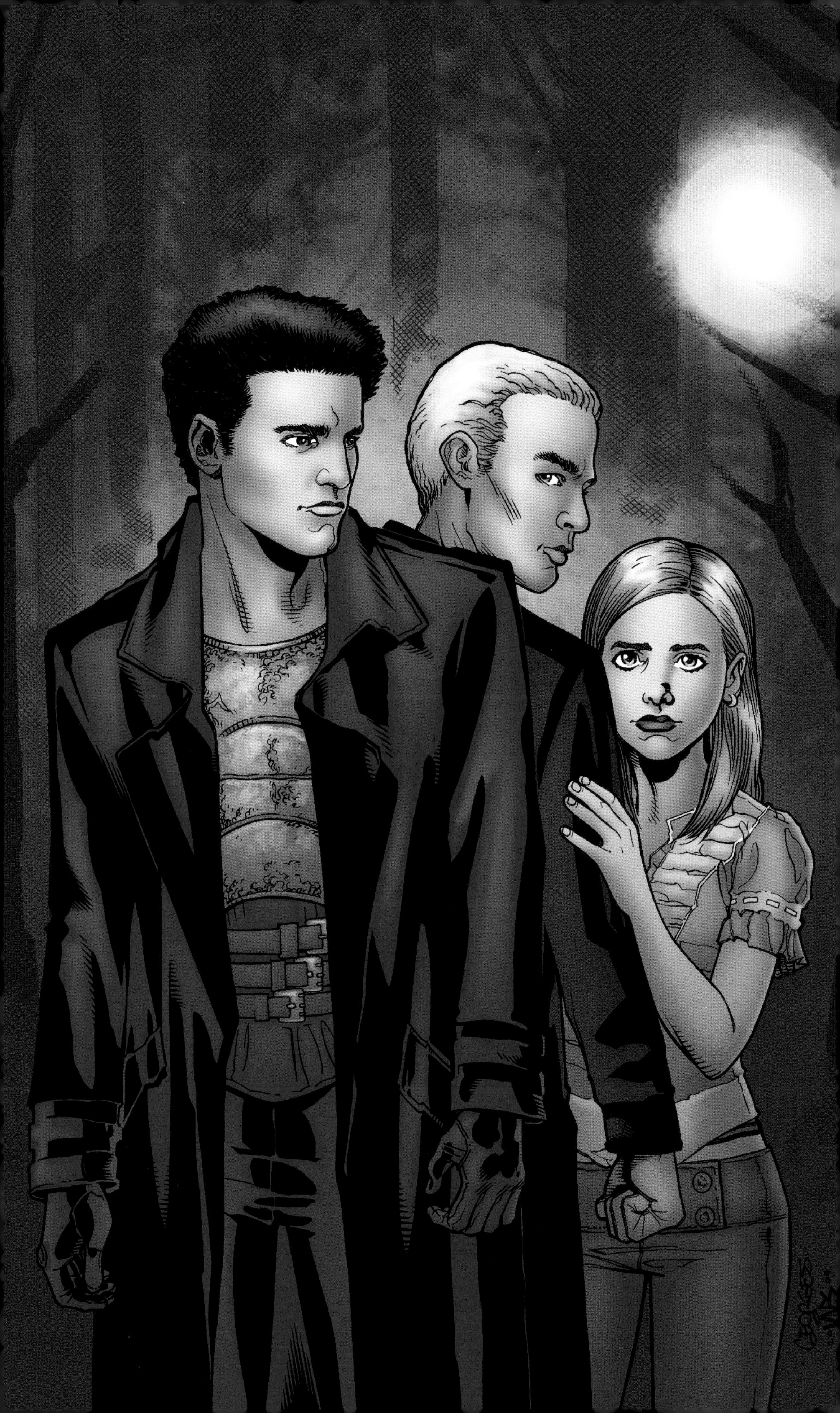

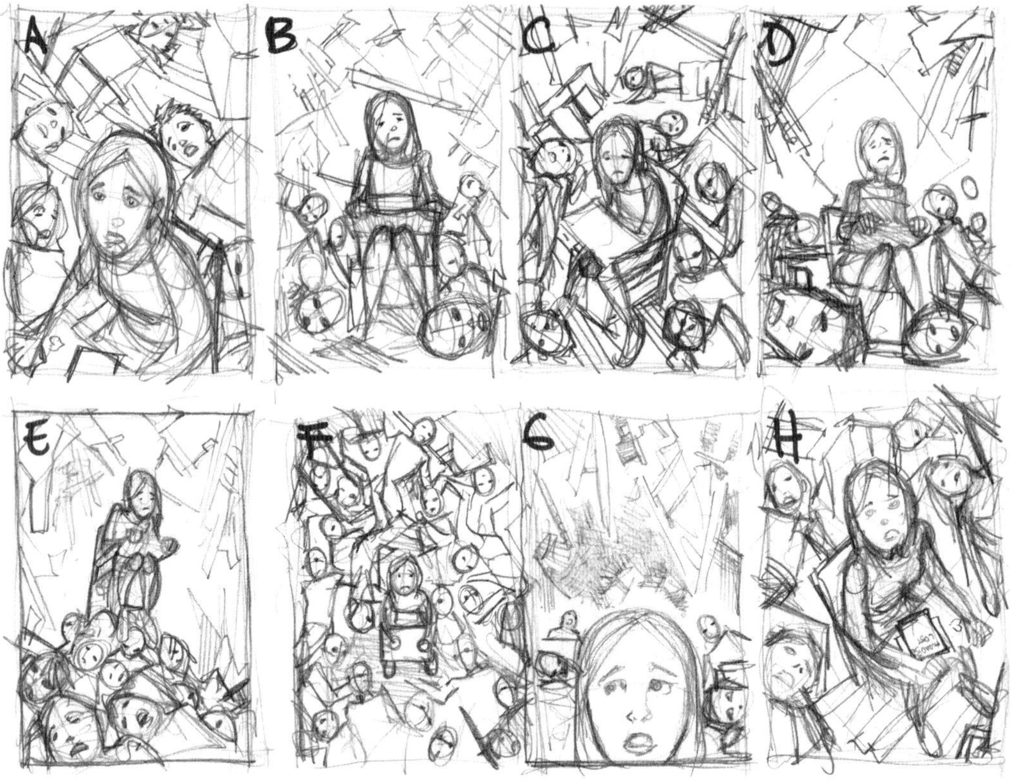
A
B
C
D
E
F
G
H

When we give Georges a basic cover concept, he runs with it! He always shows us six or more options—all of which are fantastic. We went with option D because we liked the narrative in that image. The differences in each image can be subtle, but they're there. We liked having Buffy central in the image, full figured, and with the faces of Xander and Willow at her feet in the foreground.

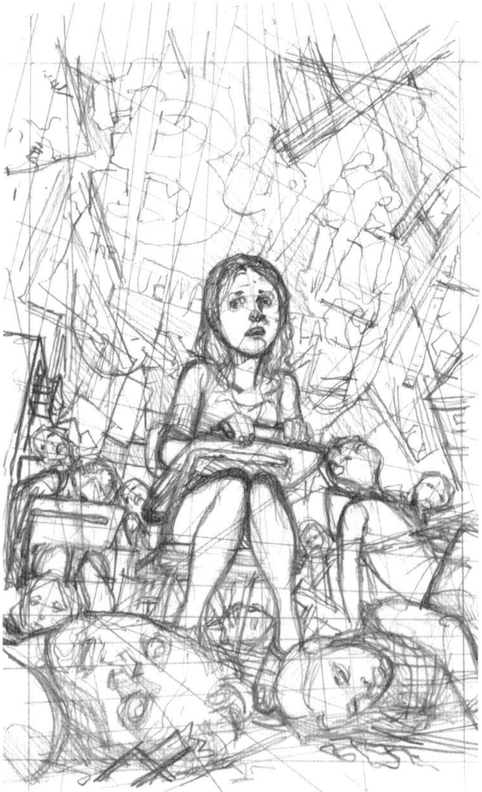

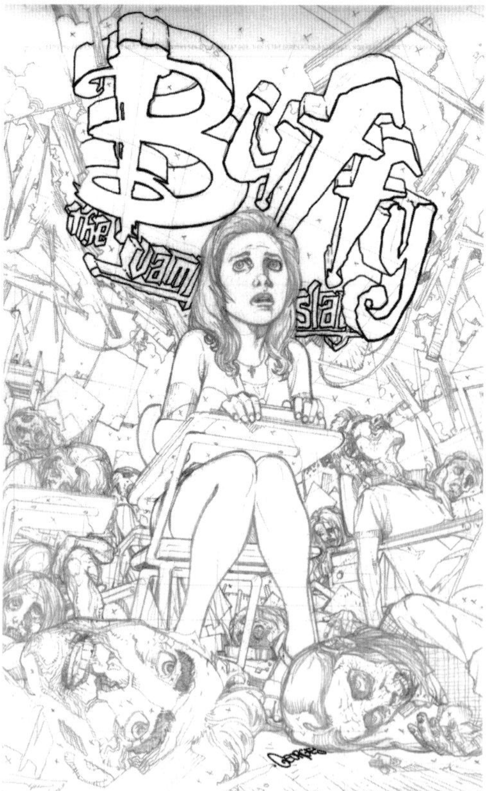
Buffy
the

The finished *Buffy* #37 cover appears on the right, showing Buffy back at Sunnydale High with her best friends as corpses in the foreground. Gruesome.

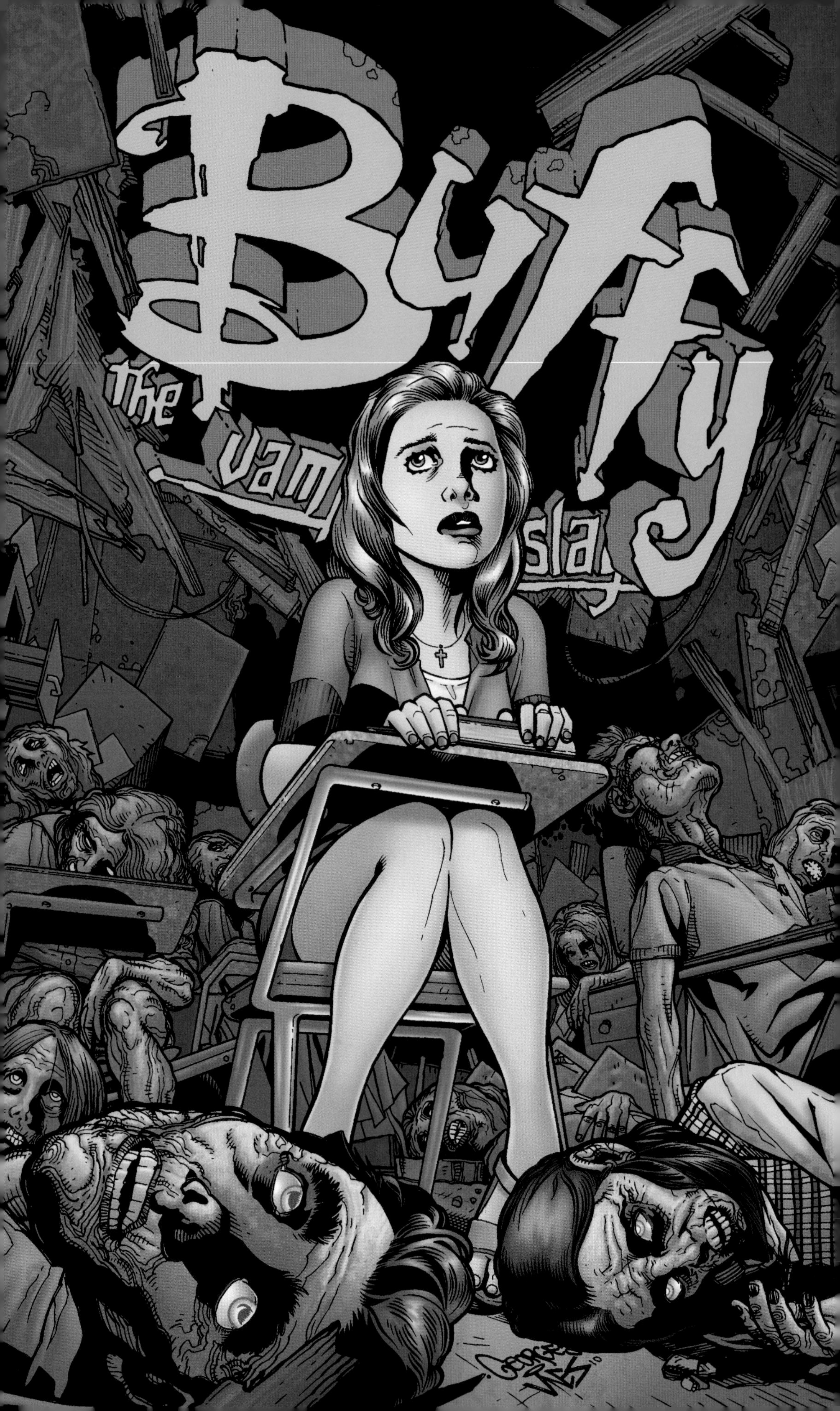
Buffy
the
vam
slay

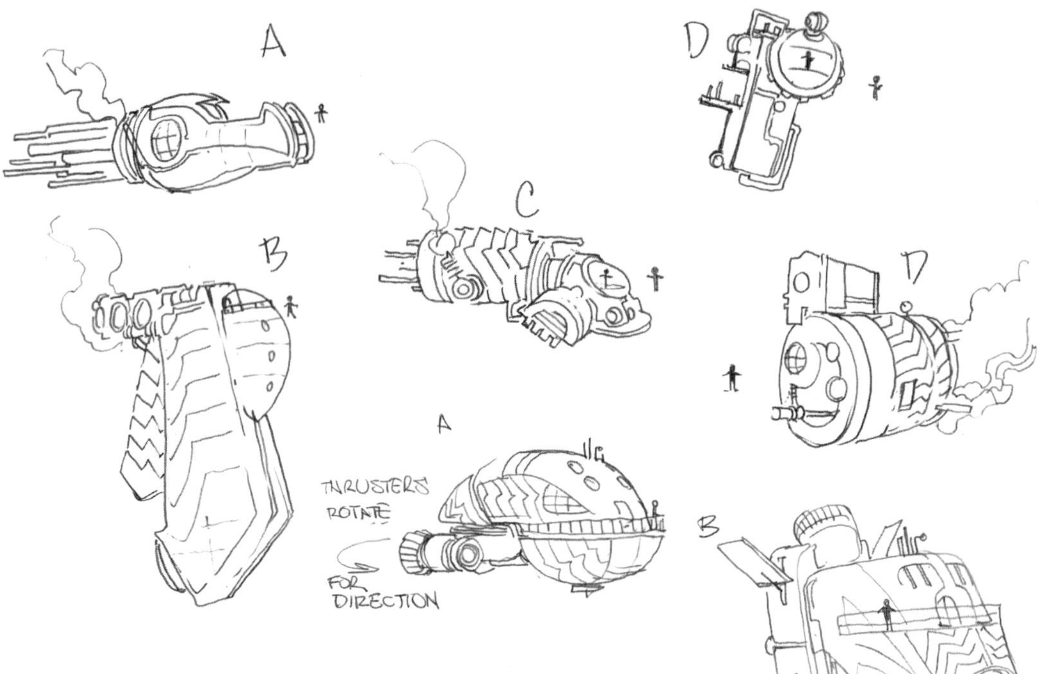

A
D
B
C
D
A
THRUSTERS ROTATE
FOR DIRECTION

Joss requested a steampunk-inspired ship for Spike to commute in, which would be manned by talking, man-sized cockroaches. (Weird? Yes. Awesome? Totally!) Once again, Georges delivered us several options to choose from.

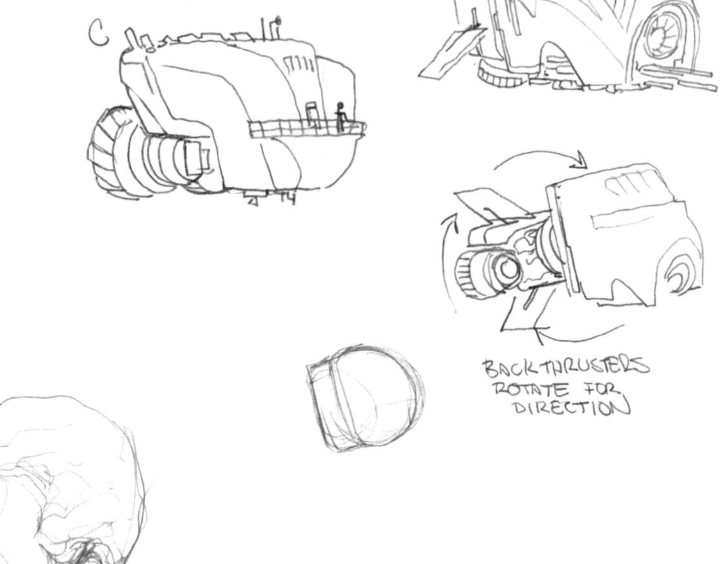

B
C
BACK THRUSTERS
ROTATE FOR
DIRECTION

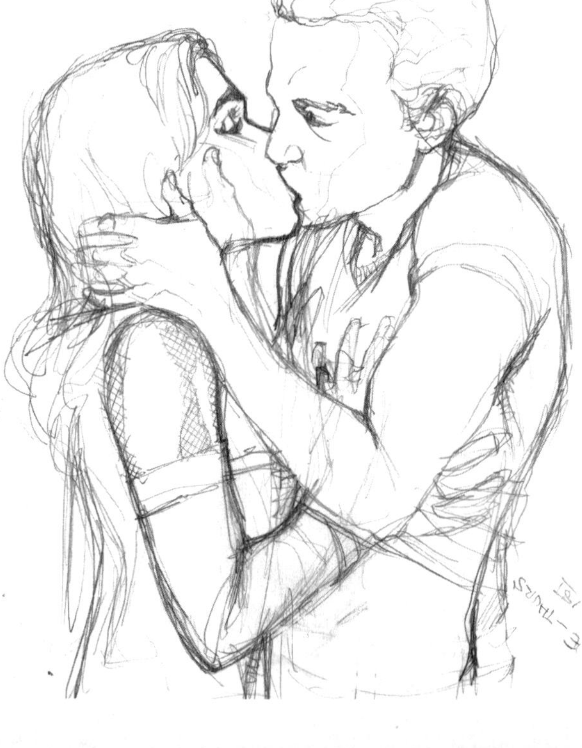

Even though the Spike and Buffy kiss is simply one of Buffy's fantasies, we wanted to give fans an image that would be both tender and sexy. These are Georges's rough pencils as he works to get this image just right. Finished drawing on pages 35 and 36.

RIGHT: *Buffy* #38 cover

FOLLOWING PAGE: *Buffy* #39 cover—a hero shot of Giles inside the Hellmouth next to the Bronze.

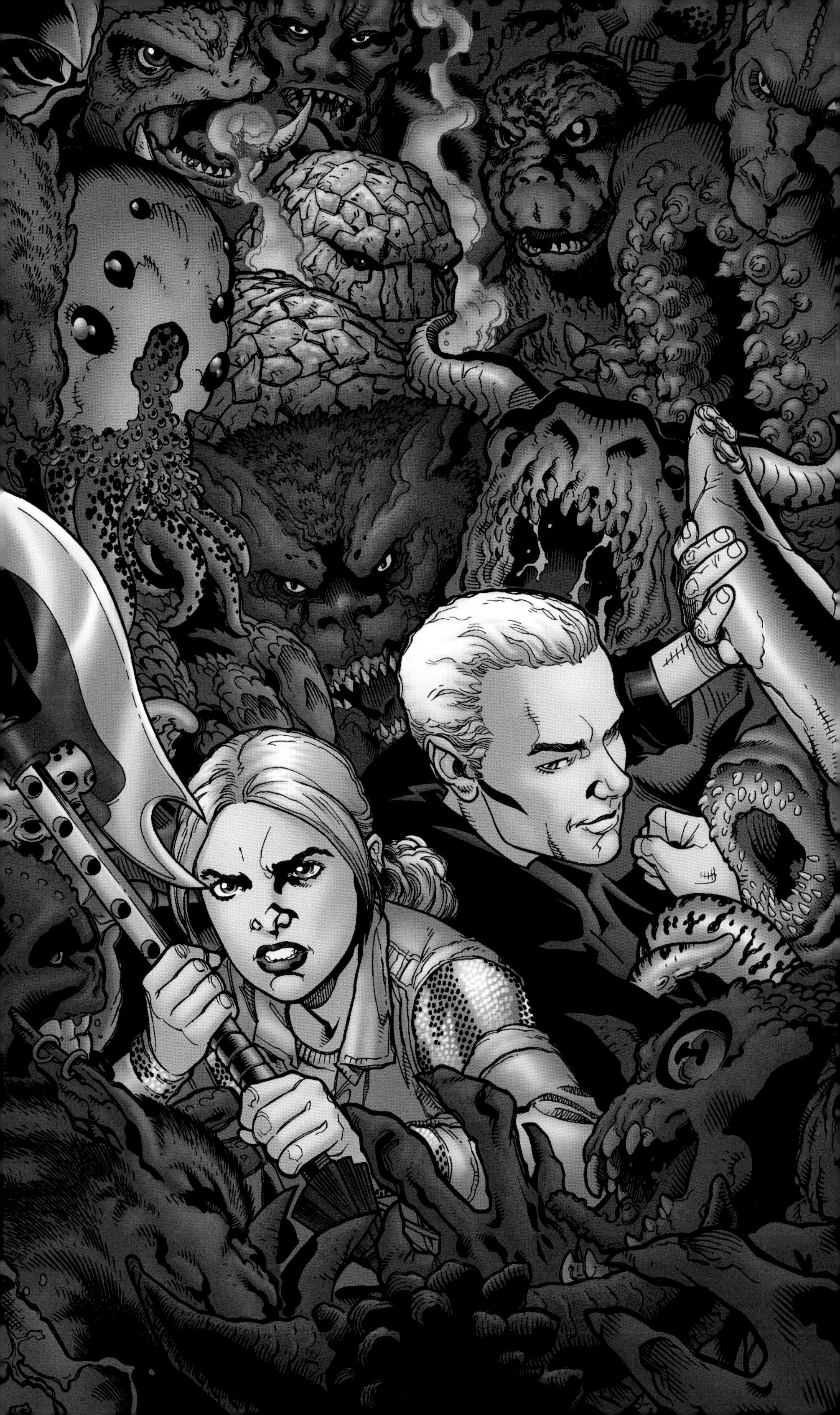

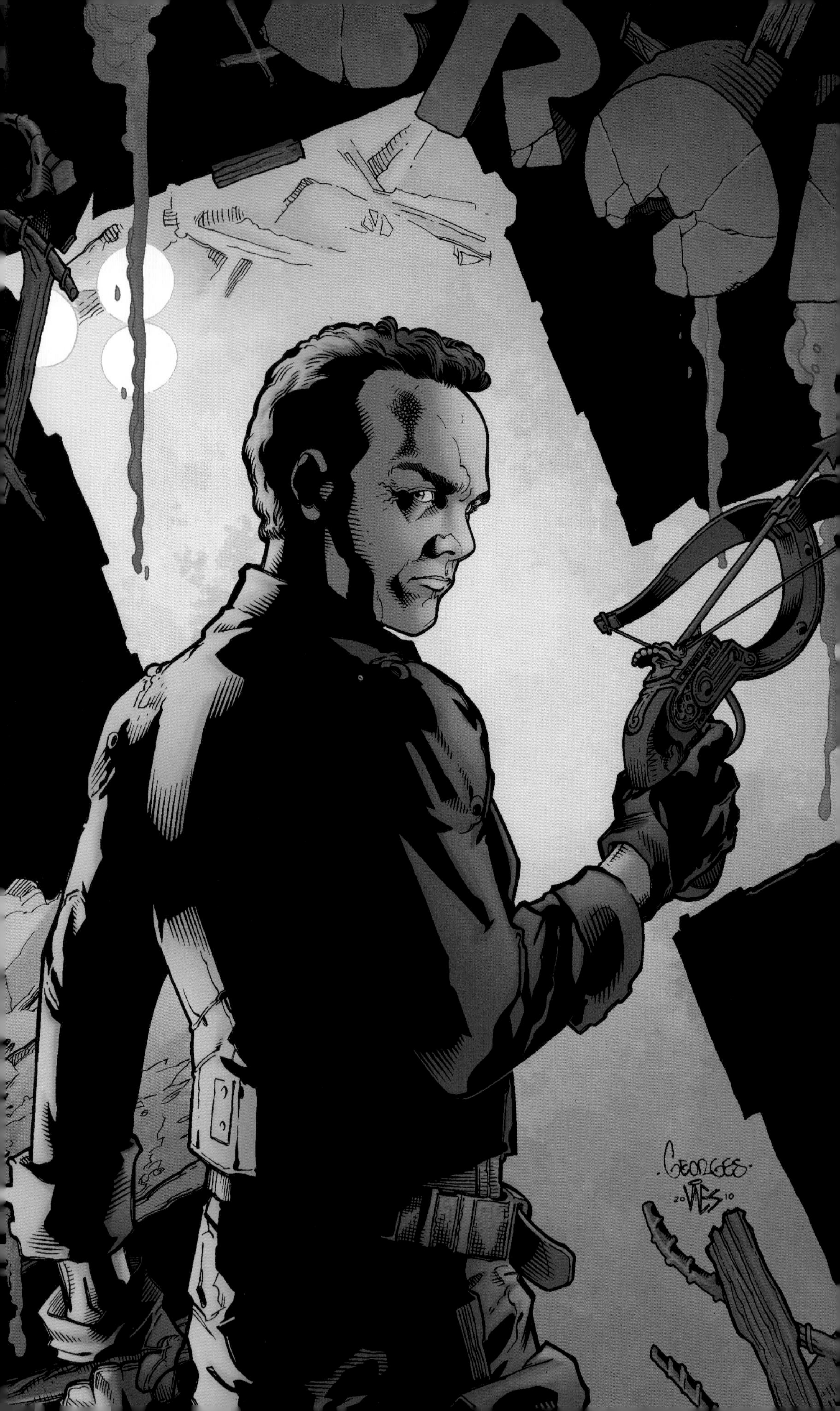
GEORGES
VIES

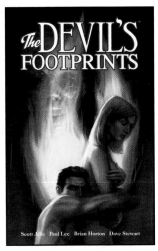

RECOMMENDED DARK HORSE READING . . .

The DEVIL'S FOOTPRINTS
Scott Allie Paul Lee Brian Horton Dave Stewart

THE DEVIL'S FOOTPRINTS
Scott Allie, Paul Lee, Brian Horton

The youngest son of a deceased sorceror, desperate to protect his family from a mysterious curse, digs into his dead father's bag of tricks. But his desire to protect his loved ones leads him to mix deception with demon conjuration, isolating himself in a terrible world where his soul hangs in the balance. The townspeople always knew something was wrong with the Waite family, and their worst fears are proven true in the fiery climax when the devil returns to New England.

$14.95 | ISBN 978-1-56971-933-6

THE TERMINATOR
2029-1984
ZACK WHEDON ANDY MACDONALD

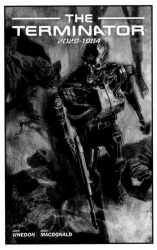

THE TERMINATOR
Zack Whedon, Andy MacDonald

Explosive action and poignant humanity in both the future and the past in this inspired reimagining of *The Terminator*! Before John Connor sent him back in time to save Sarah Connor from a T-800 with a grudge, Kyle Reese was just another man fighting to survive in a world overrun by Skynet and its terrifying army of killer cyborgs. Follow Kyle on his journey through the ravaged landscape of 2029, filled with T-800s, HKs, and rogue revolutionaries, to a world previously unimaginable to him—the glittering streets of Los Angeles in 1984!

$19.99 | ISBN 978-1-59582-647-3

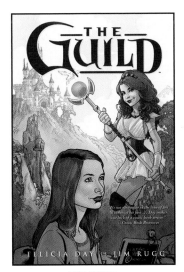

THE GUILD
FELICIA DAY & JIM RUGG

THE GUILD
Felicia Day, Jim Rugg

Chronicling the hilarious on- and offline lives of a group of Internet role-playing gamers, the Knights of Good, *The Guild* has become a cult hit, and is the winner of numerous awards from SXSW, YouTube, Yahoo, and the Streamys. Now, Felicia Day brings the wit and heart of the show to this graphic-novel prequel. In this origin tale of the Knights of Good, we learn about Cyd's life before joining the guild, how she became Codex, her awful breakup with boyfriend Trevor, and how she began to meet the other players who would eventually become her teammates.

$12.99 | ISBN 978-1-59582-549-0

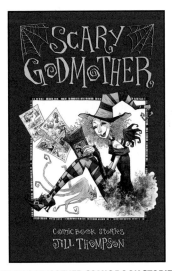

SCARY GODMOTHER
COMIC BOOK STORIES
JILL THOMPSON

SCARY GODMOTHER COMIC BOOK STORIES
Jill Thompson

Jill Thompson's award-winning children's series *Scary Godmother*—widely known from the Cartoon Network animated feature—is back with more entertainment for readers of all ages in this complete comic-book collection! Join Scary Godmother and all her decidedly dreadful friends on the Fright Side as they bring their special touch of Halloween to otherwise-terrorless times for little Hannah Marie—Christmas, Valentine's Day, summer vacation, and more!

$19.99 | ISBN 978-1-59582-723-4

AVAILABLE AT YOUR LOCAL COMICS SHOP OR BOOKSTORE
To find a comics shop in your area, call 1-888-266-4226
For more information or to order direct visit darkhorse.com or call 1-800-862-0052
Mon.–Fri. 9 AM to 5 PM Pacific Time.
***Prices and availability subject to change without notice**

DARK HORSE BOOKS

DarkHorse.com

FROM JOSS WHEDON

DARK HORSE BOOKS®
DarkHorse.com